PRAISE FOR JO KAPLAN

"Kaplan serves up an eerie feast for the senses in this addictive horror novel."

—*PUBLISHERS WEEKLY*, STARRED REVIEW

"This immersive tale is uneasy from its first pages and builds to all out visceral terror with well-executed body horror and well-placed twists. Kaplan's solid horror novel will have wide appeal for fans of many of its subgenres, such as sporror, cursed bands, and something-in-the-woods-is-trying-to-kill-you."

—*LIBRARY JOURNAL*

"*The Midnight Muse* is a found footage fruiting body of a haunted novel, a heavy metal mycelium monstrosity—imagine Iron Maiden replacing its lead singer with the Blair Witch—that echoes through your skull long after reading it."

—CLAY MCLEOD CHAPMAN, AUTHOR OF *WAKE UP AND OPEN YOUR EYES*

"*The Midnight Muse* is a gorgeously written, tense, and complex cabin-in-the-woods story for music lovers and fans of body horror."

—CHRISTI NOGLE, AUTHOR OF THE BRAM STOKER AWARD® WINNING FIRST NOVEL *BEULAH*

"Fetid, cosmic, and distinctly human, *The Midnight Muse* is a corpse paint-daubed reimagining of the urge to create art as an infection. It asks what happens when those compelled by its charge are consumed by its creeping compulsion. A must-read."

—ZACHARY ASHFORD, AUTHOR OF *POLYPHEMUS*

"One of the most effective and compelling marriages of natural and supernatural horror since Richard Matheson's *Hell House, The Midnight Muse* by Jo Kaplan is full of dazzling surprises and eerie plot twists that make it hard to stop turning pages. Thoroughly impressive horror storytelling, and an utter delight to read."

—SCOTT KENEMORE, AUTHOR OF *EDGE OF THE WIRE*
AND *LAKE OF DARKNESS*

"A pungent myco-psycho nightmare that will leave readers jonesing for Carrion Queen on ghost-white vinyl, *The Midnight Muse* pits inspiration against collaboration, individuality against uniformity, and want against need in a pagan-metal symphony of seductive survival horror."

—MATTHEW R. DAVIS, SHIRLEY JACKSON AWARD-
NOMINATED AUTHOR OF *SONGS OF SHADOW, WORDS
OF WOE*

THE MIDNIGHT MUSE

The Midnight Muse
Copyright © 2026 by Jo Kaplan
Cover by Matthew Revert
ISBN: 9781960988805 (paperback)

CLASH Books
Troy, NY
clashbooks.com
Distributed by Consortium
All rights reserved.
First Edition 2026

This one goes out to anyone who creates

THE MIDNIGHT MUSE

JO KAPLAN

ONE

There's always that one friend. The one from whom you could never stand to be apart, your hands nesting together easily as secrets passed from mouth to ear. That childhood friend whose presence was magic.

For Harlow Sorenson, Brynn was that friend.

They met in kindergarten and immediately bonded the way children sometimes do. By lunch they were best friends; by dinner they were inseparable. It was easy to be friends with Brynn, who was clever and funny and sarcastic. And bold—she wasn't afraid of getting in trouble. She dared Harlow to stay up late, to turn the lights out, to whisper Bloody Mary three times into the bathroom mirror.

Brynn kept her dark hair in frizzy waves around her face. When she was thirteen she started wearing eyeliner, unevenly applied but admirable in its thickness. Her clothes were often a size too big, but somehow they hung well on her body. She was gifted at the piano, not just in playing others' pieces but in composing her own. When Harlow came over, she rarely heard Brynn playing anything but original compositions, always tinkering with unfinished melodies. It awed Harlow, this ability to create music out of nothing. She thought it was one thing to follow notes on a page; it was quite another to conceive the notes altogether.

It was Brynn who first inspired Harlow's interest in music. Sometimes, while they were hanging out doing homework together, Brynn's fingers would dance in the air as if at an invisible keyboard. Harlow would ask what she was doing, and Brynn would shush her and say she was writing something in her head.

It seemed like another language that lived somewhere between Brynn's brain, fingers, and the air itself.

The idea of creating notes bewildered Harlow, but one thing she did understand was rhythm. Rhythms were repeating patterns. She had been tapping the tops of desks with the eraser-ends of pencils for years before she ever touched a drum, but when she did, she felt fired up by how loud, how powerful it was.

Brynn loved to talk about music. Her eyes glittered when she did. And Harlow loved to listen to her talk about music. "Did you know we have no idea who invented music?" Brynn told her once. "My piano teacher says music is so old we have no idea what the first song was. There's a flute that was created by Neanderthals like 60,000 years ago. Before that, singing was probably the first form of music. But why did they sing in the first place? Mrs. Kaszynski said it was an impulse to imitate natural sounds, like birds. Maybe that's true. But even though they were mimicking, they were creating something new."

She must have been fourteen when Brynn told her that, sitting in the shade of that big maple across from the park, because that was only a few months before Mrs. Kaszynski's swift and merciless death from pancreatic cancer. Brynn knew her music teacher was sick, and when she spoke of her a curious dread seemed to lurk behind her eyes—some innate but little-understood sense of mortality.

"She also said that in ancient times, music was believed to come from the gods. Or godlike beings. Muses." Brynn chewed the word like taffy. "I like that."

Afterward, whenever Brynn was feeling particularly inspired, she would say she had been visited by her muse. These visits were often accompanied by bouts of sleeplessness. Harlow would come over to find her holed up in her disaster of a room, caffeine-jittery, something wild in her eyes. And then, inevitably, when the muse's visit ended, Brynn became a shadow of herself, bundled into the fabric of her too-large clothing, curled up like a roly-poly, wishing the world away in a fit of despondency.

Harlow came to recognize these patterns of hers, and she arranged herself to accommodate them. Even in her lower moments, there was a brightness to Brynn that Harlow desperately wanted to absorb.

When Brynn really came alive, though, was when she put on the face of Queen Carrion.

Originally, the band consisted of Brynn on vocals, Harlow on drums, and Harlow's brother on guitar. Then they added bass, a second guitar, and a cello ("We need it," Brynn insisted. "The cello is the instrument that sounds closest to the human voice."). Brynn immediately embodied her new persona, became possessed by it. White makeup, a dripping black mouth, eyes darkened to pits. Visits from her muse led to new songs, entire albums, and even, eventually, a cult-like fanbase.

And through it all, they were still inseparable—roommates into their twenties, bandmates since their teens, best friends ever since Harlow latched onto her as a kid and did not let go. Always together.

That is, until Brynn Werner disappeared.

AFTER

She remembers the sensation of being watched back in the woods, from between the trees, and she feels it again now. Eyes hidden somewhere she cannot see. Peeking out from between the bottles behind the bar, perhaps—around the edges of Maker's Mark, Jose Cuervo, Beefeater, Grey Goose, Bacardi. From cracks in the vinyl booths standing against old brick etched with graffiti. The feeling tingles up her arms like an army of spiders, and though it's quiet, another lonely night, she can't help thinking she's never really alone. Not anymore.

She gets the bartender's attention, orders a whiskey Coke. When he sets it, sweating, in front of her, she has to lift it carefully, her trembling hand threatening to spill it over the lip of the glass. When she's downed the drink, carbonation stinging the back of her throat, she waves him down again—a Lurch of a man, balding, broad forehead shiny with grease—and asks for a shot. Something she doesn't have to taste.

Her mouth tastes like dirt, no matter what she puts in it.

She picks black polish from stubbornly short nails, flaking it off in dead pieces. Sometimes she thinks she only puts it on so she can chip it off again. Find the clean nail underneath.

The bartender slides her the brown shot, and she throws it back. "Rough night?" he asks. His cheeks are high, red. His eyes glisten a wet blue.

Her lips peel back in a grin, or maybe a grimace—she doesn't know, can't see it, but feels the tug splitting her skin. "Week. Month. Year. Take your pick."

He nods like he's heard that one before. "Get you another?"

He doesn't have to ask twice.

A wave of laughter surges from one of the tables where a group of young men sits over a menagerie of beers. Metallica chugs from the speakers, an '80s track from *Ride the Lightning*, and one from the group jams along. He has an unworried face fuzzed with a sparse goatee, and his mouth sits crooked in it, on the verge of cracking a grin. Beside him, his friend's thumbs engage in a furious dance on his phone's digital keyboard, while the other two nod and laugh and talk in words she can't make out from here.

There are different sorts of people who come to bars. She has frequented enough of them—dingy dives, the kind of venues that host underground bands—to recognize who's who in each group. She's even made something of a tarot set of them:

The Drinker is unpredictable. His only consistency is that he'll always say yes to another drink.

The Scroller never puts down their phone. Mind elsewhere. Present, but not present.

The Clown is in a good mood, cracking jokes. Wants everyone else to be in a good mood, too.

The Driver takes it easy. Orders one beer, then soda or water the rest of the night. Clear-eyed, responsible. Not very much fun.

The Troublemaker likes to stir things up. Always escalating, pushing boundaries. The one who pulls out a little baggie and says, "Let's take things up a notch."

She tries to guess at the group of men—college-aged, barely legal, or here with fake IDs. Clearly the one on his phone is the Scroller. The one jamming along to the music, she suspects, is the Drinker; his interest lies in enjoying his beverage. The other two could well be the Clown and the Troublemaker, or perhaps the Clown and the Driver. They both have half-drunk beers before them.

The previous hour saw the nodding goodbyes of a few regulars— aging bikers with long gray beards and fading tattoos. She and the group are the only ones left now as the eleventh hour slips toward midnight.

Then she spots it—a gleam of metal beneath the rainbow string lights.

One of them is the Troublemaker, after all.

"The fuck you doing—put that away," says the one with a round, clean face. Wearing plaid. Buttoned-up. Maybe the Driver.

"Protection," the knife-wielder argues, closing it with a *shick*. "I tell you how that homeless guy attacked me last week? The bums are out of control."

She tries to tune out their conversation.

Three drinks deep and she still feels she's being watched, even though she knows the boys are paying her no mind. Hairs prickle the back of her neck. She turns left, right, searching for a pair of eyes, finds none. Just the graffiti stating who loves who, and who was here, and who sucks dick in hell. The words creep over each other, forming illegible tendrils that remind her of metal band logos, spidery little messages.

One catches her eye, in the corner near the bathrooms. Scratched into the wall.

Queen Carrion was here.

She closes her eyes. Convinces herself she didn't see that. Opens them.

Queen Carrion is everywhere.

She knocks over the empty shot glass. It rolls across the bar, draws the attention of the bartender, who comes over to ask—something. She doesn't hear. Her ears are ringing. Tinnitus. Too many loud shows. And she's only twenty-eight.

Across from her, the graffiti crawls over the wall.

We're already here.

Her barstool scrapes across the floor as she throws herself out of her seat. A new song issues from the speakers, and she's half-convinced for the first few bars it's one of *theirs*, a Queen Carrion song, but then the vocalist starts, and it's not.

The group, interrupted, turns to stare at her.

"Hey, you okay?" the bartender asks. Wary concern in his eyes. Sizing her up, seeing if she's on something more than booze. She doesn't blame him. Knows how she looks: eyes charcoal-ringed to hide the sleepless bags, hair slashed jagged from botched attempts to cut it herself, clothes worn and crumpled up and worn again. In the mirrored display behind the bar, she can see a distorted version of her maggot-pale face.

She nods, head swimming, and eases back into the seat. "One more. A double."

"Don't I know you from somewhere?" he asks, eyes narrowing, as he slowly moves to pour a new drink. The group turns away, back to their conversation.

She shakes her head. Avoids looking up at the graffiti, afraid of what it will say next. Maybe it will recount the headlines from over the last few weeks, all the speculation over what happened in the woods.

"I've never been here before," she says. "You're thinking of someone else."

But the bartender's face is compressed with concentration as he tries to decipher her. She catches the moment of recognition—when something snaps into focus bchind those blue eyes. He pours the double and passes it over.

That's it, she thinks. He's seen the papers, the news. Seen her picture. Soon the whispers will start. The questions.

Did you kill them?

Why is the Troublemaker flicking open and shut that stupid pocketknife? Why does he think it makes him look cool to show it off to his buddies? Maybe he's hoping for a little danger tonight. Maybe he wants to show he can defend himself. Against bums and anything else.

She sips the drink, trying to savor it, then glances back at the wall by the bathrooms, unable to stop herself, hoping she will find only gibberish.

We're already inside.

A liquored fuzz spreads over her mind. Everywhere, the glint of light on glass bottles, the sharp eruption of laughter, the gleam of the pocketknife in the Troublemaker's hands. Her phone buzzes in her pocket, and she ignores it. A wild fantasy comes—that it's a text from *her*. A reminder, like the graffiti, that she is out there. She is everywhere. Unbound by time or place. Isn't that the way with the dead?

"...saw them live once. They used to play a lot of local shows. Fucked up, right? Didn't even find their bodies..."

She tries not to listen, but the Troublemaker's voice cuts through the music.

"You ever heard that song—'Midnight Ritual'? They say it's supposed to drive you insane."

"Like 'Gloomy Sunday.'"

"Huh?"

The Scroller types it in and reads: "'Gloomy Sunday,' also known as the 'Hungarian Suicide Song,' is a 1933 song with a sinister reputation… an urban legend claims a lot of people committed suicide while listening to it."

She squeezes her eyes shut. Tries not to listen. They can't be talking about this.

"Yeah. So I was thinking, what if they were fucking with some dark shit? Occult stuff? And that's what they were doing out in the woods. Trying to summon something. Maybe the ghost of their dead singer."

"Didn't she disappear?"

"Maybe she came back from the dead and killed them."

"I thought it was the drummer—"

There is nothing, a blank space, between clenching her hand on the glass and standing. She is simply on her feet, heart going, the stool on its side. She doesn't hear it crash to the floor, but the others do. Their eyes blaze into her, and the bartender stands frozen, staring, a wet blue stare.

Then she's at the booth. Body numb. Moving almost of its own accord. She reaches, her hand dives into the Troublemaker's pocket even as he protests, tries to push her away. But she's strong, arms corded with muscle, and if he stood, she would be taller than him.

Shick.

"Hey, take it easy," says the Drinker with an uncomfortable little laugh, hands in the air. "Why don't you give that back?"

The bartender mumbles behind her. Who is he talking to?

Shick.

"You think I killed them?" The words tumble out of her mouth, too loud. She holds out her arm, and the boys recoil, crying out. Eyes widening, widening.

In recognition.

"Holy *shit*," the Scroller hisses, holds up his phone, and it's her—a picture of her from right after it was all over, when she was still in shock, her face empty, and the headline: *Local Band's Tragedy in the Woods*.

The Troublemaker eyes his own knife with confused betrayal. This isn't the danger he was looking for. He never meant to be on the other side of the blade.

"We believe you," says the Driver, conciliatory. "Whatever you say."

The Drinker nods. "Yeah. Yeah. Why don't you tell us your story? Tell us what really happened?"

They warble, blur. Her eyes burn.

Despite their words, they look at her like she's a monster. She knows that look. The way her mother's looked at her since she was six years old. The way she looks at herself in the mirror.

Shick.

Flesh parts around the blade. Red wells in the open crevasse. Somewhere in the distance, she hears the echo of sirens.

TWO

It was a good thing they hadn't rented a van like during their touring days—something big and hulking would have struggled along these narrow forest roads that contorted into unpaved switchbacks, dense stands of pines hugging the edges. Even in the Ford Escape, Wendy drove tensed, every blind curve putting her on edge.

All she could think was that they had better get to this godforsaken cabin soon.

There were so many forests around Portland. They could easily have hit Tillamook or Mt. Hood in an hour, but no, instead they'd driven four hours through Salem and Eugene down I-5 (*the 5*, as her cousin Leah called it down in LA), then onto one of the Umpqua Forest highways, and finally through the twists and turns of roads whose names were labels of NF followed by a series of seemingly random numbers.

She knew why they had chosen this particular forest, but that didn't mean she had to be happy about it.

The Escape jarred over a dip in the pavement, and Wendy's hands clenched on the wheel. She didn't want to take her eyes off the road as it ducked behind a cluster of trees. "Lou, can you check how much further?"

No response.

The silence made Wendy glance to her right at Louella sitting shotgun, head tilted against the window, face turned down beneath a spray of lavender hair.

"I think she's asleep," Harlow's voice drifted from behind.

"She's supposed to be my navigator."

"Want me to wake her up?" Harlow kicked the back of the seat with her boot. "Hey, sleepyhead!"

With a snort, Lou came awake, jerking upright. "Wha? What'd I miss?"

Harlow leaned forward. "Well, we were relying on you to navigate, but since you fell asleep we have no idea where we are."

"We're lost?" Lou blinked around at the rising slopes of trees.

"Ignore her," said Wendy. "Harlow's just being a bitch." *Like always,* she refrained from adding.

Feeling a bit more confident, she glanced at the phone sitting in its holder on the dash, hoping it would tell her they were nearly there, that this silly schlep was almost at an end. What she saw, instead, was a map without that signature blue line guiding them forward, a gray map that said only *no signal.*

"Son of a bitch." She eased off the gas, pushing her storm cloud of hair back from her face. "Anyone have a signal?"

From the corner of her sight, she caught Lou tapping on her phone, Harlow fishing hers out of a pocket. In the rearview mirror, Thorn shifted around for his. Wendy's eyes snapped back to the screen and saw it was recalculating the route. In a moment, the GPS was back on. "Never mind."

She lamented that she was the one driving. They were deep into the woods now and she would have no idea how to get back out again if the signal cut out completely.

Wendy Mann was, or believed herself to be, a practical person. If it were up to her, they would have booked a cabin on the edge of the forest: somewhere with the feeling of being out of the city but without the inconvenience of being deep in the wilderness.

Though she didn't love the arrangement, it made sense that she was the one to drive. Thorn didn't have a car and didn't like to drive anyway (she couldn't really blame him since, being blind in one eye, he was lacking in depth perception). Lou's car was a twenty-year-old blue Corolla with a beard of rust around its wheel wells and a penchant for whining impotently rather than actually starting. And, frankly, Wendy didn't trust Harlow's driving—she drove too fast and spent half her time drunk, anyway. Besides, Wendy had the biggest vehicle, as it was hard to fit a cello into a sedan. They could have squeezed Rhys in here, too, but he'd decided to take his cherry red Camaro so that his girl-friend, Jacqueline, could come along.

Fiancée, Wendy reminded herself.

Engaged or not, she wasn't thrilled about Jacqueline tagging along. This was supposed to be a weekend just for them—just the band.

A pickup truck careened onto the road ahead of them, turning blind from some hidden offshoot, and Wendy panicked, stomped the brakes. Exhaust darkened the windshield as the truck rocked on oversized tires before surging ahead, a tattered American flag flapping from its dirt-speckled bed.

Harlow nudged down her window and stuck her head out like a dog. "Nice driving, asshole!"

Wendy shushed her. "I don't feel like getting shot today. Those are the kinds of people who swing AR-15s around to show how big their dicks are."

"Yeah, don't piss off random rednecks in the woods," Lou said.

"There's a song there," Thorn rasped. *"Don't piss off the random... rednecks in the woods... They've got guns and ammo... they'll fuck you up good."*

"Thank god *you* never wrote any of our songs," Harlow said.

The truck sped off, vanished in a cloud of dirt. Wendy glanced in the rearview mirror, saw the Camaro a few yards behind them, luckily not having rear-ended the Escape in the sudden stop. Then she caught a flash of silver in the back of the car—Harlow's flask obscuring her face.

"Hey, can you put the booze away in the car, please?" Harlow shrugged and tucked the flask into the inner pocket of her leather jacket. Wendy straightened the mirror and eased the car forward.

She was ready for this car ride to be over.

She was ready for Queen Carrion to be over.

It was time for them to move on to new things. Brynn had disap-peared a year ago, and Wendy had long since accepted that if she was ever found, it would be as a corpse. Their lead singer was gone, and there was nothing to hold the rest of the band together. Putting every-thing on hold for the past year had given her a chance to reassess. She was approaching thirty, and what exactly did she have to show for it? A classically trained cellist, she had once been a source of pride for her parents, who imagined she would go on to the prestigious world of orchestral performance, or at least teaching; when she instead joined a local metal band, they stopped bragging about her. They had imagined for her a future of comfort, but Wendy had instead spent her twenties renting cheap apartments, sleeping in vans, performing in grimy bars, living on gas station coffee and fast food, scratching by on intermittent and unpredictable cash from touring.

Maybe that was fine for her twenties, but did she really want to keep up that lifestyle into her thirties? Her forties? The future became a yawning chasm she was afraid to fall into without knowing whether there lay a cushion somewhere at the bottom.

Her phone announced a turn at the very last moment, and Wendy swung the wheel hard, sending Harlow spilling into Thorn's side. *Thanks for the head's up, GPS lady*, she thought bitterly as she straightened out the car onto the new road, which looked pretty much the same as the last one. "Did they catch the turn?"

"Unfortunately, yes," Harlow said.

"Don't be an ass."

"I don't think she can help it," Thorn said, waving his hand at his sister. "It's just… asses, all the way down."

The phone indicated they had a few more miles to go on this new road, and Wendy reached for it, one eye on the windshield, the other on the screen, hoping to check the remaining directions. As her finger met the screen, however, the directions vanished.

No signal.

"Oh Jesus *Christ*," she snapped. They rolled slowly between the trees while the others checked their phones, shook their heads. Nothing. With a sigh, Wendy brought the car to a halt. "Maybe we should turn around." Even as she said it, she cringed. Four hours—*more* than four hours—and now they would have to backtrack and make the trip even longer.

"Come on, this place can't be impossible to find," said Harlow. "It was on Airbnb, right?" She seemed so unbothered that Wendy wanted to smack that little smirk off her face. Of course she was unbothered. She'd already had a few hefty sips of whatever toxic concoction lived in that flask.

Shaking her head, Wendy clicked off her seatbelt, opened the door, and hopped out onto the dirt. She held up her phone as if the extra foot would magically bestow it with connectivity. Behind them, the Camaro pulled to a stop and the doors popped open.

"What's the holdup?" called Rhys.

The others stepped out of the Escape, stretching, calling back about the lack of GPS. Without the hum of the car, the forest buzzed with cicadas. Bright-needled hemlocks wept beads of dew, and spindles of Douglas fir pierced the low, soupy clouds. The day was as wet and gray as a funeral. Mosquitoes flitted past her face, and Wendy wished they were back in Portland.

Rhys turned. "Babe, don't you have the…"

"On it." Jacqueline dove back into the Camaro to rummage through a bag.

Slapping mosquitoes from her arms, Wendy frowned when she noticed Thorn and Harlow leaning against some nearby trees—brother and sister giving into their respective vices. Harlow sipping from her flask, Thorn lighting a cigarette. She knew he would take that stale, ashy smell back into the Escape with him.

She'd tried to get him to quit—though perhaps she wasn't very convincing, as each time they'd fallen into bed together, she always accepted, and enjoyed, the proffered post-sex cigarette. It was a bad habit, but one she only indulged in on these rare occasions. Thorn was the same for her. He was her bad habit. But she was good at not letting habits become addictions.

A shaft of sunlight cut through the treetops with an almost physical presence before the clouds rolled over. Every leaf shudder and shadow seemed imbued with life.

"Guys." Lou's voice was a hush, her eyes locked onto the distance. "Come check this out. I just saw the prettiest white deer." Twigs cracked under her feet as she stepped between the trees. "I've never seen one like that…"

Harlow pulled the flask from her mouth long enough to say, "That fuck in the truck is probably out here to hunt it. Stick its head on the mantle."

"I'd like to stick *your* head on my mantle," Rhys said.

"I'd like to see you try."

He and Harlow always seemed to be halfway between joking and cruelty—or maybe some combination of the two. Wendy worried their little barbs would turn into an actual argument. "Look, I don't want to be lost out here when it gets dark. Let's go back and regroup some-where with reception."

"Chill out." Rhys's words sent prickles of affront along Wendy's skin.

"We've got this." He turned back to Jacqueline. Her rear stuck out from the Camaro, barely contained by a pair of frayed denim shorts so abbreviated the pockets stuck out the bottom. "You got it, or what?"

"Found it." Jacqueline shimmied out of the car, brandishing a piece of paper with printed directions.

"See?" Rhys said. "Thanks, babe." He gave her a peck on the cheek. Her grin thinned her lips, wrinkled her upturned nose with its tiny diamond stud. Jacqueline was a few years younger than the others, with a haughty look and deep-set eyes. In some ways, she was the anti-Brynn: waifish and blonde and jealous. Dark eyebrows betrayed her dye job, platinum hair cut severely at the chin, crimped and frizzed, bleach-damaged.

Jacqueline was always hanging around, even during rehearsals, where she would sit and watch, occasionally interrupting to gush over Rhys's talent. "My grandfather was a manager at Capitol Records, back in the day," she never failed to boast, as if this pedigree endowed her with innate musical sensibilities. Wendy suspected it wasn't even true, though she had no proof of this suspicion. Something about Jacqueline felt like a lie.

Taking the paper, Wendy followed the directions to where she thought they must be now. Another numbered road. She wasn't entirely sure it was the right one, but if she was wrong, well, they would just spend a night lost in the woods. *Tons* of fun. "Let's get going."

"But what about the…" Lou gazed longingly into the trees.

Thorn clapped a hand on her shoulder. "Plenty more wildlife in the woods." He toed out the cigarette.

The road crossed a rickety bridge over a shallow greenish river, rocks standing in mossy clusters, and they entered a wall of pines so thick the road was like a hole cut into the darkness. Trees stood close, anonymous in their endless replication, obscuring all sense of distance.

Almost there, Wendy told herself. The sooner they got to the cabin, the sooner they could get this weekend over with.

"There should be a left turn ahead." Lou had finally decided to step up as the navigator.

The Escape slowed.

"Where?"

"I don't know, exactly." Lou pointed to the map. "There."

They crept along until Wendy spotted it.

Lou read from the map. "This must be Trail Creek Lane."

"That's barely even a road."

"It's a road."

"Well, I don't see a sign."

"It's the only left turn on the map for miles."

Wendy looked dubiously at the overgrown, one-lane path barely wide enough for her car. She was so used to cities built around the vehicle, paved highways making up the arteries that moved life along. By contrast, this dirt road was but a small intrusion on nature's sprawl.

Tires struggled for purchase in stippled mud as she eased onto the new road. Windows rattled. They passed a sign warning of mudslides and rockfall from the nearby cliff faces.

Eventually the road twisted and revealed an opening on the right, a small space in which to park beside a set of cracked stone steps leading up and into the trees, hemmed in by thickets of whitethorn brush.

"Is this it?" Wendy asked as she pulled in. To the side of the steps stood a crooked wooden pole with the faded numbers: 87.

"87 Trail Creek. That's the address." Lou tossed the map on the dashboard.

The Camaro pulled in behind, boxing them in. They stepped out.

Jacqueline tugged a duffel bag onto her shoulder. "This looks right, from what I saw on the listing. It shouldn't be too far. Right, babe?" She nudged Rhys, then turned to the others as they gazed up the steps. "Come on! This will be fun! Hey, it's kind of like your song 'Satan's Child.'" She started to sing: *From deep within her woodland hut, oh the witch is cursing! And suckles on her teat a goat, oh the witch is nursing... Satan's child!*

"*Behold the vile beast,*" Thorn intoned, voice deep and raw, the growl of his backup vocals. "*That wears its crown of thorn. The darkness drops again. It slouches to be born.*" He stuck out his long tongue, his signature move, throwing devil horns.

"Kind of butchered Yeats there, didn't we?" Wendy said with a rueful smile, glad to be out of the car.

The others laughed. Wendy noticed the look on Harlow's face, as if she'd bitten into a sour fruit. Every time Jacqueline started singing one of their songs, Harlow looked like she wanted to plug her ears.

At the top of the staircase, it came into view: a wooden A-frame ensconced in the trees, sharply angled.

Thorn nodded. "Looks like a good place to get axe-murdered."

"Shut the fuck up," Wendy laughed.

He grinned at her. He'd always loved to rile her up in one way or another. One corner of his mouth pulled taut in a perpetual half-smile. Long black hair hung down one side of his face, the other a rutted land-scape where nothing grew, flesh rippled with scars, the eye a bluish cloud. The faint musk of tobacco still clung to him, as it always did.

She tried to imagine telling her parents that *this* was her on-again off-again fling: scarred, pierced, trenchcoat-clad. This is what she reminded herself whenever she was drawn in by him.

He was fun, but then, so were all bad habits.

When they got up to the A-frame, they found the cabin already unlocked. The handle turned easily.

"That doesn't seem very safe," she said.

"Who's gonna break into this place?" Rhys held out his arms, looking around at the stretch of forest.

"Come on." Harlow shifted impatiently. "I gotta piss."

Just a few days, Wendy thought. At some point this weekend, she would tell them her plans. She would move to LA to become a studio musician. Maybe it was a wild dream, but she had been perfecting her audition tapes and thought she had what it took. If she didn't try now, she never would—and even if she failed, at least she could be proud of what she had tried. She wasn't sure how the others would take the news. Clearly, some of them had a hard time letting go.

By the end of this weekend, though, she had a feeling she would be free.

The door swung open. They let themselves inside. They didn't notice the old barbed wire fence, long since fallen and grown over, out at the perimeter.

WHAT EVER HAPPENED TO   QUEEN CARRION?

THE CURIOUS CASE OF ONE BAND'S   SELF-DESTRUCTION

Most of those familiar with the unexplained events surrounding Portland-based metal outfit Queen Carrion would believe it all began with the disappearance of frontwoman and lead vocalist, Brynn Werner —but this was not, in fact, the first strange event to befall the band.

It really started with the Wonder Room Panic, which left six injured and one dead. What caused the sudden mass hysteria that gripped the patrons of the nightclub halfway through Queen Carrion's set? What instigated the terror that resulted in the fatal trampling of 17-year-old Murphy Dunning as the crowd surged for the exits? No one has been able to say for certain, but the answer, I believe, will help us unravel the mystery of what happened to Queen Carrion on that fateful weekend one year after Werner's disappearance, when they all went out to the woods...

THREE

Even with the curtains pulled back, the cabin was dim. Flipping on the light only rendered its furnishings dusty and dated: floral bruise-colored armchairs, a corduroy sofa, rickety wooden chairs that might be better put out of their misery as firewood. A chandelier made of antlers, gauzed with the thin translucence of cobwebs, suspended a broken ribcage of spikes above a black wood stove. Above the couch loomed a taxidermied deer head mounted to the wall.

Lou draped herself on the sofa like a piece of wet laundry. Thorn toed the dirty rust-orange rug, threads hanging loose at its edges. "Nice place."

"I think you need a new definition of 'nice,'" Wendy said.

Harlow beelined past the kitchenette and found three doors: two small bedrooms flanking a bathroom. It was knotty pine as far as the eye could see. Even the toilet was a wood box with a wood lid, the sink a chipped ceramic bowl set into a chunky wood pedestal. She let several hours' worth of pent-up urine loose, relief washing over her.

Sitting here alone for the first time in hours, she pulled out a well-worn map and unfolded it. Feathery white creases split the green spread of the Umpqua National Forest, drawn over with circles and x's to rule out places that had already been searched.

Her eyes zeroed in on where they were now: an expanse of wilderness. The search had not been out this way, but what if Brynn had? There was no saying exactly where she'd gone. The name of the forest wasn't much to go on, considering its size and density. They'd started with all the more popular campgrounds, then they searched the less popular ones, hiking areas, trails, anywhere she might have ended up. It was as if she had dropped off the face of the earth. Harlow didn't understand it. Eventually, the sheriff's office thought maybe she hadn't even made it to the Umpqua, in which case, how many more places could she be between here and Portland? The range got much bigger, more impossible to cover.

Something within Harlow told her Brynn *had* made it to the forest. She knew how Brynn got when she had something in her mind: an idea, an obsession, a pursuit. She would focus on it to the exclusion of all else, make it her sole priority. She'd been like that at the time, singularly focused on going camping no matter what Harlow said.

"That's where I'll find my muse," Brynn told her. "It's like… she's telling me that's where I have to go."

Through the door, she could hear muffled laughter, footsteps creaking on old floorboards. She found herself staring at a patch of floor in the corner gone black with rot. She supposed that's what happened when you made a bathroom out of wood.

At first, the toilet only gulped. She toggled the handle until it caught, slurped down the drain. Her face was gray and smudged with grime in the dingy mirror above the sink. Water guttered uncertainly from the faucet before shooting at full gush. It smelled musty. There was no soap.

Another black patch grew from the ceiling corner. Flakes of wood peeled away from the sore like dead skin. She dried her hands on her jeans, opting against the threadbare pink towel moldering on the rack. How long had it been since *that* was put through the wash?

She hated every detail. Even though she had been determined to come out here, could not stay away from the forest for too long, she couldn't help thinking it was an evil place. It had swallowed Brynn and so many other people over the years. It was greedy, hungry. And she hated, too, that she was even thinking about dirty rugs and dilapidated bathrooms with all those miles of woodland around, all those ditches where Brynn's body might lie.

Water hissed down the drain. She pulled out her flask and took a pull, but it wasn't even a full sip. The flask was empty.

Somehow she felt both too drunk and not drunk enough. It was an unpleasant feeling.

She found it a bit unfair that there were only certain contexts where drinking was acceptable. After a show, in the glow of performance? Absolutely. Alone on a Tuesday? Not so much. On a weekend getaway? Yes. On the drive out to said weekend getaway, via hip flask? You're an alcoholic.

It had gotten her into trouble before. Whenever Harlow's back pain flared up, she found herself putting down an extra shot with each drink whenever she, Lou, and Thorn went out. Sometimes Thorn would start texting Wendy and vanish. When that happened, Harlow and Lou became each other's wing women. Sometimes, they both got wasted and went home. Sometimes, Lou found a woman to go home with. Less often, Harlow found someone to go home with.

Drinking effectively dulled the pain, but the consequences left their mark on her in bleary afternoons and stumbling late to rehearsals.

Casper, their manager, wasn't happy about it. His real name was Caspian, but they called him Casper because he was pale, soft-footed, and always working in the background. Like a friendly, albeit somewhat irksome, ghost.

When Harlow arrived an hour late to an important rehearsal and had to stop playing after thirty minutes to go puke, it was the last straw. He pulled her aside and told her she had to cut back on the drinking.

"Sure, Mom."

"I'm serious," he said. "You're making things difficult. The others are getting sick of it. It's not fair to them to have to put up with this."

"Man, unclench, it'll be okay."

"You're being an asshole and holding up rehearsals, maybe pushing back how soon we can record this album."

They had been working on a concept album at the time. *The Orchid.* The story of a flower that sprang up from the nourishment of a corpse and began communicating with other plants. This communication led the plants to kill as many people as they could because they had discovered their bodies made for good fertilizer. People were impaled upon cacti, strangled by vines, eaten by Venus flytraps. In the end, humanity died and its architecture decayed. Plants grew over and into these ruins, enjoying long eons of peace… until—

None but Brynn knew the final piece. There was one more song that acted as a kind of twist or coda, but she was still writing it.

It was the song she never finished.

Harlow reminded Casper that *she* wasn't the one holding things up.

"Just get your shit together," he said before striding off.

At that point, the hangover had been throbbing through her, the taste of vomit still sharp in the back of her throat, and she wanted to go to sleep. Being chewed out by their manager was one thing, but then Thorn said, "He's right. You might want to clean out a little."

"You're telling *me* to clean out while you suck down those cancer sticks?"

She did ease up on the drinking, at first. But then Brynn disappeared, chasing her muse, and it was the only thing that kept her going. She avoided Thorn, not wanting to invoke his condemnation. Then Lou hadn't wanted to come out anymore, so she did the socially unacceptable thing: she drank alone.

The more she did it, the easier it got.

Only now her flask was empty. Luckily, they'd brought plenty of booze for the weekend.

When she stepped out of the bathroom, she nearly ran right into Thorn. "Jesus!"

"Flattered," he said, "but no."

"Where are you taking our bags?"

"Our room." She followed him into the tiny bedroom on the left with two twin beds wearing brown paisley duvets. "Rhys claimed the loft."

"Why does *he* get the loft?"

Thorn's bag slumped to the avocado carpet. "The king and queen deserve the highest throne."

"They're not married yet," Harlow grumbled.

"Hey, it'll be like when we were kids, at Dad's place. Minus the bunk beds."

Harlow dropped back against the bed. She wasn't surprised by the ceiling. More knotty pine. Her eyes could not stop finding spots of mold in the corners, creeping like shadows.

"Seriously, though." Thorn sat on the opposite bed, which creaked beneath his weight. He nodded to the door at the foot of Harlow's bed. "If there's an axe-murderer here, he's taking you out first."

"Thanks."

Thorn pulled off the headphones that had been sitting dormant around his neck, an excuse to listen to music any time he didn't feel like listening to people. "You gonna be okay?"

"Not if I get axe-murdered." She traced grooves in the ceiling with her eyes. "Don't worry. I was the one who suggested coming out here."

"Yeah, but you're not just here for shits and giggles."

"Isn't that why *you're* here?"

He sighed. "You're here to look for Brynn."

Harlow sat up, rising like a vampire from its coffin, and she could feel it in her abdomen. She tried to remember the last time she'd worked seriously at her kit. Days blurred together. She wasn't drumming regularly anymore. "Why else would I be here?"

"I'm pretty sure everyone else is here to bury her. Not dig her back up."

"So you're giving her up for dead, too." She watched Thorn kick his bag into the corner and push Harlow's bag across the floor to her. When he straightened, he looked tired. His good eye found hers and stuck there.

He sounded resigned when he asked, "When are you going to stop?"

Harlow suspected he already knew the answer. "When I find her."

The sound of Jacqueline singing one of their songs echoed into the room. Hearing Brynn's words in her voice set Harlow's teeth on edge.

"Come on." She got up, taking heavy steps back to the main room, hoping the thump of her boots would cut off the singing. Jacqueline gave her a small, insincere smile, her teeth like little white Chiclets with thin gaps between each.

Before she could say anything, the front door opened with a rush of wind and pine needles. Rhys and Wendy stepped inside, laden with coolers and grocery bags.

"Thank god." As soon as Rhys dropped a bag on the kitchen counter, Harlow pulled out a bottle of Wild Turkey and poured a careful stream into her flask.

"Food? I'm starving," Lou said as she emerged from the other bedroom.

"Penne alla vodka." Thorn began pulling out ingredients. He paused to turn the bottle of Smirnoff to the others like some expensive brand of wine. They nodded their approval. He unscrewed the cap and poured shots all around. When Harlow went to pour a second, the first having gone down like water, he said, "Don't drink the whole bottle. I need some for the sauce."

"Yes, chef."

After checking the blade of a knife from the wooden block, he started chopping an onion, and everyone else settled in the living room.

"Oh, look." Wendy picked up a thin book from the coffee table and flipped it open. The cover read *Trail Creek Cabin Guest Book*. "What should we write? 'Queen Carrion was here'?"

"Maybe you should write the lyrics to a song. 'The Death Queen'?" Jacqueline started to hum, then broke out: "*Feed on the bones, drink of the blood, body and soul, you'll give yourself up to the queen.*"

"Brynn screams the last few words," Harlow said.

Wendy closed the guest book, dropped it on the table, and slid it away with her foot, looking put out.

"Hey." Rhys pulled a Ziploc bag out of his pocket. "Why don't we take things up a notch?" He rattled its contents: a few broken, crumbling brown squares.

"What is that?"

"That, my friend, is mushroom chocolate." He shook out a square into his palm.

"No way," Wendy said. "Last time I did shrooms, I spent an hour throwing up." Lou took one. Rhys held up the bag for Thorn, but he shook his head.

"Don't get the chef high, or who knows what you'll be eating."

When Rhys turned the bag to Harlow, she hesitated. She wanted to go out and search, but it would be dark soon, and even she realized how foolhardy that would be. She was stuck here for the night.

Might as well pass the time somehow.

She took one of the broken pieces from the bag and chewed it up, chased by a sip of bourbon.

Lou tried to play Spotify from her phone before realizing there was no wifi. There wasn't even so much as a TV to keep them entertained. Wendy dug through a stack of ancient paperbacks sitting under the coffee table and blew dust off their covers—pulpy drawings of scantily clad women running from UFOs, white cracks running through them. Jacqueline hummed snatches of their songs to fill the quiet. Rhys and Lou started debating the best album of the year.

Harlow drank, waiting for the shrooms to hit, and found herself looking at the deer head on the wall. She didn't understand the impulse to stuff a dead animal and keep it as a prize, which seemed cruel and morbid to her. Its black marble stare was somehow both empty and penetrating, and even though they weren't its real eyes, even though the animal was long dead, she felt as if it were looking at her. *Why am I stuck on this wall?* It seemed to ask. *Why would you murder me and preserve my carcass to keep me around?*

She turned her gaze, instead, to the floor, where she saw more mold. It stained the hardwood black. There must be some kind of seepage, she thought. "This place is a real shithole."

"Really? Because you seem right at home." Rhys's grin was sharp and hungry, like a shark's.

"Remember that motel we stayed at in Spokane? With the bedbugs?" Lou bent her legs under her on the couch, sitting on her knees. "Now that was a shithole. The water in the bathroom came out brown."

Wendy shuddered. "Don't remind me. I found a roach there the size of a rat. Never again."

"I think this place is kind of cute," Jacqueline said. "Rustic."

Rhys took a sip from his beer. "For eighty bucks a night? It's a steal."

"Now that you mention it, though…" Wendy frowned at the floor, at the black spots Harlow had noticed. "Isn't that some kind of safety violation? Doesn't Airbnb even check out their listings?"

"Lighten up," Rhys said.

"Seriously." Wendy stood now, pointing to the edge of the orange rug. "That wood looks rotted. Someone could fall through."

"Try jumping up and down," Harlow told her. "See if it breaks."

Ignoring her, Wendy bent down and flipped up the corner of the rug, probably to see if it was worse underneath, since that would figure, wouldn't it? Some cheapskate throws a rug over the ruined flooring so they can make a quick buck on this garbage property in the middle of nowhere, tack on some extra fees when no one's looking, wham-bam. Safety violations? Who cares, way out here?

It wasn't rotted floor she found underneath, but a hard line cut into the wood.

"What is that?"

She threw over more of the rug, expelling a cloud of dust, and there it was: a handle set into the floor with a square carved around it.

Wendy looked up. "It's a trapdoor."

"Oh, hell no," Thorn called from the kitchen, where a pot of water was boiling. "Haven't you ever seen *Evil Dead*?"

"What do you think is down there?" Lou asked, eyes wide.

"A cellar," Wendy said. "Probably filled with old junk and spiderwebs. If you're lucky, you might find a potato with tentacles."

"One way to find out." Harlow came over, gripped the handle, and pulled. The door stuck, grimed along the edges. With another tug, it groaned upward. She stood, rubbed the feel of corroded metal on her jeans, and looked down at the black square with a ladder descending into it.

"Dare you to go down." Rhys gave Harlow a wicked grin.

She shrugged. "Fine."

"Can't we just put the rug back and leave it?" Wendy asked, giving the black square a distrustful glance.

But Harlow had already stepped down onto the first rung. She lowered herself until her shoulders were level with the floor. "I'll let you know if I find any dead bodies."

She climbed down until her feet hit solid ground. Above her, Lou's head appeared in the opening. "Don't read the Latin."

Her phone's flashlight showed her pretty much what she expected to find: a small stone cellar, low-ceilinged, empty. Spiderwebs draped the corners. She called up to the others, and Wendy gave her the old *I-told-you-so.*

Harlow shined her light along the walls, disappointed there wasn't some ancient text or a cursed object or a bunch of bloodied saws. The worst, she thought, was finding nothing. They had searched the woods for weeks and found nothing—not even Brynn's bike, not a trace of her. She wanted to go to a private detective, thinking she'd have more luck with hired help, but even they turned her away, saying there weren't any clues, there was nothing for them to go on. It got to the point where Harlow wished for something terrible to happen, wished for Brynn's mangled body to be found—just so that there would be *something,* some answer.

She heard Thorn call out that dinner was almost done, but she wasn't ready to climb back up the ladder yet. She wanted to stay down here in the dark, a chill reaching up from the damp stone. She turned and looked to the other side of the ladder, where she noticed the stone wall receded into an alcove. She stepped around the ladder into the recess, followed it a few feet in, and found a dead end. She turned right —more wall. She turned left—

A set of stairs.

Going down.

"Guys?" she called, but no one answered. She thought they'd forgotten about her. They were probably filling their bowls with pasta.

The stone stairs disappeared quickly into darkness.

She hesitated. Her hand closed around the letter she'd been carrying in her pocket alongside the map of the forest for the past year, the letter she'd never been able to deliver. She knew Brynn wasn't down this set of stairs, but she felt compelled to know what *was* there. Curiosity drove her downward.

The stairs felt longer than a single flight. Wild thoughts came to her —that maybe the staircase went on indefinitely, that there was no end, that if she didn't turn back she would be trapped in an infinite downward trajectory, driven to her own destruction by her desire to follow Brynn to the ends of the earth.

She didn't know whether to be relieved or disappointed when she found the bottom. The air was even colder and smelled of damp dirt and wet stone.

Ahead of her was a cement arch, the walls smooth and gray and slick, leading deeper into the darkness.

When Harlow called into the tunnel, she heard her voice echo back in that uncanny way of enclosed spaces. She didn't know why she called out—surely there was no one in there. But where did it go? How far did it extend? Her phone's flashlight receded into nothing. She took one step, two. The smooth walls stood close.

At the very edge of the light, the shadows flickered.

"Hello?" she called again, listening to her own voice's recursion as it muddled into nothing, and her heart found its way into her throat.

She took another step and heard an echo: another voice coming from somewhere far down the endless concrete tunnel.

The phone slipped out of her numb fingers and clattered to the ground, the light going dizzy. All she could do was drop to her knees and fumble for it, feeling cold all over.

"Who's there?" she shouted as she rose, knees still bent and ready to bolt, shining the light over the damp walls, the arched ceiling. The tunnel reminded her of some vast esophagus. She backed out of it, not taking her eyes off the darkness at the end of her light.

Nothing answered. A burst of laughter snorted out of her as she realized she must have imagined it. Or it was her own voice, still echoing weirdly in the distance, some acoustical phenomenon. Wendy would know. She'd studied the technical aspects of music. She would be able to explain it.

It was just that—for only a moment—she could have sworn the voice was Brynn's.

SINGER MISSING AFTER SOLO TRIP TO WOODS

PORTLAND, OR — All anyone knows of Brynn Werner, 27, is that on Friday, June 10, she left for a solo hike in the Umpqua National Forest. Five days later, she was declared missing. For the last ten days, search parties have swept the forest, navigating treacherous terrain and dense growth in an effort to locate the missing woman.

"Every day [that] goes by, the chances of finding her diminish," says Forest Patrol Deputy Declan Arleta. "We mobilized right away knowing every second counts. These woods can be unforgiving, especially to unseasoned hikers."

Parents Marjorie Smith-Werner (56) and Griffin Werner (61) remain optimistic. "You never met a more independent kid," says Griffin Werner of his only daughter. "She always was eager to do whatever she pleased, [and] Lord help whoever got in her way. She's hiked plenty, even climbed Mount Hood once. If anyone can make it out there, it's her."

In addition to being an outdoors enthusiast, Werner is also the lead singer of Portland-based metal band, Queen Carrion. Her wide-ranging vocal skills have been described by Metal Mania Magazine as "soaring," "operatic," and "as brutal as any hardcore vocalist today."

Joining in the ongoing search are Werner's bandmates: lead guitarist Rhys Beavin, rhythm guitarist Hawthorn Sorenson, bassist Louella

Diaz, drummer Harlow Sorenson, and cellist Wendy Mann. "We're not just a band," says Beavin. "We're like a family."

The search party has yet to find any sign of Werner. "It's impossible to tell what happened," says Arleta. "Most likely she got turned around and couldn't find her way back to the trail, then proceeded deeper into the forest. There are steep inclines here. She might have fallen, hurt herself. Maybe she was hiking near a waterfall and slipped. Without a solid trail, it's anyone's guess."

Fans of the band held a vigil last night outside the Wonder Room bar and music venue, where two years ago an incident during the band's performance led to the death of one attendee.

For now, the search continues.

FOUR

Rhys wasn't surprised by the find.

There were underground tunnels everywhere. The Shanghai Tunnels extended underneath Portland, a labyrinth of interconnected basements and passageways to the waterfront. Out here, it could be something as innocuous as an aborted mine or movement of illegal goods.

Still, he did think it was pretty cool.

"We should go investigate," he said, shining his light down its impenetrable length.

Wendy laughed. "Yeah, you're welcome to, but I'm not."

Jacqueline called, "Hello!" The word became a watery echo in the distance.

"Where do you think it goes?" Lou asked.

"I don't like that this is open to whoever might get in from the other side," Wendy said. "Seems like something the Airbnb host should have mentioned in the listing."

"Yeah, '3-bed rustic cabin getaway with bonus creepy underground tunnel.' I'm sure that would've gone over great with guests," Harlow said.

Rhys laughed in spite of himself. The mushroom chocolate was hitting him now—a warmth that spread through his chest and tingled into his fingertips, hilarity ballooning up his throat. Harlow could drive him crazy sometimes, but she could also make him laugh when he least expected it. They delighted in antagonizing each other, the two of them —throwing barbs to see who would get stung first.

It was mainly how she'd always enabled Brynn that annoyed him about Harlow, even when Brynn refused to work with the others, when she insisted on writing all their music herself. Brynn would hide herself away for a week and emerge with a whole album's worth of songs sketched out: lyrics, basic melodies and harmonies, beats, even the cello part, which she would hum for Wendy if she couldn't be bothered to write down the musical notation.

"I have ideas, too, you know," Rhys had told her.

Brynn didn't care. "You write your solos, don't you?"

It wasn't enough for him. He wanted to be on the ground floor, creating songs rather than just inserting himself into her existing vision. He refused to be sidelined.

He had a vision, too.

When he tried to convince Brynn to write *with* them rather than writing *for* them, she couldn't do it. She choked. Casper had been trying to get them a meeting with Roadrunner Records, and for the first time, Rhys thought Queen Carrion might actually go somewhere. He envisioned arena shows, cross-country tours, radio play, Grammy Awards. They'd been working on *The Orchid*, and Rhys overheard Brynn tell Casper they couldn't have the meeting yet because she hadn't finished the last song.

It was after a rehearsal, and they were standing in that cheap rented room: brick walls daubed in thick gray paint and interspersed with foam panels, a tattered oriental rug thrown over the old concrete floor, the small space stuffed with equipment—mics, amps, cords. As soon as Casper left, Rhys cornered her. "The hell is the matter with you? You want us to fail?"

Brynn swiveled a microphone out of her face. "I just don't want anyone coming in and changing everything. I want us to stay Queen Carrion."

"You mean you want us to stay unsuccessful."

"I know you'd rather be a sellout than be authentic, but there are some things more valuable than money and fame." She tried to step around him, but Rhys slammed his palm against the wall, making his arm a barrier.

"Maybe you haven't noticed, living in your artsy little fairyland, but in the real world, there is nothing more valuable than money. Musicians aren't making shit. Wake the fuck up. In a perfect world, we could all just focus on the music." His sneer fell on the peeling paint, the broken analog clock stuck perpetually at 3:30—A.M. or P.M., it was anyone's guess. "But this ain't it."

He could still remember the look on her face: the downward slant of her heavy brows, eyes sharp with fury, and the blotchy color that rose to her cheeks. Sweat glistened on her chest—the air conditioning was broken—and stray drops crawled into the crevice between her breasts. "It doesn't have to be one or the other."

Rhys snorted. "If you don't make an effort to lock in this deal, I'll convince the others we can't rely on you anymore. I'm serious. We'll kick you out of the band."

"I *am* Queen Carrion!" she spat, worms of black hair sticking to her forehead. "I am the band!"

Rhys let his arm fall slack. "You think you're something special? You think no one else can put on your face?"

She didn't have the makeup on in that moment, so she wasn't really Queen Carrion, was she? She was only Brynn. Her mouth looked small without the spidery slashes of black lipstick, and even smaller with the way she had it pursed.

Rhys stepped back to let her pass. "Tell Casper to set up the meeting."

They tried working together on the last song so they could have a demo of the whole album. Every time Rhys made a suggestion, Brynn said, "That's not what it *is*," as if the song already existed and she was trying to find it.

"You don't know what it is!" he shouted. "You don't have a goddamn clue! Or else you'd be able to *tell us*."

"That's why this isn't working!" Brynn smacked the microphone, and it crashed to the floor. "You don't *get it*. You don't understand anything about the creative process. If it's at all worthwhile, it *can't* be explained."

He wanted to strangle her. He wanted to throw her down and fuck her brains out.

His anger and lust for Brynn heated him to boiling. Somehow, the more he hated her, the hornier he got. That night, back home, he had wrapped his hands around Jacqueline's throat as he thrust into her, imagining Brynn's face slathered in corpse paint, choking beneath him. Jacqueline let him do that every so often. He knew she didn't like it much, but she always brushed herself off afterward as if it had been barely an inconvenience.

After Brynn had stormed out and everyone started packing up their things—Thorn snapping the clasps of his guitar case with care, Lou wiping down the fretboard of her bass—Harlow asked if anyone wanted to get a drink.

Rhys was still heated. "Right back to it?" he snapped. "This is why we're not getting anywhere. You drowning yourself in booze—which, by the way, we can all tell when you come to rehearsal drunk because you're so off the beat it's like you're trying to play jazz—and *her*, refusing to work with anyone."

Harlow gave him a petulant shrug. "She has writer's block, or whatever. It happens."

"It doesn't happen if there isn't only one person in charge of writing."

"And fuck you, I'm on the beat."

"Eh," said Jacqueline, holding her hand out horizontally and wiggling it back and forth.

Harlow's eyes flashed. "I *am* the beat."

"Jesus, you sound just like her. Are you two fucking yet, or what?"

He hadn't expected her to rise up and push him for that, and he staggered from the blow. Just as he caught his balance and took a furious step toward Harlow, Lou said, "Guys, can you cut it out? Let's call it a night."

It was two days later that Brynn decided to go camping. She texted everyone in the group chat, saying by the time she returned, the song would be ready.

Rhys texted back: *fine, go.*

They never had the meeting with Roadrunner.

"I'm hungry," Lou announced. "Anybody else?"

They filed one by one back up the stairs and ladder, greeted by the warmth and light of the cabin. Rhys dropped the trapdoor back into place, and Wendy pulled the rug over it. They could almost believe it wasn't even there.

The pasta was ready. They ravaged the big pot, poured wine—some crouched at the coffee table, others standing against the kitchen counter. It was how they ate while on tour.

For the few minutes when they were all digging in and mumbling their appreciation through mouthfuls of penne, everything was perfect: the cellar, forgotten; the cabin, cozy and kitschy and kind of cute, really, kind of homey now; the group, together, without bickering or eye-rolling. The only thing missing was the music.

Conversation spun out as forks began to scrape against empty bowls, their mouths looking for something to do, and it came up: the almost-record deal. The taste of success, barely even grazing the tip of the tongue.

"We could have landed it," Rhys couldn't help saying. "If she hadn't gone camping, we'd probably be touring *The Orchid* right now."

"What ifs are pointless," Wendy said. "We don't know if any kind of deal would have come through. It was only a meeting."

"But it *could* have!" Rhys snapped. "That's the point. Brynn was allergic to success. She waffled over it because she was too worried about losing creative control, becoming mainstream. Which, let's be honest, is bullshit. Mainstream success is not a bad thing."

Harlow's eyes met his over the rim of her glass. "Maybe she went because you threatened her."

The stares that turned to him gave the air weight. Silence buzzed in his ears.

"What?"

"She told me about how you accosted her after rehearsal and threatened to get rid of her."

"Get rid of her?" Rhys parroted. "Shit, you make it sound like I offed her."

"Did you?"

He let the accusation slide off him like oil. The shroom cocoon shrouded him. He did, however, give an offhand, "Oh, fuck you."

At his side, Jacqueline leaned into his shoulder, and he pushed her off. He'd given her an especially large chunk of chocolate. He wanted to loosen her up. She would sing better that way. When she was coiled too tight, her voice came out strained, almost irritating. He needed her relaxed tonight.

Lou stood up and said she needed some fresh air. What she really meant, Rhys surmised, was that she needed to pay a visit to her good friend Mary Jane. She stepped out the side door from the kitchen, into the dark.

"Anyway," Rhys said as he leaned back into the couch, which welcomed him like a pool of quicksand, "Casper was a lot more annoyed with her than I was. He'd been busting his ass trying to get that meeting, and she was ready to shrug it off like it was nothing. They always butted heads, you know that."

Harlow laughed without humor. "So you think Casper lured her out to the woods to… get rid of her? And, in the process, tank the deal, the meeting he had literally just booked?"

"I'm just saying she wasn't easy to get along with." Rhys shrugged. "Look, I'm sorry to criticize the dead—"

"We don't *know* she's dead," Harlow said.

A beat of uncomfortable silence followed. Eyes shifted around, looking anywhere but at her.

Rhys poured himself more wine, limbs moving like butter. "Brynn is dead, and it's no one's fault but her own." He poured another for Jacqueline. She blinked, pupils wide, and took a tiny sip. He overturned the bottle to top her off with the last few splashes.

He figured Harlow would be a tough sell. She wasn't ready to let Brynn go, but that was okay. Harlow was replaceable. Hell, she was unreliable at the best of times.

When it came right down to it, they were all replaceable. Even Brynn. None were masters of their craft, and though something clicked when they came together to play, he believed a group of top-tier musicians was better than some mysterious "click."

They would see.

Jacqueline was the future of Queen Carrion.

Even though he was right, and the others knew he was right, and they had all accepted that what happened to Brynn was just a stupid mistake in a long series of Brynn's stupid mistakes, and it wasn't his fault, wasn't Casper's fault, wasn't the fault of any of them, Harlow had to have the last word.

"Maybe you didn't kill her," she said. "But her blood is on your hands."

AFTER

This place reminds her of a panopticon, but instead of being watched from one central tower, the watching happens from everywhere: cameras with shiny black eyes lurking where the slate blue walls meet, subtly following movement down tangled corridors. You can't see who's watching you, and you can't know if anyone is even paying attention on the other side of that camera at all, but the possibility is always there. It's like a low hum in the brain, this constant surveillance devising an invisible cage. It's like being the subject of a scientific experiment, observed in this way, and isn't that a bit ironic, after everything in the woods?

Chills and nausea chase each other up and down her throat. The insomnia is so bad she feels like her eyes are being clawed open at night, brain jackhammering against her skull. It's already catching up with her, the sobriety.

Time blurs in the artificial light.

In her sorry little cell, she sweats through thin blankets, the cotton of her pajamas clinging like a second skin. Fluorescence glares from above, making livid every bump and divot of uneven paint on the walls, bland and blank and, at least, the very opposite of the deep, lush woods.

"Withdrawal, huh?" says her roommate, Sinda Brown, sharp cheekbones pronouncing the hollows of her face, hair buzzed to an institutional bristle.

It comes and goes in waves, and she is a boat without an oar, cresting and falling. She wonders when she got like this. When the booze became a crutch she couldn't walk without. Was it after everything that happened in the woods? Or was it when Brynn disappeared? She can't remember anymore when she started drinking so much. Maybe it was after the Wonder Room Panic—after that kid died at their concert.

All she knows is that everything hurts.

The lights are too harsh, the cotton too coarse, and she wants a drink so bad she could cry. Just something to take the edge off. Soften her nerve endings.

"I've seen lotsa folks show up here in withdrawal." Sinda rakes her palm over her skull, back and forth, a comfort move. "Seems to get through most people in a week. Give it time."

"Let me die."

"Gonna have a tough time with that," Sinda says, a shrug in her voice. "In a place like this."

She drifts around in a fog, like she's drunk a capful of NyQuil. An ache radiates up from her mid-back to her shoulders. The old back pain, rearing up again. When Sinda asks why she hunches around like that, she tells her it's her back. "I fucked it up from playing drums. Bad form, going too hard, not stretching—pretty much every bad habit you can think of."

"Seems like you love your bad habits."

The days take on a dull uniformity. She eats bland chicken and rice, longs for Thorn's pasta. Wishes she had the knife in her hand again, that she could Jackson Pollock these blue walls red.

The rest of the world fades away beyond the barred windows. Sometimes she forgets where she is, wakes in a panic with the lights out, the pilled blanket and flattened pillow unfamiliar. She tries to convince herself she is safe here, zombie-walking through an existence confined to this single building, these slate blue walls. The forest is far away, and if the trees outside the windows seem to bend and sway with pendulous intention, as if to peer in at her, then that is only her imagination. She itches at her bandages, half-expecting, all the time, that something will emerge from them.

When she has a visitor, she almost can't believe it. They sit in the rec room, where canned laughter spills from a TV playing old sitcoms. Across the table, a familiar face: eyes hooded, broad eyebrows arching over the rims of tortoise-shell glasses. A turtleneck strangles her. There is a shrewdness to the narrowed eyes, a detached air of judgment behind the neutral mask.

"Wendy?"

The canned laughter shrieks, interspersed with applause.

"I almost couldn't find this place."

She blinks. "Are you real?"

Elbows on the table, leaning forward, Wendy fixes her with a scornful look. "Are *you* real?"

She doesn't know how to answer that. "What are you doing here?"

"I guess I'm here to say I told you so."

Harlow swallows. Her throat has gone dry. It does that sometimes. She feels like she's been sucking on cotton. She half expects Wendy to crack a grin, let her know she's joking.

Wendy's face is dead serious. "I told you not to go in that basement, but you didn't listen. I didn't even want to go all the way out there to begin with, but you insisted on dragging us to the middle of nowhere. I thought we should leave. You said we should stay."

"Because it would have been…" She loses her voice in a murmur, shakes her head, which feels like a dusty attic, to try to clear it. "What are you saying?"

The look on Wendy's face turns almost pitying. "I'm saying everything that happened out there is because of you."

"What?" Heat floods her—shame, yes, but horror, too. It courses through her veins like a toxin, curdling her blood. Her heart strains, hurts with the force of its pounding. Her hands feel wet, and she wipes them furiously, thinking they are red, they are covered in blood—but it's only sweat.

"Your problem," Wendy continues, "is that you never take responsibility. You hurt people and you *never* take responsibility for it."

"I do," she chokes. "I always—"

Wendy slams her hands on the table. "Feeling guilty isn't the same as taking responsibility."

"We all went out there," she tries. Someone watching the TV turns to observe her conversation, jaw hanging open. She ignores them.

"*You* wanted to find Brynn," Wendy says. "*You* wanted to go to the

Umpqua. You were so desperate for an answer. What do you think of that answer now?"

"I didn't book that place. I didn't know…"

A cough—hacking, wet. Wendy grabs her throat. "Look what you've done."

Harlow closes her eyes, but she can still hear the gurgling sound coming from across the table, cannot bear to open her eyes and see what is happening, because the woods have found her after all, it seems. The woods have found her even here.

FIVE

Louella Diaz felt the scrutiny of eyes as soon as she stepped outside.

The woods stood around her like a black wall as she flicked her lighter impotently against it, a few quick sparks marking out the quiet punctuation of a tiny flame.

Maybe it was because her hand held the sole source of light—aside from the stars ducking in and out of clouds and the cabin windows burning behind her—that made her feel like she was on stage, the audience a blur of shadowed trees. But it wasn't just that she was aware of her visibility in the otherwise blind dark; it was, as far as she could tell, that prickling feeling—almost like a sixth sense—of being watched.

"Hello?" she ventured. "Anybody out there?"

No reply but the distant hoot of an owl, the rise and fall of cicadas.

She had never enjoyed being watched. Curious, perhaps, for someone whose livelihood entailed being on stage, but it was never about the performance for Lou. It was always about the music. That's all she wanted, and something she believed she'd long shared with Brynn. The music was everything. It was the whole reason for the charade of touring and labels and all that other industry nonsense.

Perhaps it was the mushrooms making her paranoid. She could never predict how they would affect her. She sat on a stump beside an ashy fire pit. A damp chill settled in the air, the late-May reminder that summer had not yet ripened, that spring's indecisiveness could still crystallize into overnight frost.

When the others came out, someone suggested lighting a fire.

Getting it going required a search for kindling, which yielded twig-slivers and dead leaves, and the solid snap of a lighter. The wet smolder gave a breath of smoke, then crackled to life. They put their hands out for it, grateful.

The fire threw itself into the dark, which beat with hunger.

"I feel like we need to feed it with a scary story," Lou said. "The fire." It whiplashed into sparks and diminished. "It's unstable. You have to feed it, like any other living thing."

"I didn't realize fires ate scary stories," Harlow said through a haze of smoke. The light raccooned her eyes and sharpened the angles of her face.

"And here I've been feeding it wood." Thorn sat as far from the fire as he could without slipping past the event horizon of night. He certainly wasn't the type to feed a fire anything. At least, not after he'd had to feed it half his face as a kid.

Wendy poked it with a stick. Red-hot wood crumbled into glitter from the corner of a log. "I'm pretty sure fire can't digest narrative."

"I have a story." Jacqueline leaned forward until her eyes blazed. "To feed it."

"Do you?" Harlow said.

Wendy shook her head. "Oh—come on."

"The fire needs to eat." Jacqueline's fingers rippled over the flames, perilously close. "We shouldn't starve it."

A low hoot cut through the drone of insects and underbrush rustlings. They could better hear than see the movements of the woods. Trying to look out tricked the eye into thinking it was blind.

The only way to beat back the darkness, thought Lou, was to touch it. "Go for it."

Harlow's elbows dropped onto her knees. "Yeah, tell us your terrifying tale."

Jacqueline's lips curled into a smile as she leaned toward the fire. "Once upon a time, there was a girl who always felt different. She lived in a cemetery, and her world was dirt and rot. She ate bugs and drank the fluid excreted from corpses."

"Jesus," Wendy interjected.

"Still, these things fed her. Nourished her. She was like a little flame, burning bright in that dead place. Only, everything kept trying to snuff her out. Storms would roll in and beat her with cold rain. The dead would reach out from their graves, desperate for a morsel of life, of warmth—all the things they didn't have.

"One day, when she was wandering that vast graveyard, which was her whole world, she wasn't paying attention to where she was going, and she walked too near an open grave. She fell in. A six-foot wall of dirt separated her from the ground above. It had begun to rain. The dirt beneath her turned to mud, and then to a wet brown sludge that rose up her ankles, to her knees. She called out for help, but there was no one to hear her. The mud kept sucking her down into it. Worst of all, she realized she wasn't alone."

Jacqueline stopped talking. Her eyes snapped to the wall of trees. Firelight shivered on her face. "Did you guys hear that?"

Harlow snorted. "Nice try."

Wendy shook her head. "Finish the story."

After a beat, Jacqueline dragged her gaze back to the fire and blinked in its glare. She cleared her throat. "So, she was—she wasn't alone in that wet grave. As the water rose, she saw a skeleton bobbing to the surface, bits of decayed flesh still clinging to it. And it wanted her. It wanted her warmth. She felt its bony arms reaching for her through the mud, grabbing at her, trying to pull her down with it...

"She pushed it away, but she left a black handprint on the bone. She had burned it with her touch. That's when she realized: when people got too close to her, they got burned. She thought it served them right for trying to snuff her out.

"She wasn't the only little flame out there, of course. There were others. She was rare, not unique. Apart, they were small and brief, but when joined together, they would make a large, many-fingered flame.

"When the girl was able to swim out of the grave, she decided to gather them all up so they could be together. One by one, she took them into her, and as the flame ate and ate the smaller flames, it grew larger and hotter. Eventually, it was large enough to sweep away everything that wasn't fire, and the world burned with a steady, living energy, destroying the dead—and compared to the living flame, everything aside from itself was dead, or at least on its way there; the great fire was the only thing that lived eternally. Time didn't mean the same thing to the great fire as it did for the ephemeral spark: a star popping into existence and burning itself out in an instant. But after an eternity of peaceful burning, its planet drifted too close to a black hole, and it was ripped apart and swallowed, and—"

"That's *The Orchid*."

Jacqueline's mouth was still open, sentence unfinished, as Harlow sniffed and took a drink.

"I don't know what you're talking about."

"You literally stole that whole story from *The Orchid*, but you changed the flower to a flame and you threw it into space at the end."

Jacqueline shook her head, smiling. "Great minds think alike."

"Well, I don't know that I'd call it scary, exactly," Lou said. "But it was… creative."

"Jacqui's a great writer." Rhys elbowed her playfully. "Right, babe? Hey, speaking of *The Orchid*—"

"Can someone else please tell a better story?" Harlow cut in. "Something that's actually scary."

Silence swarmed in as they looked around at each other.

Lou hesitated. "Um." Eyes turned her way. "I mean… I have something that's pretty scary."

Thorn leaned back, stretching his long legs. "Go on."

"I don't want to freak you guys out too much…"

"Well, now I'm even more interested," Harlow said.

Mosquitoes lighted on her arms, and Lou pulled her sleeves down despite the fire's heat. "It's a true story. You ever hear of Ryan Kilkenny?" Heads started shaking. "Ryan was something of an outdoorsman. He and his boyfriend, Arlo, had done all kinds of things together: climbed mountains, spelunked caves, scubaed. I guess you could say they were no strangers to wilderness, or adventure. So, when their fifth anniversary was coming up, in 2018, they decided to do something a bit less strenuous and go on a hiking trip. To the Umpqua."

Wendy was already shaking her head again. "Oh, no, not here. Not a good idea."

"No." Harlow pulled out her flask, took a fortifying sip. "Tell it."

"Everything started out okay—they had their tents, their gear—but before they ever managed to set up camp, they got separated. Arlo searched for Ryan all night, calling into the woods for him, but he was all alone. The next day, Arlo made it back to civilization and alerted the forest rangers that Ryan was missing. Only he couldn't quite explain what had happened. They asked him how they had gotten separated, but he had no explanation. He just said that he knew Ryan was still out there, and they had to find him.

"They searched for three weeks, at which point—as you can imagine —they were starting to lose hope."

Harlow snorted and poured the rest of her drink into her mouth, face skyward. Wendy sat with her hands over her mouth, looking a little gray.

"After three weeks, two volunteers with the search party and a sheriff's deputy saw a figure limping through the trees. They called out Ryan's name, but they got no answer—so they pursued the person, not wanting to lose him, and when they found him—well, at first they didn't know what they had found.

"He was naked and red all over. They thought he was covered in blood, maybe from an animal he'd had to hunt to survive, but that wasn't it. When they got closer, they saw: his skin was flayed off. He was just red muscle, still holding the bloody Swiss Army knife."

Wendy sucked in a breath. "He did it to himself?"

Lou nodded. "He was delirious when they found him. And it makes you wonder—this guy, with all his adventures under his belt, couldn't handle himself for a few weeks? I mean, you or I, sure, we'd be toast, but this guy was experienced. And he went completely crazy out there. He couldn't even tell them what happened. Just kept saying, 'I think they got inside me.'"

A log snapped. Sparks flurried.

"That didn't happen," Rhys said.

"Look it up."

As she said it, Lou realized she was peaking, feeling the forest all alive around her, on the hairs of her arms. Wind shuffled through leaves like sand through an hourglass. It was as if the trees were breathing, were observing with uncanny intelligence.

The wind stirred and stilled. Flames shivered, twisted, stamped echoes of light in the air. Burning motes snapped upward like fireflies. Lou was entranced. She was reminded of the candles set in a circle, Brynn's face illuminated from all sides in the dark of her tiny studio apartment while the rain came down heavily, glittering the windows. And the humming—that familiar tune Brynn brought to the ritual she'd asked Lou to do only a day or two before she disappeared. A creeping feeling came over her, as if she could hear it again, some faint whisper carried by the cool drift of air. A suggestion of sound.

She wanted the image out of her head. Maybe that was why she told the story about Ryan Kilkenny: she couldn't stop thinking about it, so she fed it to the fire. It was impossible not to think about what might have happened to Brynn out here. What if she had gone crazy, like Ryan?

Or what if something had been haunting her, and she had been trying to get away from it?

She remembered the ritual—Brynn saying *It's like it's haunting me*, the flicker of candles, the way their curls of smoke became mist, seemed to reveal a face on the other side, or a mask, or maybe it was only Lou's imagination—but that was how she felt now, like Brynn was haunting them on the other side of the smoke.

"Did you see that?" came Jacqueline's frantic whisper.

"Don't worry, babe." Rhys wrapped an arm around her shoulders. "I'll protect you from the scary hiker with the knife."

Lou's eyes traced the tree line where the fire's ghost imprinted green echoes. Each little movement stole her attention. The forest was a sea of shifting patterns. "Oh." She sucked in a breath. "I see it."

"See what?"

She squinted in the faint light, trying to discern reality from the shudder of her own eyeballs, but she was sure she'd seen something. A pale shape moving within the trees.

"It's Ryan Kilkenny," Harlow deadpanned.

"Ryan Kilkenny is dead. He didn't even make it to the hospital."

"Or maybe he's still out here."

But the shape did not look human. It was all wrong: long and with too many legs. The strangeness unsettled her until relief finally swarmed into her body as the shape came into focus. "It's the deer!"

"What deer?"

"The one I saw earlier." She crept closer to the trees, trying to get a better view. The animal moved like liquid, smooth and powerful. A log in the fire popped. Its head turned toward the sound. White antlers spidered from its white skull. Wendy said it must be albino. Thorn said he'd never seen one like it before.

Then it streaked away, gone in the trees like smoke.

"Damn," Rhys said. "I am tripping."

And then they were all laughing and calling him high, Lou and Jacqueline and Harlow laughing because they were high too, and hell, even Thorn leaned in closer to the fire. Anything to join the laughter. And they laughed because they didn't want to say it, nobody wanted to point it out.

No one wanted to say the deer had no eyes.

FROM "WHAT EVER HAPPENED TO QUEEN CARRION?"

THE CURIOUS CASE OF ONE BAND'S SELF-DESTRUCTION

… Despite being a relatively obscure band outside of the Pacific Northwest, Queen Carrion made national headlines after they went into the woods—and not all of them made it back out. We may never know what really happened that weekend, but we can piece together the story of what led them to that point.

The trip began as a tribute to Brynn Werner, who had vanished in those same woods a year prior. One can't fault the friends for trying to find closure, but it seems they were tempting fate.

The mysterious circumstances of Werner's disappearance at first intrigued, then frustrated, true crime aficionados. What the authorities never fully considered then, but which we must not overlook now, is the possibility of foul play.

Did someone hold a grudge against Werner? Though the family of the 17-year-old boy who was tragically crushed to death during the Wonder Room Panic could not be reached for comment, they have stated publicly they do not blame Queen Carrion for the unfortunate events during their concert. Still, can we be completely sure this public statement bears out the whole truth?

The other possibility is that another member of the band was unhappy with Werner's leadership, but were they unhappy enough to take the drastic action of killing her?

Let's consider the potential suspects.

Wendy Mann: A good student in her youth without so much as a detention to her name, Mann was classically trained as a cellist before joining Queen Carrion, giving the band an orchestral flavor. Did she feel sidelined in this role?

Louella Diaz: Bassist. As a teen, Diaz began getting into Wicca and later claimed to be a practicing witch. Creative and rebellious, Diaz may have wanted a larger influence on the band's direction—something which Werner, notably, held tight to herself as the leader, founder, and songwriter. Perhaps Diaz performed a spell to diminish Werner's authoritarian rule and make her disappear?

Rhys Beavin: Lead Guitarist. Could Beavin have held ill intentions toward Werner? There have been rumors of an infatuation between them that may have turned dark. On the other hand, Beavin was in a long-term relationship at the time of her disappearance. Would he have wanted to damage the band's success?

But let's consider the two more volatile members of the band: siblings Hawthorn "Thorn" Sorenson and Harlow Sorenson. Theirs was a tumultuous childhood fractured by one key incident—when Harlow burned down their family home.

Reports indicate Harlow, six at the time, was playing with matches when a curtain caught fire. It was past eleven at night, certainly past the six-year-old's bedtime; her mother and brother were asleep, while her father was out having drinks with his coworkers. The flames quickly spread, and Harlow, recognizing the danger, walked out of the house and stood in the street until a neighbor noticed the smoke and called the fire department. Her mother, meanwhile, had woken to the sound of the smoke detector and went to her children's rooms, but by then the fire was rapidly spreading. Firefighters entered the house and found eight-year-old Hawthorn trapped in his room. His face was badly burned when a ceiling beam fell, and he spent weeks in the hospital receiving skin grafts. He also went blind in his left eye.

Did Harlow intend to murder her family that night, when she so calmly left the house without waking them? Was this merely the first indication of her violent tendencies?

Perhaps Harlow never lost the desire to harm those closest to her. She and Werner had been friends since they were young. If anyone was close enough to Werner to make her disappear, it was surely the band's drummer.

But we also cannot discount her brother, rhythm guitarist Thorn

Sorenson. His unusual features, as a result of his childhood injury, seem fitting for the band's self-professed Satanist. One marked by violence at such a young age does not escape unscathed, physically or mentally, and it's possible his mental disturbance led to a thirst for blood.

Or perhaps they all did it in order to remove Werner and install a new vocalist. Perhaps their final trip to the woods was really an effort to dispose of any remaining evidence, to throw off the ongoing investigation into Werner's whereabouts, and to select their new leader.

We may never know the truth. But let's turn our attention now to what happened in the woods that weekend, and the ultimate dissolution of Queen Carrion...

SIX

It was that time of the evening: a guitar found its way into someone's hand.

Rhys balanced the black birch Martin—his older, scuffed acoustic—on his knee. He twisted the pegs to tune it up, then strummed a few cords. "I want to play something for you guys," he said. He struck a B minor chord, then F sharp minor, C sharp major, and back to F sharp minor.

Thorn was so focused on the guitar that he hadn't expected Jacqueline to start singing.

Her voice rang through the night, sweeter than Brynn's but somehow less substantial. There was an ephemeral, almost breathy quality to it. She sang about a baby who had grown from a seed, the first new human in centuries come to repopulate the earth. The song found and settled into a groove, then deviated into an extended solo. In the end, she and Rhys fell into a final repetitive cadence: *"Take back... take back... take back... take back what's ours!"*

Rhys's eyes gleamed in the firelight. "So what do you think? Killer, right?"

Thorn had been about to agree—it had a catchy rhythm and a solid hook—until he saw the look on Harlow's face.

"Are you trying to finish *The Orchid?*" Her voice was flat.

"We have like nine-tenths of an album sitting around. We have recordings of all the other songs. We do this last one, and we've got the complete album."

"With Jacqueline singing."

"Exactly," Rhys said. "Think about the story of the album: humanity dies out, and in the end—in this song, which I'm tentatively calling 'The Return,' but I'm open to input of course—it comes back. Fresh, new, different. And that's us, that's Queen Carrion. We come back with a new voice, right at the end of the album. That's our comeback." He banged out a quick chord for punctuation.

"You can't." Harlow shook her head. "You can't take *The Orchid*. It's Brynn's."

"It's *ours*," Rhys said. "We have all these songs. Don't you want to put them out there? This is the perfect opportunity to rebrand, get away from all that 'curse of Queen Carrion' shit the Wonder Room started."

"You sound like Casper."

Jacqueline shrugged. "He thought the rebrand was a good idea."

"You mean he already knows about this?" Wendy asked.

"Casper loves it," Rhys said. "He loves Jacqui's voice, and he thinks he can get us some major press for this album. People will want to hear the last songs of Brynn Werner… and then when they hear Jacqui, they'll be hooked on Queen Carrion 2.0."

Harlow shook her head. "I won't do it."

Lips pressed together, Wendy looked around at the others. "Yeah, I don't know."

Thorn lit one of his Winstons to give himself more time to think.

He wasn't ready to let Queen Carrion go, and he had to admit it sounded like a good idea. They wouldn't even have to do a whole search for a new vocalist. Jacqueline already knew all their songs by heart, as she often liked to show off. He tried not to look at Harlow—at the ice in her eyes, the hard set of her jaw, like she was about to grind her teeth to dust. "I'm in," he said, and sure enough, Harlow whirled on him, incredulity written on her face.

"Look, half of us are high, we're all a little drunk," Wendy said. "Let's not make any decisions right now. It's a lot to think about. We should sleep on it, at least."

The guitar let out a twang as Rhys thumped it down a bit harder than necessary. "You're all bullshit," he said. Leaving the guitar propped against a stump, he snatched up the bottle of whiskey and took a swig.

Thorn receded into the shadows. His cigarette turned to an

appendage of ash between his lips. It was better to let Rhys burn through his temper when he felt slighted. This was a method he'd employed all those times Rhys had come huffing to him about *that bitch Brynn* when she shot down another of his ideas; Thorn had merely to stand there and wait until Rhys went from angry to bitter to sarcastic, and then he was all right again.

When Rhys turned to the woods, Jacqueline stood up, too. "Where are you going?"

From between the trees, shoving away branches, he snarled, "Taking a piss."

———

The crack of footfalls echoed in Rhys's wake. After a moment's hesitation, Jacqueline followed him into the trees.

Harlow turned to Thorn. "Are you *serious*?"

"Almost never."

She scooped up a clump of dirt and threw it at him. It thinned to a gritty cloud before it met his face. He closed his eyes and spat.

"We can't let Jacqueline be the new singer." Harlow's words dripped disgust.

"Why? Because you think she's annoying?"

"She *is* annoying."

"You're annoying."

She glowered. "We don't even know what happened to Brynn. And now everybody is ready to replace her, just like that."

"Hey, that's not fair—" Wendy argued. She seemed agitated. He got the sense, from the crease between her eyebrows and the way she kept chewing at the corner of her lip, that she was holding something back.

He had the urge to run his hands through her curls, then slide them along the curves of her hips, to the spot where she was ticklish. He could make her laugh if he did that. When she laughed, Wendy was transformed. That serious demeanor she wore could crack right open. If he could give her a nice time this weekend—make her laugh, show her how good they were together—maybe he could stop her from spinning away again. That's what they did: they pendulated back and forth like an uncertain clock, nearer and farther. She pulled away whenever it suited her.

He stubbed out his cigarette, feeling tired. "Why don't you think it's a good idea?"

Wendy blinked. "I can think of a few reasons."

"Such as…?"

"You know." She shrugged. "What Harlow said."

She was lying. The realization surprised him.

"And it's not just because I find Jacqueline annoying," Harlow said. "She's a bitch."

Thorn raised his eyebrows. "And *you're* so nice."

They were interrupted by a sound of frustration in the back of Lou's throat. "I'm sorry, I'm too stoned for this conversation."

Thorn raised his eyebrow at Harlow, daring her to make a comeback, but she was distracted, looking away from him toward a rustling in the trees.

Something was moving out there. He heard it now. A subtle rustling at first, but it was coming closer. Twigs snapped. Branches shook with violent motion. He rose from his seat, legs primed to run back to the cabin in case a wild animal was about to crash their bonfire. At least, he hoped it was an animal. He couldn't help thinking suddenly of Ryan Kilkenny, imagining a man filleted of skin, raw meat open to the elements as it dragged itself to their fire like a moth to flame.

He could just see it lurking within the trees, a pale shape with long limbs like birch branches.

It burst into the light, and he recognized Jacqueline, pine needles standing in static threads of disheveled hair, chest rising and falling as she caught her breath. "There's someone out there."

"Yeah," Harlow said. "Rhys."

Jacqueline shook her head. "Someone else."

"Who else would be in the woods?" Wendy asked.

"An animal?" Lou murmured, sinking into her sweatshirt.

Jacqueline's face was rigid. "It *wasn't*."

"Must be Ryan Kilkenny's ghost. He wants to cut your skin off," Harlow said with a cackle.

Crouching, Jacqueline put her hands out to the fire.

"Wait. Do you hear that?" Lou had her head cocked, fingernails against her teeth.

Thorn listened. He heard wind shuffling through the trees. The occasional scurry of animal feet. Insects abuzz. These, all part of the natural landscape, couldn't be what she meant. Just the forest talking to itself.

"I thought I heard…" Lou's gaze returned to the fire. "You guys'll think I'm crazy."

"What was it?" Thorn asked.

"You don't hear it?" Lou said uncertainly. "Singing?"

Wendy raised her eyebrows.

"No." Jacqueline was stone still. "No, I hear it, too."

"Uh huh," Harlow said. "Sure you do."

Lou shook her head. "I don't know. Maybe I'm tripping out."

"Does anything good ever happen on mushrooms?" Wendy asked. "Jacqueline saw Rhys and got freaked out. You're hearing things. Guys. You took drugs. This is the kind of shit that happens."

"I told you it wasn't Rhys." Jacqueline's fingernails clawed into her hands, and her voice rose. "There is someone out there!"

Thorn listened. He assumed his hearing was worse than Lou's, with the way he'd blasted ungodly decibels through headphones all the time growing up.

A hush fell over them.

The more he listened for the singing, the more it infected his mind. He started to think he *could* hear it. A distant voice, faint as a single leaf. A familiar pattern.

Its recognition froze him in place. He knew that voice. "It's Brynn."

Something between a squeal and a gasp escaped Jacqueline, hands clamped over her mouth. Thorn looked at Harlow, whose ashen sheen gave her an ill appearance. Her fingers were behind her ears, trying to funnel sound into them.

"You guys are hearing things," Wendy said, but now she sounded uncertain.

"It's one of our songs."

They listened. Thorn could almost make it out.

Wet streams ran from Jacqueline's eyes. She lowered her hands and sang unsteadily, *"I've become one with the night… Come find me…"* As Jacqueline trailed off, the voice in the woods rose. Became a growl. A scream.

Wendy flinched.

"It's just the song," Thorn told her. "That's where she screams in the song."

Shaking her head, Jacqueline backed away from the fire, then turned and fled inside.

All the rest stayed mutely listening.

The naked vocals sounded wrong. Thorn wanted to press his hands over his ears, but he couldn't stop listening. Her voice wound through the trees, carried between the branches. Brynn had always been closer to Harlow, but Thorn still thought of her as a good friend. Hearing her voice sent a pang through his gut. It was like hearing the voice of a ghost.

When the voice receded into a whisper, then nothing, and their continued listening returned only the silence of the forest, and they started to wonder whether they'd heard anything at all, Thorn finally said, "It had to be a recording."

"Of just the vocal track?" Lou said. "And… why?"

If someone were playing a recording of one of their songs, they had to know the rest of the band was out here. "To taunt us," Harlow said. "Scare us."

"Who would do that?" Lou argued. "Who hates us that much?"

"It's Rhys," Harlow said, sounding more sure of herself. "He's fucking with us because he's pissed we didn't immediately go along with his little plan. He's probably standing out there right now laughing his ass off at how spooked we are."

"Jacqueline said there was someone else out there," Wendy pointed out.

Harlow picked up a twig, snapped it in half, and threw it into the fire. "She's in on it! Obviously. Who else could it be?"

"Murphy Dunning's family."

They all looked at Wendy, but her eyes were on the fire.

"What?" said Lou.

Wendy shrugged. "You asked who hates us that much?"

Harlow slowly shook her head. "We met them. We talked to them. They didn't blame us for what happened."

"Their kid died at our show," Wendy snapped. "Why *wouldn't* they hate us?"

"How would they even know where we are?" Harlow argued. Thorn could tell she was getting riled up. Feeling guilty about what had happened at the Wonder Room and letting it out as anger, as she typically did.

"Could just be a couple of assholes who thought it'd be funny to fuck with us," Thorn suggested.

"Well, it's *not* funny," Harlow snapped.

Thorn raised his hands. "You don't have to tell me."

"I don't think it was a recording," Lou said.

The last flame guttered to red embers.

"What else could it be?"

Leaning forward, Lou poked at the logs with a stick. Rather than snap back to life, wood crumbled, unleashing impotent sparks. "I keep getting this feeling. Like we're being watched." She looked out at the black wall of trees.

"You know, there's this psychological phenomenon," Wendy said, "where, when you're watching something—like, looking out at the forest—your brain gets confused and thinks *you're* the one being watched. I forget what it's called."

"Could be that," Harlow said, settling back down. "Or it could be the drugs. That Rhys gave us. To screw with our heads." She raised her voice to a shout. "Joke's over! You can come out now!"

They waited. The fire died, and darkness gathered closer.

"Suit yourself!" Harlow shouted, kicking dirt over the burned logs. "Guess you can stay out there all night, then."

While she went around picking up empty cups, each of the others tried calling Rhys's name a few times. Thorn peered into the dark enclosing them, but he saw nothing, heard no movement except for the wind in the leaves. An owl gave a low coo somewhere overhead.

Wendy bit her lip and looked at him. Behind her glasses, her eyes were wide. "I don't think he's screwing with us. I think something's wrong."

SEVEN

Rhys used his phone to light the way, stumbling over pinecones that cracked under his shoes. On the other side of a precipitous embankment, the creek burbled over mossy rocks. The forest was black and cool and smelled like rain.

If he'd known this place was so remote, he might not have booked it. A passing glance was all he gave the listing when Jacqueline showed it to him before he shrugged and nodded his approval. What did he care? A cabin in the woods is a cabin in the woods is a cabin in the woods.

He took another swig. The trees rotated around him. The bonfire's glow was well past his line of sight. Each way he turned looked the same. There was no path. And no town nearby, either. No hiking trails. Just forest and more stupid forest.

The crickets' repetitive song turned into a droning shrill in his ears as he went faster one way and then the next, unsure which direction would lead him back to the cabin. His feet tangled in the undergrowth. A branch whacked him in the face.

This wasn't how he had anticipated the night going.

The others had to realize Brynn wasn't going to magically return. It only made sense to bring in a new singer. And why not Jacqueline? He'd figured Thorn and Lou would be on board, but more than that, he'd thought Wendy would see the logic in it. She knew a good idea when she saw it. The fact she'd hesitated was what sent Rhys's temper spinning, because if it had been three to one, even with Harlow's refusal—which he'd more or less expected—she'd have been outnumbered and would have, eventually, given up. Without Wendy, the split was sharper, and Harlow definitely wouldn't budge.

"Fucking Wendy," he spat and tipped the bottle back.

Jacqueline had been a little off-key, too. He couldn't help thinking she'd spoiled the moment. It should have been perfect, but she wasn't, was she? Everything was riding on her performance, and she blew it.

And now he was lost.

He willed the trees to move aside, bring him back to the cabin. He didn't know how he'd gotten so turned around, but he supposed the booze and the mushrooms may have conspired against him. He didn't think he was completely lost, though. He was confident he would find the way back, sooner or later. He really hadn't gone that far.

His confidence only grew when he spotted a light through the trees.

He chuckled at his good fortune and went toward it, ready to swagger back to the others and convince them to finish *The Orchid*, but the closer he drew, the more he slowed. There was something about the light that seemed wrong, unfamiliar.

It wasn't a fire ahead of him. The light was cold white.

Pushing away branches, Rhys discovered the light was coming from a shape—a person—skin lit by that soft pale glow.

The bottle slipped from his suddenly numb fingers as he took in the sight, disbelieving his own eyes. Recognition met with impossibility, jamming up his brainwaves. His heart seemed to stop beating, leaving him in a limbo of static that tingled through his limbs.

Lying in the dirt was Brynn Werner. He gaped at her soft, round face; her naked flesh; the curve of her hip and the points of her breasts. Pristine. Not a smudge on her. She was like porcelain. Like moonlight.

She curled her finger at him. A coy smile bent her lips.

Whiskey rushed through his chest, hot as magma. Blood pulsed in his head, surged to his groin as he traced his eyes hungrily over the body he had always lusted over, the muscular abdomen, strong milky thighs. He was harder than he could ever remember being, and he drew closer, fell to his knees.

It couldn't be real, but he felt her soft, cool lips when he kissed her, felt her body when he pressed against her. His pants were at his ankles, his tongue on her neck, his hands on her breasts.

Ecstasy crashed through him as he thrust into her. His body tingled with it. He was out of his mind with it. He didn't even consciously recognize that all her tattoos had been wiped clean. There was no color to her, no color at all. His wordless cries tangled with hers as the trees shivered above them. He came with a shudder, collapsed onto her, heart thumping, eyes closed. He inhaled, wanting to take in the scent of her, but all he could smell was decay.

His eyes opened.

Hollow sockets stared up at him from a skull blackened by rot, the body he'd clutched in the throes of passion no more than bones and cartilage held together by scraps of skin like dirty cloth. A cluster of mushrooms sprouted from a sunken chest where the heart should be.

Gagging, Rhys pushed away, but his hands slipped against the rot. Watery vomit burned up his throat. He stumbled, tugging his pants, face wet. Trees tittered as the wind rattled through them, rattled through the corpse's open jaw, laughing. Rhys thought his heart would explode out of his chest as he ran blindly, trying not to think of what he had just spilled himself into, trying not to think what might have spilled back into him.

AFTER

He is talking to her again, this irritating man. Their sessions are a series of questions—*How are you feeling today? Have you practiced what I told you? Do you want to talk about what happened out there?* She hates these questions. They are like gnats buzzing around her head. Sometimes she simply tunes him out. It's easier that way.

"I heard you had an episode the other day," he says.

"My friend came to visit."

"Why did that make you so upset?"

She curls into herself and ignores him. What a stupid question. He tries to change the subject, ask about something else, but she refuses to engage. What would be the point? She stares at the slate blue walls, tries to make her mind static. If she looks too closely at anything, she might see cracks forming, weaving themselves into messages. Into patterns.

His voice cuts through the fog:

"Why did you do it?"

Her stomach twists. Fire floods through her. Even he thinks what happened out there was her fault. Maybe it was? Her tongue is like glue in her mouth, afraid to shape words.

He thinks you killed them.

"You remember what happened, don't you? At the bar? When you took that man's pocketknife?"

"Oh." She is almost relieved to find he's talking about the incident at the bar. The thought of it makes her arms feel itchy. She scratches absently at the bandage. "Yes."

"Why did you do it?"

It isn't that she doesn't know; it's that she can't explain. How could she, in a way this man would understand? This man with a middle-aged paunch beneath his white coat, with peppery hair gone shaggy at the sideburns, with a softness, like yogurt, to his skin, his body which has never betrayed him, a body in which he has lived comfortably for perhaps fifty years.

"Was it the voices?"

She raises her eyebrows. Is he talking about the voice in the woods? The voice they all heard singing from within the dark trees?

"Are you still hearing voices?" he asks behind his clipboard. "Are they telling you to hurt yourself?"

She shakes her head. Her fingernails are scrabbling at the worn edges of her bandage again, the flesh itching as it stitches shut. She wants to scratch it open. There could be something inside, beneath the skin. "*Voices* didn't tell me to," she scoffs, digging in with her nails now. "I had to know what was inside."

The doctor frowns. "What do you mean by that?"

Her scratching has caught his attention now; his eyes slip to her forearm, where she is pulling at the soft gauze, shredding it, trying to get at the flesh beneath. "I had to know if *it* was inside. If I opened up my skin, what would I find in there?"

"Please stop scratching," he says, but she ignores him. He rises out of his seat. "Harlow." His eyes flash behind her, and suddenly there are arms restraining her, stopping her—the orderly with thick hairy knuckles—and she is outside of herself, realizes she is screaming, she is bucking against him, until she sees the needle coming and feels a pinch on her neck and then—

Nothing.

EIGHT

In the fog of her hangover, Harlow almost forgot what she'd promised herself last night.

She rolled over as silvery light spilled through the window, heard someone snoring across the room, wondered with a jolt where she was. Not that it would be the first time she'd woken in a stranger's house after a night of drinking.

When she realized it was Thorn in that pile of blankets, she remembered.

She'd intended to head out at dawn, but the light coming in was at least a few hours old, and she needed coffee, and—well, the best-laid plans when one's been into the whiskey, and all that. Perhaps if she didn't drink so much, she could jump out of bed in the morning with a spring in her step and a song in her heart, but then what would evenings be like in the coldness of sobriety? She shuddered to think.

The decision had come to her when they went out to find Rhys with their phones on flashlight mode, casting around in the dark, stumbling over roots that burst from the earth like sea serpents. When she called out his name, it came out loud, not because she so desperately wanted to find him, but because she was so damn mad at him. Her fury had been like a shot of adrenaline that made her want to punch something. Her drums, perhaps—her usual outlet when her body became an explosion. Just then, though? Preferably Rhys. She wanted to sink her fists into him. She wanted to bash his brains in.

Maybe it was stupid, her conviction that once they got here, the others would be compelled to join her in resuming the search. But Thorn was right. No one was here to find Brynn. And now this further betrayal—wanting to replace her.

It meant she was gone, that she wasn't coming back, and in that moment, when Rhys and Jacqueline finished their little song, Harlow had felt like Brynn was dying. Again. She'd felt a thousand deaths over the last year, from the start of the search to its end and after. Because there was no proof of death, that door never fully closed. Sometimes she carried on as if Brynn would return, would show up one day out of the blue, but then she felt Brynn's death again, and it was always that awful jolt, every time. How could she move on if Brynn was always dying?

"Rhys!" they called out into the night. And in their searching, Harlow had begun formulating a plan to head out on her own at first light.

There's no sense in relying on other people, Brynn once told her. *If you want something done right—or at all—you have to do it yourself.*

Self-reliance was Brynn's MO, and she embodied it like a hand in a glove. Was it being an only child, with hands-off parents, that made her that way? When they were young, Harlow admired how easily Brynn took charge. Swiped her parents' keys at fifteen, drove them out to Burnside Bridge on a permit to smoke Thorn's stolen pack of Winstons and throw the glowing butts down to the water sixty feet below, watch the bascule raise the bridge in two halves for boats to pass. And there was Harlow, begging her parents to enroll her in driver's ed. Her father, well-meaning as he was, kept forgetting. It was still on his to-do list. Her mother—well, she couldn't be bothered, and Harlow knew better than to ask something of her that would require trust. Her mother was incapable of trusting her.

If you want something done right—or at all—you have to do it yourself.

If the others wouldn't help her, then Harlow decided she would go out alone.

"Rhys!"

They called out, and the forest echoed back their voices.

A stick snapped under someone's foot. Harlow looked around, almost forgetting which direction was the way back.

"Rhys?"

Thorn held out a hand, shushed them.

Something moved in the darkness, and before they had any real sense of what was approaching, it was there: a figure, face drained of color, blasted in the sudden light, mouth a toothy grimace.

Screams turned to shouts all at once.

"What the *hell*, man?"

"Why didn't you answer?"

"God*damn*it, Rhys!"

He pushed past them, one hand raised to shield his eyes, washed-out in the glare, sweat-greased, breathing hard.

"What happened?"

He stopped. Did not turn around. "Nothing happened."

"Nice joke. Real funny," Harlow spat at him.

"What?"

She rolled her eyes. "The recording? Brynn?"

Rhys flinched and whirled around. His face twitched, something roiling beneath the surface. "The *fuck* are you talking about?"

"Nothing." Wendy threw Harlow a warning look. "Let's get back."

Ahead, the cabin appeared, a welcome shape with orange windows. It invited them back in, old floors groaning where they tread.

Harlow stumbled out of bed. It was just her luck that when she went to the kitchenette to find a pot of instant coffee cooling on the stove, the only person she found was Jacqueline leaning against the counter with both hands around a chipped blue mug. Her eyes were like darts. "Morning."

Harlow grunted in reply.

"I made coffee."

It tasted stale, but Harlow downed a cup anyway. "I'm going out to search."

Jacqueline nodded slowly. "Yeah. I figured you would." She took a breath. "And that's why I'm coming with you."

"I didn't invite you." The coffee buzzed through Harlow's nerve endings, sharpened her. "Why would you want to find Brynn, anyway? I thought you wanted to take her place." She looked at Jacqueline, at her elfin face. Those empty eyes, something calculating in them. A mocking twist to her lips. Or maybe that was just Harlow's projection onto her. She couldn't tell. She found Jacqueline hard to read.

"Easier to replace a dead body than a missing person," she said with a thin smile.

Harlow had a good six inches on Jacqueline, and every one of those inches became apparent as she stepped closer, looking down, glad, for once, that she could use her height to her advantage. "You think *you* can replace her?"

It annoyed her that Jacqueline seemed more curious than intimidated. "What will you do if you don't find her?"

The silence stretched around the question, one Harlow had not been able to consider, but she was saved from answering by the sound of footsteps.

One by one, the others shuffled down the hall, stretching and groaning, reaching for the poor imitation of coffee as they blinked themselves awake. There's a certain vulnerability about people when they first wake up. Maybe they are most themselves, or simply the softest versions of themselves, like newborns. Watching the others emerge as she laced up her hiking boots, Harlow was glad to have been one of the first to rise. She hated the idea of anyone seeing her so soft, so easily bruised.

There was only one person she never minded seeing her like that, fresh from bed, in flannel pajamas, eyes still gummy with sleep.

"I'm going out," she announced, standing. She tried to hide the unsteadiness in her step, the sick feeling that dizzied her world. All she had to do was push through it, like she always did.

"Whoa, hold on." Thorn poured the last of the coffee. "We only just got up. How about, good morning, friends?"

"Good morning, friends," Harlow said. "I'm going out. You can come if you want. But I'm going to search."

"Can't we chill for a bit?" Thorn asked.

Stung with betrayal, Harlow grumbled, "I'm not here to *chill.*" She unfurled her map, its creases soft and feathery. The Umpqua National Forest sprawled across the coffee table, most of it empty patches of pale green. It would be useless here because she couldn't pinpoint their exact location. Trail Creek Lane was not labeled, and as far as she could tell, there were no trailheads nearby. She had a compass, and that would have to be good enough.

The stairs creaked as Rhys emerged from the loft, a hangover written on his clammy face. "What's going on?"

Wendy spoke up first. "Harlow wants to go look for Brynn. As if a whole search team hasn't already done that."

Pausing on the last step, Rhys recoiled. He coughed into the back of his hand. "No."

"Why not?" Harlow raised her eyebrows. "Scared of getting lost again?"

His face soured. Blond growth bristled over his chin. Bloodshot eyes narrowed on Harlow. "You think you'll find her? There's a thousand miles of woods out there. Do the math."

"You know what?" Lou stretched. "A hike does sound nice. I don't want to stay cooped up in this cabin all day."

"I didn't exactly bring my hiking attire," Thorn said dryly. He was wearing a pair of plaid boxers and a Black Sabbath t-shirt so faded it had turned from black to gray. Harlow was pretty sure the only pants he'd brought were his torn black skinny jeans.

Wendy sighed. "Well, if everyone else is going."

In the end, Rhys was the only one to stay behind. Everyone else stepped out into the diamond-bright morning and headed off along the creek.

Harlow took a deep breath of the fresh air. She could almost forget how much she hated the woods in a moment like this, with birds calling and the breeze cool on her skin.

The others took a leisurely pace. She walked briskly, deciding they could keep up if they wanted. Then she felt a tug on her backpack, and there was Thorn, holding her back. "Stay together."

Knowing she had no other choice, Harlow slowed, but she refused to look at him, worried her anger would spill over. A realization spread over her like a fever: he didn't want to find Brynn. Hadn't he, at every turn, tried to steer her away, sabotage her search plans? Her steps grew heavy.

Daylight filled the forest's details that were invisible in the dark: gigantic trees, the spiny vertebrae of their branches furred with moss, fronds like spread fingers stretching from low ferns clustering along the forest floor. The air was steeped in thin gray mist that refracted sunlight and dampened the distance. To their left, the ground sloped over slick rocks to the creek's bank.

Lou inhaled. "The air here is so fresh."

Wendy slapped mosquitoes from her legs, put her foot down in a patch of plants that whispered against her calves. "What did I just step in?"

"I think those are dead nettles," Jacqueline said.

"They sting, right?"

"Not the dead kind."

"The dead don't bite." Thorn's lips curled in a grin. "Much."

"Don't people eat nettles?" Wendy asked. "People who are into foraging?"

Thorn struggled along in his jeans, untied hair blowing in the wind. "Pretty sure I wouldn't want to eat some random plants I found in the woods."

"You would," Harlow muttered, "if you were starving."

Brynn must have had to forage when she got lost. The likeliest choice would be mushrooms, which were abundant here. Did she know her mushrooms well, though? Did she mistake a poisonous variety for edible?

A bird shrieked and took off from a nearby branch. Harlow looked up at its flapping escape, somehow expecting to see beady black eyes staring back at her. She didn't know why, but she felt as if she were being watched. It was likely because Lou had put the idea in her head last night.

The sensation crept over the back of her neck, and she turned to look around. Trees rustled. Behind her, Lou and Wendy laughed at something. The creek chuckled around rocks.

She caught Thorn looking at her, and her eyes danced away from him.

This side of the creek was relatively flat, though still rough enough to keep them moving slowly; the other side sloped steeply upward. So far they'd kept strictly to the path along the creek—if you could even call it that, it was so overgrown and untraveled—that Harlow started to wonder at the futility of this exercise. What were the odds they would just happen to stumble upon Brynn alongside this creek, with all the vastness of the woods standing untouched around them?

Brynn died again in her mind.

She propelled herself ahead, calves flexing. This was where she belonged: pushing her body toward a purpose, adrenaline burning its way through her. This feeling carried her through long weeks of fruit-less searching, the same way it pumped in her veins when drumming on stage, in grimy nightclubs, the audience a faceless swarm in the dark.

She should have been out here with Brynn.

Sometimes she tried to piece together all the little choices that led to Brynn's disappearance. All the things she could have prevented or done differently. If she hadn't shown up so monstrously hungover to that rehearsal. If she hadn't gone drinking by herself when the others flaked out—Lou claiming she was too tired, Thorn saying, "Nah, I need to go sacrifice a goat to Baphomet," or another of his non-excuses. If she hadn't stumbled home late to find Brynn still up, deep in her notebook. Maybe they could have talked things through, if Harlow had been home that night, before it was too late.

When Brynn said she was going to go camping in the Umpqua over the weekend to finish the final song for *The Orchid*, Harlow offered to come with her. "It'll be fun."

"It's not supposed to be fun," Brynn said as she packed. "I need to be alone."

"Why?"

Brynn didn't answer right away. Harlow could see thoughts spin-ning behind her eyes as she worked out how to articulate them. "This may sound crazy, but… when I'm alone, I can talk to her."

"Who?"

"My muse? Queen Carrion? I don't know how to explain it. It's like… I can *become* her. I can become my true self."

Harlow could feel her pulling away, receding into her own internal world. "Okay, but why do you have to go camping? It's crazy to go camping alone."

"It has to be there," Brynn murmured. "Some places are special."

She tried to convince her not to go, but Brynn's mind was made up. And then, in one last desperate attempt, she asked if they could at least talk before she left. Maybe she could derail the trip—even if it meant derailing their friendship. "There's something I've been meaning to tell you."

"We'll talk when I get back." Brynn closed the door to her bedroom, closing Harlow out.

And then she'd let her go.

Harlow spent the night in her room with a bottle of Buffalo Trace, and by the time she woke up the next morning, Brynn was already gone.

She should have stopped her. She should have said what she was going to say instead of being a coward and writing it in a letter once she'd already gone. A letter she'd planned to hand over as soon as Brynn came back. A letter that had sat nestled in her pocket ever since.

"Oh my god, what is that *smell*?"

Wendy's outburst pulled Harlow back to the present, and as soon as it did, she realized she smelled it, too. Something foul, like meat left to rot in the sun. Her stomach turned over, threatened to spill itself into the dirt.

Off the path ahead, a blizzard of black flies whirled up from their feast—the source of the fetid odor.

A pile of bones.

"What *is* that?" Wendy asked.

Harlow's heart rammed itself into her throat, and for a moment all she could see was Brynn's skeleton, the ravaged remnants of her.

"It's an animal," Thorn said. "Big one. Maybe a deer?"

The air turned thick and soupy. Harlow blinked. Thorn was right. It was an animal carcass, nothing more. Relief and disappointment spun through her so hard she felt sick again. She hadn't *wanted* it to be Brynn's body—of course that wasn't what she'd wanted to see. She didn't want Brynn to be dead. She wanted her to be alive, as impossible as that might be. But for one exhilarating moment, she'd almost let herself believe they'd found her.

Lou started picking her way through the trees toward the carcass, but a few steps off the path, she tripped and went down hard.

The others ran to her, swatting damp branches. They found what she'd tripped over: a circle of stones, deliberately formed, a few feet wide. Dead wet leaves clumped in the center.

"What the hell is that?" Wendy said.

Brushing dirt from the knees of her leggings, Lou regained her feet. "It looks… ritualistic."

"Nice," Thorn said.

"Not like, devil worship," Lou explained, much to Thorn's disappointment. "People use circles like this for positive purposes. Magical protection. Creating a sacred space. Opening doorways."

Lou's clumsiness had overturned something hard in the leaves at the center, something that wasn't a rock. Something white. For a moment,

Harlow thought they had found another bone—but when she bent down she found only the melted nub of a used candle, a bit of blackened wick still stuck to the deformed wax.

"Probably some campers," Jacqueline suggested, her voice high, and Harlow was pleased that the find had unsettled her. "We should keep to the creek. Don't want to lose the path."

They backtracked to the bank, Harlow dropping the used candle back into the circle of stones. She walked astride Lou as they continued. "That looked like something you've seen before?"

"Sure. It's not uncommon." Lou looked like she wanted to say something more, like she was holding something back, but she didn't have a chance to say it because she walked right into Wendy's back, letting out an "Oomph!" Harlow knocked into Thorn, Jacqueline stumbled into her from behind, and then they were all jumbled up and asking why they'd stopped.

Wendy pointed.

Up ahead, two figures beside the creek had noticed them. One crouched by the water with a bucket while the other stood. It was hard to make out their faces, which seemed unnatural—eyes too large, round, opaque. Features insectile, empty of emotion.

Wendy's voice was a whisper. "What's wrong with their faces?"

The wind blew. The mist shifted. Sunlight struggled through.

A surprised laugh erupted from Thorn. "They're wearing gas masks."

"Huh." Wendy raised an arm and waved, but the figures did not return the gesture. She let her hand drop.

"Why?" Lou asked. "Is there something wrong with the air?"

Wendy shook her head. "Of course not."

The crouching figure set aside the bucket and stood. The round gray disks of their eyes gave them the faces of flies, their mouths transformed into hole-punched circles. They wore plain clothes and black work gloves.

Wendy backed up a step. "Could be those people in the trucks. Survivalist types, probably armed to the teeth. We should get the hell out of here."

Harlow shook her head. "What do you think they're gonna do? We can't go back now. We've barely covered any ground—"

"Harlow." Thorn said nothing more, but his tone was firm, decisive.

"Oh, fuck off." She lurched around him, took a few steps closer to the figures, waving at them. "Hey assholes! See something you like?"

She heard the others cry out in alarm before she could process what was happening in front of her.

The shorter figure extended an arm—a twitch of the hand, something in it.

A gun.

FROM "HAUNTED OREGON"

...opened by two Polish immigrants, William Hryszko and Barney Soboleski, who named the saloon after the white eagle on the Polish flag. During the Prohibition era, illegal alcohol was transported from the Shanghai tunnels to the White Eagle, but men and women were also kidnapped from the saloon and taken to the docks through the underground tunnel system. Today, the saloon plays host to apparitions of these unfortunate souls, among others, including a pre-Prohibition-era bartender and cook, Sam Warrick, said to throw things in the kitchen. The White Eagle Saloon remains one of the most notoriously haunted spots in Portland.

The Wonder Room

Originally an old bank, this downtown Portland building was later repurposed into a small nightclub that plays host to a variety of local bands. Over the years, The Wonder Room has experienced its share of paranormal activity in the form of flickering lights and other electrical failures. Few records remain from its brief stint as a bank in the early 1900s, but rumor has it the bank shuttered due to numerous unexplained events, such as patrons becoming trapped in dark vaults and money mysteriously vanishing from locked safes. One vault remains in the music venue today, now the location of the bar, where patrons report hearing eerie sounds and feeling impossible breezes when no air is blowing.

The most notorious incident at the Wonder Room was a 2019 panic that left one man dead and several injured. During a performance by the band Queen Carrion, the crowd scrambled in fear during a sudden blackout, leading to a crowd crush at the exit. The Wonder Room closed briefly following the tragedy but reopened soon after, drawing the attention of ghost hunters and paranormal experts. To this day, the Wonder Room occasionally experiences unexplainable electrical malfunctions, and some patrons have described feeling uneasy inside, though they could not explain why.

NINE

They didn't catch their collective breath until they were back at the cabin, safely ensconced within its knotty pine walls.

Wendy had been the first to run, and before she knew it the others were running too, Thorn having practically dragged Harlow with him.

Once they were back, it was all they could talk about: who were those people? Why were they wearing gas masks? Why had they pointed a gun at them?

Everyone dismissed the idea that they were hunters. It was the wrong kind of gun, the wrong kind of gear.

Whoever they were, Wendy didn't like it. Her body melted into a chair, still thrumming with adrenaline. She stifled every urge to remind the others that it wasn't a good idea being all the way out here in the middle of the woods, cut off, with rednecks and crazies and who knew what else? People were dangerous—even more so when their target was isolated.

Footsteps creaked a path across the loft, and then Rhys was hunching down the stairs. He moved as if he were trying to hold himself together, stiff and wounded. Sweat slicked a face bled of color and ringed the sleeves of his shirt. Blue eyes sat in gray hollows, typically chiseled features skeletoning him now in his pallor. A phlegmy cough erupted from the swamp of his lungs.

Jacqueline's eyes seized him. "You okay, babe?"

He tried on a grin that barely twisted his face, his mouth all wrong. "Fine. Just went a little too hard last night."

Harlow waved her hand in front of her face. "Dude, you stink."

"Speak for yourself."

She gave the crook of her arm a surreptitious sniff.

"We just saw the weirdest thing." Then Jacqueline was off—regaling him with the mysterious encounter, the thrilling race back, all the while fluttering around him like a bird desperate for crumbs of attention. Rhys grunted his way through a response.

"Couple of weirdos who probably came out here because they think the government's a bunch of child-eating Satanists," Wendy said, with a glance at Thorn. "No offense."

"I'll have you know, children are a rare delicacy."

Before long they were ravenous, ripping open bags of chips and crackers, packages of cheese and salami. The coffee table turned into a slapdash charcuterie board. The day eased into a torpid afternoon. Mist thickened, creeping up against the windows in a pale blur. Gradually, the trees retreated into a gray nothingness.

They fell into a between-time. That's what Wendy always thought of Saturdays between shows. Ears still ringing from last night's show, trying to muster up the energy for tonight's. She would often spend the day running errands or reading. Lou would smoke weed and snack and binge TV shows. Thorn would noodle around on his guitar and whip up concoctions in the kitchen. Rhys would abscond somewhere with Jacqueline. Harlow would listen to music and nurse her hangover. And Brynn? She would dissolve somewhere inside her own head, scribbling in her songwriting notebook, humming to music only she could hear.

Without warning, Rhys lurched down the hall to the bathroom and shut himself inside. "Babe?" Jacqueline asked, trailing him, knocking on the door to see if he was all right.

Harlow laughed. She didn't look so great herself, but Wendy could see her demeanor already changing after her first few sips from the flask. Her laugh was looser, friendlier. Admittedly, Wendy liked Harlow better when she was drunk, but only because daytime-Harlow—or rather, hungover-Harlow—could be so prickly and rude.

Thorn balanced a beer on his knee. "So. Should we discuss Rhys's proposition?"

Wendy pursed her lips. She didn't want to have this conversation. Maybe it was better to rip the band-aid, though.

"We wouldn't be the first band to change singers," Lou said. She shrugged at the angry look Harlow gave her. "What?"

"What do you think?"

Thorn was looking at Wendy, and she realized she had to tell them. "If you guys want to go ahead and make Jacqueline the new singer, I say go for it. But I'm not going to be involved."

"Me either," Harlow jumped in.

Thorn frowned. "Why not?"

"Because I'm moving to Los Angeles."

"What?" Thorn actually laughed, as if it were a joke. "What are you talking about?"

"I've told you I always wanted to play on movie soundtracks. I feel like it's now or never. I don't want to teach 'Twinkle, Twinkle, Little Star' to nine-year-olds for the rest of my life. I've got some cash saved. My lease is up in July." She piled salami on a cracker and stuffed it in her mouth.

"But we need you!" Lou protested.

Wendy swallowed. "You really don't. Seriously, you can still be a band without me. You don't need a cellist."

When she looked at Thorn, she found anger on his face, and it made her cringe. It took a lot for Thorn to get angry. "So you wait until now to spring this on us?"

"I'm sorry. When was I supposed to tell you?"

"You want to go to Los Angeles," he said again, like he still couldn't believe it. "You'll hate it there. The people are all fake."

Wendy laughed. "That's such a stereotype. My cousin Leah lives there, and so do my aunt and uncle. And look. Even if I *don't* go," she said, fixing Thorn with a steady gaze, "I told you…"

She could feel the awkwardness hanging in the air. Lou looked away and started crafting herself a tower of crackers and meat. Harlow stood up and went to the bedroom.

At last, she had to say it, or it wouldn't get said: "I don't want to be friends with benefits."

Thorn nodded. "Fine, so let's not. Let's be together."

"It's not that simple… Brynn was right about not dating other people in the band. Things get messy. Complicated. That's not what I want."

"Yeah, but life is messy and complicated."

"Yours is, maybe." She looked at him guiltily. "I don't want that. I want things to be simple, nice."

"So you'd rather be with Mr. Boring Normie, who works at H&R Block, lives on a cul-de-sac, wears fucking—polos?"

"That's not what I said. You're putting words in my mouth."

"I'm just trying to understand."

"Well, try harder."

Before they could say anything else, Harlow stomped back into the room. She had a notebook in her hand, loose papers spilling from between the pages.

"What is that?" Lou asked.

"Brynn's songwriting notebook. One of them, at least." She flipped it open. Extra papers slid out and scattered. "She wasn't just writing songs in them. There's all kinds of other stuff in here. Research. She was chasing something, trying to figure something out." She placed the notebook face-up on the coffee table, revealing a page scrawled over with phrases and fragments, half of them crossed out. Grateful for the distraction from Thorn, Wendy drew a finger down the writing, landing on a few lines.

the dead collect

in low places

"These aren't lyrics?" she asked. "Because they look like lyrics to me."

"This sure isn't." Lou picked up one of the loose papers, a scanned page from a book. "It's about the Wonder Room."

"I'm not surprised," Wendy said glancing at Thorn, who had sat back to brood. "She was obsessed with that place after what happened."

"What do you mean?"

"Remember how, after it reopened, she kept wanting to hang out there? I was concerned about her, so I went with her. I thought maybe it was some kind of coping mechanism, the way she seemed to want to, I don't know, recreate what happened. Not that kid's death, I mean—everything leading up to it. Like, she would play 'Midnight Ritual' on her phone, trying to trigger something. It was kind of creepy."

"Maybe she felt guilty," Lou suggested. "Like you said, her way to cope."

Harlow shook her head. "That wasn't it. It had nothing to do with Murphy Dunning. She was obsessed with the blackout."

"So you want to go digging through her private notebook?" Thorn said, arms folded. "Seems kind of disrespectful."

Lou tilted her head to the side as she peeked at the open pages. "You're not curious what she was onto?"

"She wasn't onto anything," Wendy said gently. "People tried to make it out to be something mysterious, but it wasn't. The lights went out, people panicked, the end."

"Shit, that's not all that happened," Lou said. "Come on, you were there. You know it was—*weird.*"

"Not you, too."

"Didn't you *feel* it?" Lou looked around for support. "It wasn't just the lights. It was *everything*, man. Everything was *gone.* I thought I'd gone deaf and blind. It was like being nowhere." Her gaze lingered on Wendy. "*Then* everything went back to normal, or whatever, and everyone was screaming and running. And then—well."

"The Curse of Queen Carrion."

The voice pulled their attention to Jacqueline standing in the hallway. "That's what everyone started calling it." She glanced behind her. "Hey, do you think Rhys is okay? He's acting really weird."

"He's fine," Harlow said.

"And those people are idiots," Wendy added. "They think *we* somehow made the lights go out with our music."

"Music can be used in spells." Lou raised her eyebrows at the look Wendy threw her. "What? It's not that far-fetched, is what I'm saying."

"But *we* didn't!"

Wendy didn't want to think about the Wonder Room. She had tried hard to put that behind her. For weeks afterward, every time she closed her eyes, she saw Murphy Dunning's body being carried away on a stretcher, his glassy eyes like polished stone before he was covered up. They may not have been directly responsible for his death, but it was *their* concert. He was there to see them.

She saw Harlow's hands spider into the pockets of her jacket until she found the flask and tipped the last drip onto her tongue. In a flash, Jacqueline was dangling a brown bottle in front of her face, which Harlow reached for instinctively, probably before she could even register the face behind it framed by a square of iced platinum frizz. She poured a careful stream into the narrow opening of her flask like a scientist filling a test tube, then thumped the bottle onto the table rather than handing it back to Jacqueline, as if that acknowledgment was a bridge too far.

"She came out here for a reason. It was something to do with the

Wonder Room." Harlow pointed to a note scrawled in the margin of the paper Lou was holding, which seemed to be scanned from a book about haunted places in Oregon. Brynn's handwriting added the question: *Low Place?*

"What does that mean?" Lou asked.

"I don't know," Harlow said. "She wrote a lot about it. I think maybe that's what she was looking for. She thought she might find one of those places out here."

Then, probably the last sound Harlow wanted to hear—Jacqueline, who had thus far contained herself after the reaction to her vocals last night, her voice deeper in her throat than usual as if in imitation of Brynn's alto, singing: *"Demon rises, with new eyes and, from his low place he will burn this town. Man of shadow, blood of poison, with my song now he will bring you down."*

"Congratulations," Harlow spat. "You know the lyrics to 'Midnight Ritual.'"

Jacqueline fixed her with an unblinking stare. "Didn't you notice? 'From his low place'?"

"Oh shit, she's right!" Lou burst out. "What do you think it means?"

Shame and anger flitted across Harlow's face. Apparently, these lyrics had not occurred to her when she was paging through Brynn's notes. That Jacqueline seemed to know their repertoire better than she did probably hurt, and Wendy almost felt sorry for her—or she would have if she weren't so put off by the wild conspiracies and pointless speculation Harlow had invited.

No one needed to say it, though—that was the song, the one they were playing at the Wonder Room when the lights went out and all hell broke loose.

Even if she didn't believe anything unnatural had happened at the Wonder Room, Wendy could not help feeling a little unsettled by Brynn's mysterious note.

The dead collect in low places.

BAD BANDS

50 TRAGIC & TERRIFYING TIMES
WHEN ROCK & ROLL DIED

#47 — QUEEN CARRION

Voodoo? Witchcraft? A Faustian deal? If you've heard of Queen Carrion, consider yourself a connoisseur of cursed music. Their infamous song "Midnight Ritual" instigated a mass panic at a nightclub, where someone was literally *trampled to death.* Some have said the song itself is a curse, and that listening to it can put you in a hypnotic trance that leaves you open to the spirit realm. Some people won't even listen to it, and those who do say there's something undeniably creepy about the tune.

Ramona Peters, who attended the concert, tweeted that the blackout that happened was like being buried alive, and then waking to realize everyone else was buried with you. Um, yikes! Picture this: lights out, bodies collapsed at the overcrowded exit, all to escape the terror everyone inexplicably experienced during the song. Peters said she felt something cold reaching out for the back of her neck, like the exhale of a corpse.

Was the song a curse? A ritual? Was it written by the Devil Himself? Did it send the audience into a frenzy of fear?

Chills, y'all. Not the most deadly crowd-crush incident by a long shot, but can you imagine? A band with members into the occult, an evil song, deadly concerts—no thank you!

TEN

Rhys did not look well.

His skin was tinted the gray of a bloated raincloud, and he stank—something like rancid socks. Clearly he hadn't showered today; there was dirt crusted under his fingernails.

Jacqueline had never seen him like this before, even on his worst days. Of course, he was allergic to being comforted or cared for—she supposed it was something to do with feeling emasculated by tenderness, since even though he presented strength and self-assurance, he could be terribly neurotic about how he was perceived—but when she got close to him now, in this sickened state, revulsion crawled through her.

It was the part of relationships she'd always struggled with: that the person on the other side of it was human, with all the disgusting bodily functions and baggage that brought. She wished she could fast-forward through the unpleasant parts, enjoy the times when Rhys was being clever and sexy and confident. After all, she was good at tamping down her own unpleasantness. She could make herself sensual and doting for him, or good-humored when the time called for it. It wasn't hard. All of life was a performance, in the end, so what else could Jacqueline possibly want to do with that life but perform on stage with a band at her back?

It was a delicious thought.

Then maybe other people would be admiring *her*. They would cheer for *her*. They would have to try hard to get her to like them—but when you have that kind of power and popularity, the beauty is that you don't have to be likable. Jacqueline could shed that unnecessary mask. Stop smiling to make herself pleasant for others.

But she needed Rhys. He was her anchor. He was the only person she could be even somewhat herself with.

And right now there was something *wrong* with him.

Thorn made chili for dinner, and after putting two bites of it in his mouth and giving a rough swallow, throat convulsing to get it down, Rhys's chest spasmed and he spewed tarry black vomit. It spattered the place where the wall met the floor. Bits of undigested chili swam in the black sludge.

"Babe," she said, concern tightening her throat. "Are you okay?"

Wendy clamped a hand over her nose and mouth, eyes watering behind the lenses of her glasses. "Oh my god, that is rank."

Then the smell hit Jacqueline, too: sour and fecal, like rotting fish or sewage. She gagged on it; she could practically taste it in the air, and it made her stomach turn over, made the back of her throat go hot.

Some of it speckled Rhys's shirt like dirt, and she quickly began pulling it off him. He did not resist, but neither did he help. It took a bit of fumbling effort, but she was able to yank it over his head and out of the tangle of arms. With a quick sniff, she tossed it on the floor beside the puddle of vomit.

"Why don't you go lie down," she suggested, bringing an arm around his back to guide him to the loft. He didn't look capable of making it all the way up the stairs, though, so she angled him back toward the living room, to the sofa. He took one step and then another, feet shuffling dryly along the floor, bare chest and back sheened with sweat. Meanwhile the others vacated the living room, carrying their bowls back to the kitchen, making sounds of disgust.

"I'm not cleaning that up," Wendy declared, still clamping shut her nose as she moved away from the smell of sick.

"We can't just leave it there," Lou said as she bent down to assess the damage. She didn't get very close before she had to back away. "On second thought—he who throws up cleans up."

By now, Rhys's slow gait had brought him to the couch. Jacqueline pushed on his shoulders until he sat.

"Some people really can't hold their liquor," Harlow said with a chuckle. She hadn't moved from the armchair, flask in hand, and she looked cruelly amused with the proceedings, which made Jacqueline angry, but she tamped it down.

Rhys sat up so abruptly that Jacqueline recoiled, not expecting the movement. He leaned over his knees, pulling his lips into something like a grin as he looked at Harlow with hollow eyes set upon bruise-colored bags. "She's here with me," he said, voice low, phlegmy.

"Who?"

"Brynn." His grin stretched wider, as if tugged at the corners by strings. "She says hi."

Harlow stood up. "Fuck you."

"She wants us all to be together."

They were all staring at him now, either angry or appalled. Jacqueline tried to lean closer, to tell him to knock it off, but he ignored her.

"What is your problem, man?" Lou asked.

"Isn't it obvious?" Harlow sat down again, a vicious spark in her eyes. "He's pissed because he's not getting what he's always wanted. You were so close, right?"

Thorn looked at her. "What are you talking about?"

"It's why he waited until after Brynn was out of the picture to finally propose, isn't it? Come on, we all know what he's always wanted. To be the lead guitarist, fucking the lead singer. Isn't that right? You almost got your wish, too. If only you'd been able to convince us to fold Jacqui-pie into the band."

"Okay, that's enough," Wendy said.

Rhys lurched to his feet, laughing—a grating, unnatural sound—and Jacqueline could see black bile still staining his lips and teeth. She thought it must be the black bean chili, but he hadn't eaten enough to turn his vomit that color, had he?

Everyone else was so stunned by his behavior that nobody moved to stop him as he fell to his knees and pushed the rug aside; as he pulled open the uncovered trapdoor; as he started crawling down the ladder, head and arms first, into the darkness below.

"Babe?"

Each step seemed to pound through her body. She didn't understand why Rhys would come down here—in fact, she felt like she didn't understand him at all today, which disagreed with her. Jacqueline had always thought she had a very good understanding of Rhys. She found him very predictable. He wouldn't hear of it, but it was actually one of the things she liked about him. Predictability offered a measure of control and stability, which she appreciated.

Today, he had been unpredictable in a way that unsettled her. She couldn't get a read on him—whether he was still angry with Harlow and Wendy for refusing to finish *The Orchid*, or whether he was only hungover, or whether he was upset with *her*.

She couldn't begin to understand his climbing down the hatch after making those weird comments about Brynn. When she called out to him, he didn't slow. He only flinched from the light of her phone as if it might sting him, down the stairs and into the tunnel.

Into the pitch black.

She hesitated at the entrance, staring into the darkness beyond her phone's light and wondering how far ahead he was. She took a slow step, advancing the light with her, annoyance and trepidation fighting for control.

"Babe, are you okay?"

Silence.

She listened for the crunch of footsteps moving either toward or away from her, but the tunnel gave up none of its secrets.

After a few more steps, she turned and shined the light back in the direction from which she'd come. She didn't particularly know why she did this—some gut reaction to check how far she was from the doorway that led back up to the stairs, back up to the cellar, out of this oppressive underground corridor. It felt too like a tomb. She wondered what it was like to be buried alive, the exquisite terror of discovering you are confined beneath the earth with no escape.

The tunnel receded past the edge of her light.

She turned and found a kind of horrible deja vu in seeing how the way ahead looked identical to the way back. As if they would both continue to infinity with no exit at either end.

Then she heard a faint sound, like moist chewing.

It was coming from ahead, further down the tunnel. The salty tang of sweat slipped into the corner of her mouth. With another few steps, she could see the rounded outline of his back, ghostly in the cold light.

The figure before her had no head.

Jacqueline froze.

His shape was wrong, all wrong. It was impossible, malformed.

Then she realized he was hunched over, facing the wall. The noises were coming from him. "Babe?" she said. "Rhys? What are you doing?"

"I need to get better," he mumbled, the tenor of his voice so different from his usual cutting bravado. His voice was flat and low, garbled, as if he had something in his mouth.

"Yeah, which is why you should come upstairs and stop being ridiculous—" As she said it, she grabbed his shoulder to turn him around, but she dropped her hand almost as soon as she touched him. His skin was cold and clammy, like damp putty, so unpleasant it gave her goosebumps. Though she had let go, he still turned from the momentum of her pull, and she saw that he was chewing. He held tufts of white fuzz like cotton in his hands, shoved clumps of it into his mouth.

Jacqueline stepped back. "What are you eating?" His smell hit her again, like spoiled meat. He swallowed and turned back to the wall. She came around his side, noticing cracks in the walls that widened where concrete had split and crumbled away, leaving inch-wide gaps that wept black soil.

Rhys stood facing one of these muddy cracks, spilling dirt like pus, a trickle of water staining the wall, plopping to a rancid puddle on the floor. She noticed little roots in the soil. Or, no, not roots—tiny pale worms, but they were not worms either, too thin and fine. It was the fuzz he was eating, growing from the cracks in the wall, and now he pulled free two more handfuls of the stuff.

"It will make me better," Rhys said, still in that dull monotone, and when she flashed the light up at his face, she saw his eyes like two blank balls, so empty she thought for a minute he had to be dead, even though he was standing and talking to her. The thought threaded a sliver of ice through her spine.

"What is it?" she asked, voice rising with revulsion as she watched him bring the fuzzy clumps to his mouth. "Stop it!"

"Did you see her?" he asked. "In the woods?"

Her heart threw itself into her throat.

She had decided that was only her imagination—there was no way she could have seen Brynn in the woods last night, because Brynn was dead and could not possibly be wandering among the trees—but then, how would Rhys know what she thought she'd seen?

He was sick. He was delirious.

And now he was eating some kind of mold growing from the wall.

She grabbed him by the arm and tried to pull him away, knowing if he didn't want to move he would easily be able to overpower her, but something about him seemed oddly pliable, and he let her drag him from his loathsome feast.

All she had to do was get him into bed and let him sleep it off. He would be fine in the morning.

He had to be.

Right before she turned the light from his face to guide them back down the tunnel, she noticed the fuzz still sticking to his lip, and she was sure she had seen wrong. She must have because she thought she saw the stuff squirm, crawl up his lip to find the crevice of warmth that opened up into that cold cold flesh.

ELEVEN

It was the smell that drove them outside, and though they all knew someone should clean it up, that it would continue to stink up the cabin if they left it there, no one wanted to go near the pile of sick, so instead they filed out back and got a fire going while Jacqueline took care of Rhys.

Evening had fallen again, and Harlow was still no closer to finding Brynn. After the aborted hike, Thorn had kept an eye on her to be sure she wouldn't try to sneak back out, and she knew he would stop her if she tried, so she filled her flask, emptied it, repeated the cycle. She pored over Brynn's notebook, trying to untangle its threads. The sheer size and scope of the woods was daunting to consider. She thought she might as well throw a rock into space and expect it to hit a distant star.

Brynn had once told her that nothing was impossible. It was the kind of thing Harlow expected other kids heard from their mothers: *You can do anything you set your mind to. No dream is too big. Nothing is impossible.* Not exactly something Harlow's mother had ever told her (instead, it was always, *Are you sure you can do that?*). Brynn hadn't meant it in a corny way, though. She told Harlow that what people thought of as *impossible* really meant something was *improbable*—and no matter how minuscule that probability, even if it were a one in a trillion chance, that still meant it could happen.

What if they just happened to be on the one-in-a-trillion timeline? The one where she found Brynn?

How long could she keep searching, though?

The others were talking about Rhys, poor sick Rhys, and Harlow found herself resenting him for getting sick, for taking the focus off the person they *should* be thinking about.

"Should we be worried about him?" Wendy asked as she huddled close to the fire. "What if he's really sick?"

"He is acting weird," Lou said.

"He's hungover," Harlow argued. "He'll be fine."

The mist had retreated from the cabin but still hung thick about the trees. Coyotes yipped in the distance. The cabin door opened, and Jacqueline emerged into the cool night.

"How's he doing?" Wendy asked.

Jacqueline shook her head, then came to sit near the fire.

Its crackling warmth enclosed them in a bubble of light. The quiet rustlings from within the trees made the soundscape static until another sound floated over the shivering leaves and humming insects. When she heard it, Harlow went numb. Rhys was inside, and the voice was coming from out in the forest. It couldn't be him playing a recording. But neither had it been a mushroom-induced hallucination, some collective delusion they'd managed to share, because here it was again, so unmistakable she felt the hair follicles on her arms lifting as her skin prickled. Spikes of heat chased themselves up and down her body, flushing from the top of her head down to her belly, where everything she'd drunk tonight began to churn in some unhappy maelstrom.

She knew the others heard it, too, by the shocked recognition on their faces where the firelight flickered over them, eyes round and unblinking.

Somewhere in the trees, Brynn was singing.

"How is this possible?" Wendy's voice came out as a whisper.

Harlow's heart leapt into a jagged rhythm. Even though she knew it couldn't be him, she rose to her feet and shouted, "Rhys, you asshole! This isn't funny!"

Her shout carried into the trees. The voice kept singing.

A bang made her flinch and look away.

Rhys had come outside, letting the cabin door slam behind him. He was still shirtless and barefoot, wearing only a pair of shorts that ended in a ragged hem at the knee. He stood out of the fire's glow, but there was enough light to tell he'd thrown up on himself again—or at least that's what Harlow assumed since there were black patches down his front that reminded her of that rancid puke.

Jacqueline stood and went over to him. She suggested he go back inside and lie down, but when she took him by the shoulder to turn him around, he didn't budge. He stood facing the forest, listening. Harlow frantically reached for the last thread of possibility, something to explain what was happening, but she came up empty. It wasn't Rhys doing this.

When he began speaking—in a dull monotone that barely sounded like him at all, a voice that was sticky, muddy—it was in a strange resonance with Brynn's singing.

"All that devours shall be devoured
Sinners and cowards go marching to Hell
Craven enslavers, hypocrite saviors
Reap what they sow and let justice prevail."

He was speaking in lyrics—the same song Brynn was singing, in perfect sync with her.

"Rhys?" Jacqueline said to get him to break out of his trance. "Babe?"

"We need to get him to a hospital." Wendy stood, patted her pockets, then skirted around Rhys and Jacqueline, disappearing inside the cabin.

"Maybe he's communicating with her," Lou suggested. "With—whatever is out there. Is it her?" She spoke now directly to Rhys even though he continued to stare into the trees, mumbling lyrics. "Is it Brynn's ghost? Is she haunting the forest?"

"That's ridiculous," Harlow said, even though her skin continued prickling into gooseflesh, and she could not deny the sound of Brynn's voice, so unmistakably familiar.

Rhys took a shambling step toward the trees, and it looked as if the voice were pulling him there on invisible strings, as if Rhys were merely a puppet. As he did, she got a better look at the patches on his chest, a deep gray-black with yellow crusted around the edges like dried pus. She swallowed a wave of nausea. Rhys's body lurched and he vomited again, that same tarry sludge. It blackened his teeth and gums. A small hard thing fell out of his mouth, landing in the puddle, and Harlow saw an empty space where one of his front teeth had been.

"Holy shit, dude," Thorn said.

Even Jacqueline backed away from him now, hands hovering in the air as if they didn't want to touch him anymore, didn't want to touch that blackening flesh, because Harlow was certain, now, that the patches were *not* dried vomit, but were something more like necrotic tissue, as if Rhys were rotting from the inside out.

She'd been wrong. This was more than just a hangover.

"He's possessed," Lou said. "It's something—whatever is in the woods—"

Brynn's singing grew louder. Closer.

Before she was even aware she had moved, Harlow was at the tree line, searching for the direction from which the voice came. Her body pulsed with the need to go out there, to find her, but something was holding her back, and she realized it was Thorn preventing her from going any further. She turned around, twisting out of his grip, just as Wendy emerged from the cabin with a purse thrown over her shoulder and her keys jangling in her hands, which she dropped as soon as she saw what was happening to Rhys.

He stood slumped to one side, no longer muttering lyrics, and he was moving—sort of—but not in a deliberate or even a natural way. Rather, his skin was squirming.

Something ticked in Rhys's throat like a scuttle of insect feet. Saliva dribbled from his loose gray lips. His eyes swam, though not with tears. The whites shivered. He reached out to Jacqueline, the person closest to him, opening his mouth and convulsing. His eyes were wide and going wider, the right one swelling, bulging from its lid.

"Rhys," Jacqueline said, clearly trying to keep her voice calm. "Rhys! What is it? What's—what's the matter with you? Talk to me."

He didn't, though. He stared, opening and closing his mouth like a loose hinge, and reached for her again with hands of mottled flesh, curdling black and gray.

"Rhys!" she said again—and then, maybe thinking it would help snap him out of it, she raised her hand and slapped him across the face.

His bloodless cheek never bloomed pink.

The pressure, maybe, or the force of the slap, pushed his right eye out of joint, and it ballooned grotesquely, a ball of jelly squeezed through a narrow opening, until it popped free of its socket.

AFTER

The dead collect in low places.

The phrase rings in Harlow's mind as she sits on a creaky folding chair in a circle of faces that she struggles to recognize. Her roommate, Sinda, sits two chairs down from her. Across the circle—arranged ritualistically, like a fairy ring of stones—she sees the slouching form of a woman she's glimpsed from time to time: a thin, pale creature like a praying mantis named Allison Reed. She always seems to be hiding, afraid of other people, and when Harlow catches sight of her, she is never entirely sure that she has actually seen Allison Reed.

In fact, she cannot be sure that Allison is a person at all.

Sometimes she gets a glimpse of what she thinks is a coat rack, or a department store mannequin, and when she blinks, she realizes it's a person, it's Allison Reed. But by the time she realizes this, Allison is already creeping away down the hall. She wears ill-fitting, loose-knit sweaters that hang limp from her frame. Her shoes squeak on the tile, never fully lifting. She's always turning away. Harlow hasn't managed to get a good look at her face, and even now she hunches over her knees, looking at the tile floor.

It's Sinda's turn to talk: "Do you ever feel like, sometimes, the world is *too much*? Even the day-to-day routine exhausts all my executive functioning. I have to plan and execute every last thing I do. It's not just 'get ready for work.' Hell, it's not even 'brush teeth, take a shower, and get dressed.' It's: first, walk to the bathroom, put toothpaste on a tooth-brush, turn on the tap, brush top left, middle, top right, bottom left, bottom right. Spit. Rinse. Turn on the shower. Squeeze shampoo... and on and on, every action of every moment of the day. Sometimes I wish I could shut my brain off, or hand over my awareness to something else, so that I wouldn't have to be trapped in myself all the time."

Though Harlow is listening, she finds herself at the same time trying to see Allison's face. A hood obscures all but some tufts of pale hair and her downturned nose.

She almost doesn't notice, then, when suddenly everyone is looking at her.

The attention freezes her in the chair. The group therapist—Aina, a woman in her late forties with bright eyes, narrow features, and waves of warm chestnut hair—repeats herself: "Harlow? Would you like to tell us about yourself and what you're going through right now?"

For a moment, she sputters, tries to pass the baton to the next patient, but Aina won't let her beg off speaking, considering this is her third group session and she hasn't spoken yet. At last, she is obliged to say something, and what comes out is this: "Hey. I'm Harlow. Uh, I'm a drummer. I have an alcohol problem. I got drunk in a bar and had an... accident. So now I'm here."

The man sitting three seats from Aina—twenties, unshaven, eyes set in deep hollows—leans forward, chewing the edge of a thumbnail. "I think I know you," he says. Even when Aina tries to steer things back to Harlow, to get her to talk a bit more, the young man, whose name she thinks is Kyle, keeps staring at her and saying, "I know you."

Of course he does. Her face had been plastered all over the news. *Local drummer escapes grisly fate in woodland tragedy, more at eleven.* Or one of the less savory headlines, perhaps: "Twice Cursed: Death Follows Occult-Leaning Metal Band."

They never even got any radio play, she thinks. Never topped any charts. Never won any awards. Never sold enough CDs to make ends meet. Never had enough streams to sustain them. And yet, now—now that Brynn is gone, now that everything went tits up in the woods—*now* they have some modicum of fame. Now people know Queen Carrion. Not for their music, not for their talent, but because they are cursed.

Kyle's insistence that he knows her mercifully absolves her of having to speak further at group. They move on to the next person.

That night, as she lies on the hard cot with the hall light streaming through the small square window in the door, Harlow tries to get comfortable, her back aching fiercely, her guts churning, desperate for her flask.

"Do you know Kyle?" Sinda's voice floats to her in the dark.

"No, but he probably knows my band."

"Oh yeah?"

"Queen Carrion."

A pause. "Sorry." Sinda sounds apologetic for not recognizing the name. "I don't really listen to new music. I mostly listen to, like, old-school R&B."

"That's probably a good thing," Harlow says. "Considering our music is cursed."

Long after she can hear the way Sinda's breathing has evened into sleep, Harlow lies awake, the thin blanket growing too hot, the air turning too cold, pain lancing through her body. The patter of movement shuffles in from the hall, the night shift moving between rooms, and she tries to force herself into unconsciousness because every distant sound makes her think she can hear Brynn singing. She needs a drink to help her sleep.

She hears a squeak, the rubber sole of a sneaker against tile, and she throws the blanket off, stands, energy coursing through her, energy which she would rather discard so she can *just fucking sleep*.

She steps into the hall, where the light fluoresces on white tile, crowded in by darkness where otherwise sunlight would come through the windows from the rec room on one end of the hall. It's weird being out at night. They don't lock the room doors, but still, no one wanders after dark.

Someone else is in the hallway with her.

She realizes, when she looks left, to where the corridor recedes into darkness and turns a corner, that there is someone there, just around the bend, peeking around the edge of the wall. Her heart jackhammers.

A sliver of a pale face peers out from around the corner.

She should go back to bed, but she can't; the insomnia has taken hold, and Harlow hurries down the hall to find who is watching her, whose shoes are squeaking against the floor.

Though she has pulled back by the time Harlow rounds the corner, she is able to reach forward for the shape moving away from her, turn the person around, and view them full-on.

Allison Reed.

And she realizes the reason she's never seen her face is because it's not really a face, it's a mask, it's something pretending to be a face, and it's so pale—her eyes are mere impressions in the flesh, a distant memory of the need for eyes, and her mouth is full of something like teeth that aren't, like the bristles of a baleen whale, all made of that same white stuff.

Harlow's chest seizes. The girl's face seems to ripple, to change, and from that baleen mouth, which twists up in a grin, she forms the words:

"Found you."

TWELVE

Rhys's eye, hovering several inches from his face, stared with the manic blankness of a lidless cyclops. White hairs unfurled from behind the extruded eyeball, curled over the edges of the raw socket. The pale globe swayed, held up by strands which sprouted, too, from between his lips, stretching them around a strange bouquet. His skin, great swathes of it gone gangrenous, began to split like a teddy bear at the seams, opening down the lengths of his arms, peeling back from an internal network of fine white filaments.

Unable to comprehend what he was seeing, Thorn almost laughed. What a ridiculous sight. His brain couldn't process it as being real.

And reality did seem fuzzy just then, the way it had after the fire, when his burns were still healing, the surreal experience of true agony and the almost out-of-body floating on pain medication. He remembered looking at himself in the mirror and not recognizing his own face. Thinking: *that isn't me.* Thinking: *that is a monster.*

Now he could almost convince himself it wasn't Rhys in front of him, but some monster, some impostor.

Except he knew it wasn't.

It was Rhys whose rotting flesh was sloughing off his body. It was Rhys who opened his mouth as a mass of threads sprouted, probed the air as if tasting it, stretching from his face. It was Rhys whose eye bobbed from his skull on a cord of bloodless nerves.

In spite of all this, Jacqueline reached out to him. Shock must have turned her mind to static. She took his hand because it was instinct. She took his hand because the nerves in her arm were thinking for her, desperate for the comfort of a touch. She took his hand because he was her fiancé.

Thorn understood the impulse. He wanted something to hold on to, himself.

When her fingers clutched that fishlike hand, though, and she realized what she was holding, Jacqueline tried to reel away from him.

But the hand came with her.

His arm ripped off like clothing torn at the seam.

Rhys's shoulder was now just a tangle of frayed white threads where his arm used to be.

In her haste to recoil, Wendy stumbled and fell, her glasses skittering away. Thorn saw this and threw himself down beside her as she patted the ground for them. His hand lit on the plastic frames first, and he slid the glasses back onto her face. A feathered lightning bolt scratched across one of the lenses.

Then he looked up and saw behind her: Rhys, fuzzed like a piece of old fruit, lurching on collapsing ankles.

Thorn scrabbled away on hands and knees, knocking over a half-empty beer bottle that spilled amber froth into the dirt. He grabbed Wendy, still blinking behind her scratched lenses, pulling her with him to the cabin.

They spilled inside and slammed the door shut.

Whatever thin twilight made its way through the windows gave the merest breath of light. Thorn flipped a switch, and when the bulb flickered on, it highlighted every sharp crevice and shadow of their faces. It steadied, flickered, steadied. Nothing was stable anymore. The air seemed to crackle with the pungent sting of fear.

He could barely feel his fingers as he pulled out his phone. "We need to call for help." Despite the circle with a slash through it, he dialed. Despite the silence, he held it to his ear. He clutched denial like a raft at sea. His gut couldn't decide if it was sick or numb. He'd never felt panic like this before, and he was almost surprised at how outwardly calm he was—how the panic turned him to stone, his insides crawling even as his limbs grew leaden, like foreign appendages. He moved as if underwater.

Words tumbled from Jacqueline's lips like amateur gymnasts stumbling through a routine. "We—we can't just… leave him out there." She turned to the window, the dark beyond.

"We can't let him in." Lou's voice seemed to come from far away, soft and dreamy. "He's possessed. I told you."

"He's not possessed," Wendy scoffed. "He's infected with something."

That word, *infected*, shivered the air, sparked a cringing away from the collective trauma of the pandemic. A thin surgical mask seemed a futile barrier against whatever this was. Certainly no virus.

Thorn wasn't even sure they should be talking about Rhys in the present tense anymore. He'd seen the way his body had begun to fall apart, how his insides were infested with that strange white substance. If Rhys was even still alive out there, he wouldn't be for long.

"This is so fucked," Harlow said.

On instinct, Thorn moved closer to Wendy, wanting to feel her presence near him, but she stepped away. He could see wheels turning behind her eyes. "Here's what we need to know. Number one, is it contagious? And number two, do any of us have it?"

A spear of ice lanced through his body at that question.

Harlow's boots clunked the floor as she stepped back. "If anyone has it, it's Jacqueline."

A wretched sound from Jacqueline—a laugh or sob, something of both. "Maybe *you* infected him with something. You couldn't stand to see him take over. You'd rather see him dead."

A soft thump on the window.

They all looked up.

Rhys's forehead pressed against the other side of the glass. Both eyes stood from his face on white threads, leaving wet smears.

Jacqueline moaned, "Oh *god.*"

His neck began to tear; a line opened across his Adam's apple; the flesh split, head separating from what was left of his body. It rose above his shoulders on pale ropes, bobbing. Tapping. The windowpane rattled.

"He's still alive," Jacqueline whined.

"Whatever that is," Lou said, "I don't think it's Rhys anymore."

What stared in at them with his eyes had rotted away into a nervous system of white threads bursting from every orifice, holding his skull on a wavering spinal column. Somehow, he continued tapping his forehead on the window. Could those ice-blue eyes, clouded over with death, still see?

Thorn's voice cracked. "We need to get out of here."

"No." Wendy whirled on him. "We need to stay put. If you open that door, who knows what you'll be letting in?" A gust of wind surged, battered the cabin till its bones creaked. The antler chandelier's wavering light glanced on her scuffed glasses. "We need to stay inside. Wait until morning. Then drive to the nearest police station, or somewhere with reception at least."

Though the others had turned away, Jacqueline, drifting closer to the window, stared out, holding a hand up to the glass as if to touch one of those gummy eyes through the pane.

Piloted by instinct, Thorn lit a cigarette, because that was what his hands knew how to do. He saw Harlow tipping liquor down her throat.

He wanted, more than anything, for this not to be happening. He wanted to close his eyes, open them, and find the world righted again. He wanted to pull his headphones over his ears and disappear into some deafening music. That was what he did when dealing with something that seemed too horrible to be real.

He remembered being on fire like a bad dream, and he remembered waking up in the hospital afterward, his face a shrieking wound. He remembered wishing for death rather than the pain of skin grafts stitching him back together. He remembered thinking it could not be real, that nothing could be that painful. He remembered wishing it all away.

But it hadn't gone away. He'd pushed himself through the slow, arduous recovery. Through a world of torment, where terrible things happened without rhyme or reason.

His body finally remembered how to move. He went around pulling shut the dusty curtains, blocking out the woods beyond, tucking them all safely inside. But the antler chandelier imprinted shadow branches on the walls as if to mock him. What seemed rustic and quaint in the afternoon took on new dimensions at night: wood panels infected with mold, dust webbing neglected corners.

The only window he didn't cover was the one at which Jacqueline still stood, unable to look away from the hypnotic movements of the Rhys-thing. Her hand on the glass glinted, a spark on her ring finger, a diamond on a gold band. The lights flickered again, losing stamina.

How old was the wiring? What electrical grid was this place even hooked up to all the way out here? Questions one didn't think to ask when everything was working properly, but which Thorn found himself unable to ignore. Bad wiring, after all, could start a fire.

Wendy curled up on the sofa, fingers digging into the fabric, staring at nothing. Thorn sat beside her. He wanted to drape his arm over her shoulders, to comfort her—like he had after the Wonder Room Panic, when she had spent most nights crying, guilt-ridden over the death of Murphy Dunning. Then, he had wrapped her in his arms and held her, his heart breaking over her grief, feeling her sorrow as if it were his own. And eventually, she kissed him, her lips salty and wet and desperate, and he realized, as his body came alive, that he loved her. It was like an undetonated bomb in his chest, so powerful and pent-up it could destroy him.

It was something he couldn't explain, but maybe that's what love was: inexplicable, magnetic, bright as a fire but just as likely to leave a burn. Just as likely to scar.

"I should have known," Wendy murmured.

"Known what?"

"That there was something wrong with this place." She slipped off her glasses and rubbed furiously at them with the fabric of her shirt, but she couldn't rub clean the cracks from the lens. With a sigh, she pushed them back onto her face. "I thought it was a joke or something. A gag they all decided to keep going."

"What are you talking about?"

"The guest book." She pushed the thin hardcover across the coffee table. "I flipped through it yesterday. The entries… they all mention this thing in the woods."

Lou gave up trying to get a signal on her phone, snatched up the book, and started paging through. She read for a moment, her face falling slack. "Why didn't you say anything?"

"I didn't think it was real. I figured everyone who read it decided to add to the story, to freak out the next guests. How was I supposed to know?"

Lou passed the book to Thorn. His stomach tightened as he scanned the most recent entry. "What the hell?" he mumbled. "What *is* this place?"

"What Brynn was looking for," Harlow answered. "A Low Place."

With a soft pop, the lights blinked out.

FROM "TRAIL CREEK CABIN   GUEST BOOK"

August 12

As I sit here, dawn has broken, and I am in awe of the misty morning taking shape. My family's stay at the cabin is coming to an end in a few short hours. Coming here was like being transported back in time to when this kind of forest blanketed the continent. At first the kids complained about the lack of WiFi or cell reception, but after just one hike they too expressed appreciation for the awesome power of nature—no small feat for a couple of preteens addicted to TikTok and Call of Duty!

There's nothing like immersing yourself in nature to spark the imagination. My husband Marcel (a photographer) took some incredible shots this week, and our evenings around the bonfire inspired the kids to create their own tale about the woods. Mel told us something about an ancient spirit haunting the trees, and Jack gave it a name: the Pale Form. Their creativity was so convincing I think they even started to believe it themselves!

As for me, I found a spiritual connection to the landscape. Never before have I felt God so strongly as I did

AMONG THE PRIMEVAL PINES. THERE IS A STRANGE POWER IN FEELING SO SMALL. ONE COULD ALMOST BEGIN TO BELIEVE THERE IS SOME SORT OF SPIRIT HERE, INHABITING THE DEEPEST, DENSEST PARTS OF THE FOREST WHERE HUMAN EYES HARDLY MANAGE TO PRY.

—LINA

October 3

It's almost eerie. No one for miles around. Douglas fir and spruce to infinity. Ordinarily I write in disordered spurts from my sofa, so I needed a personal writing retreat to the wilderness. Trail Creek Cabin does not disappoint. I write looking out not at a city street cluttered with traffic but a vista that should not seem so alien as it does. The isolation has physical weight here.

I hadn't intended to write an entry in the guest book until curiosity made me pick it up and I read the previous entry. It infected my mind. Last night I sat looking into the darkness and began to think I could see a pale shape in the trees. I don't believe in ghosts. How can I trust my eyes if my mind has already conjured the Form? Twisting the strange but natural shapes of the forest into an already devised pattern? We see only what we are capable of seeing. Reality is context.

Though I've only spent two days here, I feel changed somehow.

—Mathias

December 18

My husband and I wanted something simple and cozy

for our honeymoon, and this trip has certainly been both of those things! The trees are glittering and the fireplace makes for warm and snuggly evenings. But... would it kill you to clean up the place a little between guests? Just saying!

    —Danielle

March 1

All of us have really enjoyed Trail Creek Cabin as part of our pre-graduation celebration. We came here to get away from everything. At first we thought we were freaking out being in such an isolated place, even though it was exactly what we were looking for—no other people around, just us. We thought we were totally alone. But there was something in the woods. We kept the lights on, but it never came close enough to get a good look.

    —L.B.

March 30

Normally I don't like to say anything bad. My mother always told me, if you don't have anything nice to say, don't say anything at all. But I don't know what to write here except the truth. I came here with my boyfriend because it seemed so picturesque, and we've been longing for a getaway, just the two of us. But from the first moment, it's been a struggle. Hard to find, for starters. We drove around forever before we found the turnoff. And when we were ready to enjoy a nice evening, we started hearing this awful singing outside. Not even singing, really. Almost screaming. It was horrible! There was someone out there, but no matter how much we called to them they wouldn't stop. I can't imagine who would be out in the woods doing that but a crazy person.

Lee went out to tell this person to stop, since it was almost one o'clock in the morning and we'd both had just about enough. I waited and waited. But he hasn't come back in!

It's now almost three. And I hate to say it, but I think this is the worst place I've ever stayed. Because now I can hear not only the crazy person scream-singing or whatever, but I can hear Lee out there, too—he's been calling up to me, telling me to come outside with him. But I don't know why he's trying to get me to go outside! It doesn't make any sense. When I ask him, he just repeats himself. I don't like it. He's never been like this before, and I'm worried something happened, but I don't want to go out there. I don't know what to do. I had to write this down.

—Tammy

THIRTEEN

Darkness crashed down, and Lou was in the Wonder Room.

Or the Wonder Room as it had been in that moment, halfway through "Midnight Ritual," when the sound cut out like a cord pulled from an amp. When she'd felt her fingers come down on the bass strings, but they made no sound. All was void: darkness, silence, nothing. There was a smell of damp earth, as if she were underground, buried.

It might have been a moment or an eternity. Time tangled up in knots in that abyss of darkness and silence. She wondered if this was how it felt to be dead.

When the sound returned, it brought screaming, shoving, panic. Through the dark, where before there was nothing, she could see phone lights, the red glow of the exit, the shapes of bodies pressing toward it.

Lou had been haunted by darkness after that. She kept the lights on. Whenever it got too dark, too quiet, her skin began to crawl, and she wondered if, this time, she would be trapped permanently there, cut off and alone.

Now she saw a small white light. Voices—the others talking, fumbling around. More lights pierced the dark.

She wasn't in the Wonder Room. She was at Trail Creek Cabin.

Wendy was talking about needing light as she crouched in front of the woodstove with her phone blaring harshly against her face. "We need kindling."

Lou looked around. She saw Harlow clutching Brynn's notebook like a lifeline. She felt as if she were dreaming, as if she still had one foot in the Wonder Room.

Wendy tore blank pages from the end of the guest book and threw them into the stove. Thorn's lighter ignited the corner of a page, which curled like a dying insect. Dry logs caught. A warm red glow spread, moving, alive.

Lou pulled shut the last curtain that had remained open. With the windows draped and only the woodstove's light beating back the dark, the cabin felt closed-up and small. Shadows cavorted along the edges of the room.

Jacqueline stood at the window, staring at the curtain. When a faint humming filled the air, sending an electric shock through Lou's body, it took her a moment to realize it was coming from Jacqueline, who broke off her humming to whisper, voice cracking, "Do you hear it?"

She listened.

The fire crackled. The cabin cringed against the wind.

She didn't want to hear it. She didn't want to hear anything from out there, but she couldn't deceive her own ears. The voice was singing again, and she recognized the song from their second album, *The Antidote*.

The other faces in the room appeared livid in the light from the stove. Wendy was shaking her head slowly back and forth. Thorn let his cigarette become ash before he tossed it into the fire. Harlow's eyes were closed.

Jacqueline turned to them. "It's almost like she's trying to communicate with us. Listen."

Slow seconds passed. Lou caught snippets of singing as the voice passed through the woods, and she knew, she *knew*, it could not be a recording.

"See?" Jacqueline said. "It's not just one song straight through. She's singing snippets. Parts of lyrics. It's like… a message."

They listened.

My brain is on the wall, a pistol pill took my fall, and I'm splattered, shattered, I'm everywhere and nowhere at all—

—if you're afraid don't worry, you should be—

—maybe we are just a cancer in the night, maybe you and I should taste each other—

—there is no antidote, not for this life—

Then Jacqueline was beside them, taking the notebook from Harlow, flipping it open to a half-blank page, scribbling something with a dying pen. Harlow tried to grab the notebook back, but Jacqueline turned her body to keep writing, crouched over the coffee table. Convulsive firelight revealed the message she was writing down: a paraphrase of the lyrics they'd just heard. The way she'd rephrased the lines made Lou's skin crawl even more than hearing the lines sung from a disembodied voice:

I'm everywhere and nowhere. You should be afraid. I will consume you. There is no escape.

Hearing Brynn's voice brought Lou back to the last time she'd seen her. The ritual.

Her mind flashed on the circle she'd made with Brynn at her apartment: a stream of salt on laminate floorboards, candles burning. Brynn's mouth set in that interested half-grin she often wore, like she could only ever partially believe anything that was happening around her. "Does this witchcraft stuff actually work?"

"Depends on what you mean by 'work' I guess," Lou told her as she poured salt. "Are there energies around us that we can tap into with the right tools? Sure. Can you manifest your way into becoming a billionaire? Jury's out. You'll have to ask a Bezos."

"I'm trying to open a door."

"Well, that I can do," Lou said. "What are you hoping to find on the other side?"

Brynn didn't answer for a long stretch. Lou busied herself with finishing the circle. She set the now almost-empty tub of Morton's on the kitchenette counter and flicked off the overhead light, then the lamp with the orange scarf tossed over it. The only illumination left for them came from the candles and the occasional window flash of lightning as a storm rolled in. Brynn's voice broke the quiet. "You know how places can be haunted?" She studied the candle as if reading the movements its flame inscribed on the dark. "Do you think people can be, too?"

"Yeah. I guess so."

Lou asked if she'd brought her talisman, and Brynn took out a gold-plated key with jagged teeth. "It's to my parents' house. I remember when my mom gave it to me—I was maybe fifteen, morning after I'd been out screwing around with Harlow. Thought I was getting away with everything. She put it in my hand with a sigh and said if I was going to sneak out all the time, I might as well lock up on my way out." She chuckled and set the key down beside the candle.

Every time she'd done any kind of ritual herself, Lou was always left feeling invigorated, lightened, in harmony with the world around her. She often did healing spells to instill a sense of calm after intense performances, or made sachets of peppermint to energize her before a concert. She'd opened doorways to seek wisdom from the spirit world. When they were done, as she vacuumed up the salt, all the lights blazing, rain pattering down the window, she found herself wishing she'd never taken on Brynn's request.

She told Brynn to use her key to unlock the doorway—metaphorically, that is—and call forth the spirit or presence that she felt was haunting her. The candle between them juddered and sent up a curl of smoke, which thinned to a gossamer sheet. On the other side of it, impressing its shape like a foot in wet sand: a face, too blank to be human, with holes for eyes and a gaping mouth.

She'd never seen anything like it.

The vision startled Lou so much she cut the ritual short and closed the doorway, despite Brynn's disappointment. "Did you see her?" Brynn asked. "You saw her, right?"

"What was that?"

Brynn's eyes were shining. "My muse."

It had looked to Lou more like the face of a corpse.

After she'd cleaned the salt, Lou burned cleansing herbs and blew out the candle. She did not look at the smoke that trailed in the air.

Now, as she stood in the closed-up cabin, Lou wondered what she would see if she were to throw open the curtains. Would she see Brynn out there, singing? Would she see Rhys—what was left of him? Then again, it might not even be Rhys anymore. It might not be Rhys any more than the face she had seen on the other side of the smoke was a face.

She thought of that stone circle they'd found in the woods, the half-burned candle, and she couldn't help but wonder: had someone been out here doing rituals?

Was it Brynn?

Had she decided she needed to do the ritual out here instead, in this place—because the dead collect in Low Places?

If so, what had she conjured?

Something tapped on the window. Lou tried not to think of Rhys or his distended eyes pressing up against the glass. Chills traced shapes across her skin. Even with the cabin closed up, she still felt like she was being watched. The woods seemed to be alive out there, echoing with Brynn's voice.

A page flipped. There was no more room in the notebook for Jacqueline to continue inscribing potential messages, the pages filled instead with Brynn's cramped handwriting. Another loose printout flapped away.

Lou bent to pick it up and found a page full of text in splotchy old Courier font, interspersed with black bars of redacted content. At first, she couldn't tell what she was looking at. Seeing her frown, Harlow asked what it was. Lou squinted at it in the low light. "Some kind of… scientific records?" She tilted the page. "Have you seen this?"

"No." Harlow reached for it, but as Lou was handing it over, her fingers clenched on the paper, refused to let go. Her eyes had caught a faded stamp, which froze her. Breath sucked back into her throat. The paper crinkled in her grasp.

Property of the Volker Institute.

Wendy asked, "Property of *what?*"

"It's—okay." Lou scrubbed a hand over her face, then her hair, which stood in static purple threads. "You've never heard of the Volker Institute? It's this urban legend. Or internet legend, I don't know what you call it. A private research station somewhere in the Oregon woods, founded to study paranormal phenomena, that was abandoned in the '80s. Internet sleuths have been trying to find it for decades." She finally handed the paper to Harlow, whose eyes skittered down the page. "This looks like a scan of an old document from the institute. Look, it details some specimens they collected."

"Why would Brynn have this?" Harlow's fingers flipped through notebook pages, pulling out any loose paper, until she came up with a second document with that same old-school typeface. "I don't get it. What does this have to do with anything?"

"It doesn't," Wendy cut in. "Those are clearly fake. The Volker Institute isn't real. No one's ever found it because *it doesn't exist.*"

"How can you be so sure?" Frustration reared up Lou's throat. "Why are you so closed-minded about everything? Look around. Look what's *happening.* You can't tell me what happened to Rhys was normal, or just some infection. Open your mind a little. There's more out here than you think."

"Maybe the problem is that your mind is *too* open. You're willing to believe anything—ghosts, demons, Bigfoot, UFOs…"

"I don't believe in Bigfoot," Lou argued. "And, in case you haven't been paying attention, even the government is admitting UFOs are real these days."

"This is ridiculous!" Wendy's voice rose an octave. "Who cares? How is it going to help us if there is or isn't some mysterious research institute out here? Is it going to heal Rhys? Is it going to keep us from getting infected with whatever he has?"

"Maybe they were studying it," Jacqueline said. "Maybe they have information about what it is. Whatever infected him."

Lou flipped through the scanned documents. She saw nothing that reminded her of what had happened to Rhys, but that didn't mean Jacqueline was wrong. She wondered about all the esoteric knowledge buried inside the abandoned facility, wherever it might be, and why it had been vacated in the first place. What had happened that whoever was rich and powerful enough to fund such a venture would abandon something that provided evidence of things beyond our preconceived notions of the world?

"Look at this stuff," Wendy said, gesturing to Brynn's notebook. "You're trying to find reason where it doesn't exist. She was putting together puzzle pieces regardless of whether they fit together in any kind of coherent picture."

The fire snapped just as Harlow's eyes—which had been closed, her hands over her face—popped open.

"She was looking for Low Places," she said, eyes going to the corner of the rug that remained rumpled, disturbed.

The dead collect in low places.

"What's the lowest place here?"

SPECIMEN UF-56

Description: Hydnellum peckii (common name:
Devil's tooth); white cap with tooth-like projec-
tions beneath its fruiting body, 8 cm by 5 cm.

Origin: 43.2940° N, 122.3417° W

Incident: During routine mushroom foraging,
██████████ came across a stipitate hydnoid fungus,
identified as Hydnellum peckii. Initial observation showed no unusual features. The fungus exhibited red guttation droplets commonly found on
young fruit bodies (Note: accounting for the
common names "bleeding Hydnellum," "bleeding tooth
fungus," and "Devil's tooth"). While inspecting,
████████ perceived an unusual humming sound,
described as "what you hear when you close your
lips and hum a low note, and the sound buzzes
inside your head." The sound seemed to be
emanating from the fungus. Upon closer inspection,
the guttation droplets appeared to be vibrating
"like water droplets on the surface of a speaker."

Samples taken from UF-56 were later confirmed to contain human DNA. Guttation tested positive for human blood. All samples originated from inside the fungus. No samples matched ███████.

The humming sound is not yet accounted for. Prolonged exposure leads to spontaneous bleeding from the eyes and nose.

Recommendation: Specimen should be handled only for short periods while wearing earplugs. It should not be handled by those currently taking anticoagulant medication. Further testing recommended.

FOURTEEN

"I wouldn't go down there if I were you," Jacqueline said.

Harlow's shoulders tensed. "Why not?"

"That… *stuff*… that came out of Rhys? It's growing on the walls of the tunnel. I saw it when I went to bring him back up." Then she added, almost like an afterthought: "He was eating it."

The trapdoor's slam coughed up a cloud of dust as Harlow let it fall back down.

"First of all, gross," Lou said. "Do you think that's what happened? He ate it and… it grew inside of him?"

Jacqueline was slowly shaking her head. "I don't think so. He was already acting weird before that. I think it was something else. Maybe it was already inside of him, and it gave him the urge to feed it or something."

Considering her fiancé had decomposed before their eyes, Harlow thought Jacqueline was taking all of this remarkably well. The initial panic had worn off, leaving behind something clinical, calculating, unemotional.

"When did he start acting off?" Wendy asked.

"Last night," Thorn said. "Right? When he got lost."

"You think something happened in the woods?"

He shrugged. "That guess is as good as any. If it's something out there—the voice, the Pale Form they wrote about in the guest book—it'd make sense if that's where he got infected with it."

The stuff that had come out of Rhys reminded Harlow of when she was eighteen, and she and Brynn had found themselves on the edge of a field of dandelions after getting lost on a weekend road trip. It was late summer and the field had gone to seed. Brynn had thrown the car in park, lobbed herself out into the field, blowing with puffed cheeks and windmilling her arms. White tufts flurried into the air like snowfall. There was something magical about it. Harlow had followed her, hands slapping dandelions, sending their seeds airborne. They blew them into clouds and laughed and lay down in the field, staring up at the gentle blizzard they had created.

Brynn had turned on her side, propped up on one elbow, and looked at Harlow. They were inches apart. Harlow felt tingly and her stomach kept swooping like the blown seeds. She was close enough to see the crinkles at the corners of Brynn's eyes, the sliver of white teeth behind slightly parted lips.

When she reached out, Brynn was on the other side of a pane of glass. She could never reach her. Dark eyes transformed into blue, Rhys's eyes pressed against the glass, jarring her out of the memory.

Mercifully, there was no more thumping from outside. Maybe Rhys was dead. Though it was an awful thought, she nevertheless found it more comforting than the alternative. She tried not to imagine his rotting remains shambling around out there, puppeted by those white strings, jaw opening and closing.

The lights sprang back on, blinding her in the bright shock before they flickered and died again.

No cell service. No wifi. Bad electricity. Mysterious infections.

Harlow *really* hated the forest.

As the others discussed how to get the lights back on (was there a fuse box somewhere?), Harlow found herself staring at the deer head mounted on the wall. It stared back with those black marble eyes, filling her with the sensation, once again, that she was being watched. She knew it wasn't because Lou had put the idea in her head. She could feel it.

The deer's eyes, close-up, were not identical. One of them was clearly a glass eye, a good imitation of the real thing, but the other did not match. In fact, it didn't look like an eye at all. It was black, and the circle at its center did not so much look like a pupil as it did an electronic lens.

"Hey, guys?" she said. "I've got a weird eye over here."

Of course it was Lou who wandered over first, interest piqued by the unusual phrase. She frowned and leaned in, squinting from one eye to the other, face close enough she could have brushed her nose against the dead deer's fur.

Fuck it, thought Harlow. She reached up, dug her fingers into the hardened flesh around the edges of the weird eye, and pulled.

It popped free: a rounded lens trailing wires back into the deer's skull.

A camera.

Harlow let go of the device. It dangled from the deer's socket, swinging. She tried, and failed, not to think about Rhys's eye standing from his skull.

Lou gently lifted the mechanical eye and waved a hand in front of it. "Has the host been watching us this whole time?"

"Pervert," Harlow said. "The power's out, though, and this is wired. Unless it has a backup battery, it's probably not on right now."

Wendy wrapped her arms around her body. "Jesus. This is the last time I stay at an Airbnb."

"Maybe whoever's watching saw something," Thorn suggested. "Maybe they'll call for help."

"I wouldn't count on it." Harlow grabbed the little lens and yanked, tearing thin cords which frayed at the ends. She dropped it to the floor and slammed her boot down with a satisfying crunch.

"What if there are more?" Wendy asked.

The question sent them searching the cabin's corners. The hall turned up nothing. The bedrooms, likewise. Jacqueline and Wendy climbed to the loft, returned shaking their heads. Either there weren't any more, or they were too well-hidden to find.

"Wait," Thorn said. He reached up to the smoke detector high on the wall near the kitchen. It took a bit of yanking, but he came away with another little black lens and held it up.

The air rushed out of Harlow. "What the *fuck*."

"Why would they be watching people staying at a vacation rental?" Wendy asked, face ashen. "What is going *on* here?"

"Home videos," Thorn said. "America's fucked-up-est home videos."

Wendy turned to Thorn. "You were right. We need to get out of here."

"Make a run for it?" he said. "Get to the car, drive the hell away?"

"I thought you said we should stay put," Harlow pointed out.

"Yes, when I thought it was safe inside." Wendy found her purse and dug through it. "But now that I know we're being *watched*—" She unzipped a pocket, stuck her fingers inside. "—I think our stay at Trail Creek Cabin should come to a swift end, don't you?"

"You heard Brynn out there, right? I'm not leaving."

"Then *stay*," Wendy spat, turning over the purse and dumping its contents onto the floor.

Her keys were not there.

"No," she murmured, looking frantically around. "They have to be here. I had them. I thought Rhys was sick and we needed to take him to a hospital…" She sucked in a sharp breath, clapped a hand over her mouth. Looked at the curtained window.

Harlow remembered the clink of her keys hitting the ground when she dropped them.

Wendy lowered her hand. "Shit."

"I'll go find them," Thorn announced, and Harlow had to stop herself from rolling her eyes.

"How heroic. Will you lay yourself down across mud puddles so she can walk on your back, too?"

The pale meat of his blind eye reflected a tongue of flame as shadows shuddered like waves on rippled scar tissue. "If you have another way out of here, I'm all ears."

"Jesus, stop it." Wendy stepped between them. "They're *my* keys. I'll go get them."

She instructed the others to open the curtain and have someone watching through the window along with someone standing by the side door—the one at the end of the kitchenette, closest to the firepit—while she went out. The keys had to be between the cabin and the firepit, a stretch of about fifteen feet, but it was dark out there, and she wouldn't see anything coming if she was busy on her hands and knees in the dirt.

Thorn tried again to offer himself up, but Wendy shut him down. "I don't need you to do this for me, okay?"

Lou pulled open the curtain, and Harlow held her breath as she looked out into the dark.

Nothing.

No eyes against the glass, no rotting body, no Rhys.

Thorn grasped the doorknob and turned it, slowly swinging the door open. Rusty hinges belched.

Wendy followed her phone's light outside.

Cool night air breezed into the cabin, smelling of damp pine. Harlow watched through the open doorway as Wendy bent at the waist, light aimed at the leaf-littered ground, debrised with stray twigs and the tangle of weeds.

What would they do, she wondered, if Rhys lurched out of that darkness? If he grabbed Wendy and infected her with whatever was in him? Would they give her up for dead, as they had with Rhys, and close the door before she could make it back inside? Would they listen to her thump against the window, begging to be let back in while her eyes detached from her skull?

The minutes stretched on. Wendy's fingers danced across the ground, increasingly erratic. Wind moved through the trees beyond. Wendy's light flashed frantic patterns across the dirt, caught the edge of the firepit gone to ashes and embers, dark liquid smears on the ground the only sign of what had happened there.

She wasn't going to find her keys. Of this, Harlow felt almost certain. She wasn't going to find her keys; they would stay here for the night; she would have one more chance to try to find out what happened to Brynn. She felt like she was getting closer to figuring it out. The voice in the trees, the documents in the notebook, it all had to mean something.

Then Wendy screamed.

"Found them!" Wendy called as she stood, one hand above her head, keys glinting from between her fingers. She dashed back to the door, and Thorn closed it behind her once she was inside, breathing hard but filled with victory.

A long, slow exhale released from Harlow's chest.

That was it, then. They were leaving.

They gathered up their things as best they could, throwing

discarded clothing into duffels, leaving the coolers, the contents of the kitchen, behind. All except for the slim knife Harlow tugged from a wooden block on the counter. It wasn't very sharp, but she felt better with it. She folded it into a dirty washcloth, tucked it into the pocket of her jacket, hoped it wouldn't cut through the bottom.

"Everybody ready?" Now with a clear path forward, Wendy sounded calm, assured. She hiked her bag's straps onto her shoulders, nodded at the others as if to bolster them. "Straight shot down the stairs to my car. Fast as you can."

"Aye aye, cap'n." Thorn gave a quick salute.

The front door swung open, admitting an eddy of leaves. Their shoes crunched the dirt. A half-moon struggled through thin clouds overhead.

The damp stone stairs slipped beneath their feet, nearly sending Lou tumbling before Thorn snatched her backpack to hold her upright. The mist-gauzed moon revealed the cars below, side by side.

Wendy's SUV was blocked in by Rhys's Camaro.

Thorn swore as they hurdled the last few steps. "It doesn't matter," Wendy said, keeping her voice low. "Get in. I'll get around it."

They piled into the Escape, Thorn stealing the front while Harlow, Lou, and Jacqueline squeezed into the back, bags on their laps.

Worry threaded Thorn's voice. "I don't see how—"

"I'll *get around it.*" The engine cranked, hiccupped, puttered. Wendy turned the key, tried again. Tears filled her words. "Oh, god *damn* it."

"Let me check." Thorn got out of the car as Wendy popped the hood. He pushed it up and vanished behind it. All they could see out of the windshield now was white. The woods beyond—and whatever may inhabit it—vanished behind the raised hood.

When Thorn finally stepped back around the car, his eyes were saucers. He looked in at them through the window, shook his head. They had no choice but to get out and see for themselves.

The engine was a mess of tangled vines, pale and thin. They wove a snarled web through every inch of machinery, plugging gears and tying up chains.

Wendy unleashed a wail of frustration and slammed the hood. Her chest heaved.

"What about...?" Lou turned to the Camaro, but no one had Rhys's keys, and even if they did, they suspected they would find the same chaos within.

"What are we supposed to do?" Jacqueline now stared at the cars with glazed-eyed horror. "How are we supposed to leave?"

Wendy wiped tears of frustration from her eyes. "We should get back inside."

They headed for the staircase, but they did not ascend. A familiar shape stood at the top of the stairs, bathed in moonlight.

Rhys.

FIFTEEN

Rhys was standing there impossibly, perfectly alive.

"Babe?" Jacqueline breathed.

He fixed his blank eyes, like cue balls, upon her. Eyes she had seen burst from his skull just before his skin split and his limbs peeled away.

But here he was, pale and nude and perfect. White as a man of snow.

It was the second time this weekend she had seen someone who was supposed to be dead.

He was her only tether here. Jacqueline Price had never fit in with the others. They had never accepted her, although she had tried, all her life, to be accepted. To be admired. To be loved. While she wasn't naive enough to believe Rhys's love was perfect, it was, at least, a kind of love she'd never anticipated having. He *wanted* her in a way no one else ever had, and it felt so good, so deliciously *good*, to be wanted.

Socially, things didn't come easy for her. She often had the sensation that she had to pretend to be human, that she was an alien learning their customs, their mannerisms, how to make them laugh. There wasn't anything that came naturally to her, not like guitar came naturally to Rhys or singing came naturally to Brynn. She wasn't like them. She had to *try*. So hard. All the time.

It made her want to scream.

But here was Rhys, standing on the stone steps, as beautiful as the first time she saw him take off his clothes, the first time they made love, in a dingy little back room after a Queen Carrion concert, when she had discovered the joy of an infatuation fulfilled, which might as well have been love. That was it, she'd decided: she was in love.

And he was standing right in front of her.

Lines of muscle chiseled into the marble of his chest. A trail of fine white hair pointed down from his belly button.

Hardly even aware of herself, she careened up the stairs. She yearned for his embrace, for him to tell her everything was okay, he wasn't dead, all would work out. All their plans, their dreams—it wasn't over.

A sharp yank skidded her to a stop.

She turned and saw Wendy behind her, hand on her wrist, pulling her down and away from Rhys. "That's not him."

Jacqueline almost laughed. "Of *course* it is. Look at him!"

She saw their future still ahead of them: sold-out stadiums, the crowd's cheers ringing in their ears as they fell into bed with the hunger of newlyweds. The wedding, beautiful and perfect. The wedding night.

Rhys did not walk so much as glide down a step. "Don't you leave." His voice sighed with the shudder of leaves in the wind. His eyes were two unblinking bulbs. "Won't you stay? Won't you come with me?"

Thorn finished the phrase, "Out of the fire, into the dark."

Lyrics. Yes, that was it. He was speaking in Queen Carrion lyrics.

She couldn't help herself. She continued the song: "*Out of the mire, into my heart. Oh won't you stay, down here with me in the dirt?*"

As she sang, she realized someone else was singing, too. A voice out in the trees, which sounded too much like Brynn.

Brynn—who was supposed to be dead.

She clenched her hands into tight little fists.

Rhys drifted down another step, the bottoms of his feet skimming the stone. His legs did not lift and step like they should. It was as if something on the soles of his feet were propelling him.

If Jacqueline believed in ghosts, she might have thought him one. She nearly considered it. Her brain touched on the idea like a toe testing the temperature of water, like a tongue testing a new recipe.

The idea dismissed itself from her mind. Ghosts were not real. Rhys was standing in front of her, telling her not to leave, telling her to come with him. He was solid. He was real.

Jacqueline wrenched her arm from Wendy and lurched up the steps toward him, her bony arms outstretched, ready to embrace her betrothed. Someone shouted behind her, but she ignored them, as they had always tried to ignore her. As she drew near, Rhys's mouth stretched wide, and a tongue protruded from between his lips—or, no, not quite a tongue, but a woven braid of white threads lurching up from his throat, lengthening, probing the air. It reached out as Jacqueline ascended, five steps from him, four steps, three, the tip splitting into a thousand filaments that fanned out.

One of the hairlike strands brushed her cheek—delicate, the ghost of a touch—and the sensation, feather-soft, was somehow horrible. She lost her balance. Her foot caught on the rough edge of a step, and she stumbled, slipped away from that yawning embrace.

Behind her, someone else ran up the steps. Harlow slashed out with a steel blade, which sank into Rhys's cheek. What passed for flesh was soft and spongy, yielding.

On her hands and knees, Jacqueline slid herself down a few steps, away from Rhys as he pulled the knife out of his face and let it fall. It clattered down the stairs and away into the night. He sucked his rope-like tongue back into his mouth.

The ragged hole in his face began to stitch itself over.

Something snapped in Jacqueline's mind. His blank eyes, devoid of pupil or iris. The too-long tongue-like appendage. The flesh that was not flesh, healing itself bloodlessly.

Not Rhys.

Something else.

A broken scream surged all the way up and out of her throat as she scrambled up the steps and around him to get back to the cabin.

SPECIMEN UF-93

Description: *Zenaida macroura* (common name: mourning dove) infected with unidentified parasite.

Origin: Unknown

Incident: Specimen discovered during birdwatching excursion. ████████ (24) and his father ████████ (51) heard the telltale song of the mourning dove, but both acknowledged there was something unusual about its cadence. They pursued the source of the song, which they discovered to be a repeated set of notes described as "somewhat mechanical, like it didn't even know it was singing, more like a tic." When they found the bird perched on a low branch, ██████ observed a long protrusion extending from the bird's head, with an orb near its terminus. Protrusion appeared consistent with the genus *Ophiocordyceps* (Note: this parasitic fungus is only known to infect insects, typically ants. There are no known cases of *Ophiocordyceps* growing on any creature in the class Aves. Comparison to *Ophiocordyceps* is only due to similarity in attributes).

When ▮▮▮▮▮▮▮ attempted to approach the bird, rather than taking flight, the specimen slid horizontally across the branch in a stilted motion and proceeded to vocalize a mating call characterized by its plaintive tones. When ▮▮▮▮▮▮ reached for it, fearing the bird injured, the specimen attacked, driving the point of its beak into ▮▮▮▮▮▮'s eyes.

Later, while under observation ▮▮▮▮▮▮ (herein referred to as Subject) began to exhibit signs of infection. After 2 hours of observation, Subject developed uncontrollable muscle spasms and vomiting. Subject's speech became stilted and repetitive. Over a period of 36 hours, Subject deteriorated until he had lost all control of his body. Verbalizations were gibberish. After 37 hours, Subject's body adhered itself to the floor and became locked in place. At this point, a fungal stalk grew from the crown of Subject's head. Subject remained alive for another 13 hours before death.

Subject's remains have been labeled a biological hazard and are sealed in container ▮▮▮▮▮▮.

Recommendation: Incinerate remains and destroy container ▮▮▮▮▮▮. Keep Specimen UF-93 in current location.

SIXTEEN

Brynn always did her makeup a certain way for shows: black shadow around her eyes, sinking them into caverns; foundation two shades too light, almost gray; black lipstick dripping jaggedly down her chin. Her corpse paint. It was the face of Queen Carrion, and when she had it on, she was transformed.

By some trick of the firelight, they all had a bit of that face to them now, their eyes lost in shadow, lips twisted in a rictus of fear.

"We can't get away," Wendy murmured, clutching her keys so hard they left jagged imprints in her palm.

"We'll wait till morning and go on foot." Thorn chewed on the end of a cigarette. "We'll follow the road."

The fire burned itself into Harlow's retinas. She wanted to sear away the image of Rhys pulling the knife out of his cheek, slurping the braided rope back into his mouth.

It was Lou who finally voiced the question: "What *is* he?"

Suddenly, mortality felt too close. It should have been a distant thing, a subject for songs and stories. They all knew they would die someday, but it was a far-off experience with little relation to them now. Such is the delusion of the young—not that they will live forever, but that they will live long enough for it to feel forever-like before the years begin to shorten. The truth was something Harlow almost couldn't stand to think: that time is little enough as it is, and the end of it might be much sooner than she thought.

It came to her in the way of revelation, a voice from nowhere: *Death is the thing that drives us all—away from it.*

Except it didn't drive Brynn away, did it?

"I'm going to die this year," Brynn had said the moment she turned twenty-seven. At the time, did the words send a shiver down Harlow's spine, as they would when she recalled this moment later? She couldn't think of that pronouncement—Brynn having just blown out a candle on a cupcake with black frosting, its smoke still smudging her face— without a chill. She didn't remember what that moment used to be, but now it was eternally spooky in her memory.

Brynn had been obsessed with the 27 Club. Jimi Hendrix. Janis Joplin. Jim Morrison. Kurt Cobain. Amy Winehouse. "Think of them all."

"Just don't start doing heroin or anything."

"I think it's a curse. Doesn't it make you a little nervous?"

Harlow shrugged. "I'm not nearly talented or famous enough to join the 27 Club anyway."

Now Harlow couldn't help feeling that, in going out to the woods on her own, Brynn had gone looking for her entrance into the 27 Club.

Maybe she'd gotten what she wanted.

But now Rhys, too. Of course, he was twenty-nine, too late for the club. It hit her hard in the chest, though: even though she had never particularly *liked* Rhys, and he had often driven her crazy, the realization that he would never turn thirty was like curdled milk in her gut.

And for maybe the first time, she felt sorry for Jacqueline, whose eyes tripped around the room, who looked so lost and afraid and, in that moment, terribly young. Her voice was small when she said, "He can't get in, can he?"

Wendy shook her head. "We closed everything up."

Somehow, that didn't seem good enough. How did they know that would keep it out? Harlow's skin tightened. Even her leather jacket failed to warm her.

She looked down at the rumpled rug, the trapdoor.

"Maybe we can find out what he's made of." Her eyes found Jacqueline. "You said that stuff was growing in the tunnel, right?" She felt her way to the kitchen in the dark before powering on her phone's flashlight. The battery sat at thirty percent. Enough for now, but it was time to start conserving.

Thorn followed her. "What are you doing?"

She dug an empty wine bottle from the trash, glad, for the moment, that they were all musician-poor, as it was a screw-top rather than a cork. She rinsed red dregs down the sink, then started opening drawers that rattled with utensils, worn and half-rusted. She found a pair of tongs, tucked them into her back pocket as far as they would go. They stuck out, prodding her back with every step.

When she pulled open the trapdoor, Wendy let out a little moan. "You're crazy." She looked at Thorn. "Tell her not to go down there!"

"She's right. You don't know what's in that tunnel."

"Exactly," Harlow said as she tucked the bottle under one arm. "I want to find out." She lowered herself onto the ladder, then down into the dark.

———

With no real light coming from above—just the faint flicker of fire glow—the cellar became an abyss. Her phone's light, cold white on stone, diffused quickly at the edges of the beam.

Through the alcove and down the flight of stairs, an underground chill permeated her veins. Ahead, the arched tunnel sucked away the light. She hesitated at its entrance.

The concrete was cold under her palm. She curled her hand into a fist, rapped her knuckles three times against it.

From deep in the tunnel, something knocked back.

Harlow threw herself back, whirled around, and slammed into a solid mass. Her phone's light went wild. The tunnel echoed back a ghost of her cry.

"Whoa, chill."

Steadying herself, she realized she'd run right into Thorn. Relief melted to fury. "What the hell, man? Why did you sneak up on me like that?"

A shrug as he peered behind her down the tunnel. "I thought you shouldn't be down here by yourself."

She turned back to the darkness. Even with both their phones lit up, she couldn't see far.

"Something's in there."

Thorn shoved her gently. "Don't fuck with me."

"I'm not."

"We should go back up."

Neither moved. Harlow called into the tunnel, "Hello?" It only gave back an echo of her voice. "Hold the light for me." She put her phone away and pulled out the tongs, then stepped forward.

If her hands were free, she could reach out to either side and touch both walls. The tunnel retreated into black ahead of her. She glanced over her shoulder, but Thorn was just a hulking shape behind the blast of light. "Where do you think this goes?"

"Disneyland." The hiss of his voice echoed against the narrow walls. "This is a dumb idea."

"Don't you want to know what we're dealing with?"

"Honestly? No. My adrenal gland is leaving me no room for curiosity. I'm all cortisol. I'd sell my soul for a helicopter out of here right now."

"Didn't realize you still had one."

"A helicopter?"

"A soul."

"Yeah." A dry chuckle burst out of his throat. "It's a little burned up, but still usable."

Harlow stopped. There, at the edge of the light: the growing crack along the wall, white fuzz spilling out of it like a thick net of spiderwebs. As she approached, she had the awful feeling they had sensed her —they were pulling further out of the dirt, they were knotting together. An amorphous *something* strained through the crack. Something that began to stitch itself into the semblance of a face. The edges of its neck, where it met the wall, stretched into a thin network of fibers, tethering it there.

The darkness seemed to spin around her.

The mouth gaped open as those white strands emerged, reaching out—long tendrils weaving through the air toward her—

Harlow stumbled back from the tumorous growth in the wall.

"Quick," Thorn said. "Do it quick!"

As the mouth opened and those probing threads spilled out, Harlow darted the tongs toward it, closing around the fuzzy edge of the face where it met the wall, and tugged. Threads broke loose, a piece the size of a cotton ball wedged in the tongs, its edges stretching out like cilia.

She brought it to the lip of the bottle and pushed the fibrous clump against the opening until it fell inside, then she screwed on the cap.

The rope extended further from the open mouth, twisting and reaching for them from the wall as they backed away.

They couldn't get out of the tunnel fast enough.

They passed the bottle around in a strange parody of what they'd done earlier, only this time, no one drank from it.

The specimen tried to climb the slippery glass walls of its prison, seeking a way out. Harlow lifted the bottle, the fire sending orange flares through the glass. Up close, it looked like a clump of spiderwebs, hairy and amorphous. Its movements were deliberate, somehow, *directed.*

What sort of sentient growth could perfectly imitate Rhys's body and Brynn's voice? What could be such a capable mimic?

"You know what that looks like?" Lou said, leaning closer to the bottle. "Fungal hyphae." Her eyes found Wendy, a brightness brewing in them. "Do you remember that documentary we watched? The one about mushrooms?"

A wry little smile turned the corners of Wendy's lips. "You mean the one about magic mushrooms?"

"It wasn't *just* about psychedelics. They did a whole segment about mycelium, the network under the forest floor, moving nutrients around. Like a way for trees to talk to each other. The Wood Wide Web."

"You're saying this is a mushroom?"

"The root structure," Lou clarified. "Mushrooms are the fruiting bodies."

A spasm arced through Harlow's back, and she realized she had been hunched over, tensed into a low posture. She forced herself to straighten, breathing through the pain. When it had passed, she took a drink from her flask, hoping to numb the lingering ache. She tried not to notice Wendy pursing her lips or the way Thorn stared at her, both eyes burning holes through the air, even the one that couldn't see.

She took a second, longer drink, daring them to judge her harder.

Sitting farthest from the others, on a chair set nearly out of the stove's reach, Jacqueline did not take her eyes off the bottle. She hardly blinked. "That was inside him."

"I think it's… what he *is* now," Harlow said as she screwed the cap back on her flask.

"But it started out inside of him." Wendy seemed to realize it as she spoke. "How did it get there? If something happened last night, when he got lost, that means it took a little under twenty-four hours until…" Her voice thinned to nothing. "If we don't know how it got inside him, then we don't know if it's inside any of *us*."

"There's one way to find out."

Harlow went to the kitchen and checked her options from the knife block. She picked a small paring knife this time.

"You want us to cut ourselves open?" Thorn sounded more annoyed than surprised. "This isn't *The Thing*."

"How else will we know for sure? We'd see it, wouldn't we? If it's inside us?" She had just pressed the tip of the blade to her palm, piercing the upper layer of skin, when Thorn grabbed her hand and held it fast.

"This is ridiculous," he said.

Harlow snarled and wrenched out of his grip. "Let go of me."

He stepped back.

The knife had cut deeper than Harlow thought. A bead of blood welled on her palm, slithered down her lifeline. She held her hand palm-up for a moment, watching it spread.

She thought of how the stuff had come out of Rhys. How it had *eaten* him from the inside out.

A terrible curiosity compelled her to snatch up the bottle, and before she could stop to consider if this was a bad idea, she unscrewed the cap. The others gasped and shouted as she held her palm over the top until the drop of blood fattened and fell, dribbling a thin red stream down the glass. She quickly fixed the cap back in place.

Ignoring the wave of admonishments, Harlow watched as the specimen crawled up to meet the blood. Its tendrils reached out, testing it, absorbing it. The trail of red turned black before the cluster of threads licked the rest of it up.

"Did it just… eat your blood?" Thorn asked.

"Fungi excrete an enzyme that processes nutrients from the environment," Lou explained. "That allows them to digest things externally."

"Yeah," Harlow said. "I think it just ate my blood." Purposefully. With intention. "Let's feed it something else."

"Let's not," Wendy said.

Harlow was already creeping along the room's edges, guided by her phone. Dust particles drifted and spun in the beam of light. Cobwebs collected in the corners. Something small and dark scuttled down the wall from its web. Harlow grabbed one of the loose papers from the table and held its edge to the wall. She coaxed the spider onto it, then carried it over to the bottle and overturned the paper flat against the mouth. She tapped a few times, and the spider fell.

It landed at the bottom. The specimen crawled closer, reaching out. The spider seemed too stunned to move, and then it was enveloped in a white cocoon. There was some sort of justice in it, predator becoming prey. For once, the spider learned what it meant to be caught in a web.

When the specimen moved away, all that was left of the spider was a black smear.

The cluster of white threads began pulling together, forming a shape. A rounded body, pinched in the middle—head and thorax. Eight bent legs that rose and fell in unnatural jerks.

"No," Thorn said. "No way."

"It imitates what it eats," Harlow realized.

"Kind of like pseudo-flowers." Lou brought her eyes level with the bottle, watching the spider-thing crawl up the glass. "A kind of fungus that mimics flowers to attract bees. The bees land on them and get covered in spores, which they leave on all the other flowers they land on. So it's like—the fungus mimics the flowers to find new hosts."

The pseudo-spider reached the curve of the bottle and crawled up into the neck. Two forelegs extended toward the underside of the metal cap, trying to figure out how to open it.

"You need to get rid of that thing," Wendy choked out.

"It can't get out."

"You don't *know* that."

They watched the pseudo-spider crawl down the other side of the neck.

"We're still learning about it," Harlow said. "We can figure out how to kill it—"

"Look what it can *do*. Look what it *has* done," Wendy burst out. "We shouldn't be messing with it." She looked around helplessly, clearly waiting for someone to agree with her, but no one spoke up. Fear and anger strained her face. "Fine. If you won't get rid of it, I will."

"Stop!"

But the bottle was already in Wendy's hand. She held it by the neck, away from herself, trying to keep her eyes on it while also looking around for where to take it.

"Put it down," Harlow said. "Give it to me." She grabbed for it, but Wendy held it away from her.

Harlow lunged.

There was a scramble of fingers slipping on glass, each trying for purchase. Thorn and Lou shouted at them to stop, but Harlow couldn't seem to help herself: she tried to wrest the bottle out of Wendy's hands, spitting "let go," but Wendy held on, snarling at her to back off.

When Harlow managed to yank it free, the bottle's momentum spun it into the air, throwing flashes of refracted firelight, until it cracked against the floor.

AFTER

"Do you know why you're here?"

The question haunts Harlow. Why is she here, surrounded by these slate blue walls? Why is she here, alive at all for that matter, eating her three square meals a day, shuffling from the rec room to the dining hall, existing just for the sake of existing?

Why didn't you die out there?

Perhaps if she could curl into herself, she might just disappear.

Brynn once told her that she always tried to make herself small. There was disappointment in her voice, Harlow remembers. *You pretend to be a badass,* she'd said. *But still you do what so many women do: make yourself small for others.*

Maybe it was the hunching. Over the years, Harlow's back has curved into a question mark as a result of her drumming and the way she leans her weight forward into her arms. If she were to stand up straight, there might be another inch or two to her stature than with the hunch she has never bothered to try to correct.

But Harlow could never be small, not really. Edging toward six feet, she always towered over Brynn, with her shorter, curvier body. By contrast, Harlow has always been flat and athletic. When she was younger, she was sometimes teased by kids who thought she was a boy.

She thinks of Thorn, also tall, and wonders if she *had* been born a boy, would she have tried to make herself small? Or would she have embraced her height?

A bizarre fantasy: she shrinks and shrinks until she has gone out of existence, until she is simply not here anymore.

Why *is* she here?

"You're here because you've gone through a significant trauma. I think it's time we finally talk about what happened in the woods."

It's the doctor who asks and then answers his own question. Doctor Merriweather, a name that made Harlow want to comment on just how *merry* the *weather* is here in rainy Oregon when she first heard it.

She shakes her head. She does not want to talk about what happened in the woods. She knows the murmurs that have traveled across the internet. "Everyone thinks I killed them."

The doctor's eyebrows furrow. "Did you?"

Perspiration prickles Harlow's forehead. The question, asked in such a neutral tone, feels nevertheless loaded with accusation. *I might as well have,* she wants to say. *I should never have made it out of the woods.*

What she does say is: "What if it was my fault?"

"How could it have been your fault?" He flicks open the file folder on his knee and peruses it with a frown. "The reports say you and your friends were attacked by a bear. Now, as far as I can tell, you don't have any special ability to control bears, so I'm curious to know how it could have been your fault."

She feels foggy. She tries to remember what happened. Attacked by a bear?

She shakes her head.

"Can I have a piece of paper?"

Frowning, Doctor Merriweather flips open his notebook to a fresh page, tears it free with a breathy *schiiick.* Hands it over to Harlow. She folds it in half, carefully tears along the crease until she has two pieces of paper. "Have you heard of Low Places?"

"I can't say that I have."

"Let's pretend this piece of paper is—everything. The whole world. The whole universe. If you could take all three dimensions and squish them down into two." Now she holds both papers up horizontally, one in each hand, half an inch apart. "You could stack up universes that way."

"It sounds like you're talking about parallel dimensions," the doctor indulges her. "It's an interesting idea, but what does this have to do with what happened to you in the woods?"

"Just let me finish." She pinches at the paper, pressing little folds and creases into its flat surface. "The world isn't smooth. You know the Mariana Trench? We barely know what's down there. It's the lowest place on earth." She holds the papers up again, the pinched one on top. "Like the Mariana Trench, there are these—I don't know, topographical defects—in the universe. But they don't go *down* like the Mariana Trench, because remember, this is everything in two dimensions. So this space outside the paper? We can't access that. It's not really *down*. It's *outside*." Holding the papers close together now, the trenches in the top one dip far enough to touch the page below. "When one of these spots is low enough, it reaches the next layer down. Another place. Whatever is down there, below our world. The Underneath."

Doctor Merriweather looks carefully at the papers, at the points where they meet, and nods. Leans back, uncrossing his legs, recrossing them in the other direction. His gray pants hike up to reveal plaid golf socks. "Harlow, would you say you often retreat into distractions when you're faced with difficult truths?"

"What?" She lowers the papers. "You're not listening to me. The woods. There's a Low Place there. That's why everything that happened *happened*. Brynn knew it. That's why she went there. And then I followed her there, and brought everyone else."

"You're a drinker, aren't you?" The doctor asks, tapping a pen against his knee. "Maybe you could tell me what it is you like about drinking."

"I like drinking so I don't have to listen to pretentious dickwads ask me why I like drinking."

Doctor Merriweather nods. "I'm only trying to help you."

She stares at him.

"All right," he says. "Let's talk about something else." He glances down at his file again, adjusting his glasses, which leave red marks on either side of his nose. "Maybe we can talk about the fire that burned down your house when you were a child?"

"Because everything leads back to childhood trauma? Is that your professional opinion?"

He ignores this. "Do you remember how the fire started?"

"Not really," she says.

"Do you feel as though the fire was your fault?"

"You are aware I was the one who started it."

"You were a child. It was an accident."

"So what? What does this have to do with anything?" She waits, but he doesn't answer. A pressure valve bursts inside of her. She stands up. "You have no idea what's going on. You have no idea what you're talking about." She turns to the window, where twilight throws long shadows on the parking lot below. Shadows creep into the trenches between streetlamps and the crevices around the window frame. She turns away, to the blank wall—an old wall, the plaster worn, a hairline crack running up to the ceiling. The crack draws her eyes, and she imagines it widening, making room for the darkness behind it to squeeze through. Her heart throbs in her head to a particular rhythm, one she feels thrumming through her whole body, a rhythm that makes the crack seem to dance before her eyes, to wriggle like the too-long body of a parasitic worm, trying to form words—

Queen Carrion is here.

Queen Carrion is everywhere.

She steps back, knocking her knuckles against her ribcage to trip her heart into a different rhythm, clearing her throat to remove the distant ringing of a tune in her ears. Doctor Merriweather is talking to her, but she doesn't hear. In a blink he is beside her, a comforting hand warm on her shoulder, and she flinches away from the touch. The ringing vanishes; her hearing comes back; her heart returns to a regular gallop.

"Don't touch me," she snarls.

"I'm sorry. I wanted to know if you were all right."

"Stop—stop being like that," she spits. "Stop talking to me like you *know*. You *don't* know." Her lip curls. "You don't know what happened. You don't know it wasn't my fault." She thinks back to the smear in the bottle, the broken glass. "You don't know I didn't kill them."

SEVENTEEN

The bottle was a shatter of shivering firelight.

It reminded Wendy of the broken glass of her car window reflecting the sunset like a fiery spiderweb, two weeks after the Wonder Room Panic. She had been having dinner with Brynn, and when she'd gone out to the parking lot, she'd found her window smashed up and a rock on the ground, glittered with glass grains, a piece of paper tied to it via rubber-band.

There was one word written on the paper, in red marker: MURDERERS.

The incident had left her shaken, and the police were little help. They'd said it was probably a friend of Murphy Dunning, someone who had seen them out in public having a nice time and who had acted out of grief. Still, Wendy had felt targeted. Unsafe.

Even then, she had begun to wonder whether it was all worth it—if she wanted to be someone recognizable, someone easily targeted by deranged fans with an ax to grind.

Staring at that broken bottle, now, she felt unsafe.

The pseudo-spider was gone. It could be anywhere.

Wendy saw the horrified expression on Harlow's face and said, "You shouldn't have brought that thing in here."

Lou toed the shards, swept them over the empty floor. They clattered and scraped at the wood. "I don't see it."

"Let's find it." Thorn switched on his phone's light, and the others followed suit. They split off, scouring the floor. Wendy ended up in the kitchenette, examining the corners, the counters, but the scratch across the lens of her glasses clouded her field of vision. She tried taking off the glasses, but that wasn't any better; her unfiltered eyesight blurred everything to basic shapes and colors.

Not being able to see clearly sent a dull panic pounding through her heart. Her shoe crunched on stray glass shards thrown from the bottle. Everywhere she looked she thought she saw a scuttle of white, and she had to peer through her good lens to see that it was only her light reflecting on a spoon, a bundle of dust.

The edges of the pine cabinets were stained dark. Rot and rust gunked up the drain in the sink. All these details struck her more intensely in the focused light of her phone, livid against the dark, and her gorge rose. Was that mold in the grout? Was it fungus?

She wondered what her parents would think of her now. She imagined them shaking their heads with shame.

It was Brynn's belief in her that had kept Wendy from backing out of the band early on. She'd told Wendy that Queen Carrion wouldn't exist without her. "You might think we don't need you," she'd said when Wendy was weighed down with her parents' disapproval and suddenly unsure of what she was doing with her life. "But we do."

When she played, she thought about the register, the tone, the emotional tenor of a bow stroke; how her cello resonated like a voice, and it was *her* voice. Her voice, made of strings. Maybe she had never been meant for professional orchestras, and what's more, she didn't want to be part of some stiff ensemble still playing the corpses of long-rotten men. She wanted to do something new.

"Queen Carrion needs all of our voices," Brynn told her. "Even the ones we don't make with our throats. I think you're the final piece of the puzzle."

Brynn wasn't here anymore; maybe that was why they were falling apart. Without her, they were motes of dust, scattered. Wendy imagined them disintegrating like Rhys, all because Brynn left. Maybe they were all bound for that same fate, and Rhys was only the first to go.

When she turned around, Thorn stood at the entrance to the kitchenette, blocking her way. "Do you see it?"

She shook her head, and Thorn let out a long, slow breath. She heard footsteps creaking down the hall, rummaging in the bedrooms.

"You shouldn't have let her bring that thing up here," she said.

Thorn bristled. The corner of his mouth pulled into a smirk. "You think I have any control over what she does?"

"We were safe before that stupid little science experiment." Bitterness slipped into the words. "We would have been safe in here."

"You don't know that."

Everything she had kept pent up for the last few hours threatened to burst free. Her eyes bubbled over with tears, obscuring her already imperfect vision. They spilled over. Her breath hitched. She couldn't hold it in.

Then Thorn's arms were around her, and her face was pressed into his chest. That familiar funk of sweat and tobacco, of old smoke, enveloped her, and for the first time all night—if even for just a moment—she felt safe.

She pulled back enough to look up at him. Their faces were very close together. She felt the heat of his breath against her. The world seemed to spin.

Their lips met, and then their tongues, and Wendy became lost in the moment, in the rush. What came next was less a thought than it was a feeling, an instinct: that maybe she was making a mistake in planning to leave. Maybe it was a mistake to always push Thorn away. For so much of her life, she'd felt like she wasn't good enough, that she could never live up to the expectations placed on her. But Thorn had never made her feel that way.

They broke away from each other when Harlow cried out, "Holy shit!"

Reality doused Wendy once more with cold fear. She and Thorn, still holding onto each other, turned to see what Harlow had found. They stumbled out of the kitchen as Lou and Jacqueline came running down the hall.

Harlow stood over the spot where Rhys had vomited earlier. Wendy had entirely forgotten about that.

The black puddle had completely fuzzed over white.

And there was more—spreading up the wall, long tendrils reaching out from the corner of the room, unspooling across the floor.

She felt a moan rising from the bottom of her throat.

Maybe they deserved it. Wasn't it true they'd never been punished for Murphy Dunning's death? Hadn't they never paid for what had happened to him? Maybe this was some divine punishment, the universe setting things back in balance.

A high-pitched twang cut the air. Wendy startled. It was the pluck of a guitar string. Rhys's acoustic guitar leaned up against the wall of the living room, its strings still faintly humming.

She pulled away from Thorn to go see. Behind her, Lou prodded the dying fire with a poker, sent it roaring back to life.

Something scuttled into the guitar's dark interior through the soundhole, faster than she could see what it was. She thought about smashing the instrument into pieces and feeding its wood to the flames.

The others were talking about what to do: douse it in alcohol? Would that kill the stuff? Maybe throw blankets down? It would find a way through, though, wouldn't it? Maybe, Lou suggested, they should try to book it on foot—but they saw fuzz growing, spreading along the edges of the front door.

It was *everywhere.*

Looping up from the floorboards, one of the tendrils grew bulbous. A naked eye bent on a thread of nerves, lolling, surrounded by fine white lashes, staring blindly.

With a shout, Harlow tried to stomp on it, but the threads only scattered beneath her boot. Wendy grabbed Rhys's guitar by the neck and slammed its body down. The strings threw a clash of sour notes as the wood smashed into the growing fuzz.

"Guys."

Jacqueline's gaze was on the ceiling. With dreadful slowness, they all looked up.

The antler chandelier was webbed in it. Wendy wondered how long it had been up there. She wondered how long they had gone on assuming it was cobwebs.

A long thread dangled, drifting loose, thin and delicate like a string of spun glass.

She took off her glasses to rub at them with her shirt, staring up, blinking, mouth open as she struggled to make out the details, to figure out just how far it had spread.

It had been here this whole time. She was wrong; they had never been safe from it, after all.

She didn't see it coming.

And the strand was so thin, so fine, the others barely noticed it either, until it was already there: the pseudo-spider hanging on its thread, descending, legs curling and fanning, until it dropped right into Wendy's open mouth.

SPECIMEN UF-121

Description: *Actaea pachypoda* (common name: Doll's Eyes)

Origin: 43.346306° N, 122.269444° W

Incident: While on a trip to investigate claims of an unusual growth by a local mycophile, ███████ and ████████ observed peculiar psychological effects of this Specimen while in its presence. They described it as "like being watched" and "the unshakable sensation of eyes on the back of one's neck." These sensations were described as occurring *before* either observer was made aware of the presence of the white baneberry growth, often compared to eyeballs on fleshy stems.

Because it is not native to the Pacific Northwest, its discovery aroused suspicion. Testing revealed similarities to *Actaea pachypoda* but with slight abnormalities. The flowers grow in a racemoid structure in spring and produce the white fruit, roughly 1 cm in diameter, whose shape and coloring resemble eyes, hence the common name "Doll's Eyes." As the berries develop, the pedicels turn red and may be compared to retinal arteries. In effect, the clustered berries resemble a bouquet of eyeballs. The plant is also severely poisonous, containing cardiogenic toxins. Ingestion of berries can lead to cardiac arrest and death.

Specimen UF-121 exhibited the abovementioned traits, in addition to the physical and psychological reactions experienced within a vicinity of roughly five meters of the plant. Physical reactions included horripilation, perspiration, and shortness of breath. Psychological reactions included intense uneasiness and paranoia.

The effects of Specimen UF-121 were observed on ten test subjects. Subjects were blindfolded and entered a containment space empty except for the Specimen. Of these ten, nine experienced horripilation, eight experienced perspiration, and six experienced shortness of breath in the presence of the Specimen, even though they were unable to see it and did not know it was in the room. All ten subjects experienced uneasiness and paranoia, and all described a sensation of being watched which they had not experienced prior to entering the enclosure. Seven subjects were able to remain in the enclosure for the full five-minute duration of the test, while two expressed a desire to leave after three minutes, and one urgently exited the area with an elevated heart rate and significant symptoms of anxiety after 97 seconds.

Recommendation: Specimen to be kept in container ▮▮▮▮▮. Should be handled with caution. It is not recommended that anyone with a preexisting anxiety disorder or heart condition be within 5 meters of the Specimen for a duration exceeding 30 seconds.

EIGHTEEN

Hawthorn Sorenson was no stranger to trouble. He'd been burned, spat on, judged, ridiculed; he'd had angry evangelicals scream in his face. None of this held a candle to the sight of Wendy clawing at her throat with terror in her eyes.

She hacked, spat, and a wet fuzzy glob popped out, sticking to her lip. A gasp scraped out of her throat. The glasses slipped from her fingers and sprayed across the floor.

Fine white hairs reached up and crawled into her nostrils.

Her fingers scrabbled at the thing on her face as she shouted a half-coherent plea to get it off, get it *off*, but the whole of it had disappeared into her nose by now. She snorted like a bull, a sharp expulsion of air. "It won't come out," she mumbled. "It won't come out!"

"Try holding one nostril shut, blowing with the other," Harlow suggested. Wendy huffed, pinching first one side of her nose and then the other, but it was no use.

Thorn had almost allowed himself to think everything would be okay. He could still taste her lips on his. Wendy was the only woman he'd ever been with who didn't look at him like some kind of freak or fetish, and the realization that there was something inside of her now taking root, something that would eat her from the inside out and turn her into something *else*, filled him with unbearable dread.

If Wendy followed Rhys's timeline, then in less than twenty-four hours, she would be dead. Her eyes would burst out of her head, and her skin would rot open as a flurry of white fibers spilled free.

He saw this realization pass across her face—the way her eyes grew round and vacant. "It's okay," he said. "We'll figure something out." He pulled her close, crushing her against his body with such force he thought he might hear her bones crack.

"She was right," Wendy mumbled into his chest. "We are cursed."

"Come on," he said. "You don't believe in curses."

He felt her head shake against him, something wet on his shirt. Her voice came out high and keening. "I don't want to die."

"You're not going to die."

He looked over the top of her head at the others, who gaped back at him—all except Harlow, who was looking around the cabin at all the places the fungus was creeping, all the cracks and crevices through which it squirmed, her eyes moving from the webbed chandelier to the hyphae around the door.

Wendy jerked away from him with a sneeze. When she lifted her head, a thread hung from her nose. A dribble of blood loosened from one nostril. She sniffed, and the thread spooled back up, leaving only a smear of drying blood on her lip. Thorn licked his thumb and wiped at it. She flinched from his touch.

"We need to get off the floor," Harlow said, stepping carefully around the cracks in the floorboards like they used to do on the side-walk as children—*step on a crack, break your mother's back!* At least, Thorn had avoided them. Harlow had always made sure to step on every crack they passed.

She hopped onto the steps, where the fungus had not yet managed to creep, and the others followed up the stairs to the loft.

They entered the open space at the top, where the ceiling sloped down at the edges, low enough for Thorn to bang his head if he wasn't careful. It rose to a sharp peak in the center of the room. Black windows framed the bed's pine headboard, opposite which sat a little writing desk scored by years of wear. Rhys's jacket hung on the back of the chair. The bed's plaid comforter hunched in rumpled lumps. All of this was only a sketching: the light from below rose as a dim glow in the air, turning everything hazy.

"I need to get to a hospital," Wendy said. Coming up from behind, Thorn put his arms around her, but Wendy slid forward, away from him.

A bead of light swiveled around, a quick survey of the loft area, then clicked off. Jacqueline lowered her phone. "First, we need to find a way out of here."

"What we *should* do," Lou said, "is figure out how to kill it. If the Volker Institute was studying it—if we could find the right document—"

"If, if," Harlow cut in. "That's a lot of *if.*"

Thorn tried again to reach for Wendy, to hold her close as if she were in danger of slipping away if he didn't have hold of her, but Wendy sidled past, pushing herself from him, toward the edge of the loft and the waist-high wooden railing that looked down on the living area. "What?" he said, arms flopping at his sides.

He knew she was looking at him, but the stove's light was behind her, so he saw her only in silhouette. Her voice came out a whisper. "I don't want to infect you."

"You won't," he said. "I don't think that's how it works—"

"We don't know how it works!" Wendy shouted, hysteria blooming in her voice. "We don't know anything. We don't know what this *is.* We don't know where we *are.* We don't know—we don't know *anything.*"

"Hey." Thorn reached forward. Her arms went up in front of her like a shield, and when he tried to gently push them back down, they flailed against him. She was shivering, twisting away, her breath coming too fast.

All he wanted was to lend some small ounce of comfort. To grab onto her and not let go. But the more he reached out, the more she pulled back. His grasping grew increasingly desperate as her refusal took on a wild insistence, and he had one clear moment in which to think that he had only just, maybe, regained her affection, and now she was doing what she always did, pushing him away—and a tiny seed of resentment sprouted as he wondered how many times he should keep reaching out only to be rebuked.

Why was he trying to grab her hands, to still her arms, to calm her? Why was he trying so damn hard when she clearly didn't want it?

He let go.

Suddenly her legs were where her head had been, her feet pointed up—the most peculiar position.

Then she disappeared over the railing.

There was a terrible crunch.

It was a long moment before Thorn could bring himself to peer over the railing to the floor below.

Wendy lay in a wreck of limbs, her head canted at an unnatural angle, her neck bulging in an angry knot.

A turbid pool spread around the frozen cloud of hair, black in the firelight. The silence broke around the snap of a dying log in the stove, and then another sound: a soft gurgling, choking.

Wendy's throat convulsed. Blood popped from her lips. Her eyes rolled, lids twitching.

Thorn's knuckles turned white from clenching the railing. He pulled his hands away, looking at them as if they had betrayed him. As if they had pushed Wendy over the side.

Look what you've done.

His feet slid down the stairs, though he could hardly feel himself moving. He knelt in the spreading pool of blood, reached for Wendy's face—he didn't know why, didn't know what he could possibly do, it wasn't as if he could snap her broken neck back into place—but as he did, he noticed Wendy's eye wriggle and roll toward him, seize on him.

Thorn went still with the realization that he was watching Wendy's life drain away, the cliché of light leaving her eyes, and he reached around Wendy's head, grasped mostly hair, sticky and wet. His breath came in erratic hitches. All the blood in his chest turned to oil and ignited.

A slow drain of air, like the last bit of a deflating balloon, released from Wendy's chest, and she went still.

A ball of grief lodged in the back of his throat when he saw Wendy's eye move again. Not the pupil, which stared with the emptiness of death, but the rest of it *squirmed.*

Thorn pulled his hands away.

The squirming intensified, something trying to wrest its way free from a dying prison. The eye dissolved in its socket like the goo of an egg white. Thorn slid back on his knees, dragging smears of blood with him.

As he watched, Wendy's face collapsed into a puddle of rot, and the white fuzz already teeming inside devoured the blackening flesh. A spray of feathery threads emerged from the sunken well of her face until there was no longer anything recognizable about her. As if the fungus within had realized its host body had died prematurely and there was no reason not to simply devour it now.

Thorn felt someone dragging him away, back to the stairs. His wet hands slipped on the edges of steps, on the railing, but he could not look away from what was happening to Wendy: from the writhing mass growing over her body, rising, gathering itself into a tower. A tall thin figure—narrow as a skeleton, on two slim stalks for legs—molded itself like clay.

Somehow, Harlow managed to drag him over the top step, back into the dark of the loft, so he could no longer see the monstrous form weaving itself together below.

NINETEEN

Sometimes, when a thing is broken, it can't be fixed.

Like the house.

It stood black and gaping in Harlow's mind. Her memories of the inside were mostly impressions now: her room, pillow-soft and sun-dappled; the kitchen, oven-warm, with its oval table and white fridge; the living room's corduroy sofa and tube television.

Because the image of the burnt house had seared itself so firmly into her mind, all her happy memories hid behind it. Life before the fire barely existed anymore, like a dream.

She'd seen it because her dad had brought her back, expecting there to be a house to return to, perhaps damaged, perhaps requiring some significant cleaning—but he hadn't expected to find the house a blackened wreck, its windows shattered into beads of glass, walls buckling under a crooked roof. When she could stare at it no longer, she looked at her dad, whose gaze melted from shock to despair. Something left him in that moment. Whatever stability had upheld his life fell away over a precipice.

He stood staring at the house for a long while. It had taken everything for him to build this home, having come from a family with almost nothing, and it was all gone. Though he didn't know it then, his marriage was gone, too, or would be soon enough.

They did not go inside. The problem was that it was all made of wood, with brick only around the foundation, and the flames had spread too quickly for the firefighters to contain.

When they got back to the hospital and relayed the news to her mom, she looked at Harlow and said, "What were you thinking?" She turned toward the window to Thorn's room. "Look what you've done. Can you at least explain yourself?"

Harlow could only shake her head.

"I need an explanation."

But Harlow had no explanation. She didn't know what to say.

Her mom wept and beat at her husband and said she wanted an explanation, until she eventually cried herself out against his chest.

The more Harlow tried to find an explanation, the more mute she felt. Unable to form words. They were stuck in her throat and wouldn't come out. She wanted to cry and bang on something, too.

Her mom kept asking. Eventually, she would ask it in that weary way, eyes blank, voice low and dead, no longer expecting an answer but asking anyway. "Do you have an explanation?"

Each time, Harlow's tongue curled back into her throat.

For weeks, that was basically all her mother said to her. Eventually, it started to seem more like a taunt than a question, as if she thought she could torture the answer out of her. Her mom was desperate to know *why* this had happened, but even though Harlow had lit the match, she didn't know how to explain why. She had been trying to do something, but it seemed so unimportant now, after what happened, that her brain had left it behind.

As the weeks of Thorn's recovery wore on, Harlow started to ask herself her mom's question. Why? Why did she do it? And, as with her mom's line of questioning, the more she asked herself, the more the answer receded. Just as she thought she was grasping the clear, bright memory of what happened that night, it was snatched away, and she ran through so many scenarios that she could no longer tell which one was real and which was imagined. Everything before the fire was already becoming like a dream. The more the memories and dreams grew jumbled, the more she asked herself why. The more she searched for her own explanation.

Her dad would often pull her mom aside when she started asking and speak quietly but sternly to her, which usually left her in or near tears, pushing him away from her, asking him how he could just accept it—living in a motel room, everything they owned gone, their son mangled in the hospital as it ate up their life's savings.

That image of the house—likely further twisted by her mind, still smoking even though it must not have been (the fire had long gone out by then), grotesque, its windows and doors turned to dark hollows— gripped her heart, even now.

There are some things you can't fix.

Like a friend on the floor, shattered into pieces.

Harlow realized she was still gripping Thorn's arm and let go. They crawled as far from the staircase as they could get, huddled against the far wall. She could feel him shaking.

"We need to get out of here," Jacqueline said again.

A soft thump came from below, delicate enough to almost ignore. For one desperate moment, Harlow tried to pretend she hadn't heard anything at all. She willed the house to silence. The house, however, refused to obey, and the creaking floorboards below shattered the momentary illusion of safety. Something was moving. A shift in weight. A footfall.

"We can't go down there," Lou whispered, pulling her knees to her chest. Her back was pressed against the wood planks of the wall. Beside her, a white sock, inside out and pebbled with tiny balls of fuzz, made a pale tumor on the floor. A sock for a male foot. One of Rhys's.

Harlow looked around the loft, widening her eyes to adjust them to the low light. They had managed to get themselves cornered. She regretted having come up here to this dead-end room where the only exit was the staircase.

Its bottommost step groaned.

She cast about the room, but the only other openings were the windows on either side of the bed. Desperation pushed her toward them, trying to see out. "These open, right?"

"I know what you're thinking, but it's too high," Jacqueline said. "Land wrong, and your legs are broken."

The stairs spoke again, weight shifting from one step to the next. No one dared look down.

"I think I'll take my chances," Harlow murmured, but her plans to throw herself out the window were interrupted by another sound, this one not from the staircase but seemingly from everywhere. She could feel it raising the hair on her arms.

The cabin was humming.

"Is that…" Lou frowned. "…a cello?"

She was right. Harlow recognized it: Wendy's cello part from one of their songs. She couldn't tell which one, though—strange to hear the part on its own. Wendy always practiced by herself. Harlow didn't think she'd ever actually heard any of the cello parts played solo.

She only recognized the song when Brynn's vocals joined in, materializing as if from nowhere.

"Don't give in to the lie," Brynn sang, accompanied by cello. *"Killing ourselves is the fastest way to die…"*

It was impossible to tell where the voice was coming from: whether it was nearby or on the other end of the cabin. The echo of sound made it seem to come from everywhere at once, and Harlow could not help but imagine it was only a thousand pseudo-mouths forming on the web that had begun to creep over the walls, the threads becoming vocal cords stretched across the cabin, tendrils unfurling like kudzu. The whole structure was now one big throat, and this was the voice it had chosen.

She didn't like that thought.

Now she imagined breaking her legs on the fall out the window— dragging herself across the dew-slicked grass while tendrils followed, licking their tongues at her ankles, the cabin dragging her back to it by the jagged bones of her legs. Pulling her into its great hungry maw while it sang in Brynn's voice.

She stepped back from the glass as the stairs groaned again with the advance of whatever was creeping up from below.

"The side door," she said abruptly, thinking of the one that led behind the cabin to the firepit. They'd all seen the fungus growing over the front door, but she couldn't recall if she'd noticed the same on the narrow door at the end of the kitchenette. And even if it was grown over? They'd just have to bust through. Jacqueline was right—and wasn't *that* a jarring thought?—getting away from the cabin was essential. The whole structure was infected. They could not stay here.

"But…" Lou stared past her at the emptiness on the staircase landing. She didn't need to say it.

They knew what was coming.

Harlow wanted to take a drink to fortify herself. She longed for a slug of whiskey, something sharp and acrid to soften the sharp edges of the horror she had somehow stepped into, but there was no time for such indulgences. There was no time for anything.

She crossed the room and forced herself to look down.

Below, the fire was dying, gone down to a few smoldering red embers, but there was enough light yet to see what was coming up the stairs.

Wendy—or otherwise a perfect replica of her body spun from spider silk. The blank bulbs of her eyes seemed almost to glow. A smile cracked across her face. Every detail was perfectly rendered, yet it was so clear: her eyes were not really eyes, her teeth were not really teeth. Every bit of her was composed of the same material, like strings of cheesecloth woven into shape. Every bit of her had been bled of color, of individuality, rendered in cold white.

She was not a thing, but a living replica. A Pseudo-Wendy.

When she opened her mouth, strings shifting somewhere inside the tunnel of her throat, what emerged was more of that cello music. It rang out as if her vocal cords were made of catgut.

All that was left at the bottom of the staircase was a black smear on the floor.

Pseudo-Wendy took another awkward step, still finding the rhythm of her movements like a newborn lamb.

"Run to the road." Harlow threw one lingering glance behind her. The others were only shapes in the darkness, but even so, she could feel Thorn's gaze, could almost see him opening his mouth to tell her not to do what she was about to do.

Well, too late.

She threw herself down the stairs, bulldozing right into Pseudo-Wendy halfway down, sending them both tumbling. Her elbow jarred against the edge of a stair; the world spun; the floor slammed into her, whiplashed her neck, and she skidded on the wet smear reeking of rot.

Pseudo-Wendy's tendrils extended and wrapped around her, knotting at her back, holding her in place. Pulling her closer to the white face. From its open mouth and nose, the edges of its eyes, more threads reached out to Harlow—her ears, her nose—trying to feel their way inside.

That was what it wanted: to get inside. And once it was inside, it could destroy you, digest you, recreate you in its own image.

A rotten funk thickened the air until Harlow could taste it in the back of her throat. Her lips pressed tightly together even as the threads probed at the seam of her mouth, and she tried not to gag.

Shapes rushed past her peripheral vision. She didn't know how much longer she could hold herself shut until the feeling hyphae found ingress to her flesh. They crept toward her squeezed eyes. Against her lids she saw Wendy broken on the floor, neck bulging; she heard that awful choking gurgle; she was overcome with the fetid stink of decomposition, and she could not contain it any longer.

She opened her mouth to scream.

AFTER

There are cracks in the walls.

Harlow tries to ignore them, like she tries to ignore the pale face that seems to lurk behind her own when she looks in the mirror. At night, in the dark, when Sinda's breathing indicates she's fallen asleep, Harlow lies flat on her spasming back, pain flaring up whenever it wants, and keeps her eyes wide on the echoes of light dripping in through the window.

There is too much in the haunted house of her mind. The charred house is inhabited now—not just dead and blistered, still emitting its polluted exhalations of smoke, but filled with living things. Pale Forms that slither just out of sight, that change their twisted shapes. With visions of Allison Reed, who she could swear is not really a person but only an imitation of a person, a pseudo-person. As far as she knows, they might all be pseudo-people. But she doesn't know. Sometimes she doesn't know if what she's seeing is even real.

"You're living in your head," Thorn tells her when he visits. His face swims in and out of focus. It looks wrong, lopsided.

"Isn't that where everyone lives?" Harlow asks. "Isn't the world filtered through our perception anyway? Doesn't everything that happens just happen, at least to us, inside our own minds?"

Rain lashes the windows. "You sound like Brynn." Thorn scratches at the flesh around his bad eye. It's covered with a patch.

"You look like a pirate," she says.

Thorn laughs. "Yo ho ho."

"Where's the bottle of rum?"

All at once, his laughter sours. His lips turn down. "You look terrible."

"Wow, and you wonder why you can't hang onto a girlfriend." She realizes what she's said as soon as it's out of her mouth. She wants to suck the words back in, make it so she never said them.

"You said the drinking wasn't a problem. Just for fun. But *look* at you." He shakes his head. "You look like Ozzy Osbourne after a bender. You're like Dad."

"Well, which is it? Am I Brynn or Dad?" She frowns, but she is relieved he ignored her girlfriend jab. "Or Ozzy Osbourne?"

A man Harlow has come to know as Carl stands up with his hands over his ears. He shouts about how it's too loud. The rain sounds like needles on a tin roof. He says it's too loud, it's too *loud,* and an orderly comes at once, tries to calm him down. He won't. Another comes to lead him out of the rec room and down the hall.

Thorn watches him go. "Remember when we were kids—the Vile Hornets? We would play until, like, midnight, because Dad didn't care. But he had that one neighbor—Mr. Fenton? The vet?—who would stomp over to complain we were making too much noise. But instead of making us stop, Dad would yell at him. And there was that one time he chased him away throwing beer bottles. We thought it was hilarious." Thorn shakes his head. "I think about that sometimes. What if one of those bottles had hit him? Could have cracked his skull open. What if all the noise we made gave him flashbacks? What if he had PTSD? We were stupid kids, but Dad should have known better."

"Shut up. Dad was the best. I hated going back to Mom's every week. It felt like a prison."

"You talked about any of this? With, you know, the doctors?"

"What good will it do?" she asks. Cracks expand in the slate blue walls around her. She senses, without seeing, probing white tendrils reaching out for her. "They don't know the half of it."

"Don't you want to get out of here, though?" The gray outside deepens. All that's left is the buzzing fluorescents shedding their artificial glare on the drab, institutional room. "This feels like a prison to me."

"It is," Harlow says. Her gaze flicks to the security camera in the corner of the ceiling. "They're watching us. All the time."

Thorn starts to say something placating, then shivers. She thinks he must recognize it, too. The feeling of being back at Trail Creek Cabin. Of being watched.

"If you let them help you, then you can leave," he says at last, scratching around his eye patch again. "And then you can help me."

"How can I possibly help you?"

Thorn leans in. "I've been looking into them."

"Who?"

He glances left and right. Rain pings on the roof. "The Escher Society."

Harlow shakes her head. "You're not really here, are you?"

"Of course I am," he says, but she doesn't know what to believe anymore.

The cracks in the walls grow and spread.

Reality has fractured.

TWENTY

Breaking through the shock, like a shaft of sunlight through fog, came a spark of urgency: Thorn saw his sister pinned in place with a web of threads folding around her.

Adrenaline shot through his body. A green glint flickered on the floor in the gasp of firelight. The neck of the bottle, still intact, made for a good handle, fit easily in his palm. He moved on instinct. As if from far away, he watched himself swing the bottle at the hyphae, glass shards slicing through until the threads retracted. With his other hand, he grabbed the back of Harlow's jacket—that old leather thing she'd picked up at a thrift store six years ago and had barely taken off since, as if it were a child's comfort blanket—and pulled her away.

Pseudo-Wendy swallowed the excess threads, slurping them up like spaghetti noodles. The sight made Thorn wonder if he would ever be able to eat pasta again. Her cloud of hair lifted, each individual hair alive and moving of its own volition, each one an individual appendage, one of thousands, wavering and seeking entrance to the warm bodies ahead. Thorn wondered what it would be like if every one of his cells were alive, in the way *he* was alive as a composite of those cells—if each one could move and act on its own, his body just a squirming, unstable conglomeration of millions of sentient *things*.

If this were true, he could shear off the dead parts of him—scar tissue and the pointless orb of his blind eye—and simply remake these parts, like a salamander regrowing its tail. The thought held its appeal. Who wouldn't want to be able to heal wounds at whim, the way Pseudo-Rhys had after Harlow stabbed him? All the pain of healing—which, truthfully, was worse than being burned in the first place, it was the agony of healing that nearly undid him, made him almost want to stay wounded—could be removed in favor of this eternally shaping and reshaping cluster of component parts.

Weren't humans all made of component parts, though? Cells, bacteria, proteins, all humming along in perfect harmony to support the consciousness that you had determined was, in fact, *you.* What made Thorn *himself* aside from the collective dream of thirty trillion cells all imagining his conscious existence?

Was Wendy something separate from her component parts?

Could something fully recreate her from these component parts?

He looked at her now, not dead, not broken upon the floor, but standing before him and alive in so many ways.

"Wendy."

Her name escaped his lips like a prayer.

He wondered if it were possible that whatever made her still existed in those component parts—even an echo of the *real* her, a ghost of Wendy, something that could retain a kind of memory of itself.

Was Wendy still in there, or was she gone, wiped clean, and the Pale Form was like a photograph, a replication of the real thing with none of its soul, none of its *self*?

Pseudo-Wendy opened her mouth. A mournful cello melody emerged. One of their gentler songs, a ballad from *The Antidote*.

A cool breeze traced a path across the back of Thorn's neck. It came from behind him—the kitchenette.

The side door was open.

Lou called out, "Come on!"

Thorn didn't move. He could not stop looking at Pseudo-Wendy's face, struck by how much it looked like her, how much it *was* her. It made his arms prickle with gooseflesh.

He could still hear the wet crunch of her body on the floor. The moment she had disappeared over the railing was imprinted on the backs of his eyelids. But here she was, in front of him, and so very alive.

He had to know.

He stepped closer, aching with the sight of her, the possibility that he had not ruined everything.

"Is that you in there?"

"Thorn, stay back." Harlow's voice was a warning.

His legs would not cooperate. The broken bottle gleamed, sharp edges out, in his hand. He'd almost forgotten it was there. But had the cells in his fingers forgotten? Maybe they had been keeping track for him.

It wasn't the cello sound, now, that came from her, but Wendy's voice: "I don't want to die."

She said it in exactly the same way the words had emerged from her mouth less than twenty minutes before.

It wasn't *really* her. It was just the memory of the way her vocal cords had once moved.

Before he could think, he jabbed the broken end of the bottle at her.

Pseudo-Wendy simply moved away—not by sidestepping him, but by *morphing*, her left side scattering into a spray of threads and then weaving back together. She shifted out of the path of jagged glass seemingly without effort, without even moving her legs, without taking a step. Tendrils of hair reached back, tried to wrap around the bottle, and Thorn flinched, his weapon slipping from his hand.

Pseudo-Wendy pressed forward, gliding along the cilia on the bottoms of her feet, and Thorn lurched backward, nearly went tumbling over the armchair. He saw Harlow duck to his side and snatch up the fire poker with its deadly tip—a tip that would do no good against whatever the Pseudo-Wendy was made of, whatever mycelial substance it was that could shift and change and form new shapes at will.

He and his sister locked eyes, and in the way they used to silently communicate all the time, he knew they were thinking the same thing.

Harlow thrust the poker into the dying fire. A log collapsed, spat ash, refused to spark up. She patted her chest, dug the flask from her pocket, and unscrewed the cap. Before she could give her actions another moment's thought, she dumped its contents into the stove.

Flames whooshed up as Pseudo-Wendy's hair reached out to envelope him, and Thorn turned, took her in his arms—feeling the shape of her body one last time, the dip where torso flared to hip, the slope of shoulder meeting neck—and thrust her into the fire.

The head and its attendant cloud of hair, shoved into the stove, caught.

Sizzled.

Popped.

Blackened.

The edges of her began to curl.

The sound Pseudo-Wendy made, rather than a scream, was like the earsplitting scratch of a rosined bow sliding too close to the cello's bridge: an inhuman, atonal, nails-on-a-chalkboard screech. Thorn let go, pressed his hands against his ears as the thing in the stove—stuck there, face melted, glued to the metal—writhed, lost its shape, collapsed into a mass of fibers.

His ears rang. His limbs felt like dead weight. He saw Harlow's mouth moving, and it took some moments for her voice to cut through.

"Let's go." She grabbed his arm. "Let's *go!*"

He scooped up the broken bottle, feeling safer with it in hand, and stumbled after her toward the kitchenette where Lou waved to them from the side door. Harlow urged him forward even as he kept looking back, watching flames arc over Wendy's dissolving form, the billow of smoke rising up from it.

She did not let go of his hand until they had cleared the doorway. Cool night air swept over him like an ocean tide, sweeping away the stench of rot and singed hair and coppery blood.

He looked back one final time—saw the spray of hyphae twisting into agonizing shapes, nothing like Wendy any longer, if they were ever really like Wendy to begin with—and realized she was *gone* in a manner more final than death.

Her body was gone.

There was nothing left of her.

Outside, Thorn exhaled and looked up.

He allowed himself this one brief moment to think: *It's over.*

The thought invited a wave of melancholic relief.

A dusting of stars sprayed the black sky. He'd never noticed how many you could see out here, so many thousands and millions of them, scattered like grains of sand. All the times he'd come into the woods with Harlow trying to find Brynn, he'd never bothered looking up. He had always kept his gaze on the ground.

Had Wendy not looked up at the chandelier, maybe she would be out here with him. Had he only held onto her—not let her fall over the railing—not let go after that last ephemeral kiss—

These thoughts rose in him like helium. He felt giddy and perilously close to vomiting.

Wendy was dead. They were outside the cabin; the fungal thing was still in there burning; he could breathe the fresh air—but Wendy would never breathe again.

What brought him back down to earth was the peculiar silence around him.

The others were not moving, not making their way to the stone staircase that led to the road.

Thorn tore his gaze from the sky.

Three pale figures stood blocking their way.

TWENTY-ONE

They stood ranged around the path that led to the stairs, the cars, the road.

Rhys.

Wendy.

Brynn.

All of Harlow's internal organs plummeted. Vertigo tipped her, threatened to send her sailing off an imaginary cliff. She could still smell Pseudo-Wendy burning in her nostrils, sharp and acrid, but here she was again, perfect and whole, face curved into a crescent moon smile, as if none of that had happened.

And beside her—Harlow felt her insides twist—was Brynn.

For the past year, her desperation to see Brynn again, to find her, had driven Harlow to sleepless nights poring over her songwriting books, whiskey-fueled benders, selling anything she had lying around for enough cash to keep going, keep looking. Working extra shifts bartending to keep her afloat as she poured everything into the search. She had fallen, exhausted, into her pillow after fits of rage and begged the universe to give her something.

Now Brynn stood before her, and she could barely focus her eyes, which turned everything into a smeary blur. She wanted to throw herself on the figure, wrap her arms around it. Even knowing what it was made of, she worried she would fall right through and the ghost of Brynn would disappear with a laugh in the wind.

It wasn't really Brynn, though, was it?

Her tattoos had been erased; her color melted away. Her green eyes had gone to snow; her black hair twisted into pale ringlets.

Though she had heard her voice singing from the woods, the truth seemed to hit Harlow all at once. It stared her in the face like a vapid eye. There was only one answer to the question of what had happened to Brynn.

After all, the fungus only mimicked what it had digested.

Years ago, in the early days of Queen Carrion, when they were just figuring out who they were together, what their sound was, how they meshed, Brynn and Harlow ended every session with a breakdown: the cello needs to come out more, the bass is too splatty, Thorn's rhythm guitar should be crunchier, or groovier, or louder. They picked apart the sounds, and then it spilled over into the people who made those sounds.

"Rhys is totally into you."

Brynn rolled over with a laugh. "Ugh, I know! I feel like I'm giving him these very obvious signals that it's never going to happen, but he doesn't see them."

"Or doesn't want to."

During rehearsal: the way he kept showing off, peeling away into wild licks, stealing glances at Brynn. Afterward, when he kept crowding her space, trying to talk, and she ducked away from his outstretched arm.

Brynn, on the couch, propped on her side, looked down at Harlow sitting on the floor, back against the cushion. "Some people really can't take a hint."

"Rhys is so full of himself. I couldn't even imagine what it would be like trying to date him."

"Even if I *were* attracted to him," Brynn said, "I'm really not interested in dating right now."

Harlow leaned her head back into Brynn's hand, which absently played with the split ends of her hair. "How come?"

"I mean…" Brynn's gaze turned distant, face pressed in a frown.

"Well, I'm focused on Queen Carrion right now. Dating would be a distraction. Plus, it's always a bad idea to date within a band. Screws everything up, you know?"

It was written on her face that this wasn't the whole truth, but it was enough of the truth that Harlow didn't push it. Maybe she didn't want to know what the whole truth was. Still, she couldn't help but ask: "What if the perfect person came along?"

A shrug. "I don't think there is a perfect person for me."

"Right." Harlow tried on a laugh that died in her mouth. "You're married to your muse."

Eyes darkening, like the shadows at the bottom of a forest. "Exactly."

"Well, you'll always have me." Harlow tried on a smile this time, but it only rose halfway up her face. Did Brynn know? When Harlow brought dates back to the apartment, back to her room, did Brynn know she was only filling the hole of her with all these people who did not really matter? How could she tell her?

"Good," Brynn said, lying back on her arms. "You're the only person I want to be stuck with."

Pseudo-Wendy's cello-humming, Pseudo-Brynn's voice: the forest filled with the unmistakable strains of "Midnight Ritual," that cursed song. It left Harlow rooted to the spot. She wanted to touch her, but she knew the strange spongy texture that would meet her fingers if she did. She couldn't forget the way the knife sank into Pseudo-Rhys's face, like slicing a vegetable. Distinctly not human or animal flesh.

Pseudo-Brynn's voice, however, was identical to real Brynn's voice. It was unmistakable. The song enveloped her.

"A stew of bodies
Frankensteining
Bits of flesh I've harvested:
Eye of rapist
Toe of preacher
He will rise now from the dead."

All three of them—the dead—had made it impossible to get down to the road.

The dead collect in low places.

Harlow tried not to let the song work its way into her veins, but she couldn't help it. It was the song that had initially put them on the map, and it was the song that had led to the death of Murphy Dunning.

The song was about a witch who cursed the town that hated her by performing a macabre ritual, which involved adding different body parts to a concoction she was brewing. When the ritual was finished, a demonic figure emerged, composed of those body parts and shadows, and she sent this figure to terrorize the town. By the end of the song, the listener discovers that the witch has even sacrificed her own tongue to the creature, who uses it to sing a cursed song that will make all who hear it go insane.

Thinking of the song now, Harlow fought a swell of hysterical laughter. She certainly *felt* insane.

"Is that what you're doing?" she said. "Harvesting?"

Pseudo-Brynn stopped singing. But hers was not the only voice in the forest.

From between the trees, others were singing, other Brynns, voices made strange by distance. How many of them were there? Did the number even matter? The mycelium was as large as the forest, perhaps —a vast network of roots—and from its thousands of miles of thread, it could weave as many Brynns as it wanted, as many Wendys, as many Rhyses. It could form deer and maybe other shapes, too. It could be anything. It could be multitudes.

All at once, Harlow felt incredibly small. And that was no mean feat for someone who had spent much of her life towering over the heads of her peers.

She was only one, but this thing was legion.

As aware as she was that it was only some *thing* that stood before her, still she felt, deep in her bones, that she was looking at Brynn.

Her fingers brushed the letter in her pocket. She wanted to pull it out and give it to her, as she'd meant to do as soon as Brynn returned from camping.

She heard her name being called—the others behind her, trying to call her away from the pale figures—but what was the point? She had found what she was looking for. Brynn was right in front of her; that was the end of it. What did it matter if it meant she would be consumed? Maybe it was better this way. It would be like going back and staying in the burning house this time, letting it erase her from the world. It was only fair.

Pseudo-Rhys's arms were no longer arms but ropes reaching out, feathered at the ends where hands ought to be. They would like to loop around her, slither down her throat, but she instinctively reeled away. As she did, a shout pierced her ears from just beside her.

Thorn was there, lashing out with the broken bottle. He severed a few hairs from the end of Pseudo-Rhys's rope-arm, which floated up and spun through the air, nearly weightless, like hair caught in a breeze. Thorn's teeth were bared, scarred flesh pulled back from that grimace, his hair throwing itself behind him like a black banner in the wind.

He thrust the bottle again, sending Pseudo-Rhys back a step—or a *glide*—and giving them at least an arm's length of space. Pseudo-Wendy and Pseudo-Brynn also hesitated at the provoking edge of the broken glass and did not advance.

The brief respite allowed Harlow a moment of bright, clean clarity as she realized she did not, in fact, want to be eaten from the inside out. The image of fibers bursting from Pseudo-Wendy's sunken face made her guts squirm. She felt filled with worms just thinking about it.

She turned, with gratitude, to her brother. They had saved each other now, each one pulling the other back from the brink of destruction. Maybe it wasn't enough to make up for what she had done to him as a kid—maybe nothing could ever make up for that—but she realized that Thorn had always been on her side, even when she'd thought he wasn't. He was always looking out for her, even when she failed to look out for him.

Now she did, though. She turned to him, ready to fight their way out of here together.

It was only the moonlight and the faint glow of the hyphae that revealed the bits of fluff drifting in the air like the blown seeds of a dandelion. One of them found its way to Thorn. Harlow opened her mouth because he didn't see it—*couldn't* see it—as it settled into his clouded eye.

Her body felt like a scream.

In her peripheral vision, she could see Lou and Jacqueline backing away into the forest, taking shelter in the cover of the trees away from the Pale Forms. She could not turn to track them, though, because she was unable to look away from Thorn. They had locked into a mutual stare. Understanding crept across his face.

And she could see a faint wriggling in the meat of his blind eye.

She rushed to him, but Thorn pushed her back, just as Wendy had done to him.

"Go," he said.

Behind him, the pale figures began to advance.

This was wrong—it was all wrong. She couldn't leave him. "No," she said. "No!" Her heart felt as if it had been stomped by a spiked heel. Her lungs burned; she could not breathe. Thorn nodded at her to go, but she shook her head. "I won't."

"You have to."

She saw the blackened house set back to flames that tongued a sky of smoke; she saw herself standing, in shock, watching as it burned; she saw her mother dragging Thorn through the front door limned red, the patch of black over his face like a mask.

She couldn't leave him.

Not again.

"I'm sorry," she said. "I'm sorry."

He pushed her, held up the broken bottle, and turned his back, turned to face the pale figures.

Someone grabbed Harlow from behind—Lou, she saw a flash of purple hair—and pulled her away. The fight went from her quickly. Her body was like lead. She let herself be pulled, wanted to feel nothing, wanted to be doused in alcohol and thrown in the fire. The movements of her legs were distant as they ran into the trees. Her mind was a wash of fog.

Lou let go as the trees closed over them, and Harlow slipped on wet grass sloping down to the creek. She caught her balance, briefly came back to herself, and stopped.

No, this wasn't right.

She would not leave Thorn behind.

She turned, trying to give Lou an apologetic look as she glanced over her shoulder, prepared to go back to the cabin, to the figures, and to whatever might await her there, even if it was death.

That's when she heard it—Thorn's bloodcurdling scream—and it stopped her cold, turned her veins to ice, told her she was already too late.

Dear B,

Do you remember that time we went swimming at the Willamette River, and I almost drowned because I was a terrible swimmer and forgot to tell you I'd never taken swim lessons? We were twelve, and it was one of those super hot summer days that we would both hate now but that we loved back then, when summer was lazy and special and never long enough. You dove in and I followed, feeling like I would somehow be fine because you were there, but it was windy that day, and the river was kind of choppy. It was ice-cold when I jumped in, so much that it shocked my muscles numb, and I ended up flailing in the current. I don't think I was actually anywhere close to drowning—there were tons of other people nearby, and the current wasn't strong—but I somehow swallowed a big gulp of water, which made it feel like I was drowning. You had to pull me out onto that little sandy outcropping, and I thought for a minute, with you leaning over me, your wet hair dripping in my eyes, that you were going to try mouth-to-mouth.

Obviously, you didn't need to. I was fine. But I realized, in that moment, I really wanted you to. I wanted you to put your lips on mine. I didn't even know why at the time, but I wished I'd tried to drown a little harder. It was only later that I understood: it was because I wanted to kiss you.

That was before I realized I was bi (and, goddamn, didn't THAT take way too long for me to figure out?), and I always thought I just wanted to be really good friends with you. I thought it was normal, to be obsessed with your best friend, to be jealous when she wanted to hang out with other people, to feel possessive of her. I didn't realize, and I thought there was something wrong with me for wanting to kiss you. I guess that's always my first instinct: to assume there's something wrong with me.

This is all stuff I don't know how to say out loud. It's too sentimental, I guess, and you know I hate sentimentality. Maybe it's good you told me we could talk when you get back. Some things are easier to write on a piece of paper, you know? Then again this has taken me like an hour to write and it's not even that long, so maybe it's not easier after all.

What am I really trying to say? The phrase I should write seems to be "I have feelings for you," but that sounds so lame and generic. The truth is, ALL my feelings are for you. They've always been for you, even before I knew it. I can sleep with every groupie that comes my way, but you're the only one I want to be with. I want to tell you this, but I also don't want it to be weird. I don't want it to screw everything up, which is why I waited so long to say anything. I didn't want things to change between us. I didn't want to ruin everything.

What I'm trying to say is, if this is going to screw up our friendship, you can rip up this letter right now. No harm, no foul. Pretend it didn't happen. It's okay. I'd rather be friends than nothing at all. But if, for some reason, you happen to feel the same way, then when you're done reading this, pretend I'm drowning and come give me mouth-to-mouth resuscitation. Because I'm only alive when I'm with you.

Oh my god that was so corny,
H

TWENTY-TWO

Lou had no idea where they were going.

Rather than empty her mind, as running often did, it left her thoughts flying alongside her body. She could not pull her mind away from the Pseudo, for that was how she'd come to think of it: not just Pseudo-Wendy or the pseudo-spider but the pseudo-anything, the stuff that could become other things through rot and replication. She wanted to know how it worked. If it could, somehow, *think*. Her mind worried at it like a wound.

They ran along the creek. Brynn continued to sing, her voice here and then faraway, trading phrases between the many voices of the woods. Lou tried not to let herself believe the flickers she saw from the corners of her eyes were Pale Forms struggling up from the dirt. Once the idea was in her head, though, it had already taken root. She wondered how far the Pseudo extended beneath the forest floor. Acres?

The idea of such a vast entity so consumed her, she stumbled, not seeing the branches, like teeth, hung from trees astride their path.

A part of her still could not believe any of them were dead. Even though she had witnessed their deaths, in some ways, those events were like a dream. She had seen them, heard their voices, as if they were alive, and though it wasn't quite *them*, it was so close as to confuse the notion that they were really gone from this world.

Or maybe it was just shock.

When her breath came too hard and stitches split her side, she had to slow. They all did. The singing was now such a distant echo, it might be mistaken for the wind. With ragged breath she clambered down the embankment and dropped to her knees, palming cold water to her mouth. When it splashed her face she rubbed it on her hot flesh and burning eyes, then leaned over her knees, dripping.

"I think we lost them," Jacqueline said, which Lou found funny, somehow. *Them*—as if there were three separate people, who looked like Brynn and Rhys and Wendy, coming after them. It wasn't three, though. It was one; it was a million. It could be anywhere or everywhere.

And if that was the case, then they hadn't lost anyone but themselves.

She looked around at the pines in every direction, or what little she could see of them in the dark. There was no way to tell where they were except for the creek, and all she knew of it was that in one direction lay the cabin and the Pseudo, and in the other the unknown. You always follow water though, right? It sounded right to Lou, but she wasn't sure where she had heard that. All they could do was keep following the creek.

It was so dark. A shiver passed through her. Any kind of dark reminded her, now, of the Wonder Room, and the unnatural dark that had descended there. But this dark was not unnatural—only unfamiliar. The moon struggled through the treetops. She fumbled to turn on her phone, saw the battery symbol gone red. Still no signal. She tucked it back into her pocket, wishing she could use it for a light and knowing the battery would drain that much faster if she did.

Sounds amplified in the dark. It was all leaf-rustle, footfall, twig-snap, heavy breath, and whatever pounded an endless rhythm inside her brain. The drone of insects crept across her nerves. The scuttle of nocturnal animals. An owl offering a low, mournful call. Lou reminded herself to pay more attention to where she was going. Uneven ground pitched up and down; brambles snatched at ankles; left, right, forward, backward became interchangeable.

Jacqueline fished a fallen branch out of the dirt and held it upright like a walking stick, jabbing it into the ground as she went. "There were no reviews."

"What?"

"The listing. For the cabin. It had no reviews. I didn't think anything of it at the time."

"Huh," Lou said. "Do you think the same thing happened to the people who wrote in the guest book?"

Jab, step, jab, step. "Wouldn't that have been on the news, if they all disappeared?"

It was a good point. Lou didn't know. Maybe it was in the news, but then again, people disappeared in the woods—multiple people every year. She might not have even noticed.

"Well, if we make it out of here alive," Jacqueline said, still jab-stepping, "I'm writing a terrible review."

A guffaw spilled out of Lou's throat, which surprised her. She clapped a hand over her mouth.

She was even more surprised when Harlow spoke up, her voice flat: "'A carnivorous mold ate my friends, and I ended up lost in the woods. One star.'"

The laughter was contagious. It spread through them, giddy and manic, until it morphed into wheezing, into tears. They gradually wrung themselves dry and solemn.

Then they kept going.

Feet stumbled, hands grasped at bark scratched and scarred with age, scaled with lichen. Lou tried to see up the dizzying height of a nearby tree, searching for its top. She craned her neck. They were so small down here. If they could ascend to the canopy and look out, they would see the forest stretching around in all directions, but from down here, in the thick of it, they were like flies caught in its web.

"In any other circumstances, I would think this place was like a fairy tale," she murmured.

It did seem like it, with moss-furred trunks and lush underwood. Deep in the old-growth forest, it was easy to imagine the world the way it must have been millions of years ago, when gigantic conifers grew in vast unbroken networks; when all was wilderness and unfamiliar life thrived in forests so dense and extensive that one could only imagine the mysteries that lay shrouded at their hearts.

It was so different from the city. The constant barrage of lights, even in the middle of the night, making visible the nooks and crannies. Cars buzzing by at all hours. There was a sense that you were never really alone.

Never had she felt so alone as she did then, walking deeper into a forest teeming with strange life that wanted to invade them, digest them, *become* them. Every sound put her on edge. Was it an animal scuttling through the underbrush, or roots bursting from the dirt to form a human shape? Were those crickets chirruping, or only a thousand little cotton balls mimicking the sound of crickets? Was it all around them, just under their feet?

Lou looked down, but all she saw was dirt.

Shivers wracked her shoulders. Night's damp chill had fully settled, piercing through her sweatshirt, worn thin at the elbows. She could feel the fabric sticking to cold sweat. Stiff fingers clenched and unclenched to find some blood flow.

"Do you still have your map?" she asked, and Harlow reached into her pocket and dug out the folded paper. As she did, another paper slipped out. She let go of the map to snatch at it.

"What's that?" Jacqueline asked.

"None of your business."

They crouched around the map, holding a light against its surface. Even when they found roughly where they thought they were, no one could exactly pinpoint the location of Trail Creek Cabin, let alone the creek they'd followed way out here.

Harlow sighed and leaned back against a tree. Lou could see the energy drain out of her. Still clutching the second paper, she carefully unfolded it. At an angle, Lou saw it was covered in writing.

"I wrote her a letter," Harlow said. "When she went camping. I was going to give it to her when she came back. I never got a chance to tell her…"

"You loved her," Jacqueline supplied as though it were obvious.

It hadn't been obvious to Lou, but now that she thought about it, she should have seen it sooner. Of course Harlow loved Brynn. They were practically inseparable. But Harlow kept certain things private.

The paper shook, its edges crumpled in Harlow's hands. "I kept thinking she would come back, and I would be able to give it to her. But she never did, so… I kept it."

"Come on." Jacqueline stood. "Let's keep moving." Her phone lit the grass in ghostly hues.

"You should save your battery," Lou told her. When Jacqueline looked down at the screen, her face blanched in the glare. She turned it off, and they blinked into darkness.

Anything could be out there.

This thought, fleeting and intangible, should not have unnerved Lou the way it did. She had already seen the worst of what could be out there. She could imagine nothing more horrible than what they had already encountered back at the cabin. Yet somehow, the oppressive dark of the woods bearing down from all sides, not knowing what secrets it hid, felt worse. At any moment, they might stumble on the next awful iteration of fungal architecture, or a thousand cadaverous Brynns looming out from the dark. A pale hand might burst up from the dirt at their feet, stitching itself together to grab them and pull them down into the earth.

Sugar pines stretched their jagged limbs over a sky fuzzed with moonlit clouds. Lou put her hand against one, felt the rough bark, estimated the diameter of the trunk to be about six feet. The trees here were massive and exceptionally old. What had they witnessed in their hundreds of years standing sentry?

When Lou stumbled, Harlow caught her by the elbow before she could go down. At her feet, she discovered twisted metal grown over with vines. A corroded razor-wire fence, collapsed, half-buried, and a sign, long-faded, with the partially obscured words: VATE PERTY.

Frowning, Lou uncovered the rest of the sign with her shoe. "Private property? In the national forest?"

"Are you sure we're still *in* the national forest?" Jacqueline reached for Harlow's pocket to retrieve the map again, but her hand was swatted away. "It didn't seem like you had any idea where we were on that map."

"Well, excuse the fuck out of me for not being a master cartographer," Harlow snapped. "Don't you have a map from Airbnb? Didn't it tell *you* where this place was?"

"Shh," Lou hissed.

They quieted enough for the distant sound to make itself known. Somewhere, far away: voices babbling.

"Hello?" Lou called out. "Is someone there?"

The voices, still indistinct, continued.

Jacqueline put out her arm to stop them. "Who else could be out here? It's the middle of the night."

"*We're* out here," Lou pointed out.

The voices dipped and rose again. Quiet as radio static. First they seemed to come from ahead, then it was as if they were echoing from behind. Lou turned around, then around again, trying to pinpoint the right direction. She knocked away Jacqueline's restraining arm and took a few steps through the trees. If there was someone else out here, they could help.

Ahead of her, she saw a shape.

A person.

Her mouth was already open again, chest filling, primed to call out, when she noticed how pale the figure was.

She sucked a breath through her teeth as the figure, faintly illuminated with its own effulgence, turned to face them, or at least she thought it did—the eyes were blank hollows in a blank face. It lifted one leg, moving as if underwater, unpeeling from the dirt like Velcro, trailing broken threads from the bottom of a malformed foot.

Lou's instinct was to run.

To the right, the way was too dense with growth. They wouldn't make it far.

To the left, then.

She slid down the embankment to the creek. Icy water shocked her ankles. On the other side, she clambered up an incline of broken rocks, scoring her palms with their edges, and then she pitched through the dark, guided by the wildly flailing light of Jacqueline's phone like a roving white eye in the darkness.

She couldn't go very fast. The way was too rough, too rocky, too threaded with low-hanging branches. Lou glanced behind her but could no longer see the Pale Form. She tripped, caught dirt in her mouth. Up again, she spotted Jacqueline's light ahead of her. She could barely hear their footfalls above the wet throb of her pulse in her ears.

As she pushed to her feet, she noticed something growing from the dirt. Sprouting, like the shoots of a young plant in fast-motion, then gathering into a white knot, braiding into some new shape. She sprang away from it, then hopped again, seeing more shapes crawling up from the dirt, and she knew: it was *everywhere*.

Jacqueline's light vanished.

For a moment, horror lurching up her throat, Lou was alone in the dark with the Pseudo all around her.

Where had it *come* from?

The question sprang into her mind like a missile.

She thought of Brynn and the ritual—how she had wanted to call something up, the thing that was haunting her, the face that was not a face, but more like a corpse.

She thought of the Volker Institute—all the strange things they had supposedly studied and documented.

She thought of the Wonder Room—the unnatural dark that had spilled in during their song, the way she had felt displaced in that moment, as if she had been transported somewhere *else*.

She couldn't fit it all together in her mind.

Then she saw the light appear from behind the trunk of a tree. She rushed toward it, nearly knocking into the others.

"We need to get inside," she panted. "Somewhere it can't follow."

Her forearms stung with the whippings of thin branches swept aside. Her heart was in a puddle at her feet. Slick grass rose in a slope, a hill, and Lou nodded. She would go to the top, use the last bit of juice in her phone to look out from there, try to see if there was anything nearby, if there was anywhere for them to go. She surged ahead, taking long strides past the others, quads burning, until she reached the top of the mound.

The trees were taller still. She could not see anything.

The battery icon of her phone flashed, and the screen went black.

She slid down, hunching over her knees. The ripe smell of sod rose around her. The mound was treeless but overgrown with grass and weeds. Any moment, the Pseudo would catch up, would find them.

From below, she heard Jacqueline say: "Hey."

She blinked. She could just make out Jacqueline pointing to the side of the mound. Sliding down, Lou came around the side. She looked, but at first she did not understand what she was seeing. It didn't make sense. It didn't seem to fit.

There was a door in the side of the mound.

TWENTY-THREE

One of Harlow's sharpest memories was the first time she saw Thorn after the fire. He was a mummy, gauze-wrapped. The burn unit was like a trip to hell: screams echoed down the halls as if its inhabitants were being tortured rather than healed.

She had to gear up in scrubs and pull papery booties over her shoes that whisked against the tile floor. Until she saw him, she'd thought only the worst—that he was charred from head to toe, that he was dead or near to it.

When she stepped into the room and saw him sitting up, half his face buried under his dressings, she felt a shock of relief, her stomach untwisting for the first time in a week. There he was, and it wasn't a spent matchstick or a corpse. She ran immediately to him, opened her arms. Her mother snatched her back. "You shouldn't touch him. You'll only make it worse."

She shrank back against the wall. If she touched him, perhaps the burn would spread over the rest of his skin like a disease. Thorn couldn't really speak. His voice was barely a rasp, and the burn extended to his lips, preventing him from moving his face much at all. The uncovered eye roved to her, glazed with pain and medication, but she could not read anything in that one-eyed stare.

They grafted skin from his thigh for the worst of the burns on his forehead and cheekbone, the third-degree portions that had melted through flesh and singed off his nerve endings. The second-degree edges blistered and popped.

Weeks passed before he could leave the hospital. By then, Harlow was living in an extended stay motel with a rotation of one parent or the other, whoever wasn't at the burn ward any given day. They found an apartment before Thorn's discharge, a two-bedroom, with a second-hand pair of bunk beds for the kids. Obviously Thorn got the bottom bunk. Sometimes, Harlow would wake in the middle of the night and dip her head over the side to watch the rise and fall of his chest, making sure he was alive.

The doctors said his skin would be sensitive to sunlight as it healed. At first, it was their mom who stopped him from going outside without a hat, an umbrella, a thick slather of sunscreen, but after a while Thorn embraced the routine. When the clouds parted, he hissed like a vampire. He said if he stood in the sun too long, his skin would start to smoke.

While their mom lamented his disfigurement, always looking at him with those wounded eyes, Thorn embraced it, started wearing black, wrapping himself in chains and studded belts.

After several bitter years in which their dad spent nights on the living room sofa, their parents having low-pitched arguments they couldn't keep from seeping through thin walls, the divorce was a mercy kill.

When all was said and done, their mom moved into a new house—a two-story Victorian farmhouse set back in the trees, painted buttermilk yellow, with lace valances on the mullioned windows—while their dad ended up in a manufactured home in the Pinewood Mobile Estates. They shared custody, but there was more room at Mom's, so Thorn and Harlow lived there during the weeks and spent weekends in Dad's cramped little home.

Harlow loved Dad's place, even if it was small and made of tin. She always felt at ease with her dad. Whenever he had a beer in his hand, he was happy, goofy, easygoing. He didn't discipline her. He bought her a drum set as a kind of consolation prize and let her practice at all hours, for as long as she wanted, without ever complaining. He let her stay out late without question. He *trusted* her, and it was the exact opposite of the rest of the week she spent at her mom's, where she could barely go to the bathroom without her mother expecting her to blow something up, where curfews were precise to the minute.

Once Harlow had the drum set, Thorn got a guitar.

She and Thorn became a two-person band. They called themselves the Vile Hornets. They even had a hand signal for it: right hand making a peace sign, left hand throwing devil horns: VH. Their songs mostly consisted of riffs interspersed by extended drum and guitar solos that often devolved into nonsense, explosions of dissonance ultimately won out by laughter. They spent entire weekends cramped in that shared little room—more bunk beds—playing, making new songs. They didn't write them down or record them, so the songs existed as fleeting things, experienced once and forgotten, continually slipping back into the ether.

That was what Harlow thought a life was: an unrecorded song that exists for a particular duration and then slips back into the void, the bubbling froth of creation.

Dad would let them play while he sat on the couch with a beer, or while he went visiting his neighbors for evenings of card games.

When they were at Mom's, there was no music. Thorn would plug headphones into his electric guitar and noodle silently, which made Harlow feel completely alone. She had to tiptoe around her mom unless she wanted paranoia and criticism, she couldn't play with her brother, and she had no drums. The house was suffocatingly quiet, tucked away from the main road, in the trees. She wished fervently to be back at her dad's and would count down the days each week until she could return to her real home on Friday.

Thorn started smoking in his teens, and he would bring his cigarettes to Dad's to hide them from their mother, knowing Dad would hardly notice, or particularly care. "I eat fire," he would say between Vile Hornets jam sessions, exhaling smoke.

His voice had changed, too: throat singed, it took a few weeks for it to be anything other than a rasp, then a growl, then a sound like chewing gravel. The cigarettes didn't help. He said it made him sound cool.

The only saving grace during the long, quiet weekdays was that Brynn lived closer to her mom's house. The less time Thorn spent with her, the more time she spent with Brynn. And though Brynn likely saved her from herself, Harlow always missed Thorn when he wasn't around. It was like his absence, rather than his presence, reminded her of the blackened house, the ruins of an innocent childhood. The guilt she carried grew heavier when he wasn't around.

It was always heavier when he wasn't around.

———

And now Thorn was gone.

The knowledge beat in Harlow's heart like a drum.

If she were alone, she'd have stopped running long ago, but the urgency of Jacqueline and Lou had pushed her onward, keeping pace. Her long legs ate up the ground faster than theirs, anyway.

Having come this far—and she didn't know exactly how far that was, with the creek snaking between trees to form a serpentine path—they had to slow, to stop, unable to keep running indefinitely. Momentum broken, Harlow was on the brink of giving up, letting the dirt claim her, until Jacqueline pointed out the mound's unusual feature.

She regarded the door. It stood against a vine-threaded triangular facade under the man-made mound, which had been easy enough to mistake for a natural hill until they noticed the flat side. The door was a gray slab, cold to the touch, like stone.

Jacqueline tried the handle. It didn't turn.

"Where do you think it goes?" Lou asked.

The mound wasn't very large. If Harlow had to guess, the door led to a space the size of a small shack, some little one-room hovel. What she couldn't guess, however, was what it was doing out here, far from any path or road, hidden under a roof of sod. It was a minor wonder they'd even noticed it in the dark, except that Jacqueline kept turning on her phone's flashlight to see where they were going.

Her first question unanswered, Lou added: "You think someone lives here?"

"I doubt that very much," Jacqueline said.

Harlow's fist slammed a percussion on the door. "Hey! Let us in!"

"Maybe we can break it down," Lou suggested.

Rearing back, Harlow kicked. Her boot connected solidly with the door, but it didn't budge. "There's your answer," she said and sagged against the stone wall. With a frown, Lou stepped away from the mound, still looking around. It was only a matter of time before it found them. Harlow wondered if this was what happened to Brynn: if she had gotten lost, tried to run, and eventually succumbed to the hungry forest.

It seemed a fitting end for the rest of them.

"We're all gonna die."

"No, we're not." Jacqueline's voice was firm. Uncompromising. It wasn't optimism so much as it was determination, a refusal to give up.

For all her distaste of Rhys's fiancée, Harlow found the attitude admirable. Now she looked at her, this girl she had spent so much time despising. Her bleached hair was ragged, studded with bits of leaf; her wiry arms bent at sharp angles with hands planted firmly on her hips; her elfin face, no longer simpering and smug, was set in a stubborn grimace. She didn't look frightened, though Harlow knew she must be.

A rush of regret rose, sour, up her throat. Why was she still holding onto this stupid grudge? She may not like Jacqueline, but right now she and Lou were all Harlow had. They were the only ones left. She thought of all the times she'd been a jerk to Thorn, all the things she'd never gotten the chance to apologize for. And now, standing here, lost in the forest, with death looming in every shadow, she felt compelled to say something. "I don't really hate you, you know."

Jacqueline looked up, eyes widening. "What?"

"I've been a bitch to you," she said, surprising even herself. "I mean, I *am* kind of a bitch, but to you especially, and you don't deserve that."

A flash of something, pain or guilt, crossed Jacqueline's face. "It's okay. You can hate me if you want." Her grimace twisted into something almost like a smile. "The truth is, it was my idea to take over vocals. I let Rhys think he came up with it. But it was my idea. I wanted it." Her eyes gleamed.

Harlow expected the confirmation to ignite her ire, but all the anger had gone out of her. There was no room for it anymore. So what if it had been Jacqueline's idea? Could she really blame her for that? "Whatever. Either way, I'm sorry. Sometimes, I think I'm so mean to myself that I forget how to not be mean to other people. You know?"

"Actually, I do." Jacqueline frowned, like she was trying to work out what to say. Then she grabbed Harlow's wrist, the bones of her fingers like a bird's claw. "I'm sorry about Brynn." Her eyes blazed into Harlow with breathless anticipation before dropping to the forest floor. "I *am* sorry."

Harlow could only nod, glad that Jacqueline had picked Brynn's name for her apology rather than Thorn's. The thought of him was too raw. Her mind tried to dance around the scream they'd heard. She thought if anyone said her brother's name right now, that would be it, she would be done.

"I'm not a good person," Jacqueline said suddenly.

"Yeah, well." Harlow huffed a laugh. "Me neither."

After circling the mound, Lou started pounding on the door again, until her knocks grew lighter, knuckles singing. Defeat in her posture, she slithered around with her back against the door and slid to the ground.

That was it, then. Their one chance at refuge, foiled by a locked door. Harlow wondered how long it would take for the Pseudo—that's what Lou had called it—to catch up with them. And it would, she was sure of that. They had outrun it for now, but it was only a matter of time.

It wasn't until Lou's back jolted that Harlow had any reason to think otherwise.

She turned.

With a click, the door creaked open.

EXCERPT FROM AN INTERVIEW WITH BRYNN WERNER OF QUEEN CARRION

METAL MANIA MAGAZINE

MMM: Where does your inspiration come from, and how does the songwriting process work for Queen Carrion?

BW: I don't know. Magic? Dreams? I have to be in a certain mindset. Receptive. Open to suggestion. I don't know where that suggestion comes from, but it usually appears as a little nugget, a seed… could be a specific lick, a few notes or chords, that haunt me until I run with them. From there I find the rough structure of the song, and then the collaborative part of the process comes in. I take the proto-songs to the others and we build the more complex parts from those seeds, from whatever I tapped into. Call it a muse whispering in your ear. But what the muse is—I think that idea is just our attempt at embodying the fleeting access to some higher level of consciousness, some plane of collective intelligence and creativity that exists nowhere and everywhere at once.

MMM: Do you mean God?

BW: No. I mean—well, sure, call it God if you want to. I don't think of it like that. It's too complicated. God feels too simple. Like a copout, easier to swallow than whatever's really out there.

MMM: Your vocal work is some of the best of the women-led outfits coming out of the indie scene right now. You manage to blend the melodic and the gritty in an artful way—at times soaring and operatic, and at other times as brutal as any hardcore vocalist today. Who are your strongest influences?

BW: We have a lot of influences as a band, but as far as vocals? Amy Lee, Cristina Scabbia, Maria Brink, Tarja Turunen, and Tatiana Shmayluk, to name a few.

MMM: Tell us more about your concept album, *Tomb of the Sphinx*. How did that come about? Are you interested in doing more concept albums?

BW: The album as a whole really evolved from the song "Speak, Cleopatra." I had this image of her in my mind: this brilliant and savvy leader. What do most people associate with Cleopatra, though? That she slept with Julius Caesar and Mark Antony, that she was seductive and beautiful, that she killed herself with an asp. A bit phallic, no? Ultimately, she was framed as a whore. But did you know Cleopatra spoke at least nine languages? That she was educated in politics and economics, that she commanded the army and navy? The song is a call for her to speak her truth—for all women throughout history remembered only for their sexuality, or not at all, to be heard. In that song, the chorus is a spell to summon her, saying, "Speak, Cleopatra. We've opened up our ears." And when she finally does speak from beyond the grave, her voice generates a cataclysm that shakes the world to its foundations, rendering listeners mute with the ancient power of her voice… the ancient intelligence buried in the Egyptian sands, waiting eons to rise again. She destroys to create anew. A better world.
But as far as other concept albums… stay tuned, and keep your watering can ready. I've got a seed germinating, and it's just about ready to flower.

TWENTY-FOUR

A face swam out of the dark.

After almost toppling, Lou whirled and caught her feet as the door creaked inward. From its opening peered a woman who might have been a rough-worn thirty or a spry forty-five. Suspicion and surprise tightened the lines of her narrow face. An oversized UC Berkeley sweatshirt—yellow font gone spotty on navy fabric, old and worn thin—slumped on her shoulders. She wore a pair of gray joggers and thick white socks. "How did you get here?"

"You need to let us in," Harlow said.

"Please." Lou held up her hands. "We need help. We're lost, and it's not safe out here."

The woman's eyes flickered warily behind them. "Why should I let you in?"

"If you don't, we're going to die," Jacqueline said. "There's something out here."

The reminder, stated so matter-of-factly, set Lou's heart pounding hard enough she could feel it in her fingertips. She wanted to push this woman and storm inside, but she hesitated when another figure appeared over the woman's shoulder: a man in his thirties, spectacled, clad in army green cargo pants and a thermal shirt. His voice was soft, gentle. "Audrey. We should let them in."

The woman's mouth tightened. "I don't think it's a good idea."

"We can't just leave them out there."

"Please," Lou begged. The back of her neck prickled. She told herself not to turn around. If she turned around, Audrey might close the door, and they would be left out here.

The door eased open. "Come in, then."

A light buzzed on, revealing a sparse white-walled room with a sunken concrete floor, the lowered bottom making the room larger than it had appeared from the outside. A desk with a green banker's lamp stood to the right. A pair of sleeping bags sprawled on the floor beside an agape backpack and a camp stove.

Gratitude and relief rushed through Lou in a heady mix. "Thank you."

"Do you have a phone?" Harlow asked.

Audrey sighed and went to the camp stove, setting a kettle on it. "We're completely off the grid." She poured from a pitcher of water and clicked on the stove. "This place is powered by a generator. Vic." She looked at her companion. "Don't be rude to our guests." Her intonation on the final word was sarcastic. She clearly did not want them here.

Nodding, the man opened another door to what appeared to be a storage closet and emerged with two rolled-up sleeping bags, which unfurled on the floor like blown party horns. "Sorry," he said. "I'm Victor. Have a seat. You're safe."

Lou collapsed onto one of the bags, a cramp making itself known in her right leg. Her fingers dug into the muscle to ease it.

"Do you know what's out there?" Jacqueline asked, voice carefully neutral.

Audrey shrugged. "Animals. Bears."

As the kettle shrilled, Lou looked up at Jacqueline and wondered if she was going to tell them the truth. But how could they even explain it? She could tell, however, from the sharpness in Jacqueline's eyes that she, too, was wondering: what if it got inside? Who was to say it couldn't get in here like it had gotten into the cabin?

She clocked Vic sliding a lock into place on the front door. He turned and saw her watching him. "You said you were in danger. Don't worry. See that door? That's three inches of reinforced steel and concrete." He rapped his knuckles against it, as if to prove it.

"What is this, some kind of bunker?" Jacqueline said.

Accepting the chipped mug Audrey offered her, Lou wrapped her hands around it, letting its warmth spread through her palms. The tea was some herbal concoction, thin and a little grassy. "It helps with anxiety and indigestion. I always drink this when I've had a bad night," Audrey said as she passed around the mismatched mugs: one with a pattern worn to static, another bragging *World's Best Dad*, the third missing a handle, just ragged white porcelain where it should be connected. Harlow and Jacqueline took theirs and joined Lou on the floor.

"How long have you been here?" Lou asked.

Audrey's reply was sharp. "Why?"

Lou shrugged. She thought Audrey was worried they'd been caught squatting, but Lou really didn't care about that. It was none of her business. As long as they were safe.

She hadn't realized how much adrenaline had been driving her until she had the chance to stop, to sit. Exhaustion turned her blood to sludge. Involuntary tremors rippled through her arms. Her stomach looped into a figure eight. All she wanted to do was lie down and drift away from the world.

"We've been here a little while." Vic leaned against the desk. "What happened to you? How did you get all the way out here?"

"We were staying at a cabin," Jacqueline said after a beat. "We were having a bonfire, and we got spooked—an animal, I think. We made a run for it, which was stupid, because we got lost." The lie came so smoothly from her mouth, even Lou almost believed her.

"It's lucky you found us," Audrey said. "Not much around here for miles."

"There has to be a road nearby." Harlow frowned into her mug.

"It's a bit of a hike," Vic said, adjusting his glasses. "We can take you tomorrow. Parts of the woods around here are tricky to navigate. Very easy to get turned around."

"Do you have a map of where we are?" Jacqueline asked.

"No." Audrey gathered the mugs and set them beside the cooling kettle. "Why don't you get some rest? You'll need it if we're going to head out in the morning."

Lou didn't need to be told twice. Even the tea hadn't warmed the chill in her bones, so she crawled into the sleeping bag, which smelled faintly musty, like sweat and feet. Beside her, Jacqueline slid into the other one. Vic offered his to Harlow, but she shook her head. "I don't think I can sleep."

Despite the leadenness of her limbs, Lou found her mind unable to lose itself to slumber. The overhead light switched off, but the desk lamp offered a soft green glow. She closed her eyes, listening to the faint whispers of Vic and Audrey from somewhere far away, their shifting movements.

She began to drift, still half-conscious but sinking, now, into the fuzzy realm of her mind.

Audrey struck her as anxious. Maybe a little twitchy. Her eyes were large but hooded, like a nocturnal creature, and her pallor did nothing to deter this impression. Her hair was a brown scraggle over her shoulder, and she looked as if it had been a little while since she'd washed up. Drugs? Lou wondered. They didn't behave like junkies, as far as she could tell, but she wouldn't be surprised if they were holed up here with a stash. Maybe they were out here mushroom harvesting, looking for psychedelics.

Whoever they were, whatever reason they had to be here, it didn't matter.

The door was closed. The Pseudo couldn't get in.

At least for now, they were safe.

TWENTY-FIVE

Harlow came awake all at once. Her head ached on the hard floor. The air smelled of dust and neglect. A light buzzed hungrily above.

She didn't know when she'd fallen asleep. She didn't even know where she was. It could be one of any number of off-brand motels they'd stayed at while touring up and down the coast. She couldn't even count how many times she'd woken up on the floor with a rockstar hangover, mouth foul with last night's excess, skull fit to burst.

Her mind drifted in a fog, slow to catch up. She felt groggy, disoriented.

"You're awake," came a voice. She blinked up at Audrey, sitting cross-legged nearby.

"What time is it?"

Audrey checked her watch. "A little after eleven."

The world tilted as Harlow sat up. Nausea roiled in her gut, but she was no stranger to that, and she managed to keep it down. "I thought we were going to hike to the road."

"You showed up so late last night." Audrey looked bright and fresh, but the red rims of her eyes betrayed a lack of sleep. "It was, what— three, four in the morning? We thought we'd let you sleep in." She pressed a mug into Harlow's hand. "Tea?"

Harlow gave an obliging sniff—earthy, a slightly different blend from last night's cup—and set it down. She wished it was coffee instead. Something with the perk of caffeine.

The lumps that were Jacqueline and Lou lay still, buried up to the nose. Harlow nudged their shoulders until they were both groaning themselves awake. Audrey offered them cups of tea, and Lou took hers with a nod.

Now that she was awake, Harlow wished she were asleep again. At least that had been blissfully, mercifully blank. Awake, her mind could not help but call up everything that had happened last night, which seemed like some awful nightmare: Rhys, bursting at the seams; Wendy, choking on her broken throat; the Pale Forms mimicking them; Thorn's scream. She felt like she could hear it still, and it made her want to tear her ears right off her head.

To distract herself, she looked around the room, noticing it in a way she didn't last night when she was high on terror, numb with shock. The walls were bare, crumbling with old paint worn gray. No windows. The air was stale, musty. Along the wall furthest from the entrance sat three more doors: the storage closet and two mystery doors. All three were closed.

Jacqueline lifted the mug to her lips, breathed in, then set it down. Her eyes were January-cold.

The front door belched open with a spray of wet morning light. When it closed, it snapped away the daylight as if it were never there, but it deposited Vic into the room, bearing a wicker basket and wiping a red-stained hand on his pants. Forest dirt had made its inescapable way into his clothes: staining his knees, the ends of his sleeves, the crusts of his fingernails. Without windows, the ceiling light burned him from above.

"Breakfast?"

Harlow looked from the basket to his red hands, wondered if there was something dead in there, if blood would start to pour through the wicker from the mangled rabbit inside, or Thorn's severed head, both eyes blind now. Her lungs seized. She couldn't breathe.

The basket lowered, and she saw what was really in there: berries.

"What are those?" she asked. "Blueberries?"

"Similar. Salal berries. And these ones are salmonberries." He pointed to a cluster of what looked like raspberries but paler, more of a coral color. "In a few months, there will be blackberries growing every-where, but it's a bit early for them now."

Lou popped a few into her mouth. "Oh my god, that is so good."

Despite her pounding heart and the swooping feeling only just beginning to fade, Harlow's stomach rumbled. She grabbed a handful. They were sweet and juicy, fresher than supermarket fare.

Audrey looked at Jacqueline. "You should have some. You'll need your strength. It's a decent hike to the road from here, and the terrain is somewhat unforgiving."

Nodding, Jacqueline reached into the basket and took a salmonberry, looking at it as if she didn't trust it. She still hadn't drank any of the tea. "We should get going."

"What's the rush?" Audrey asked. The lights gasped and flickered. She frowned at the ceiling. "Sorry about that. The generator is ancient. Doesn't always cooperate."

"Same thing happened at our cabin," Lou said as she grabbed another handful of berries.

"Why don't you point us in the direction of the road, and we'll find it ourselves," Jacqueline suggested.

The smile froze on Audrey's face. "Oh gosh, there's no way you'd find it. It's a limited access road, unpaved, very easy to miss. We'll have to take you. Go even a little off course, and you're heading into deep wilderness. It's incredibly easy to get lost. And then you've got to deal with ravines, cliffs, all kinds of things that make it even more difficult to navigate."

"If it's so hard to navigate, how did you guys find your way here?" Jacqueline pressed.

Audrey shrugged. "We stumbled on this place. Same as you."

"But what were you *doing* out here?"

"Camping."

"And you just... decided to stay in this weird old bunker?"

By now Audrey's smile had grown brittle. She crossed her arms, pulling her shirt taut. Clavicles stood out below her long neck. "What would you like me to say? That I lost my job because I was too busy taking care of my dying father? That I have nothing to go back to? Does that satisfy your curiosity?"

"Aud," Vic said, voice low.

"If you'd prefer to decline our hospitality and try to find your own way, there's the door." She nodded to it. "But don't forget what's out there. *Animals.*"

Harlow hadn't noticed Lou wandering around by the desk until she pointed to an old piece of machinery behind it and asked, "Is that a ham radio?"

Jacqueline looked up quickly. "Could we use it to call for help?"

Vic shrugged. "I can give it a try."

Harlow and Jacqueline came over to see the old metal box covered in dials, connected by a coiled cord to a handheld transceiver. It was dirty and corroded, but maybe it still worked. He fiddled with the dials, then spoke into the device: "Hello? Can anyone hear me?" He let go of the button, listened to silence. "I'd appreciate it if you wouldn't hover. I'll keep trying and let you know if I get anyone on the other end."

He seemed to know what he was doing, so they stepped away while he continued trying to reach someone over the airwaves. If he could reach the park rangers or sheriff, they would be able to send help directly. They wouldn't even need to make the trek to the road, at which point they would still have to follow it and hope it arrived somewhere useful.

Harlow pulled out her flask and remembered it was empty. She'd dumped it into the stove last night.

"Where does this door go?" Jacqueline asked, taking the handle of mystery door number one. Before Audrey could answer, she pulled it open to reveal a grimy little bathroom on the other side. The sight of the toilet reminded Harlow how full her bladder was.

"It won't flush," Audrey said. "The water doesn't work. Take it outside if you need to go."

Harlow, Jacqueline, and Lou went out the front door and separated into the nearby trees to release their bladders. By day, the forest felt less threatening. There was a cool, loamy breeze. Sunlight sparkled on dew. There were no voices. Harlow thought maybe the Pseudo was more active at night. It seemed to prefer the dark. Wasn't that the way with fungus? It thrived in moist, dark spaces? As long as they got to the road, or made it through to someone on the radio, before dark, they would be fine.

But a part of her—an awful, lonely, nihilistic part—wanted to see the Pseudo again. Even if it was only an imitation, she craved the sight of Thorn's face, the sound of Brynn's voice. They didn't have to be gone forever. If she stayed until nightfall, she could see them again. Lou and Jacqueline could go, but she thought of Audrey saying she had nothing to go back to and wondered: what exactly was waiting for Harlow at home? An apartment with Brynn's things still haunting the empty bedroom? A mother who would hate her even more now that she had let her only son die? Her shitty bartending job where she often snuck drinks on the clock, knowing she would someday be caught?

Maybe she should walk into the forest now, lose herself in it, wait for the dark to descend and the Pseudo to ensnare her.

Instead, she pulled up her pants and turned back to the sod-roofed mound.

As the three of them converged, they discovered the door yawning open, Audrey standing there with her arms crossed, waiting for them to come back in. "Didn't want you to get lost."

The contrast between the outdoors and the inside of the bunker was stark. Sunlight vanished behind the door, enclosing them in a room both stuffy and dim, motes of dust suspended in the dry air.

Shaking his head, Vic stepped away from the desk, his back still hunched from bending over the radio. "Nothing yet, but we can try again later. I'm sure we'll be able to get through to someone if we keep trying—and that will be better than hiking to the road. Much safer."

Harlow sank to the floor, boneless and drained, back against the wall. Jacqueline sat down next to her, close enough to touch. Just as Harlow was about to sidle away to keep a barrier of personal space, Jacqueline whispered from the corner of her mouth, "Do you know where your phone is?"

The question momentarily unmoored her. Why was Jacqueline asking about her phone? Why wouldn't she know where it was? "What's the point? It's dead anyway," she said even as she stuck her hands into her pockets—first her jeans, then her jacket—and came up empty. She knew she'd had it with her when they got here. Where had she put it?

"We can't trust these people," Jacqueline whispered, eyes locked on Audrey and Lou engaged in a conversation about the wild fruits growing nearby.

"Why would they take our phones?"

"If they did, they'll have put them somewhere. See if you can look around without seeming suspicious."

Harlow stood, stretching, while Jacqueline joined Audrey and Lou beside the camp stove and the backpack. Harlow didn't know how she was going to check inside the bag without arousing suspicion, but her presence did provide the perfect distraction for Harlow to slip inside the storage closet.

It went back a few feet with shelving on either side. The door ticked shut behind her, and for a moment she stood in a well of darkness. Then she found a dangling chain, pulled, and a dull yellow glow flickered on.

Two deflated duffel bags sagged beside an electric lantern gray with dust. Little else occupied the wire shelves, but even if it did, she wouldn't notice, because her attention lay on the hooks against the back wall, on the familiar shapes that hung from them—the large gray disks for eyes, the insectile mouthpieces.

She had seen these masks before.

FROM "WHAT EVER HAPPENED TO QUEEN CARRION?"

THE CURIOUS CASE OF ONE BAND'S SELF-DESTRUCTION

… killed in a bear attack. Oregon is home to somewhere between 25,000 and 30,000 bears, but attacks are few, and fatal attacks are even rarer. In fact, the state doesn't have any documented fatal bear attacks, unless you believe that Queen Carrion was, in fact, beset by a vicious bear on their trip to the Umpqua National Forest, which seems dubious at best.

After all, no bodies were ever recovered. Doesn't that seem a little strange? For there to be no remains at all? It isn't as if a bear would consume a person whole, bones and all.

It's as if they vanished, the way Brynn Werner had vanished a year before. But what are the odds of that happening twice? It seems to me like something has been covered up. Someone has covered their tracks to keep secret what really happened out there in the woods.

To add to these strange circumstances, Sorenson revealed to police that the group had stayed in an Airbnb called Trail Creek Cabin, but no records remain of any such property on the Airbnb website—or any other rental site, for that matter. If she was telling the truth, then what happened to this mysterious cabin, and why has it vanished from the internet? If she wasn't telling the truth, then why would she lie?

What was Harlow Sorenson hiding?

TWENTY-SIX

Jacqueline Price was not a trusting person. As far as she was concerned, everyone carried with them some hidden motive and would act first and foremost in their own self-interest if given the opportunity. Perhaps it is the untrustworthy who most readily spy untrustworthiness in others, like the ability to identify kin; whatever the case, so it was with Jacqueline.

It took very little—a passing glance, the whiff that they were holding something back—for any trust she may have had in Vic and Audrey to dry up and wither.

Now the mystery of the missing phones consumed her. It was no coincidence both she and Harlow (and likely Lou, if she asked) had somehow misplaced their devices. She imagined Audrey reaching into her sleeping bag, hand moving along Jacqueline's warm unconscious body to find where the phone had slipped from her pocket, then slowly extricating it to avoid waking her.

Despite the phone being dead, Jacqueline felt naked without it. Her phone was never far from her hand, ready to entertain her with videos and social media. Being without it heightened her senses, made her feel singularly untethered. Disconnected.

Alone.

She wasn't really alone, though: Lou and Audrey sat cross-legged by the camp stove; Vic hovered nearby, observing with eyes so black the pupils melted into the irises. As Jacqueline knelt down beside Lou, her movements became especially, consciously clumsy—elbows too pointed and abrupt, knees unsure of their location.

"So, what do you guys do out here?" she asked, keeping her voice light, making the question innocuous rather than interrogating. "Do you go hiking… hunting…?"

"Vic's a botanist." Audrey turned her face up to him. "He spends a lot of time observing and documenting all the different plants that grow around here. He's planning to get his PhD."

"Oh, that's cool," Lou said.

At this mild show of interest, Vic brightened. "I want to study comparative morphology. It's how we determine the evolutionary relationships between different plant species. Not only does that help us find out what organisms share common ancestors, but it can also help us cultivate and breed new kinds of plants too—ones that are more resilient or beneficial… or delicious." He chuckled and gestured to the nearly empty basket of wild berries.

"And what about you?" Jacqueline turned to Audrey.

"I like to read. Lots to catch up on."

"What kinds of things do you like to—" As she spoke, Jacqueline leaned back too far, fumbled for balance. She reached out to ground herself and grabbed hold of the backpack, pulling it onto its side. Its contents spilled to the floor: notebooks, clothing, a toothbrush, a pill bottle. With her other hand, she found the nearby mug of cold tea she'd left there and knocked it over, splashing a translucent brown puddle across the floor.

"I'm so sorry," Jacqueline said as Audrey lunged over and started mopping up the spilled tea with a shirt that had tumbled out of the backpack. Jacqueline's fingers found the pill bottle—white, something over-the-counter—and turned it so she could read the label. "Melatonin?"

Audrey paused her wiping, shoulders rigid. "It helps me sleep. My circadian rhythms get thrown off sometimes. I like to read late at night."

The bottle rattled in Jacqueline's hand. "Did you put this in our tea?"

The question made Lou set her mug down warily. Even the brief hesitation as Audrey finished soaking up the tea was confirmation enough for Jacqueline. When Audrey straightened, her jaw was set, eyes darting out from deep hollows. "You all looked like you'd been through the wringer. I thought it might help you sleep."

"So you drugged us."

Audrey scoffed. "Melatonin is hardly a drug."

"But you put it in the tea this morning, too, right?"

"Of course not."

But Jacqueline could tell she was lying.

"Look, I'm sorry," Audrey said, giving a little laugh. "I didn't think it was a big deal. It's just a supplement. I always find it soothing when I've had a bad night, and I thought you might too. You're acting like I roofied you or something."

"Maybe, like… tell us next time." Lou's voice was conciliatory. She was so trusting. She wanted to see the good in everyone. She wanted to believe the world was a more fantastic and hospitable place than it really was.

When Jacqueline looked up, she saw Harlow standing outside the door of the storage closet and tried to determine from the look on her face if she'd found anything in there. Her eyes were blank, mouth set into a vague frown. She suspected if Harlow had found their phones, she would be holding them, but there was nothing in her hands.

Though no phones had fallen out of the backpack, that didn't mean they weren't buried in a pocket somewhere. They had to be around here somewhere. She wondered again: why take them? Why put off bringing them to the road? What did these people want from them?

Audrey tossed the tea-stained shirt into an empty bucket while Vic gathered the mugs scattered around the room. He opened the front door and poured the liquid into the dirt.

As Jacqueline backed away from them, she found herself at the desk and sat down on the chair. Making sure no one was watching her, she slid open a drawer, thinking the phones might be there, but she found only a sheaf of stationery and a clatter of pens. She swiveled the chair to the radio and started turning dials, but she didn't see or hear anything happening on the device—no lights, no static. She found the cord at the back and followed it down to where it curled on the floor like a dead snake.

It wasn't plugged in.

That was it for her—phones or no phones. "We should go." She looked across at Harlow, whose eyes were wide, trying to communicate something.

But then Vic was inside again, the door shut, and he towered over her. He suggested they wait while he tried the radio again, positioning himself between Jacqueline and the room's only exit.

"What's going on?" Lou asked.

"Don't lie to me," Jacqueline said to Vic. "I know you didn't really try to call for help. I know you took our phones."

Then Harlow said what she had clearly been trying to communicate silently: "They're the gas mask people."

Jacqueline let out a surprised laugh. She'd almost forgotten—it felt so long ago, that morning hike, finding the figures in the gas masks by the creek as they filled their bucket, which she now recognized as the one that contained the shirt-cum-tea rag. She remembered telling Rhys about the strange encounter, but he was already sick at that point, already infected with the creeping fungus from the forest.

A sigh deflated Audrey. She reached under her large sweatshirt to the small of her back as if to press on an ache. "I'd really hoped it wouldn't come to this."

When her hand came back around, it was holding a gun.

<hr>

Time seemed to slow.

The black eye of the gun—a small snub-nosed revolver—bled into Jacqueline's vision, larger than it really was. She thought it funny how death could exist in such little things: the brief barrel of a gun, a switchblade concealed in the palm. It was so easy to make a choice—pull a trigger, slash a knife—that could not be undone, and she didn't put it past Audrey to depress that trigger on a whim, end her life as easily as a twitch of the finger.

Instead of shooting her, Audrey merely tilted her head to the final mystery door against the back wall—not the closet, not the bathroom, but the other one, which hadn't been opened yet. Obliging, Lou turned the handle and let it swing.

"Go on."

The threat of death urged them all to follow.

On the other side of the door lay an abbreviated hallway lit only by a red light to the left. Two steel doors stood under that light. Audrey reached over, pressed a button, and the doors slid open onto the interior of an elevator.

Another surprise. Where could an elevator go in this one-room bunker?

The answer—once Audrey handed the gun to Vic, who took it awkwardly and ushered them inside, then stepped in behind them—was *down*.

"Containment room 4-B," Audrey said, handing a plastic key card to Vic before the doors closed in her face.

He slid the card into a thin slot in the wall, then pressed the button labeled *4*. Jacqueline noted seven such buttons. Seven levels hidden beneath this unassuming mound of earth.

Where on earth were they?

With a jolt, the elevator began to descend. Sickly light fluoresced from the ceiling, buzzing down on them as they ground unsteadily downward.

Even with the weapon, it was three to one, and despite Vic's lumbering height, he seemed more nerd than jock. Jacqueline liked these odds. She lunged, reaching for the gun, but the solid metal struck her eye like the flash of a grenade, and the blow threw her head back into the steel wall, turning everything to bright static, a high whistle of pain.

"I'm sorry," Vic said. "You surprised me. Please don't do that again."

Her vision returned as the elevator lurched to a halt. The doors slid open onto a black abyss into which Vic ushered them. He threw a switch, and lights stuttered to life in a long room lined with smaller rooms, each with a large window looking in. The electricity here sounded like a brood of cicadas. Dull metal tables, desks, and cabinets hulked in the center of the room.

On the far wall: four people lurking, utterly still.

Jacqueline's exhale went back into her throat.

No, not people. Flayed human skins, suspended in the air.

She blinked, vision swimming from the blow to her head.

Another look revealed them to be some kind of protective lab suits, coveralls, a dingy, spoiled yellow.

Vic guided them to a door, which he opened with a puff of stale air. "Get in."

Jacqueline thought about trying to tackle him again. What were the odds he could get a solid shot off before she had him on the ground? But her head was like a mosquito zapper, and her vision had gone watery. Nausea spun through her.

She trailed the others into the containment room. The door hissed shut behind them. The room was small, maybe five feet by eight feet, and completely empty.

Lou sucked in a breath. She turned to the window to look out at the metal tables and cabinets under a failing light. "You guys." Her voice was a cold breeze. "I know where we are."

Jacqueline shook her head, trying to settle the painful thump behind her eye. "What? How could you possibly—"

Lou cut her off. "This is the Volker Institute."

AFTER

Harlow doesn't expect another visitor, but when she goes out to the rec room, she sees her, waiting: faded lavender hair, wide dark eyes, the tip of her tongue running over the edges of her teeth.

"Lou," she says, feeling time slip out of joint; the slate blue walls recede into the bilious sky behind a canopy of black spidery branches; the room stretches. Every shadow becomes a looming pine. "Why are you here?"

"Duh," Lou says, rolling her eyes. "Because you know what's out there. You can't just hide in here."

A slight young woman whose t-shirt drapes her like a tent grunts from the couch in front of the TV. An older woman, white hair like sparse cotton candy, wrests the remote from her and laughs. By the window, one of the men playing checkers plugs his ears, the better to ignore her.

"I'm not hiding," Harlow argues. "I'm institutionalized. They think I'm crazy."

A frown tugs Lou's face. She looks older. The grooves of the forest etched themselves into her skin like bark. "I mean, you did slice your arm open in a bar."

"You know why, though."

The way the light hits Lou's face, it seems to shiver. Like the snap of a lighter, the shock and shudder of a bonfire. It's the flicker of changing TV channels, the screen dancing from one to the next fast enough to cut off snippets of voices so they become almost inhuman. Or maybe it's because the ceiling light is going. It fluoresces and dies in heartbeats, which quicken in Harlow's chest. Where she isn't looking, the air seems to solidify into glass walls.

"Am I trapped here?" she asks. "Have I never left? Am I still in the Institute?" Her mind spins. Maybe none of this is even happening. Maybe she went crazy in the woods. "I feel like I can't tell what's real anymore." A tidal wave looms over her. She brings her hands to her face, pressing the heels of her palms into her eyes.

"When you experience something that seems impossible, reality gets hard to hold onto."

"No one believes me."

"What did you expect?" Lou snorts. "A bear attack, right?"

Laughter bursts from Harlow first, then Lou. They laugh themselves into tears. Eventually, Lou's stop, but Harlow's don't.

"I don't know… I don't…" The words can't make it out fully formed.

"Hey." Lou's hand hovers above Harlow's. "It's okay."

The older woman has landed on a channel. She clutches the remote to her chest and sits on the lumpy couch, transfixed by the TV. She found some non-broadcasting frequency, and now she sits watching the static. Watching nothing. Just the effervescent buzz of snow. Harlow can hear the sound of it in her bones, like thousands of tiny hair-thin threads scratching at her from the inside. Her skin itches. Somewhere in the droning froth of sound, the meaninglessness becomes voices. The voices from the woods.

Stop it, she tells herself. She wants a drink. The soft cushion of whiskey like a blanket for her brain. At least if she's drunk, she's not back there. She's not in the woods. At least the alcohol seems to kill those particular brain cells.

It's just that she keeps going over it, trying to rewrite it in her mind. What if she had stopped them from stepping inside that door when Audrey opened it? What if they had kept walking? They probably all would have died, she reasons. Maybe they could have turned around when the GPS cut out on the way to the cabin. Just gone back. None of it would have ever happened. She tries to fix it all in her mind, going even further back, sticking Band-Aids where the wounds are. She could have gone camping with Brynn. She could have stopped everything that happened after that. But then, if she's already doing this, if she's already letting herself rewrite reality in her mind, why stop there? If she had never told her brother they should start their own band, call themselves the Vile Hornets, would Queen Carrion ever have existed? If her parents had never divorced—well, her mom would never have let her get a drum set, that was for sure.

And if she never sat in the dark lighting matches with small, clumsy child's fingers? Delighting in seeing that spark of light abruptly blister the darkness?

She might as well go all the way back and wonder if she was never born.

And there is the smoking, blackened house at the end of her mind's world, waiting for her. She might go to it. There's nowhere else to go. When she steps inside, its disease will be contagious: she, too, will blacken and rot, her skin smoking as it chars and crumbles.

Come on in, the darkness is fine.

A burst of sound yanks her from the house. Fake swells of laughter. Some old sitcom. The younger woman has managed to steal the remote back and has changed the channel. The older woman howls at her.

"Brynn said she was cursed," Harlow says. "Maybe she was right."

"The curse didn't die with her, though, did it?" Lou rubs her leg with the phantom memory of pain.

Harlow struggles to keep her gaze on Lou. She won't look at the cracks snaking along the walls behind her. "Curses never die." She won't look, at least not directly, but the cracks are there all the same. "I'm seeing things that aren't there."

"How do you know they're not there?" Lou asks. "Maybe you're just the only one who can see them."

The cracks widen, yawn open. From somewhere behind them, in the recesses beyond the walls, thin white filaments, like hairs stuck in a comb, creep through and unfurl. They find their way through the narrowest slivers of space, through the veins and arteries of this world.

There are Low Places, sure, but there are also cracks in the foundation that can spread higher.

Harlow scratches at her healing forearm, at the itch coming up from underneath. She thinks of that long red slice of hyphae spilling from parted flesh. But it was only blood that spilled out in the bar. Maybe she should have dug deeper. Maybe it was lurking way down deep, wrapped around her chalk-pale bloodless heart.

Lou leans over the table toward her and says something Harlow doesn't catch at first. "What?" she says, but something inside of her *did* hear, because her heart is drumming again.

Lou's lips stretch into a smile, as if she's about to tell Harlow a secret. "If you're afraid, don't worry, you should be."

TWENTY-SEVEN

"What makes you think this is the Volker Institute?" Jacqueline asked.

Lou sank to the tiled floor. "How many hidden research facilities do you think there are in Oregon?"

Shadows clustered at the edges of the large room beyond, where the overhead lights—long fluorescent bars half burned out, the rest guttering feebly—struggled to reach. Old laboratory skins dangled from the back wall like hanged victims. Harlow looked across the room to the partitioned spaces on the other side and wondered how many of those windows were truly clear, and how many were two-way mirrors. She wouldn't be surprised if some of them were. At least they had been placed into a room with an actual window. Not being able to see out would have made her feel even more trapped than she already did. After sealing them inside, Vic had taken the elevator back up and left them here on their own.

She imagined this floor as it might have been forty years ago, with lab-coated scientists bustling around the desks at the center, moving from room to room with clipboards to observe whatever was happening within. Writing down notes on the various specimens they were testing.

Harlow tried to remember the details of the scanned documents they'd found in Brynn's notebook. She'd only glanced through them, their descriptions strange, black bars of redacted information interrupting the sentence flow.

"Vic and Audrey didn't stumble on this place. There's no way. They must have been looking for it." Lou looked around at them. "What do you think they're doing here?"

"Nothing good," Jacqueline said. "We need to find a way out." She pounded a fist against the window, then looked at Harlow, eyebrows lifted.

If anyone could put some power behind her blows, it was the drummer. But no matter how hard she punched, it didn't leave a dent. The glass was the kind of unbreakable polycarbonate-laminated stuff that could stop a bullet. Whatever this place once kept in these containment rooms, back when the Institute was running, they wanted to make damn sure it couldn't get out.

Shouting didn't do much, either, except echo in the small space. Even if their voices could penetrate the walls and the reinforced glass, who would be able to hear them?

The pummeling left Harlow winded, and eventually she gave up, leaned back against the wall.

Across from her, Lou sat chewing on the end of her thumbnail. "What if they found whatever the Institute was researching? Supposedly, there was some kind of accident that closed down the facility, and that's why it was abandoned. What if the thing that caused the accident was still alive?"

"I'd say they were morons for letting it out of its cage." Jacqueline ran her fingers around the edges of the door, desperately seeking a way out of *this* cage.

"Or maybe it was already out. Either way… maybe Vic and Audrey are studying it." Lou nodded to herself as she spoke. "Maybe they locked us up so that we don't interfere with whatever they're doing. They might have a good reason. We should hear them out—"

"Have they tried to explain their 'good reason?' No. Did they force us in here at gunpoint? Yes." Jacqueline whirled around. "Stop giving them the benefit of the doubt."

Harlow leaned her head back against the wall and closed her eyes. "What else can we do? There's no way out of here."

Jacqueline's voice dripped venom. "Then let's just give up, I guess."

For a moment, Harlow lost herself in the hush, and she wished Brynn were here to fill it, or at least her voice.

"Someone's coming."

She opened her eyes at Jacqueline's statement and looked out the window. Audrey stepped out of the elevator, washed-out in the unnatural light, skin sallow and broken out, yet there was something proud in her bearing, like a queen in her domain, autocrat of an abandoned underworld and all its defunct machinery. She flipped a switch on the wall, dragged a metal chair over, and sat in front of the glass with her knees slightly parted. Her posture was the hunch of an academic, someone whose hours pass in research, but she held the gun as easily as if it were a pen.

In a moment, her voice crackled through a circular arrangement of holes in the ceiling like the head of a sunflower. "Listen, I'm sorry about all of this."

"Why did you lock us in here?" Lou asked.

It must have been a two-way speaker because Audrey acknowledged her, even if she did not provide an answer. "I know it's not ideal, but we had to."

"What are you doing at the Volker Institute in the first place?"

Surprise slipped across Audrey's face. "How did you know?"

"Our friend was looking for this place, too," Lou said. "And we've been looking for *her*."

"Well, no one else has been here, so your friend didn't find it. We did." Audrey bristled with pride. "Now, why don't you tell me what really happened last night?"

Jacqueline snarled, "How about you let us out first?"

"I'm sorry, I can't do that."

"Why not?"

Audrey's fingers brushed the gun, petting it like a cat. "Because it isn't dark yet." She pulled out a bent pocket-sized notebook and a pen, flipped to a clean page, and looked up. "Now, tell me what happened to you at the cabin."

Harlow wasn't interested in playing this game, and Jacqueline clearly had no intention of giving Audrey anything she wanted, so it was Lou who began to recount the last two days: the way Rhys had fallen ill and then become something else, the way the Pseudo imitated the forms of those it had eaten. Audrey jotted down notes as she spoke.

"And you think it was mimicking them?" she asked.

"It was," Lou told her. "Perfectly. Down to their voices."

Audrey tucked the notebook away and looked up. "Thank you. That was very helpful."

As Audrey stood, Jacqueline banged her fists against the window. "What are you waiting for? Why are you keeping us in here? What do you *want* with us?"

"We can't do anything right now," said Audrey. "It doesn't seem to like the daylight. Nocturnal, I guess, if you can categorize it in such animal terms. I think it retreats back underground during the day."

"You already knew about this thing." Jacqueline rubbed at the reddened sides of her hands where she had slammed them into the glass. "So… what, you just wait around for people to stumble on this place so you can study them? Experiment on them?"

"Wait around?" Audrey's lips tugged into a smile. "Who do you think put up the Airbnb listing?"

Vic replaced Audrey in the chair. She told him she wanted to go compare notes, though what exactly she was comparing, Harlow hadn't a clue. She could see Jacqueline and Lou were still reeling from the knowledge that not only did Vic and Audrey know about Trail Creek Cabin, but they were the ones who had lured them here in the first place.

"You know we're famous, right?" Jacqueline said, voice raised so it would come clearly through the intercom. "We're a band. People are going to come looking for us."

Harlow didn't bother to correct her. *She* wasn't in the band. Then again, Queen Carrion was effectively dead if the only two surviving members were the bassist and the drummer.

The speaker played static.

"There are records of us coming out here," Jacqueline continued.

"Audrey's good at wiping things like that."

"Have you been watching us?" Lou asked.

A flash of guilt passed across Vic's face. "I haven't collected the footage yet, if it makes you feel any better."

"It absolutely does not."

After pacing the room—the cell, more like—Jacqueline turned swiftly back to the window. "I need to pee."

"Can't you hold it?"

She arched an eyebrow. "No. Would you like me to contaminate this room by pissing all over it?"

"Just… hold on." With a sigh, he stood. Audrey had passed him the gun when he replaced her as sentry, and now he held it up. "Just you." His eyes flickered to Lou and Harlow through the glass. "You two stay back, okay?"

Before Harlow could even think to jump to her feet, he had opened the door and pulled Jacqueline out by the arm, then slammed it shut and turned the lock. She followed compliantly to the elevator, and then they were both gone.

"Think they'll come back?"

"Of course they will," Lou said.

Harlow wasn't so sure. If Jacqueline got the opportunity to make a run for it, she probably would. Harlow wouldn't blame her, either. Why risk her life to come back down for them, two people who had often found her more of a nuisance than a friend?

"If they *do* come back," she said, thinking out loud, "I'd rather not just sit around."

"What should we do?"

The plan—if you could even call it that—was for them to stand on either side of the door. When Vic opened it, Lou would grab Jacqueline and drop them both to the floor while Harlow kicked the gun out of Vic's hand, punch him in the face, and generally pummel her way through him. Meanwhile, Lou would grab the gun and turn it on him.

"Easy-peasy," Harlow said.

"There's only about a million things that could go wrong."

"You got a better idea?"

She didn't.

Sooner than Harlow anticipated, the elevator doors slid open on Jacqueline—disheveled, red-faced, irate—and Vic urging her on with the gun. Something had happened.

They approached the door.

Adrenaline turned every instant bright and shiny, time tracing itself through the slow and heavy thump of each heartbeat.

Victor turned the lock and pulled open the door. As he did, Lou dove for Jacqueline, who didn't even have the chance to look surprised before she was taken by the shoulders and pushed down, as if Lou were trying to dunk her underwater. Their knees smacked the floor. Harlow jackknifed her leg, swiveling so hard to the side she felt, but did not see, her boot connect with the outstretched gun.

The air cracked and filled with the smell of burning. The gun spun out of Vic's hand, the report loud enough to crowd out everything else, turning Harlow's ears to wells of tinnitus. Her brain felt stunned, scrambled by the shock of the noise, the high ringing. She couldn't track where the gun had landed.

For a moment, she felt like she was underwater—sound muted, every move trapped in slow motion—as the others lifted their heads, dazed, making sure the bullet hadn't found its way into them.

Harlow sprang to her feet and pushed out the doorway, past Vic, who she forgot to punch, though he was still recoiling with his hands over his ears, and she had to wonder if he'd ever even fired a gun before. She darted out under the sputtering lights, the soles of her boots squeaking with a sound so distant she could barely hear it. Behind her, Lou and Jacqueline were only just climbing up from their knees, still inside the containment room.

Vic grabbed her from behind. She flailed, throwing him off and, in the process, throwing herself entirely off balance. The edge of a metal table cut into her brow, gouging a sharp crevice, and her head exploded. Her brain felt like it had been rattled against the edges of its cage. She flung out a hand to catch herself and latched onto a freestanding cabinet, which she pulled to right herself. It toppled over, landed with an explosion, spilling its contents: glass bottles collapsing into glitter, papers scurrying to the floor, a few of them whisking through the open doorway into the containment room.

The way ahead was clear. Harlow could make a run for it.

But the others were still in the room. Still blocked by Vic. She didn't even know who had the gun. The urgency in her brain told her to run, but her body refused to move forward. Suddenly she was back in the forest, leaving Thorn behind with the pale figures, leaving him to burn, to rot, to die—saving herself while he screamed.

She couldn't leave them behind. Preparing to tackle Vic, to sink her fists into his face, to do whatever it took to give the others an opportunity to escape, she turned back.

Vic reached under a table—reached for where the gun had skittered off—and then he had it in his hand, swiveling it up to Lou and Jacqueline in the doorway. They raised their arms and stepped back into the room.

Harlow stood where she was, panting, as he turned the gun to her. Warm blood dribbled from the cut on her head. Normal sound returned in increments.

"I don't want to shoot you," Vic said. "Please. Just get back inside."

Heart unsteady in its gallop, she swallowed dryly and did what she was told.

Once the door was shut again, Vic left them, probably to go tell Audrey what had happened. They were alone.

"Good try," Jacqueline muttered. "You should have kept running, though."

"What happened up there?" Harlow asked.

"I tried to take off once we were outside, but I didn't make it very far. He tackled me."

Harlow could see, now, the dirt on her elbows. "They're not going to let us go," she said as she sat, gingerly touching the hot, throbbing spot on her head. Across from her, Jacqueline's eye was blackening where she'd been hit with the gun, and Lou rubbed her knees where they had slammed into the unforgiving floor. Harlow couldn't help it: she laughed. It was almost funny, wasn't it? They'd made that whole trek from Trail Creek Cabin to get here, a place they thought would be their sanctuary, only to meet their deaths anyway.

"Yeah," Jacqueline said. "This is all super hilarious."

"What's this?" Lou picked up one of the stray papers that had flown out of the fallen cabinet. Several lay on the floor, and she gathered them into a pile. "There's stuff about the Institute here," she said as she flipped through them. "Look, it references what's on the different levels. Maybe there's another way out."

EP 21

BSL-4 Containment Breach Evacuation Protocols

The following containment breach protocols are in place for Levels 3-4, 6-7, per the classification system designated in Section 9 of the VI Handbook, in the following Events:

(a) In the Event of a Class 2 BSL-4 containment breach, all parties within proximity should proceed to the autoclave, remove protective clothing and place in biohazard bins, and continue to LL 1 for documentation.

(b) In the Event of a Class 3 BSL-4 containment breach, all parties on the floor should proceed to the autoclave, remove protective clothing and place in biohazard bins, and continue to LL 3 for decontamination and debrief.

(c) In the Event of a Class 4 BSL-4 containment breach, elevator access to lower levels 3-7 will be locked down using emergency protocol M-12. All parties in lower levels will proceed to emergency stairwell and continue to LL 5 for incineration procedure.

EP 22

Fire Evacuation Protocols

The following protocols are in place in the Event of fire:

(a) For small fires, use the nearest fire extinguisher (pull pin, aim, squeeze hand, sweep side to side). Use emergency phone to alert Director of Safety and Operations.

(b) For large fires, activate the fire alarm,

evacuate through stairwell (do not use elevator), and seal doors to contain fire. Follow fire evacuation procedures according to current Level:

(i) LL 1 - Proceed to LL 2 and use access points to residences. Await further instructions.

(ii) LL 3 - Proceed to LL 1. If cleared, use elevator to ground level.

(iii) LL 4 - Proceed to LL 3 and await instruction.

(iv) LL 5 - Shelter in fireproof control center, use emergency switch to deactivate incinerators and activate fire suppressant system. Notify Director of Safety and Operations via emergency phone.

(v) LL 6 - Proceed to LL 3 and await instruction.

(vi) LL 7 - Proceed to LL 3 and await instruction.

<u>Section 9</u>
9.1 CLEARANCE LEVELS

Clearance Level 0 - White. No access to operations information or lower levels.

Clearance Level 1 - Green. Limited facility access. Required for: janitorial, equipment engineer, and logistics personnel.

Clearance Level 2 - Yellow. Limited data and operations access. Required for: research technicians and clerical personnel.

Clearance Level 3 - Orange. Direct access to test subjects and containment data. Required for: laboratory research staff and security personnel.

Clearance Level 4 - Red. Direct access to live biological specimens and potentially hazardous material. Required for: biomaterials specialists, containment specialists, and senior laboratory research staff.

Clearance Level 5 - Black. Full access to sensitive data, classified document archives, site operations, and long-term materials storage. Required for: senior administration, site director, and cryogenic specialist.

9.2 LOWER LEVEL SECURITY ACCESS

GF - Entrance Lobby. Clearance Level 0. Controls external and emergency access to facility.

LL 1 - Operations Management. Clearance Level 2 entry, Levels 3-5 required to access document archives and management offices.

LL 2 - The Hub. Clearance Level 1.

LL 3 - Equipment. Clearance Level 1.

LL 4 - Observation. Clearance Level 3.

LL 5 - Incinerator. Clearance Level 1 entry,
Level 4 required for operation.
LL 6 - Vivarium. Clearance Level 4. Quarantine
and decontamination required for entry and exit.
LL 7 - Cryogenic Storage and Effluent Decontami-
nation System. Clearance Level 5.

TWENTY-EIGHT

The documents were about as illuminating as they were inscrutable—much like the scans Brynn had probably discovered in some obscure corner of the internet. It was a puzzle that occupied Lou's thoughts so she didn't have to contemplate being trapped in this tiny room four stories underground.

"Level 4. Observation." She looked up. "That's what these rooms are for." Her finger dragged along the page. "And look. Level 2, The Hub. This emergency protocols document says there are access points to residences there."

Harlow leaned over her shoulder. "Some kind of dormitories?"

"Do you think they'd want to house people *inside* the facility?"

"They'd need to keep everyone who worked here close, wouldn't they?" Harlow said.

"That's not really helpful though, is it, unless we can actually get to Level 2," Jacqueline said. "What we need to do is get out of this room and get the key card Vic used in the elevator."

"You're right." Lou sat back, frowning. "That's how you access the different levels. With the key card that has the right security clearance."

The lights did their little dance—a flicker, a twitch, a desperate buzz. The yellow suits seemed to shiver, making them appear strangely alive. Pockets of dark dropped half-seconds of emptiness, and Lou begged the lights to stay on. She imagined the power failing now, their blindness complete, stuck here without even Vic and Audrey able to come get them with the elevator frozen wherever it stood.

"But the elevator can't be the only way between floors," Lou murmured. "That's crazy. It's a fire hazard. There must be a staircase somewhere. Here—it says to use the stairwell."

She wished one of the pages that had wound up in their cell had diagrams or floor plans. Their vantage point was limited to the window's view, and though it was large enough to see much of the room beyond, the far wall seemed like it had hallways that extended further. She couldn't be sure. She had no idea where the stairwell might be.

The elevator doors clanged open, and Vic stepped out. He came up to their observation room, set down a bowl and a cup on the floor, and flicked the switch that operated the speaker. "Brought you something to eat." He flipped up a latch near the floor that looked like a prison food port, then slid the cup and bowl into the square of space that opened up beneath the window. Lou took them, and the port snapped shut.

"What is this?" Jacqueline asked.

Creek water filled the cup. Lou took a sip, relishing the cool liquid in her throat. She looked down at the bowl filled with dirt-speckled lumps.

"Porcini and oyster mushrooms," Vic said. "And I added some fiddle-heads, too, which I cooked on the stove, so you can eat them."

Lou took one of the green spirals and bit into it. It tasted a bit like asparagus, but not as sharp. As soon as she took a bite, she realized how hungry she was. Her stomach came to life, urgently requesting more, and she ate some of the mushrooms (trying not to mentally equate them with fungus) before passing the bowl to Harlow.

Without taking one, Harlow asked, "What time is it?" She passed the bowl to Jacqueline.

"About three o'clock," Vic said.

"And what's going to happen to us come nightfall?"

His lips pressed together. He gave no answer.

"You know what'll happen," Jacqueline filled in. "They're going to kill us."

Despite everything, Lou could not believe that. They were scientists, or at least Vic was. Clearly they were using Trail Creek Cabin to lure in test subjects so they could study their interactions with the Pseudo via the hidden cameras. Maybe they hadn't even realized how deadly it was. Maybe they were in over their heads and trying to figure out what to do next.

She thought of Wendy, Rhys, Thorn, and a hard lump formed in the back of her throat. Vic and Audrey couldn't have meant for that to happen. "You're not… you're not a bad person," she said to Vic. "I can tell."

Jacqueline swilled some water and cleared her throat. "Even serial killers can seem normal on the outside. You never really know."

Lou watched Vic carefully. He sat on the chair with his head down and hands together. No gun. Maybe Audrey didn't trust him with it anymore. She seemed to be more comfortable with it, anyway.

"You're *not* a bad person," Lou said again, hoping he would look up. "You don't need to do this to us."

His voice trickled through the speaker. "I can't let you go."

"Why not?"

"Because of Audrey."

"Why? What does she have over you?" Jacqueline said.

Vic shook his head. "You don't know what she's capable of."

"But you're not a killer," Lou tried again. "You're a botanist. That's why you're here, right?" She saw his eyes brighten, if only slightly. "What kinds of things have you found here, anyway? What makes this place so special?"

"It's unbelievable," he said. "There are things endemic here, to this very specific area, that no one's ever heard of—that no one's ever seen before. And there's so much the researchers who used to work here discovered. When we got here, a lot of the file cabinets had been cleared out, but there was enough left to give us tons of reading material. Audrey's working on cataloging what's left."

Lou didn't think he could see the papers on the floor of their cell, but still she slid the pile beneath her. "How big is this place? There are other levels, right? What did you find there?"

Suspicion colored his features, and Lou worried she'd pressed too much. Then a grim little smile cracked his face. "Why, you want to go exploring? I wouldn't recommend it. Something happened below five… we don't go down farther than that. The levels below are contaminated. Unsafe."

"And yet you stuck around," Jacqueline said.

For a long moment, Vic said nothing. His excitement about exotic plants went cold. His face was filled with ghosts. At last, he said, "There were four of us, originally."

"What happened to the others?"

Vic scratched the back of his neck, looking down again. "I mean, you have to understand how much Audrey wanted to find this place. She was determined. I don't think any of us really believed her about it until we saw it for ourselves. We didn't know what we'd find. I'd expected to spend some time in the woods, documenting different species. Eva studied biology. Greg did chemistry. But none of us were working in our fields. There aren't enough jobs. I mean, Eva taught, for a little bit, but she didn't make enough money to live on. We were all kind of desperate, adrift. And then Audrey said she was going to find the Volker Institute.

"It was amazing, at first. We'd found this goldmine of information that no one knew about. Eva wanted to take it public as soon as we got here. We'd all be set for life with this kind of find. We could write books about it, give lectures, get grants to continue whatever they were studying here… but Audrey was adamant about keeping it to ourselves, at least until we'd gone through everything. She made a good point. This stuff didn't belong to us. If whoever once owned this place was still around, they could snatch it all away before we could do anything with it. She thought it would be better if we knew exactly what we were dealing with before we said anything. She wanted to stay here to go through it all.

"But Eva hadn't signed up to stay indefinitely in an abandoned facility in the woods, with no running water, no cell service… and nothing Audrey said could convince her. None of us realized Audrey had brought a gun, either. She blocked the door and, kind of, threatened Eva. Forced her to stay."

"I knew she was a bitch," Jacqueline said.

"Eva realized she would have to sneak out when everyone was sleeping. She didn't make it very far. We woke up because we heard her screaming, and when we found her…" His eyes turned glassy. "Well, we only found half of her. The other half was… decomposing."

Lou sucked in a breath.

"Greg said we had to leave. We had to contact the authorities. Everything we'd found until that point was basically paperwork, but this was *real*. Audrey knew it had to be something the Institute had been studying. She said we needed to find the file for it before we did anything.

We had to understand it, whatever it was. There was no way Greg was going to stay. And there was no way Audrey was going to let him leave. When he tried to push her out of his way, and things got physical—she shot him."

"Jesus," Lou murmured.

"It hit him in the shoulder." Vic shook his head, rubbed his eyes. "But it was bad. He bled a lot. I thought she must have realized what she'd done because she opened the door and told him to go. The sun was just starting to set. I didn't realize she'd gotten the cameras to work, these old security cameras set up at the perimeter, but like I said, she's good with electronics. She was able to get the generator running for this whole place. She showed me the control center, and we saw Greg on the cameras, and… we observed."

Lou felt her skin, grimy with sweat and dirt, flush as heat rolled through her. They knew. They *knew.*

Vic and Audrey were going to kill them, and they were going to *watch.*

"Just let us go," Jacqueline said.

"Even if I did, you'd get lost out there. For every right direction, there are a dozen wrong ones. By nightfall, it will find you anyway. And the outcome is the same, except we gain nothing." He looked up. "Is that what *you* want?"

"Option three," Jacqueline said. "You lead us to the road, like you said you would."

"If I did that now, I wouldn't make it back before dark." He stood, turning from them. He was agitated. Frightened. Of course he was. He'd seen it—through a fuzzy black-and-white screen, the strange shape that grew out of the ground, bloomed across Greg's body as he kicked, screaming without sound, and the curdling of flesh, the way his body must have melted beneath its touch, until there was nothing left of him. Not even a body. Total annihilation. The only body left would be that of the pale mimic that from the loamy earth would sprout again the next night, and every night, to taunt them—unless they found other people it could taunt instead.

Harlow finally spoke up. "If you stay here, sooner or later, it will get you, too."

His expression suggested this possibility had already crossed his mind.

"This is such bullshit," Jacqueline said. "You people have no idea what you're doing. Clearly you're not *actually* scientists. You're a couple of frauds. Playing pretend." She slid the half-empty bowl back through the port, eyes locked on Vic, who also refused to look away even as he unlocked the hatch on his side and reached in for the bowl. As he did, Jacqueline's hand snapped out and she grabbed him by the wrist, pulling until his arm bent through the port, pulling until he was pressed up against the glass, wide-eyed, her fingernails digging into his skin. A vicious smile quirked over her lips.

"If you don't open this door, I'm going to start breaking your fingers."

He pulled, but her grip was unrelenting. She bent his wrist around the edge of the opening to lock him in place.

"What do you think… pinky first?" She struggled to keep his arm in place as he flailed, pressing her knee to his wrist to pin him there. Almost tenderly, she took his pinky finger and bent it backward, pulling the flesh taut. With one sharp thrust, there was a crack like a stick breaking in half, a second of silence, and then a wail that echoed strangely through the speakers. Tears squeezed down the sides of Victor's cheek, pressed to the glass, his mouth fishing open.

"How many fingers will it take?" Jacqueline asked as his moans died away. "Two? Three? All of them?"

His head shifted back and forth, trying to tell her no, even as Jacqueline took hold of his ring finger, the pinky dangling, loose and crooked beside it. "I'm not going to stop until you open the door."

She pushed the finger back.

"Okay, okay!" he cried. With his free hand, he reached to his side, stretched his arm out, fumbled with the lock and handle. The door clicked and swung gently outward.

"Thanks," Jacqueline said—right before she slammed the heel of her hand down on his ring finger.

TWENTY-NINE

Screams ricocheted through the observation level as Harlow pounced on Vic, holding him down—not that he resisted much, too busy wailing over his broken fingers jutting out at wild angles, swelling purple like fat worms—while Lou dug through his pockets until she came up with the key card.

Leaving him prone on the floor, they ran for the elevator. Jacqueline frantically pressed the button again and again until the doors belched open. They fell inside, collapsing against each other at the far wall, then had to fumble to get the key card into its slot.

Harlow pressed the button labeled *GF*—Ground Floor.

The doors groaned as they slid shut. In the narrowing gap, she saw Vic struggle to his knees, clutching one hand in the other, his mouth open. Then he was gone, and the elevator squealed and rumbled as it ascended.

Above the doors, they watched the glowing red number shift from four to three, then three to two. The elevator stuttered and whined. Harlow worried its old gears and wires would break and send them plummeting to the bottom.

The number changed from two to one.

The elevator slowed. Ground to a halt.

Jacqueline hit the *GF* button again, but the doors were already peeling open. Audrey stood waiting on the other side, her eyes capturing them like the shutter snap of a camera, her gun already raised, aimed.

Audrey held a walkie-talkie to her mouth and pressed the button. "It's okay. I've got them." Static crackled as she clipped the device to her pants and shifted both hands to the gun.

Harlow knew what she would do next: bring them back down to that same little room and lock them inside. And this time, they would never get out.

Well, she was sick of being locked up.

Her life had been a cage: her mom's house and its distrustful warden, the burned house in her mind that imprisoned her childhood memories, the barbed wire snare of regret that snaked around her. Even if it meant taking a bullet, she would not return to that enclosure down on level four.

Before the elevator doors could begin to close, she shoved her way through the opening and rushed at Audrey, taking her by surprise. Plowing into her, Harlow stumbled, sending Audrey to the floor where the brown carpet—some industrial-grade low-pile—just barely cushioned the crack of her skull.

The central space was lined with doors to offices and storage rooms. Hallways cut canals of darkness into the buttermilk walls.

The others followed Harlow out of the elevator. Jacqueline threw herself to the floor, wrestling with Audrey for the gun. "Come on!" Lou said, pulling Harlow further into the room. She tried a door. Locked. The next one opened, and they ducked inside, flipping on the light to reveal an office lined with filing cabinets, a desk bearing the dust-gauzed cube of an '80s-era IBM. Lights bore down from the ceiling panels, bright but for one that sputtered with mosquito-zapper frequency.

As Lou began yanking open desk drawers, Harlow asked, "What are you doing?"

"I don't know! Looking for anything that might help us."

A glance out the door revealed Audrey and Jacqueline still tussling on the floor, the gun swinging in erratic arcs, grasping fingers perilously close to the trigger.

Harlow joined Lou at the desk, pulling open a drawer and shoving papers aside. Beneath them lay another key card, which she pocketed, and a stapler, which she snatched up. It was heavy, made of metal. She leapt over the desk and out of the office—stumbled toward the figures on the floor, where Audrey was getting the upper hand, pinning Jacqueline beneath her—and slammed the stapler into the back of Audrey's head.

She collapsed to the side, somehow still clutching the gun, refusing to let it go.

Jacqueline stared up at Harlow, panting. "Thanks." She took Harlow's outstretched hand.

"Watch out!" Lou shouted from the office doorway.

Instinct made Harlow duck as the gun fired, the aim wild from Audrey's position on the floor. The bullet punctured the wall next to Lou, pluming plaster dust into the air.

They took off.

Down a hallway, they put as much distance between themselves and Audrey as possible. But that also meant they were moving farther from the elevator, deeper into the facility.

The hallway turned a corner and ended with a nondescript door. Lou pushed it open with a weighty groan on hinges that sang with disuse. "Stairs."

She was right: just beyond lay a stairwell. The light was thin. Metal steps turned abrupt corners along walls that shone a dull green. On the other side of the door, though, when Harlow turned away from the passage downward to head up, she found herself confronted with a concrete wall.

"What?" Jacqueline slammed her palms against it. "No!"

Behind them, the door that had swung shut began to open again. Jacqueline threw her back against it to hold it closed.

"What do we do?"

The door pushed against her back as Audrey shoved it from the other side, and with a wordless look between them, they bolted down the stairs.

Steps rattled under their feet, the metal banister swaying with loose screws. They could only see as far as the immediate half-turn of the stairwell. Its rusted creaking threatened to send the whole structure tumbling into the abyss below.

Above, the door banged open, followed quickly by another gunshot.

The echoing report, the clang of their running, all of it reverberating tenfold up and down this seven-floor stairwell turned the world into cacophony, someone knocking over a dozen drum kits and kicking them. Harlow careened through each turn, long legs taking her down level after level, body on autopilot—

The door marked 4 swung open as she passed it, and Vic—face bloodless, eyes shot through with red spiderwebs—tumbled out, grabbing at her. Limbs tangling, they both fell, the metal stairs jarring Harlow's elbow, her knee. Jacqueline and Lou sailed past as she tried to rip Vic's hands off her. Spotting his purple fingers, she took hold of them and squeezed, eliciting a scream. His other hand let go of her. When she had gained her footing, she stomped on his broken hand, then fled down the stairs after the others.

They were nowhere to be found.

She could hear Audrey's steps clanging down the stairs above and knew she would be here in moments. One more level down, Harlow grabbed the handle of the door marked 5 and pulled.

Locked.

Then she remembered the key card in her pocket. There was a slot above the handle. She pushed it in, and the door clicked open.

The room smelled of stale ash.

A faint red glow issued from somewhere ahead, enough light to tell she stood in a vast open space. No hallways or containment rooms on this level.

She took a moment to catch her breath, let her eyes adjust to the low light. Her head throbbed dully, and her ears still rang with the clang of gunshots and metal stairs.

"Lou?" Despite the softness of her call, it reverberated around the empty space. "Jacqueline?"

The echo died to nothing.

Her footfall resounded where boot met concrete floor. A suspended metal ceiling hovered high above. Following the wall, Harlow saw a row of grimy blue and yellow bins, followed by racks of lumpy red bags with black labels composed of three interlocking circles. More yellow skins hung from the wall like deflated bodies.

That burnt, acrid smell was everywhere. The air was thick with it, fine particles swimming lazily against the red lights. It stung her nostrils and sent her gut roiling, as the smell of burning sometimes did.

She stepped into the burnt house in her mind, blackened but still smoking. She could smell Thorn's burnt flesh like roasted pork. In her mind, a shadow peeled from the wall, and though only part of his face had burned, she found herself looking at Thorn's charred corpse, reanimated, eyes like tiny moons staring out from the crumbling charcoal shell. Her eyes conjured him in the low light, and out of the thick silence, her ears rendered the growl of his voice inquiring why she had left him there to die.

The house stretched out around her, or what was left of it. A jaundiced haze gave alien form to dark and twisted shapes. Ash swirled, powdering the crumbled foundation with strange snow, white as chalk. Stepping into the blackened structure, Harlow began to recognize familiar details in the unnatural gray soup, like seeing human bones unclothed by skin, stark and naked and *wrong*. Kitchen appliances lurking amid destroyed cabinets. A molten lump where the armchair once sat. Everything was ruined. Their home—its rooms dusty with untidy living and sagging couches, piles of mail, cords snaking into outlets, all the things that were the hallmark of a home well-lived-in—was gone. Guilt crawled up from Harlow's gut. She reached into her memories and came up only with obscuring smoke.

Thorn loomed in the mist, ash settling on his dark hair, turning it white. Harlow squeezed shut her burning eyes. "I'm sorry." She felt the heat of his breath on her face and caught a whiff of his Winston cigarettes, but when she opened her eyes, he was gone.

The black house receded into her mind and closed itself up even as the smell remained. She recalled Brynn telling her once that out of any human sense, smell has the strongest connection to memory, the olfactory bulb connected directly to the amygdala where emotion is stored. Harlow wished she couldn't smell anything.

She was alone in an unfamiliar, underground room that was not her childhood home. The ceiling stood high above. Taking up most of the space before her was a piece of machinery composed of huge metal tubes surrounded by scaffolding. It went all the way up to the ceiling. Decades of abandonment had rendered it rusted and dull.

Level 5. The Incinerator.

She came around its side, finding an open metal container the size of a dumpster at the end of a chute. It was filled with pale powder. Ash.

Of course—that's where the smell came from, haunting the air even though it must have been sitting here for years. Small chunks sat in the otherwise fine powder, and Harlow brushed at it, coming up with what looked like small white rocks.

They must have used this to dispose of potentially hazardous substances. Maybe to destroy specimens similar to the one at Trial Creek Cabin—the one that looked like Wendy, which Harlow and Thorn had shoved into the woodstove, watching it burn. A brief thought crossed her mind that she shouldn't be touching the ash with her bare hands, but it didn't bother her enough to pull away.

There must have been several cubic feet of ash, at least, in the container. She thought of all the things that had to have burned in order to accumulate this level of debris. As she sifted, she came across a larger chunk that hadn't fully burned, somewhat curved, smooth. She brushed it clear, saw a rounded hole in it, and realized it was not a rock.

Red light glared down on the eye socket, the partial skull embedded within the pile, and Harlow reeled away, wiping her hands on her jeans, feeling the grit still stuck beneath her fingernails.

She had assumed all the ash in the container came from specimens, but it was people.

They had incinerated *people*.

Hurrying away from the hulking machine, past the bags of biohazard waste, she followed the red light, hoping to reach the elevator. She clutched the key card in her hand, willing those silver doors to appear. She didn't want to spend another minute alone here with this dormant dragon waiting to awaken after its long slumber and breathe fire onto her.

Lou and Jacqueline had to be *somewhere*. She had to find them.

Before she could, however, she heard a voice call her name.

CATALOG OF COLLECTED
SPECIMENS UF-100 – UF-199

The Volker Institute is a subsidiary of Escher
Industries, Inc. All contents and data herein are
the intellectual property of, and may not be
reproduced except by, Escher Industries, Inc. and
its subsidiaries. The following proprietary information is for research purposes only.

Contents:

THIRTY

Lou spiraled downward.

Something knocked on the back of her mind, telling her she wanted to go up, not down, but right now she had no choice, since *up* led to Audrey with the gun, and by now Lou knew she was perfectly capable of shooting them if she wanted to.

But Vic and Audrey didn't go down past level 5. Maybe they wouldn't follow her. Maybe the danger below would deter them, but as for Lou—well, she would have to take her chances.

Without any other choice, she ran down the stairs, sneakers skimming the bumpy metal, until she hit the bottom.

Another dead end. To her right stood the door to Level 7.

She had the key card, which bore a little black square in the corner —that was the highest security clearance she'd seen on the document, wasn't it? Sliding it into the slot, she held her breath, hoping it would work.

The door gave a mechanical whine and clicked. She pulled. The hinges squealed in protest, but the door opened. She bolted into the dark, driven by adrenaline.

Her heart pounded in her ears. She didn't even hear the door slam behind her and couldn't see where she was going until she nearly ran into a tall metal box.

Silence.

She turned, realized Harlow and Jacqueline were not behind her.

For a moment, she considered going back out to find them, but what if Audrey and Vic were there, right outside the door, waiting for her? What if Harlow and Jacqueline were already dead?

The air was chill. All dark, but for a few dusty beacons hovering in the nothing, like streetlamps spaced across the stretches of a country road. Pools of shadow thickened in the empty space, and Lou thought of the Wonder Room, its impenetrable dark, the nothing into which she had been transported.

A shiver wracked her body. Not just a chill: the air was like ice. She waded toward the beacons of light, which shone on those gray boxes, rows and rows of them, with vents at the bottom, each one labeled a series of numbers.

A memory, abrupt as a struck match, sprang to life: she and Thorn playing video games between concerts. Him telling her, "You can hide here," as the character crept into a cabinet or a locker, watching through the slats for the monster to pass. These would be big enough to hide in if a monster came stalking through the dark.

She grabbed the handle of the nearest box and unlatched it, the door hissing open onto metal racks lined with labeled jars. Though the inside was the same temperature as the outside, the power no longer sustaining the container, Lou realized it was a freezer.

The lower-level security access document, which she'd tried to memorize, swam to the surface of her mind.

Level 7. Cryogenic Storage.

Overwhelmed by curiosity, she reached into the freezer and took a jar, turning it to see the label. UF-23. Time and warmth had clouded its contents, fermenting whatever was being preserved into black sludge.

In the silence, she heard a faint sound: the squeal of a door opening. Hope ballooned in her gut. She opened her mouth to call out, but another voice beat her to the punch.

"I know you're in here."

Audrey.

Lou shrank back against the freezer. The jar slipped from her hand and shattered, spreading a liquid pool through the broken glass. She leapt away and realized Audrey would have heard. Footsteps pounded in her direction.

Fleet of foot, quietly as she could, she hurried down the row of freezers, found another corridor leading off in a new direction, another row of freezers extending into the dark.

It settled into the pit of her stomach.

If every one of those jars contained a specimen like the one Harlow had captured in the wine bottle—and every freezer contained a dozen of these jars…

Exactly how many invasive species had been preserved down here?

Careful not to touch another freezer, she eased down the corridor. Her breath was too loud in her ears, her footsteps like the clomping of elephants. Even her heart seemed to pound out of proportion, and she was sure Audrey could hear its every beat.

"You know it's not safe to be down here," Audrey's voice drifted ethereally down the storage-lined halls. Lou tried to gauge how far away she was, but the echo prevented any clarity on distance. She tried to keep to the darkness, even knowing anything might be lurking there, even wondering if the darkness might snatch her and pull her away into the abyssal realm that lay beneath this Low Place.

Passing here was like moving through an alien crypt. More corridors, more turns, and she lost track of which way she'd come from, each hall identical to the last. The fear of getting lost—seven levels beneath the earth, in a freezing and barely illuminated labyrinth filled with bizarre things preserved in jars—warred with the fear of Audrey finding her.

She was shivering hard now, the cold seeping into her bones. She pressed her teeth together so they wouldn't rattle.

She remembered Wendy poking fun at her for having a low tolerance for the cold. "Your skin is too thin," she'd said with a laugh, giving Lou a delicate little pinch.

Thinking of Wendy left frost crystallizing the edges of her heart.

Though she couldn't hear her, she knew Audrey was stalking somewhere, ready to shoot. She couldn't keep wandering. She had to find somewhere to hide.

Perhaps she could fit herself into an alcove between two freezers and sit there, snug, in the dark.

"If you three want to play hide and seek, I'm game," Audrey said, closer than Lou had expected, making her heart jolt. Her words offered a spark of hope, though—*you three*. That meant she hadn't already killed Harlow and Jacqueline. She thought they were down here with Lou. They were out there, then, somewhere.

Trying to make herself as stealthy as a cat, Lou crept to the end of the corridor and picked a new direction, but there were no freezers here. At the end, she found a doorway to a pit of darkness. She hesitated at the entrance—one step, and she might slip out of reality altogether—but surely Audrey could never find her in here.

Holding her breath as if about to plunge into a cold pool, she stepped inside.

She kept the wall beside the doorway at her back. Her eyes gazed blindly into the void, and thus deprived, began to conjure awful shapes: broken jars spilling toxic contents into the air, half-formed pseudo-creatures crawling out of cracks in the walls, the mask-like face—or face-like mask—that had pressed up from the other side of the smoke with Brynn.

Her back slid against the wall as she sidled away from the door. The sharp bones behind her shoulders scraped a small protrusion from the wall, which clicked, and the ceiling lights sputtered on.

A burst of terror—Audrey would see the light, she would know Lou was in here—nearly compelled Lou to shut the light back off, but her curiosity, and the deeper fear of sending herself back into that abyss without first seeing what was in the room with her, stayed her hand.

Not broken jars or grotesque creatures, but a large device with metal barrels and piping, indecipherable gauges and knobs.

On the other side of the room, though, was another doorway— another hall—and without bothering to shut off the light to hide her movements, she darted around the hulking machine and into the hallway.

Behind her, footsteps followed.

At the end of this hallway, she saw something that made her gasp with relief.

The elevator.

She called it with a few frantic pushes of the button, Audrey's pursuing footfalls ricocheting off the walls as the elevator rumbled down the shaft.

The doors slid open just as Audrey shouted from down the hallway behind her, "Stop!"

Lou ducked into the elevator, turned to the row of buttons. The ground floor was like a siren song, but she knew Harlow and Jacqueline had to be on another floor, and she couldn't leave without them. She fumbled the key card into its slot while Audrey appeared, fury twisting her face, blood running down from her hairline into one eye from where Harlow had bashed her with the stapler. The doors began to close. Her mouth twisted into a mad rictus as she raised the gun.

The shot was like a bomb going off in the enclosed space. Deafening.

Suddenly Lou was on the floor, feeling like she'd been hit with a sledgehammer.

She looked down and realized she was sitting in a growing pool of blood.

THIRTY-ONE

The door to level 7 closed behind Lou before Jacqueline could reach it. Pulling the handle did no good, as the lock had already engaged. She pounded on it, but when it did not reopen immediately, she realized Lou was not coming back for her.

Though she couldn't exactly blame her—if given the opportunity, Jacqueline wouldn't go back for Lou—the closed door still left her full of foul feelings for Queen Carrion's bassist.

On the stairwell above, Harlow and Vic struggled against each other. Jacqueline backtracked one level and tried the door, though she expected it, too, would be locked. To her surprise, the door to level 6 swung right open. The handle hung loose in its socket, the door somewhat out of joint.

Just ahead stood another steel door, this one with a wheel set into it, but it stood ajar. At its top was a faded sign that read: Proceed with Caution. Hazardous Material.

Closing the door behind her, she pushed through the second one, wondering if all the levels had this additional barrier and warning. She blindly felt the walls on either side until she slapped a paddle switch. A solitary light struggled to life, brightening and failing before finding a mostly steady glow. The other lights seemed to be burnt out.

More empty suits hung nearby, along with respirator masks and safety goggles too grimed over to see through. Jacqueline took a step, and her shoe crunched on shattered glass.

This floor seemed to be set up like level 4, with enclosures along the walls, but where the observation rooms on level 4 had used a window to see in, these seemed to be made entirely of glass—and most of them that she could see were badly cracked or completely smashed open. Damp walls glistened, furred with moss or lichen. Black, rusty stains sprayed the floor.

It wasn't only abandonment that tanged the air, but something more. Something sweet, musky, vegetal.

This space had been closed up for—well, who knew how long? So why did it seem like there was something *alive* down here?

The idea prickled hairs on the back of her neck to standing. Yes, she was sure something was in here with her. The feeling reminded her of Friday night, when she had first glimpsed Brynn in the woods and had allowed the panic and paranoia to crash over her, brain trying to disbelieve what her eyes had seen. She'd thought it an impossible sight because Brynn was *dead*. She *knew* she was dead.

Now the world had shifted on its axis. Things she once thought impossible weren't any longer. The dead could return. No wonder Vic and Audrey wanted to harness its power. Jacqueline supposed anyone who had ever lost someone would want the power to revive the dead.

She wanted to laugh. She had been so careful, but it didn't matter. Brynn was still lurking in the woods. It was a wonder she hadn't divulged to everyone what had really happened to her. Then again, the thing mimicking her probably did not retain her memories.

Small comforts.

She crept forward, between the destroyed enclosures. The light sputtered over pale mushrooms sprouting from concrete walls, playing tricks with their shadows, making shapes where there were none. Striations of brown and red climbed the broken glass in spidery veins, roots growing over all these man-made structures, reclaiming them. The air seemed to breathe. It was thick with the smell of rot and earth.

Something pale skittered into the recess of a hallway, or else it was just the flickering light. Jacqueline's tongue felt heavy in her too-dry mouth. "Is anyone in here?" she called out, not expecting a reply. Her voice deadened in the air, fell away, gave nothing back.

She remembered, then, what level 6 was.

The Vivarium.

Hadn't Vic said the lower levels were contaminated? Maybe that's what shut down the Institute in the first place. Whatever it was, though, it was not connected to the Pseudo—it couldn't be. It had been trapped here for decades.

That lone defiant bulb gave an electrical pop and died.

Darkness.

From somewhere far away—so far that Jacqueline had to wonder how large this level stretched before her—she heard an echo belatedly return her question: *"Is anyone in here?"* The voice sounded like nothing human, like rubber trying to squeak out words against a chalkboard, like someone sounding out a language they did not understand with vocal cords made of catgut.

She had to get out of here.

But the darkness was absolute, and she had turned enough times to lose track of the way back to the stairs.

Moist sounds dripped around her. Soft, slow, squelching movement.

This whole time—even after being locked up, even after watching Rhys die—Jacqueline had been certain, somehow, that she would survive this. She would do whatever it took to get out of here, and this thought brought her comfort. Even when the way was uncertain, she had never once truly thought she might die.

Now she realized just how close she might be to death, and a kind of leaden horror swelled in her gut.

All her life, she had felt like an outcast. No close friends. No one who'd ever really understood her—not even Rhys, if she was honest. And now she was going to die six stories underground, alone and utterly forgotten. At least Brynn had something to be remembered by. At least Brynn had gotten to be Queen Carrion.

Jealousy replaced horror, burned like a flame.

She started to sing—the new song, Rhys's song, *her* song—and her voice floated and echoed in the dark, cushioned her as she moved through it.

Something began singing with her when she repeated the song, recognizing it the second time around. A rough saw of a voice.

At least she could hear where it was now. Her teeth clicked together.

And she saw it, too, at least in silhouette—for a shard of light suddenly pierced the dark ahead of her as two doors parted, and the yellow spill backlit the amorphous shape with many limbs, like flapping tongues, before it shrank and squealed away into the dark.

In the wake of her and the creature's duet, the light emitted a piercing scream.

Inside the elevator, Lou slouched back against the wall with one leg extended and one curled beneath her, sitting in a pool of tacky blood.

Jacqueline leapt between the open doors and crouched to assess the damage. Sweat sheened Lou's face, which had gone gray. Her leggings were soaked red, a hole punching through the thigh. "Let's get out of here," Jacqueline said, rising to face the buttons. Lou's key card—the one she'd gotten off Vic—still sat in its slot.

"Harlow…" Lou panted, seeming to have screamed herself out.

Jacqueline shook her head. "Not with me."

"We… we need to check…"

"Every stop is an additional risk."

"*Please*…" Lou gulped. "I left Audrey… on seven…"

Squeezing her hands into fists, Jacqueline sharply exhaled through her nostrils and pressed the button for level 5. "There. Happy?"

The doors met in the middle, and the elevator gave its mechanical whine as it lurched up a floor. As soon as the doors squealed open, Jacqueline prepared to send them up the rest of the way, but still she gave a cursory shout into level 5, not expecting a response.

"Harlow?"

Her finger hovered over the button to close the doors, then pressed down just as Queen Carrion's drummer came sprinting into the elevator, the doors clipping her heels as they closed. She threw herself upon Lou, hands dancing over her with concern, asking what had happened.

"Audrey," Lou gasped, breath shuddering in and out. "She was with me on seven… she'll probably use the stairs… to get back up…"

Jacqueline stared at the changing numbers above the elevator doors, willing them to decrease faster.

5… 4…

All they had to do was make it to the ground floor before either Audrey or Vic called the elevator from the other side on one of the floors they were passing. As long as they could get the elevator to the top and hold it there for even a moment, they would have the head start they needed.

3… 2…

The grinding squeal of gears decades out of date did not inspire confidence. The elevator lurched and slowed, bringing them up in uneven bursts that must have jarred Lou's wound with the way she hissed, the high whistles of pain she let loose.

The elevator crawled past level 1.

And then the doors—almost unbelievably—were opening at the ground floor, onto that tiled hallway that led out to the lobby where they'd all slept last night, and the door that opened onto the woods, the wide-open world.

Though Jacqueline wanted to run to freedom, she forced down this instinct to grab one of Lou's arms while Harlow took the other, and together they hefted her up. A single step out of the elevator left Lou howling, tears slipping down her face, her right leg crumpling beneath her. They dragged her down the hall as the elevator doors closed and its gears whirred to life, lumbering back down into the bowels of the facility. By the time they made it to the front door, they had already left a significant trail of blood in their wake.

"I can't," Lou moaned even as Harlow assured her they would not leave her behind.

Jacqueline turned the lock, and late afternoon sunlight washed over them, gold trickling through the canopy. She pulled Lou's arm over her shoulders, and they limped out into freedom.

She could not help but feel they were moving too slowly. Every step was painstaking, every breath a moment too long spent in the vicinity of the Volker Institute. Insects whirred in the trees, keeping a brisk tempo as if to highlight how little they could move with each step, saddled together like this.

They had gone perhaps ten paces from the mound when Jacqueline heard heavy footfalls behind them. She looked over her shoulder.

Vic and Audrey must have gotten to the elevator once they'd vacated it, and now they stepped outside, Vic still cradling his purple fingers, two of which had ballooned to limp sausage links. Audrey held up the gun.

"Will you *stop?*" she shrieked. "Who else do I need to shoot?"

She and Jacqueline locked eyes, and Audrey's seemed to say: yes, you. She recognized that look, and she knew if she didn't move, Audrey would shoot her as easily as anything, and it wouldn't be in the leg, either.

Before Jacqueline could duck out from under Lou's arm, though, Vic stepped between Audrey and the others. "What the fuck are you doing?"

"Hobbling them," she said. "It will make it easier."

He threw himself at her, pushing her arm up, forcing her to fire a shot at random into the sky. The crack echoed. A flurry of squawking birds erupted from the branches.

Here was their moment, free and clear: instead of letting go, Jacqueline gripped Lou's arm more firmly and *pulled*. She and Harlow dragged her like some kind of five-legged creature, into the forest, sheltered and shadowed by an inverted sea of leaves and pine-fractaled branches, away from the Volker Institute and into the trees.

THIRTY-TWO

It wasn't long before the crunch of footfalls caught up with them.

They hadn't made it far—couldn't go fast enough with Lou sandwiched between Harlow and Jacqueline, color draining from her face—and when Harlow heard the pursuing tread, she ducked free of Lou's arm and turned.

Her head was pounding, as if someone had driven a spike through her eye; she felt giddily delirious with exhaustion, body humming like a struck tuning fork; an ache radiated from her lower back to her shoulders; her mouth was impossibly dry, and the vestiges of a hangover sweated from her pores.

Physically? She felt like shit.

Mentally? Well, she was reaching the end of her rope.

All she could do was turn around and see which of them had followed. At the very least, she could slow them down, give the others a bit more time. Pretend Audrey was a drum: lay down a sick beat on her face, supplement with double kicks to her gut.

Since no one was currently shooting at them, it was without surprise that she discovered Vic skidding to a halt behind them, hands thrown into the air. Harlow leaned back on her heel and tightened her fist.

"Wait!"

Leaning against a tree, clutching Jacqueline, Lou stared from Vic to Harlow. Even that single shout had left her winded, and she squeezed her eyes shut. "He can help."

"You can't be serious," Jacqueline said, voice flat. "Harlow, punch him."

"Don't," Lou protested. "We don't know… where we're going…"

Though Harlow could feel her knuckles straining, eager to make contact with his face, she resisted the urge. Lou was right. He was the only one who knew the way to the road. "Where's Audrey?"

"I left her." Vic kept his hands in the air. "I knew she wouldn't leave the Institute. You were right. I—I can't stay there. I don't want to die."

Jacqueline sniffed. "It would serve you right."

For a moment, Harlow considered decking him anyway. "You're a piece of shit."

"I know." His head ducked in a nod. His two broken fingers stood up like crooked fence posts. "I'm sorry. Things got way out of hand. Please. I need to get away from her. I can show you to the road. We can all get out of here."

Jacqueline frowned at him. "Why should we trust you?"

He shrugged helplessly. "Why would I be out here, helping you? I never wanted to hurt anyone. Everything… it's all just so messed up. Please." His eyes glistened and his lips trembled, wet and red. "I'm sorry. I let her get in my head and make me think what we were doing was right, but I can't. I can't do it."

Harlow observed the remorse twisting his face, and though her hatred for him was undiminished, she wondered what this world would be without second chances. Without the opportunity to fix things, make them right. There were things she couldn't fix, things she had majorly screwed up, but if Harlow thought even for a moment that she deserved a second chance, then why shouldn't Victor get one, too?

"Show us how to get to the road."

———

They trekked through thick brambles and boxleaf, ferns weaving dense green mats across the forest floor. Douglas fir stood tall and narrow, with measurable space between them, but with no trail they had to weave a circuitous course. Thin arms spidered from their trunks, catching strands of hair where they hung low.

Harlow and Jacqueline followed Vic's back, dragging Lou between them. Each step seemed an agony for her, as every jostling movement left her emitting high whines and grunts of pain that made Harlow wince in sympathy.

It was nearly impossible to get her over the more uneven terrain. They pulled her up ridges and slid down muddy slopes veined with the protuberances of knotty roots. When Lou's weight came down on her foot, she cried out and fell, then let loose a scream. Jacqueline tried to shush her in case Audrey was following, listening, or maybe because she worried the forest was listening.

The forest was always listening.

Harlow couldn't tell how fast the sun was dipping behind the trees. Daylight shifted to a deeper gold.

In spite of the difficulty of maneuvering Lou through the forest, in spite of her hatred for this endless sea of trees, Harlow took a deep breath of the fresh air. They had made it out of the underground facility. They would make it out of the woods. A part of her, though—a deep and rotten little piece of her heart—wasn't sure she wanted to make it out.

Her thoughts spiraled downward, ever closer to the yawning doorway of the blackened house in her mind. She could feel her body slowing, and Jacqueline must have noticed because she looked across at her, determination hardening her face. "Come on. We have to keep going."

Between them, Lou sagged, eyes gone glassy, breaths coming in feeble pants.

They pushed onward. Trees stretched in endless replication on all sides. She had no idea where they were, if they were any closer to the road. Ahead of them, Vic picked his way carefully through the wilderness, pausing every so often to assess their direction.

"How much farther?"

He glanced over his shoulder. "Not much."

Lou's attempts to keep going flagged. Her eyelids kept sliding shut. Harlow tried to keep her alert by talking, making mindless observations, offering snatches of hope. "Once we're at the road, we'll flag down a car. Head straight for the nearest hospital. They'll dope you up on all the best painkillers. You'd better share."

"Not a... chance," Lou breathed, a whisper-thin laugh exiting her mouth.

"Bitch." Harlow held back a smile. "Guess I'll have to get my own drugs."

"We may have to walk a while when we reach the road. Not many cars pass through here," Vic said.

"We'll find someone eventually. I mean, hell, there were people out here when we drove in. We saw that truck, right?" She turned to Lou, whose head nodded forward, hanging toward her chest. Harlow prodded Lou to keep her awake. "Remember? Don't piss off rednecks…" she murmured, trying to remember the stupid lyrics Thorn had made up in the car. It was like groping into the aching hollows of childhood memory, fuzzy with distance even though it was less than two days ago. His voice receded in her mind; she couldn't catch it. Her throat turned full and heavy.

"I'm not a redneck," Vic said.

His words surprised a laugh out of Harlow, maybe because the only red to his features were the blossoms of blood in his cheeks from physical exertion. The laugh felt oddly good. She couldn't even remember the last time she'd felt good. But here she was, hauling her injured friend through the woods, strung out, a wreck of drained adrenaline, stomach squeezing itself with hunger, and damn it, she actually felt good. Every vibrant detail of the forest came alive in her senses: the verdant smell of soil, sunlight crystallizing on latent dewdrops clinging fiercely to the edges of leaves like beads of glass, the rough texture of tree bark under her steadying palm.

The road couldn't be far now.

They were going to make it out of here.

"Just ahead," Vic said, picking up his pace. He vanished momentarily between the trees. They struggled to follow, calling for him to wait up, slow down.

Ahead, there was an opening, and Harlow could almost weep for joy. This was it, at last—the road that would lead them away from here.

Only she didn't *see* a road.

Jacqueline called out for Vic to wait for them as they tried to catch up. They came to the break in the trees, each step slowing as a familiar landscape unspooled before them. They had seen that cluster of bushes before. Harlow recognized the crooked lean of this tree.

In the clearing stood the face of a triangular building with a mounded sod roof, and a woman holding a gun, a smile on her face, a thick coil of rope in the grass at her feet.

Victor had led them in a huge circle, right back to where they started.

AFTER

Thorn is back.

He sits across from her, shoulders hunched, elbows resting on the table with an unused checkerboard between them. His eye darts around as he leans in further, voice akin to the low rumble of distant thunder.

"I got in contact with them."

"Who?"

"What do you mean, who? Who have I been telling you about?"

Harlow's mind lives in a fog. Her eyes are two clouded windows, everything beyond them like something glimpsed through a dirty glass filter, muffled and vague. *Stop coming here,* she wants to tell him and all the others who have shown up, trying to pull her back to the woods. Putting words to all of this feels like more effort than it's worth, though, so she tries to communicate her exhaustion through a shake of her head.

"Who do you think founded the Volker Institute?" he asks. "It wasn't government run. It was privately funded. So, who funded it?"

She shakes her head again to indicate she has no idea.

"The Escher Society. They go back at least a hundred years, probably more, but they're super secretive, so there's almost no info on them. But there's plenty of speculation. The Society was founded by a group of radical thinkers, influential people, and wealthy donors interested in pushing the boundaries of science. Basically, it's a bunch of powerful people you've never heard of—because they got rich profiting off of unorthodox research and unethical or unregulated experimentation."

"Okay."

"Suffice to say, they dabbled in some shady shit, and it paid off. The Volker Institute was just one of their ventures, of which there are... shit, who knows? What I *did* find was a parent company with direct ties to the Society. Escher Industries, Incorporated. And you wouldn't believe how many ventures they've funded over the years."

At this, Thorn pulls out his phone and starts scrolling through screenshots. "There are a few places I found specific mentions of because they all seem to have a common purpose. A South African diamond mine called the Coetzee Mine, whose real purpose was to dig for a passageway into the *anderwereld.*"

"Uh... huh."

"Some kind of other world—I've seen it referred to as the Underneath—that they could find, if they dug deep enough." He checks some notes on his phone. "There's also the Macaw Research Station in Belize that—again, *supposedly*—is studying environmental conservation and wildlife, but is actually studying parts of the jungle, particularly a local cave system, that locals have all kinds of weird stories about. Bizarre animals no one's ever documented. Plants that don't behave like they should. And there's one in Siberia—some outpost called Lytkin Station, studying what's under the permafrost."

"Stop. Just stop."

"This is important," Thorn insists.

Her brain is torturing her again, trying to bring her back to everything she would like to escape.

"Harlow. Come on. What are these places they're looking into? These various underworlds, or places that might lead to some underworld?"

She shakes her head.

"Low Places."

As Harlow tries to process the rabbit hole of information Thorn has managed to dig up in his research, her muddled mind catches up to the start of the conversation. "Wait, you said you got in contact with them?"

"Well... I mean, I sent them a letter. And an email. Okay, a couple of emails. I haven't heard back yet, but someone is going to have to pay attention. Someone is going to have to realize that something dangerous got loose at their abandoned facility. Someone will have to take responsibility for it."

"You sure put a lot of faith in rich people."

Her attention is captured by another patient wandering by. Every person who passes draws her eye, now, begging her to check their face, to make sure it really *is* a face and not some blank mask, some pale imitation. She's constantly looking out for Allison Reed.

Thorn glances from Harlow to the direction of her gaze.

"She's followed me here," Harlow says.

"Who?"

"Queen Carrion. Somehow, she got in here. She's like—I don't know, a patient? I don't know. But she's *here*. She's coming in through the cracks."

"Okay. So—let's get you out of here, then. You need to demonstrate you're not a danger to yourself, that you're—that you're okay. And then you can come with me."

"What if she finds me wherever I go?" she asks, looking into the corners of the rec room, into the hallway, the doorways beyond. "What if she doesn't stop? What if she'll always be there, somewhere, waiting?"

Even now, she wonders whether she'll see her if only she turns her head fast enough. She knows Queen Carrion is there, creeping in the shadows. She presses up from the translucent boundary between worlds, stretches impossibly thin limbs into narrow cracks and crevices, trying to feel her way inside.

"Are you sure it wasn't just in your mind?" Thorn asks.

She looks at him, and she hears his awful scream echoing from the woods, and no, of course she isn't sure; she can't be sure of anything anymore. She has seen impossible things, things which have irreparably broken the world.

What is real?

Sometimes she doesn't know if what happened in the woods really happened at all, or if it is only her brain now creating some wild scenario to account for it. For their deaths. This place, with its patchwork furniture and paper cups of pills and slate blue walls, seems less real than the towering pines of the Umpqua. Maybe she is still back there—maybe this is all part of an elaborate experiment somewhere deep in the earth.

Maybe she is still in the Volker Institute.

THIRTY-THREE

It may not have been an ideal situation, but Lou was hard-pressed to feel anything except relief once she was finally sitting down, legs stretched across damp grass, back resting against a tree trunk. The fire in her thigh had burned itself to a peculiar but merciful numbness.

Somehow, Lou had never wondered what it felt like to be shot. She steered clear of guns, having no interest in ever firing, let alone holding, one. Why would she want to mess around with something that could kill a person with the twitch of a finger? There was no sense in it. Wendy had asked her once if she would consider using a gun for self-defense. It was after the Wonder Room Panic, after someone had smashed up her car, and she was paranoid that whoever had done it might follow her home. Even for self-defense, though, Lou wouldn't touch one.

Getting shot had really only cemented her feelings about the damn things. Trying to hobble around the woods with a gunshot wound in her leg hadn't helped matters in the least. Leaning back now, closing her eyes, she could almost ignore the thick vines of jute rope coiled around her wrists, snaking across her torso, pinning her to the broad fir, but she felt a tug as Vic finished tying a knot in the rope and tested its strength.

"I'm sorry about this," he said.

She snorted. "No, you're not."

"I know what you must think of us." He sat back on his haunches. "You were right, though. We're not bad people." He glanced over his shoulder at Audrey, who had retreated to the Volker Institute's doorway. "Audrey's dad used to work here, a long time ago. He signed some kind of extremely strict NDA. All she knew was he worked at a lab with chemical and biological components, and she figured, from there, it was something to do with pharmaceuticals."

He wound a length of spare rope around his hand carefully, so as not to nudge his two broken fingers, before continuing, "Anyway, not too long ago, her dad got sick. Pancreatic cancer. It was already stage four, so there wasn't much they could do. But Audrey, she wouldn't give up. She found clinical trials, experimental meds. Her dad, he was all she had left. She begged him to tell her about this place, if there was anything here that could help him, any kind of research they did into cancer treatments. But he wasn't exactly a forthcoming guy. Either he was dead serious about that NDA, or he just didn't want to talk about it. So she found it on her own."

Harlow audibly scoffed. She was tied to her own tree, Jacqueline on the other side of her. "That's your sob story? You're looking for a cure for cancer? To save Audrey's dad?"

Vic shook his head. "He died once we were already out here."

"So what's the point?"

"This is bigger than Audrey's dad. Way bigger. We had no clue till we got here." There was an unsettling shine to his eyes. "You've seen it. It's not just a mimic. The more we feed it, the smarter it gets. The more it understands human beings."

"What are you talking about?"

Wrapped in a fog of pain and the sweet numbness that had begun creeping through her, Lou closed her eyes and listened. She could hear the eagerness in Vic's voice, of the same variety she'd recognized when he was talking about plants.

"I'm talking about a consciousness that can absorb other consciousnesses, like—like an organic supercomputer. This is Nobel Prize big. This is change-the-world big. Prototaxites Pseudoparenchyma—that's what I call it—can take on the form of whatever it consumes, yes. But it doesn't destroy what it digests. It breaks it down and recreates it, using its own material. It's a compound organism. Made up of itself and everything it eats."

"I don't understand," Harlow said.

"You will."

By the time Lou opened her eyes, he was already walking away, leaving them here, and she understood her critical error in thinking she could appeal to his humanity, in thinking she could convince him to help them. Vic was every bit as zealous as Audrey, and every bit as willing to leave them here to die.

It wasn't fair—for a gun-hater to get shot, for a person who'd always tried to be kind to others to be so carelessly stomped on. She tugged on her restraints. They held.

Gloom fell fast around them. The last bit of light faded behind tree-tops hungry for shadow. Jacqueline's and Harlow's faces became gray shapes.

Lou almost wished the pain of the gunshot wound would over-whelm everything else again, but still she could feel the uncomfortable stickiness of blood drying on the stiffened material of her leggings, the bite of protruding bark stabbing her back, the coarse rope pulled tight around her wrists. During their trek, she'd had to keep telling herself *one more step, one more breath*, just to get through each excruciating moment, but now the moments were piling up, and she wondered how many more of them there would be, after all.

A security camera hung from a branch above like a watchful eye, aimed directly at her, and the other two beside her, tied to their own trees. The perfect vantage point for Vic and Audrey to watch them die. A tiny red light indicated it was on.

"Maybe it won't find us," Jacqueline said, voice soft in the gathering dark.

Grunting with exertion, Harlow lifted her arms and brought them back down, sawing at the rope with the tree's rough skin.

"At least we'll see them again soon," Lou murmured. "We'll get to be with them."

Harlow stopped sawing. "Don't say that. It's not true."

"Didn't you hear what he said?" Lou's mind spun. "It *is* them. It's all of them, somehow, wrapped up together with whatever the Pseudo was originally. They're *part* of it." As she said it, the idea expanded in her mind, exhilarating and terrible all at once. A morbidly curious part of her wondered what it was like to become part of such an entity. She'd had the experience, on LSD, of becoming one with the universe, the edges of her form bleeding out until her atoms got mixed up with the atoms all around her, until she was formless, no longer consolidated into a single identity. It was only a trip, but it had felt profound at the time.

She wondered if it would be anything like that—the world's most insane trip through a compound consciousness. Becoming one with something far greater than herself.

If only the entry fee wasn't death.

She tried to settle herself more comfortably against the tree. If ever there were a time to reach out to the spirits of the woods, to summon strength and peace and healing, now was it. Though she didn't have any herbs to burn, she had noticed a dandelion waving its head nearby, and she figured its presence would have to do, as she had nothing else to offer.

As she sat, eyes closed, attuned to her breathing, she tried to let her mind slip away from the discomfort and pain of her body. She listened to the steady chirp of crickets, felt the cool breeze that moved across her face. She opened herself up to the energy of nature. The world fell away; it was only her and the pulsing bass and her heartbeat and the tree behind her, anchoring her to the earth, and with her mind she called out to the positive energies of the forest.

As she did, she could hear something in the wind joining her mental bass line. A tune. A melody. Something familiar, deep in the brain, like a lullaby retrieved from the strange lands of distant memory.

A voice.

Words carved themselves out of the night, and she recognized the opening lines of "Midnight Ritual."

The forest spirits had shown up, all right. Just not the ones she wanted.

Brynn's voice wove between the trees.

At every moment, Lou expected to see the edge of a Pale Form emerge from behind a trunk, skitter between the trees that stood like black columns.

Even if it did appear, her arms were stretched taut around the tree trunk, her legs a pile of useless meat. She looked down, wondering if she would even be able to gain her feet if she was somehow able to get free of the rope. Her wound had clotted over, but her thigh, in the faint glow of the camera and the moonlight, wore a black cast of dried blood and felt like a fat piece of rubber. The grass shivered underneath her, and there, she saw it, sprouting from the dirt: a thin white stalk.

Its shoots stretched out like antennae. It gathered, extended.

She couldn't pull her leg in, though she wanted to tuck her knee beneath her chin; it wouldn't bend, wouldn't obey. It lay there like a dead thing. All she could do was watch as the white stalk pulled itself up out of the earth, growing to a foot in height, two feet: a mass of writhing hyphae, shapeless, reaching up.

With her good leg, she kicked at the dirt, shoe digging a trench. She heard Harlow gasp and knew the others had seen it, too. Fear raced like the prickle of chills as a shape began to form—tall and slender, then filling out, plumping with curves.

Brynn dragged herself out of the dirt, pale enough to be luminous in the dark. Eyes like spider egg sacs. Black hair bleached white. Face split into that mischievous smile she always wore, filled with danger.

"Brynn?" Lou heard Harlow's voice crack over the word. "Is that you?"

The Pseudo turned to her, still smiling, hairs crawling back from the stretching lips, as its voice continued to sing from the trees. When Pseudo-Brynn spoke, she did not need to move her mouth at all; the vocal cords within plucked themselves, something behind the lips shaping the words.

"We are all here... in this fucked-up world."

Lou recognized the song. "The Anthem."

"If we burn, we burn... together."

A pale hand reached out. Tree bark bit the back of Lou's scalp, tugging at stray hairs. For a moment, she imagined Queen Carrion, together again: all of them as one, no more infighting or petty squabbles, everyone entirely in sync, slotting together as one perfect being.

The moment passed, and instinct took over. With her good leg, Lou kicked out, the blow meeting Pseudo-Brynn's midsection with enough force to knock her backward, to cave in the soft tissue holding her together. A flurry of hyphae exploded from her folded torso, and like the spread of crystallization in honey, the resulting chaos rippled through the rest of her, disrupting the solidity of her form. Pieces of her dissolved and reshaped, dangling loose threads like a half-finished garment on a dressmaker dummy.

The Pseudo lurched as it struggled to reshape itself. White vines grew from its back like tentacles as it steadied.

It was hypnotic, in a way. Lou understood, in some sense, Vic and Audrey's desire to study this thing. It was so unlike anything she had seen before. It was a wonder. Seeing it filled her with awe, that something so beyond her own imagination might exist in the strange, vast reaches of the universe.

She gasped.

Having been so focused on Pseudo-Brynn, Lou no longer paid any attention to the threads still sprouting up from the dirt. She hadn't noticed one of the pale tentacles that had slithered toward her across the grass. She hadn't noticed until she felt the squirming discomfort, its pointed tip probing the bullet hole in her leg, slipping through the torn cloth into the meat beneath.

Dear Audrey,

If you are reading this, it means I'm gone. You should be receiving this with my will. I'm sorry for not giving it to you when I was still alive, but I am too much of a coward.

I know how badly you've wanted to learn about the work I used to do. You've asked me again and again, but I've had my reasons not to tell you. It isn't only the ironclad NDA, though that's part of it. There are things I've done. I worried you wouldn't see me the same way. I had intended to take this with me to grave, but the more the cancer eats at me, the more I feel you deserve this final truth. You deserve to know why I was gone so much when you were a kid, why even after I came back, I was still gone in a way you could not possibly understand.

I tried to be a good father. I tried to do right by you. But I know it was never enough. You're smart, Audrey. You always were. And you're strong. That's why I think you can handle knowing the truth now. It's a truth no one else knows—except for a few people, and I have no idea what happened to them after everything. They might be dead by now, like all the others.

I ask only that you never share this information. Doing so could put you in danger. The people who ran the Institute are powerful. I don't know what they would do to you if you shared this, so please, if you keep reading, do not ever breathe a word of this to anyone. This is only for you. So that you can finally know who I am.

My work at the Volker Institute was in documentation. I wasn't some great scientist like you thought. I worked in an office filing papers. I didn't have direct access to what was going on below; everything underneath the offices was like another world that I only read about in the reports. I was also in charge of documenting any use of the incinerator, if something needed to be destroyed, or if there was a containment breach. This didn't happen often.

It was all fairly mundane during most of the years I worked there. I would do my month-long stints, then come home for a week to see you. Your mother wasn't happy with the arrangement, but we needed the money, and it was very good money. As much as I wanted to see you, I dreaded coming home because I knew your mother and I would spend most of the week arguing. She wanted me to quit, but I always insisted I stay on a bit longer to build up our nest egg. Put money away for your college education.

And then the Incident happened.

I can't tell you exactly what occurred, but there was a major containment breach in the Vivarium, which is where they studied living organisms in specially designed habitats. There was a breach, and one of the organisms got out. Someone on that level, in a panic, opened the door to the stairwell, and a lockdown was triggered for the whole building.

Everyone in the levels below the offices was told to proceed to a certain area for a decontamination procedure. I had to document it. I had to witness it. It wasn't my decision—that came from higher up—but maybe I could have tried to put a stop to it. Maybe I could have done something. But all I did was watch and document, and I think that makes me just as culpable as the management team who made the call.

It wasn't a decontamination procedure. Audrey, we burned them all. We burned them alive.

I will never forget it. It is seared into my mind, following me into my final days on this earth. It's something I don't think is possible to atone for. All those people, even the ones who weren't on the contaminated level—all of them, sent to the incinerator.

And I did nothing.

That's why I came home with that large bonus. Blood money. I could never tell your mother what really happened, and I think that's why we could never again be as close as we once were. I was holding this back from her, this terrible thing, inside of me all this time. This secret that has eaten away at me for so many years. I was only following orders, I told myself. But that isn't justification for what we did. What I did.

Audrey, I am so sorry. I am sorry for everything.

I love you,
Dad

THIRTY-FOUR

Time slowed to a crawl. It was like every bad memory ripping at Harlow's mind, all at once, every awful thing, and—why didn't she see it? Why didn't she stop it?

The Pseudo's pale tentacle dug deeper into Lou's wound, and her voice rang out from pain or terror, it was hard to tell.

Panic crashed at the shores of Harlow's heart. She let out a scream, sawing her arms up and down, trying to fray any bit of rope she could. Her wrists chafed, rubbed raw. Lou tried to shake out her leg as the tentacle wriggled deeper. Harlow threw herself to the side, hoping to tear the rope, but she felt something in her back pop with a dazzle of pain. Her fingers scrabbled at rough bark as she yanked at the bindings.

"No, no, no, no, no." The words slipped from her mouth in a stream. She locked eyes with Lou and saw in them a dull acceptance.

It was cowardly, but she couldn't watch. She closed her eyes. She wanted to see nothing, to be nothing. The darkness swirled with looping tendrils of color as if it had followed her even to the insides of her eyelids.

A *snick* snapped them open again. She looked—and wished she hadn't.

Bones protruded like sticks of birch out of the mud, a black puddle of rot where Lou's legs had been.

It crept up her torso, vining toward her face, but in its quest to devour her, it had eaten through the rope, which snapped, freeing Lou's hands. She had managed to retrieve the lighter from her pocket and she was flicking it, sparking short-lived bursts of light that snapped right out in the wind. Harlow wanted to ask what she was doing, but she remembered the sizzle, the crackle, of the mycelium when she shoved it into the wood stove about a million years ago.

"Burn the fucker," she said.

The lighter caught, but when Lou tried to hold it to the encroaching fungus, it merely shrank away. She pressed it up again, and the Pseudo shifted its malformed body from the juddering flame—just a small bead of light, too small to do any harm.

Harlow's heart plummeted into her gut.

Then Lou leaned hard to the side and held out the lighter like an offering. At first, Harlow didn't know what she was doing—it wasn't as if she could take it from her, and even if she could, why would she? The fungus crept up Lou's torso, turning her skin necrotic, but she held the little flame steady.

Harlow almost told her to stop before she realized what Lou was doing.

"It's okay." Lou's words slurred together. "I'm going to be part of it. I'll get to see what it's like…"

The rope singed, charred, and finally snapped, falling into loose coils around Harlow. She pulled her arms free.

Seeing this, Lou dropped her hand, the flame whisking out. The lighter landed somewhere in the dirt.

"Here!" Jacqueline shouted.

Harlow crawled over, working her fingers into the stubborn knots of rope lashing Jacqueline to her own tree, shrugging off the rope trailing behind her. Though Jacqueline urged her on faster, her hands were shaking, her fingers were numb, it was hard to grip the rope—and the Pseudo was rising again. She glanced over her shoulder to see it behind her as it finished its meal of Lou, whose face was gone, and now it would be turning its sights on them as it assembled whatever form it might take now.

"Come *on!*"

At last, the knot came loose, Harlow pulled the rope, and Jacqueline tugged free. Harlow patted the ground, searching, until her hand found the still-warm lighter—just a red plastic BIC, half-full of juice—and, this in hand, she took off after Jacqueline.

They ran.

It was the kind of blind run that had low branches slapping her in the face like razor wire, that sent her careening off the trunks of trees, bruising shoulders and knees, falling and getting up again, but it didn't matter as long as they could put some distance between themselves and the Pseudo.

But they couldn't—not really—could they?

Around them, the song began again. Brynn's voice called mournfully, echoing so they lost all sense of where it was coming from. Ghostly images emerged between the trees—Pale Forms, the manifestations all too familiar: Brynn, Rhys, *Lou*.

How could they outrun it?

The Pseudo was everywhere.

"Stop!"

The shout sounded distinctly human, but then, the Pseudo's voice sounded human too. Harlow stumbled; Jacqueline grabbed her. Flashlight beams zigzagged toward them. Coming up fast now: two masked figures. The black gleam of a gun.

"Oh, for fuck's *sake!*" Jacqueline screamed. Before Harlow could stop her, she had thrown herself at the approaching figures. The gun went off and skittered into the underbrush as Jacqueline and the taller figure, which must have been Victor, went hard to the ground.

Seeing them with the gas masks on made Harlow want to pull her shirt up over her mouth, but she had no idea why. What could be in the air? Maybe they were trying to avoid what had happened to Wendy, to Thorn—a hair-thin filament floating on the breeze, accidentally finding its way into an orifice.

Audrey was distracted. Though she could not see Audrey's face, she saw the direction of her gaze, back through the trees where they had come from.

Toward the Pseudo.

Toward Brynn.

No, she could not let herself think about that right now. What Vic had said about it being a compound organism was too much for her to try to unpack. Still, it knocked at the door of her brain.

It wasn't just pretending to be Brynn.

It *was* Brynn.

Audrey darted off, following the pale figure, and Harlow wondered if she'd ever seen it without being filtered through a screen, through cameras. Jacqueline, meanwhile, was no match for Vic on her own. He had gotten the upper hand, straddling her with his hands around her throat.

That was enough to spur Harlow to action. She knocked him over, pulled off his gas mask, and pried the flashlight out of his hand. She aimed it down, whitewashing his face, and he cringed from the light.

Good. She hoped it blinded him.

She didn't realize what Jacqueline was digging around for in the underbrush until she heard the click.

The gun was cocked, aimed down a Vic, whose eyes watered and spilled over as the light blasted directly into them.

"You fucking liar," Harlow growled, feeling vindicated, powerful. She wanted to scare him. She wanted to hurt him. In her mind, she brought the flashlight down on his face, bloodying his nose, again and again, until he was unconscious. The idea thrilled her. He deserved to suffer, after what he had done to them, after everything he had put them through, and Harlow would have no qualms about bludgeoning him until he begged for mercy.

"I'm sorry," he said, covering his eyes with his hands. Always apologizing, she thought, but he never meant it, did he? "You just—you have no idea—"

What, exactly, they had no idea about, they would never know.

The blast momentarily deafened her. It left her ears ringing.

Vic gasped, mouth hanging open. His throat convulsed. Blood popped from his lips. Pupils shrank back from the light, then steadied, staring, and Harlow thought there was no way he could stare directly at the light like that.

Then she saw the red on his shirt, recognized the smell of gunpowder.

"Good riddance," Jacqueline said as she let her arms fall slack, the gun hanging at her side.

Harlow thought she should have been horrified, but she had seen multiple people die this weekend and imagined there must be some kind of limit to the amount of horror a person could feel before their adrenal system just said, *you know what, fuck it, let's go get a pizza.*

She realized she could really go for a pizza right now.

It was such a bizarre thought to have while standing over the dead body of one's captor, the chuckles rising up her throat threatened to dissolve her into a puddle of manic laughter. She managed to swallow down the hysteria. All it took was feeling the weight of the lighter in her pocket and remembering that Lou had saved her while she died.

"She trusted you," Harlow spat at Vic's body. A wave of sadness crashed over her. The torrent of different emotions made her want to slip inside a bottle.

Jacqueline had other plans, though. She was already heading off again, glancing back with her eyebrows raised. "Audrey, too."

The words barely penetrated the muted sludge of Harlow's brain. "What?"

"We need to get her too. Or this isn't really over."

She was already following Jacqueline through the trees when she realized what she had meant. *We need to get her.*

They were hunting Audrey.

Harlow's stomach flipped over. She didn't want to see anyone else die. She wanted to tell Jacqueline to leave her, but that cold determination had come over Jacqueline's face again, and she suspected no amount of convincing would stop what was going to happen.

"There," Jacqueline said, pointing ahead, taking off at a faster clip. Not wanting to lose her, Harlow followed, aiming the flashlight low ahead of her, bringing a circle of forest into view as she went.

Something clunked at her side—the gas mask, which she was still hanging onto with her other hand, smacking a tree trunk—and Harlow hurried to keep up. With her elbows she batted away leafy tendrils, tall grass climbing up to her thighs. Something fell on her back, skittered up her neck, and she smacked herself with the mask before she could even figure out what kind of bug it was.

The woods grew rougher, denser. The way ahead was obstructed by thick underbrush. "Hey," Harlow said as Jacqueline slipped into the darkness between shrubs. "Slow down!" She lurched after her, wondering how much longer she could continue.

Then she spilled out into the open air.

The trees cleared.

Something else was growing here.

Pale pillars stood in a ring at the center of the clearing: tall and cylindrical, like trees but otherwise bearing no resemblance to what grew in the rest of the forest. Each one tapered to a point somewhere above. Instead of bark, their flesh was smooth, slick. They were like great pale fingers emerging from out of the earth.

Audrey stood before them. She pulled off her gas mask to better gaze up at the faintly luminous columns. "We found them," she said. "Victor!"

"Victor's dead."

Audrey turned, saw them standing at the edge of the clearing.

Everything about this area seemed wrong. The air had a thickness to it, as if the darkness around the palely glowing shapes had a physical form. Harlow blinked against the strange overlapping effect this created: seeing the tall growths through the physical darkness, seeing both at once, made her woozy. Still, she could not stop staring at the fleshy protrusions from the earth. There was something alien about them.

"What are they?"

Audrey's eyes gleamed. "The fruiting bodies." Another look, and Harlow could see it now: the flesh was not perfectly smooth. There were gills along the sides of the pillars. "It led us here." Audrey turned back to the ring. She stepped forward, raising a hand. Lay her palm against one of the growths. "I've been trying to find this, and it finally brought us… It wanted us to see."

The gills fluttered as with breath, then exhaled: half a dozen plumes of silvery mist expelled into the air.

Realizing now what it was for, Harlow pulled the gas mask over her face.

Audrey, meanwhile, dropped her own mask and turned. Spores dusted her hair like snow, powdered her face, crawled into her open mouth. In a flash, Jacqueline dove for the fallen mask, but the cloud of spores was already descending, dispersing on the wind. She pulled it on.

"Did you get any on you?" Harlow called. It was impossible to read the look on Jacqueline's face, which had disappeared behind the insectile visage of the mask.

Joy spread over Audrey's face. "I can hear it," she said as her eyes clouded over white. "I can hear it inside my brain. We understand now." Her eyes twisted and rotated in her skull. Her skin glimmered.

"Come on," Harlow said. "We have to get out of here."

Jacqueline didn't move. She turned back to Audrey, arm raised.

The gun went off.

Audrey stared back at them, grinning. There was a gaping hole in her skull. In a moment, it had stitched over.

"We understand," she said. "You were Queen Carrion. Now We are Queen Carrion."

Jacqueline shot her again, this time in the heart, and Audrey screamed with a thousand voices, spores swirling from her mouth. The gun gave an empty click as Jacqueline pulled the trigger a third, fourth, fifth time, and then she threw it to the ground.

"We need to get out of here!" Harlow shouted, reaching for Jacqueline's arm to drag her out of the clearing.

Audrey was beginning to change. The mycelium had taken root, reshaping her body into something that was no longer her body—something wholly *other*.

Jacqueline shook Harlow off. "I need to destroy it."

"I won't go without you."

For a moment, Harlow thought Jacqueline was about to nod and follow her. Instead, she pulled off the gas mask and let it drop with a thump. An urge to grab it and smash it back over Jacqueline's head had Harlow reaching out for it, but then she saw Jacqueline's eyes. They looked strange—silvery, pale.

"I didn't get it on in time," she said. "Go. I have a plan."

Behind them, Pseudo-Audrey collapsed and contorted, growing new limbs. Harlow's feet wouldn't move. She shook her head.

Jacqueline growled in the back of her throat. "Let me do this for you."

It was almost funny: yesterday, she hated Jacqueline. Now, she wanted to grab her and hold on, wanted her to be okay, to not be infected by those floating spores. She didn't want to lose her like she had lost everyone else. She was the only one left.

Jacqueline pushed her away and said something that took several moments for Harlow to understand. Even when she did comprehend the words, they made no sense to her. Jacqueline repeated herself.

"I killed Brynn."

The air vanished from Harlow's lungs. "What?"

Jacqueline's teeth were gritted together, her eyes bright. "You shouldn't try to help me because *I killed Brynn*. I followed her here. I slit her throat. I wanted to be... I wanted to be *her*. I wanted Rhys to want *me*. I thought we could come out here, and it would cross this area off your list, and I could make sure no one ever found her. But we *did* find her. She's not even really dead." Jacqueline's eyes became white balls. "You need to go."

"You… you…" Harlow backed into a tree at the edge of the clearing, her brain stuttering as Jacqueline turned back to the thing Audrey had become—some inhuman shape, maybe the real form of the Pseudo, or maybe just one of its many forms, maybe it had no true form—something fractious and many-limbed.

Harlow's brain stuttered. She refused to accept it. Jacqueline was lying, she had to be—lying to push Harlow away, to get her to leave. She couldn't have…

But Jacqueline hadn't been around that weekend. Try as she might, Harlow could not call forth a single memory of those days that included her. And now a yawning chasm was opening inside of Harlow as her brain spat up every moment she had spent in Jacqueline's company. All this time, she had been in the presence of a killer. Brynn's killer. She had always thought there was something wrong with Jacqueline, but she had never imagined her capable of murder.

All of this was because of Jacqueline.

Chills raced across Harlow's arms, and her stomach swooped. Her breath came too fast. She felt like she was hyperventilating. She felt Brynn dying, again and again.

She didn't wait to see what Jacqueline was going to do.

She threw herself back through the dense foliage, scrabbling at branches and weeds that smacked her, and she ran in what she hoped was the direction of the road, without looking back.

MMM: Where do you see Queen Carrion going over the next few years?

BW: Evolving. Becoming ourselves. I've been thinking… okay, bear with me here.

Have you ever thought of a band as an entity in its own right? "Emergence" is what it's called when something becomes more than the sum of its parts. An entity that has properties that its parts do not have on their own. A band is like that. On our own, we're people making sounds. Together, we're a unified entity making music.

Emergent phenomena are like… flocks of birds or schools of fish. The way they move together in a swarm. Or snowflakes—how they reveal a larger pattern in their creation, even though each one is distinct.

Maybe consciousness itself is an emergent property of the physical complexity of the brain. Maybe creativity is an emergent property of consciousness. I mean, it makes sense, right? Atoms are simple forms that combine to create molecules. Molecules are simple forms that combine to create much more complex things. We don't think of ourselves as being composed of billions of tiny particles, each one with its own identity. No, our identity is the *whole*, not the parts. That's emergence. When the identity becomes the whole, the unity. We can't even imagine what it would be like to be a single molecule in our bodies. How could we? We are so much more vastly complex than the individual parts we are made of. And if consciousness is an emergent phenomenon, then that means human beings aren't some kind of special creations with a soul or some magical creator—it means anything can become conscious with the right level of complexity. Maybe we're just early in the process of the universe waking up to itself. Maybe everything wants to be conscious.

So, I think of Queen Carrion like that. It is an entity beyond us as individuals. A whole. A unity. Imagine if multiple consciousnesses combined to create an even more complex consciousness. What would that be like? The ultimate creative force. It would be like… becoming your own muse.

I'm sorry, what was the question?

THIRTY-FIVE

She could feel it blooming in her mind as the spores latched onto her brain cells, as tendrils grew into and between her nerve endings. At first, it was like insects scratching in her head. Then, the sounds took on more definition, notes, frequencies, speaking in tones rather than words, like the low hum of a bowed string.

Audrey stood before her, or at least something that had once been Audrey, something that was now part of Jacqueline as well, a Great Web that connected them—and she could feel the way it stretched out beneath the forest, sending electrical signals across the miles of its brain.

Jacqueline ran her hands over her face, feeling it both with her own flesh and with that *other* stuff, recognizing and memorizing its shape, and she remembered the last time she was out here, filled with both horror at herself and a wild joy, agony and ecstasy, after slitting Brynn's throat, ensuring she would never sing again.

She could hear her now, still singing—in the forest or in her head, she could not tell. She could no longer tell the difference between *inside* and *outside*—between *self* and *other*.

All their individual deaths ceased to matter from this new perspective. Even Rhys's death was unimportant now. Maybe it had only really mattered when Queen Carrion was still a possibility. Now the whole thing had fallen apart, right when it was about to be fixed, about to be *perfect*, with her, *her*, at the helm. Maybe it wasn't really Rhys she loved after all; it was Queen Carrion.

She would be part of it now. Oh, yes—she would be part of Queen Carrion, and so much more.

Clinging to this realization, clinging to the clear bright sense of *herself*, she found her hands on the Audrey-thing and *ripped*.

Cords of mycelium screamed in her head as she tore the many-limbed thing to pieces. Where her hands pressed against Audrey, what was left of her decomposed, and Jacqueline realized the power she now held—to rot something with a touch.

Audrey collapsed into an unformed pile of mold, and Jacqueline felt her own body changing, too, but she willed it to rebuild itself even as her old flesh rotted away, willed the new material to reshape as it consumed.

And as she did, she clung to *herself* so that she would not be ripped away into the soup of mixed-up consciousness that was the Great Web that threatened to split her across its miles of matter, so that she could be part of it but still retain something of herself.

Maybe she was special, after all.

She turned to the fungal stalks, and she could see them but also beyond them, into the other world underneath this one from which they had grown, both overlapping in this low spot. If she let herself unravel, the hair-thin parts of her could slip down into that other place, but it was so dark there, and so cold.

There was so much more to consume in this world.

As she became part of it, she could also feel its purpose: to get back to people, though it did not really understand how or why. It was a drive that some of its recent integrations had, a lingering echo of their desire to get back home.

But Jacqueline's drive was stronger.

She was hungry.

She was Queen Carrion.

Not quite, though, not *completely*. She didn't have every single member inside of her. She could sing with Brynn's voice, she could play Wendy's cello, but she needed *all* of them, she realized, in order to be whole. She saw that now, with the gift of this newfound spread-out consciousness—she, We.

We were hungry.

Imagine having all of them together again.

A smile crawled over her face. "The music we could make."

BEFORE

When We were Brynn Werner, or rather when Brynn Werner was not yet us, she heard our singing. She listened. She could not recall the first time she'd heard it—the tune that haunted her—only the first time she became aware of it. Possibly, she'd been hearing it since she was born, or even before, as a melodic pulse in the womb. Memory is a shoddy thing before four or five, childhood amnesia stealing the first few years of one's life entirely.

She became aware of the tune when she was five years old.

It started with simple patterns: *Red. Red Green. Red Green Blue.* And so on. Brynn had mastered these basic beginnings. But then the Simon's pattern became longer, more complicated. It helped that the colors matched the tones, so she could start to remember the tune itself and use that to hit the right buttons. She had been able to do this by associating the tones with their colors.

Brynn was in her room, legs stretched out, door mostly shut, concentrating on the notes, the patterns, the repetition.

When the tune grew longer, she began to feel, inexplicably, that she recognized it. She felt as if she must have heard this tune before, though she could not remember where or when. It simply seemed familiar. She wanted to hear more of it, keeping pace with the faster and faster series of notes, but it was getting harder to do. Then it seemed to her that the buttons were no longer playing the right notes at all. It sounded as if there were more notes coming from the buttons than were possible on the toy. Try as she might, it was all coming apart, spilling over. She couldn't keep up, hit the wrong button—

In that instant, there was something like a flashbulb in her head: bursting, then burning out. And on the other side of it, darkness spilled in, just like the fuzziness after a camera flash pierces the retinas. Looming in that sudden shock of darkness, its shape emerging by degrees as her eyes adjusted, was something like a person, but not a person. A figure bleached the color of bone, as if its details had been erased, or as if it had been sculpted out of clay, the eyes two thumb-print divots. Not so much a face as a mask. It seemed to be pressing up from the other side of something, reaching out of that *other* dark. Over-lapping tones ululated from its throat, the tones the Simon toy had made, and the mouth yawned open, or seemed to be pushed open by marionette threads.

Something was going to come out of that mouth as the jaw stretched wider, Brynn was sure. Then the darkness receded, as if her eyes had adjusted too much and the light of her room had to remind her it was there. She blinked, and it was gone.

The Simon lay inert on the floor. The game was over.

She tried to recreate the tune on the Simon again and again, but it never quite came out right. She needed more than four notes.

She needed a keyboard.

When she finally got one, after asking and asking, and she plucked out every note from top to bottom, all the white ones and all the black ones, she still could not recreate the tune that had summoned the figure, which now lurked at the edges of her mind. She tried humming it, but it was never exactly right. She got closer with her voice. The human voice can create all kinds of sounds, all kinds of in-between notes that are not feasible on most instruments with standard tuning.

Brynn was a precocious child, and not one to be deterred. She would keep trying.

She had heard us.

And We noticed.

It is difficult to communicate through the cracks in the world, but We did our best, and Brynn tried to reach us in return, tried to mimic our voice—our greeting—our tune.

"Should we enroll her in piano lessons?" She overheard her parents talking in the kitchen. "You see how she's taken to it."

"She's just plunking out nonsense."

"It sounds like music to me. Anyway, isn't that what the lessons would be for?"

When asked, Brynn readily agreed. She thought a teacher must know the special tune. She had no name for it, nor a way to articulate what it was—not that she had the chance to try. Her piano teacher was an elderly woman with skin like a raisin and a voice like a razor. Her body was stretched taffy, long and unnaturally thin, but her fingers were liquid on the piano keys. She wore oval spectacles on a chain around her neck and her hair in a silver bouffant.

"Back straight," Mrs. Kaszynski said, taking Brynn's wrists. "Hands here."

"There's a song," said Brynn. "I want to learn—"

"You'll start with the basics. C." She pressed Brynn's thumb onto a key, the note ringing out. "D. E." And they went on like that, one by one.

"Have you ever heard—"

"Curve the fingers." Brynn rounded her hands into a claw. "Relax." She loosened.

The first lesson was mostly about holding her hands over the keys and saying the note when she played it. Later, she learned how to play scales, read sheet music, pluck out simple melodies, and then chords. At first, Brynn was frustrated and unfulfilled. She wanted to learn the tune she'd heard. But the more she studied, the more she realized she would have to master the technicalities before she could recreate it.

She continued to take lessons until she was fourteen, when Mrs. Kaszynski passed away. In the previous year, she had traded her silver bouffant for a scarf tied over her skull, and her already preternatural gauntness, now exacerbated by disease, had made her almost ghoulish. Brynn tried not to notice her deterioration. Mrs. Kaszynski was like a force of nature in her life. Indestructible. Unstoppable. Seeing this frailty in her felt wrong.

"Can I play something for you?" Brynn asked. "I've been working on it since—well, since before I even started taking lessons. I don't know where it came from. I think maybe I dreamed it. But it's been there, in the back of my head, ever since. I feel like I can only ever half-hear it." She set her fingers in place, took a breath, and began to play.

It was messy. Not fully formed. But it echoed the tune. It was like hearing the tune's shadow. As she played, a powerful feeling came over her: she seemed to slip outside of herself, enter the slipstream of creation. And she thought she saw, even with her eyes closed, the vague shape of a figure, far in the distance but not far at all, pressing up against the thin fabric of the world, a face she almost recognized, a face like that of a corpse—

Possessed by the music, Brynn kept playing, even beyond what she had been practicing on her own. Her fingers came down to strike the keys as if she could not fully control herself, or she was so deep into the rapture of the music that it did not feel like control.

All the while, the face pressed further and further through the mist, against the translucent scrim at the edge of everything, trying to break through. A foul odor filled the room: something rotten, like the dead squirrel she had found in the backyard once the snow melted one particularly cold winter. Like black soil. The mouth seemed to yawn wider as the stench intensified, and Brynn's hands dropped off the keys to press against her nose.

"What was that?"

Brynn blinked. The smell was gone. She realized Mrs. Kaszynski was asking about the music.

"It was…" She could not quite form words.

"Did you write that?"

She did not know how to answer. How had the tune first come to her? Had her own brain conjured it? Or had it come from the gods— from something beyond?

In the end, did it matter?

As Brynn left—and it would be the last time she set foot in Mrs. Kaszynski's elegant but overstuffed living room with its walnut floors, velvet sofas, shelves of sheet music, and that beautiful Steinway set before the bay window looking out onto her overgrown hedges—Mrs. Kaszynski stopped her on the threshold, her hand on Brynn's wrist with the same dry strength as the first time she'd touched her eight years ago, and said, "You have something. Don't lose it."

Within the week, Mrs. Kaszynski was hospitalized. And within the month, she was dead.

Brynn would never forget her piano teacher. It was Mrs. Kaszynski who taught her what a muse was, after all.

So that is what she called us. Her muse.

Just as she sought to mimic us in replicating our voice, We, too, made our attempts at replication—one of our strongest skills. The face We crafted, while rudimentary, offered a visage similar enough to pass for human, as We believed it would be her preference to see us like she saw herself.

Such a curious creature, Brynn Werner.

She tried so hard to reach out to us, but each time she got close she became afraid.

When her piano lessons had come to an end, she joined the school choir. The problem, she realized, was how cheesy she found the music: church songs and show tunes that got stuck in her head with maddening clarity. She hated them, but at least they drowned out the *other* tune, the one that kept trying to worm its way into the back of her mind, maddeningly *un*clear, driving her crazy.

Case in point: she stood in the girls' bathroom (the one in the west hall of the high school that most people avoided because it always smelled, for some reason, like old fish), having just finished scratching a bit of graffiti in the stall door to let everyone know *BW was here.* Besides her, the bathroom was empty. She turned on the water to wash her hands, looking up in the mirror as the stall door swung shut behind her. She'd been humming one of the songs from choir and didn't even realize when her mindless humming morphed into a different melody altogether.

You can't help what gets stuck in your head, can you? Sometimes it repeats so much it loses all meaning, becomes something else.

Something banged on the stall door behind her. Brynn stopped humming, cold water running over her soaped hands. "Hello?" Her voice echoed on the tiled walls.

No one had gone in there. She'd have noticed someone slip into the stall she'd only just exited.

There was another bang, like a hand slamming against it from the other side. The door swung slowly outward.

Brynn watched in the mirror, breath frozen in her chest, as the door's movement revealed the edge of a pale face—too pale, no color at all—and then the crater of a partially-formed eye socket.

Not even realizing it, she had called us with her song, and though We remained on the other side of things, still We were able to peer through.

"Go away," she said, breath coming shallow. "Leave me alone."

The bathroom door opened.

"Brynn?"

Harlow Sorenson slouched in, hands in her pockets.

Trying to regain control of her breath, Brynn turned to the stall behind her and found it empty, of course.

"You okay?" Harlow asked, looking around for whatever Brynn was trying to find.

"Yeah. Hey, does this water smell like a yeast infection?" She flicked her wet hands at Harlow, sending droplets onto her face.

Harlow rubbed at her lips. "Don't make me puke."

Brynn shut off the water and dried her hands on her jeans, mentally dispelling the tune, banishing us, filling her mind with the first awful earworm song she could think of. Grabbing Harlow by the shoulders, she belted out the prolonged "hey" from the 4 Non Blondes song.

"What's going on?" Harlow said.

Brynn kept singing.

Eventually, Harlow cut her off. "No, seriously, what's going on with you? You've been out of class for like fifteen minutes. I had to convince Mr. Freeman to let me come find you, make sure you didn't fall in a toilet."

Brynn turned back to the mirror so she could rub her fingers over her scalp, lift the roots of her dark hair so the waves stood taller, wilder. "I honestly thought hanging out in the bathroom would be more entertaining than Freeman's five-hundredth lesson on the Civil War."

Already, she wished she had another song to replace this conversation. To distract her.

She'd tried for years to recreate her muse's tune, but she'd never been successful. Sure, she would come close—would recognize its ghost in birds calling and trucks honking down the highway, would almost manage to sing it before it flitted away again—but the closer she got, the more she felt *noticed*.

She sensed the eye of something peering out from the cracks

between doors, those slivers of darkness which seemed to lead some-where else.

The idea of something watching her—drawn by echoes of the tune, waiting to hear it in full—became more disturbing the older she got. At five, it was like being watched by Santa. Delightful in its own way. Even at fourteen, when she played a glimmer of the tune for Mrs. Kaszynski, she had still felt equal parts fear and exhilaration that she might tap into something beyond her world. She felt special. She had a muse.

But at seventeen, she wanted to be normal. She wanted to worry about the same mundane things as everyone else, not to be haunted by a faceless creature who watched her even without discernible eyes, who *perceived* her through some other sense that Brynn could not even imagine.

It was the noticing that bothered her. She thought her muse was haunting her because it had noticed her all those years ago, when she'd stumbled on something she shouldn't have while playing with the Simon toy. The muse noticed—and then noticed that *it* had been noticed, and started looking back. And now it was always looking at her. Wanting to possess her.

That is what she thought of us.

And still, she could not let us go. She could pretend, for a while, to be normal. She could temporarily abandon her search for the tune.

But in the end, she could not stay away. Our voice was an addiction she could not quit. We tried to teach her our language. We spoke to her and gave her music, and this she could not ignore.

We gave her everything she wanted. All We asked, in return, was that she come find us.

Brynn quit the school choir and told Harlow she wanted to start a band, and since Harlow already played regularly with her brother, it was an easy transition. The band became all-consuming for Brynn. Queen Carrion was everything.

"You look like shit," Harlow told her at school.

"Thank you for that thoughtful assessment."

"You need to stop falling asleep in class. I can't keep kicking your chair to wake you up."

"Noted."

Harlow looked at her. "Haven't you been sleeping?"

"Not really. I've been staying up all night writing music. I think I'm on the verge of a breakthrough."

"What do you mean?"

"Nothing—it's just, I'm inspired. My muse is visiting."

"Okay, well, you might want to tell her to visit during daytime hours."

Brynn had begun to view her muse as the source of her creativity, the way muses have been viewed for thousands of years, and she decided We were essential for her success in making music. She began to understand our desire to communicate. Maybe, she thought, the people who had claimed to have muses in history—writers, artists, poets—had merely been the ones to take notice when a muse was trying to communicate.

Curiosity and hunger still at war with trepidation, she decided she wanted to communicate. She worked tirelessly to get the tune just right, neglecting her studies.

We gave her music, and she fed it to Queen Carrion. Many different tunes came to her over the years, springing to her brain in fountains of inspiration when she opened herself up, when she listened. None of them were the original tune, but they didn't need to be. They were alive in their own way.

One of them came close, though.

It was an echo of the tune. A shadow. A reflection. Not the real thing, not quite—but close.

She called it "Midnight Ritual."

It was this song that opened up her world when she played it at the Wonder Room. When the venue seemed to slip down into the earth, into some below-place, for several heartbeats before it resurfaced.

A part of her recognized that place. She had seen it, smelled it, when playing the piano for Mrs. Kaszynski.

It was where her muse lived.

She read up on the history of the Wonder Room. She researched strange phenomena, and the places—like the Volker Institute—that studied them. She stumbled onto the notion of Low Places: where the two worlds became close, where one might even slip from one to the other.

It took her years to collect enough information that she understood any of this, however. And during that time, she kept writing her music.

Until it dried up.

She had been working on her album, *The Orchid*, so much of which We had given her, but she reached a point, before she was able to complete the final song, where she felt unable to continue. A black swarm of depression buzzed over her, shrouding her from us. This happened sometimes, but it usually passed and deposited her into a state of wild creativity, of manic inspiration, that opened her to our influence.

This time, however, it did not abate. We could not reach her. She was cocooned in it, and it stifled her ears, turned down the volume of her reception.

She became desperate to finish her album and turned to Louella Diaz for help.

"We can do a ritual to open the door," Lou told her, and they cast the salt circle, lit their candles, and called to us.

We were there only a moment before Lou shut the door, having caught a glimpse of our face, but Brynn knew it would not be enough to reach us. We whispered what We could through the cracks in the world to make her see that she needed to do the ritual in a Low Place.

Brynn had always been receptive to such things. As a young child, she had learned a game—something like Bloody Mary—where you light a candle in a dark room, then look in the mirror and say, "The door is open. Please come in." If you did, a spirit would come through. She tried it, thinking the face would appear again, like when she was playing with the Simon, but nothing happened. Eventually, she gave up, but she did convince her friend Harlow to try it.

Unfortunately, something *did* happen to Harlow when she played the game.

Though they never spoke of it, Brynn knew she bore some of the blame for what had fractured the Sorenson family. It was at her urging that Harlow had tried the game in front of the mirrored door of her bedroom closet. Had she seen something looming on the other side of that mirror? No one would ever know, because she fumbled the match. The flame bloomed and spread throughout the house.

Brynn knew she had to find a Low Place. She uncovered scans of documents from the Volker Institute and recognized its purpose: to study these places, and what emerges from them. She believed she had to go there to access her muse. She had to connect, or she feared she would never write another song; her creativity would vanish and never return.

When she found the area where she suspected the Volker Institute must be, she knew she had to go there, to the woods.

We helped her, of course. We urged her on.

We were waiting for her.

Brynn arrived in the forest and knew she had chosen the right place. The air here felt different. Resonant. Alive.

With stones she had found, she constructed a circle, lit her candle, and placed it within. The key—her anchor—she held tightly in one fist, the metal warming against her skin.

She had waited for dusk, thinking it a more appropriate hour for such communion, and she had spent the day playing Queen Carrion's repertoire on her phone, filling the forest with its sounds, its tunes, its patterns that were already so recognizable to us.

We squirmed with joy. We were so close.

All she had to do was play the right frequencies, in the right order, to invite us through—she had to play the tune. The one We had been trying to teach her all these years.

As she sat at the circle, keeping one hand around the candle to stop the wind from stifling its little flame, white wax melting down its side, she played the next song from her phone: "Midnight Ritual."

She could not help herself. She sang along.

But as she sang, the song changed, minutely, in her mouth. She got it *right*, finally, her voice transcending herself, and she sang *the tune*, which widened the cracks enough for us to slip through, reaching up into the bottom of this Low Place. Our temporary face unraveled like a sweater with a pulled string, all our thin hyphae scrambling *up* and *through*.

Though others from our world had gotten through before, We had spent so long trapped in the darkness, We had not been able to hear the way—

Until now.

We stretched up, expanding, spreading thousands of tiny filaments into the dirt.

Brynn did not get to see us, though.

The candle tipped over, snuffed out. Brynn found herself staring up at Jacqueline Price, Rhys's girlfriend, who stood there with a knife in her hand.

Brynn laughed.

There was shock—that Jacqueline was standing before her, must have followed her all the way out here—and there was, also, despair in that laugh, because she believed, in that moment, her ritual had not worked, that it had all been in vain, that her muse had left her for good.

If only she had known We would never leave her.

The look on Jacqueline's face was cold, blank, more like a mask than a face. She raised the knife, blade-out, pointed at Brynn. And Brynn, besieged by her own failure, and not really thinking she would do it, said to Jacqueline: "Go ahead."

She did.

The knife slashed across Brynn's throat. Blood sprayed Jacqueline's face, which had fallen slack with surprise at what she'd done. She watched as Brynn clutched the second smile weeping open on her neck, gouts of blood spurting with every pulse of her heart.

Jacqueline dug a hole for her, though it was not very deep. She did not even realize, as she rolled Brynn into it and covered her up with dirt, that Brynn was still hanging onto life, if only by a thread. She continued to wheeze and gurgle blood even as soft earth piled over her, the life leaking slowly, so slowly, from her body.

From below, We reached her at last, our Brynn, our pet, and We embraced her.

She was right. We did want to possess her. We took her into ourself and thought it a mercy. She was so delicious.

Now she is part of us, forever, and she has introduced us to the wonders of this overworld. There is such a diversity of life here—so much living matter.

So many interesting things to consume. To become.

THIRTY-SIX

Harlow's breath echoed inside the mask.

Everywhere looked the same—the same trees in every direction, the same dark slivers between them, the same canopy scratching a muddy black sky and the smeared ghost of a moon. Her lungs tapped out and she had to slow, a hand pressed against the gallop of her heart.

Everyone was dead, and she was alone in the woods.

She couldn't help but wonder: what was the point? Where was she going?

All she had wanted was to find Brynn, and instead she had destroyed everything. Her mother was right about her. She couldn't be trusted. Everything she touched turned to ash.

I deserve this, she thought.

A glimpse of white ahead, in the space between trees, peering out from behind a trunk: the edge of a face, a shoulder.

The figure emerged: a Venus carved from marble. Harlow didn't want to stare, but Brynn's naked, alabaster body was gliding toward her on cilia-lined feet, and she ached with the sight of her. She lost all the energy and willpower to run, and after all, where else could she possibly want to be except for right here, with Brynn? Not just some imitation, either—she felt it in her bones, had known it as soon as Vic revealed the truth about the Pseudo.

It was itself, and everything it consumed.

Brynn opened her arms to embrace her, and Harlow thought, why not? Why not go to her? She could be with her, at last—she could be with *all* of them. It was like Lou said. They could all be together.

There was something she had meant to do, though.

She slid the letter out of her pocket, paper crinkling as it unfolded, edges smashed and wrinkled from a year of fragile hope. Her throat was too tight for words, so instead she held the letter out, and Brynn took it. Blank eyes roved over the writing, and tiny wavering threads crawled out from her fingertips, feeling their way across the paper, tasting her words. Within moments, black spots of mold bloomed across the page, which curled in on itself, eating away the scrawls of ink until the paper fell, a damp and rotten ball of mush.

Harlow pulled off the heavy gas mask and let it drop, freeing her face to the cool, damp air. She expected the tips of Brynn's fingers to be fuzzy, but the edges of her form behaved. The sensation was strange as she brushed Harlow's cheek, the texture sending a shudder all the way down her body.

Brynn leaned closer, opening her mouth, and it was the kiss Harlow had always quietly longed for, the one she had requested at the end of the now-destroyed letter. She wanted to entangle with this creature even if it was not quite the Brynn she'd long loved, even if it meant being consumed—and maybe she would have, if it weren't for the wriggling hairs in place of a tongue, probing for a new mouth in which to embed themselves.

She pulled back.

Dozens of threads hung loose from Brynn's gaping mouth, like the jaw of a baleen whale, and Harlow tried to reconcile this: that she was looking at Brynn, but she was also looking at a monster. That Brynn was a monster.

"You killed them," Harlow said as the realization came to her, brain trying to catch up with her heart. "If it's still you... how could you? You were willing to kill them—kill all of us?"

The baleen curled in on itself and formed the semblance of teeth. *"All our tombs are full of bodies,"* Brynn sang. Harlow recognized the song, "Secrets Bleeding in the Sand," from their album *Tomb of the Sphinx.* *"You say, 'Open Sesame.' I say, 'are you sure?' Every heart a pyramid with tunnels in its soul. None escape the sands of time—none of us are pure."*

A twig cracked underfoot as Harlow backed away.

Brynn had allowed herself to become a monster in the endless pursuit of her muse. She was so desperate to chase the source of her creativity, she had allowed herself to be consumed by it, transformed.

It wasn't just Brynn anymore. She was also Jacqueline. Audrey. The Pseudo, and whatever inhuman mind had evolved in the darkness of the world beneath their own.

Though it would be so easy to give in to the temptation, to let Brynn consume her, to give up, Harlow realized she did not want to become a monster.

She stumbled away as the Pseudo reached out again.

Brynn's singing haunted her ears, the lyrics sparking an idea in her mind.

Tunnels.

She was back again at the place she had tried so hard to escape:

The Volker Institute.

She'd wandered in what felt like a dozen circles until she was able to find it, tracing her steps back through this long and terrible night. The woods lurked, unsettled, beyond her flashlight, rustling with secrets.

When the triangular facade appeared, it was like coming home—to a haunted house laden with terrible memories. She reminded herself that Vic and Audrey were dead. Even so, when she opened the front door, she half-expected Audrey to be standing there with the gun raised. When she crept under the blinding lights, she glanced over her shoulder, waiting to see Vic's hands reaching for her.

Her heart struggled to return to anything like a normal rhythm.

The first thing she did was grab the pitcher of water beside the camp stove and pour it into her mouth so fast that half of it sluiced down her cheeks, rivulets meeting at the chin and spilling down her front. She didn't care. She gulped, not having realized how dry her mouth had become until the water met it. She set down the pitcher, panting and wiping her face, which turned into little slaps against her cheeks to snap her from the dazed fatigue that threatened to drag her down.

Rest was tempting. She could lie down, if she wanted to. She'd locked the door after her. No one could get in. But she refused to remain here a single moment longer than necessary. Instead, she rummaged through the storage closet to see if there might be anything else useful in there. She found Audrey's backpack and overturned it, unzipping interior pockets.

Three phones clattered to the floor.

Each one as dead as the next.

She stared at the useless black bricks and wondered if there was a charger around here. This took her to the desk, where she froze at the sight of the ham radio. Dropping to her knees, she found the cord and plugged it in. "Hello?" she said into the transceiver once she'd powered it on. "SOS? Mayday?"

Static.

She nudged the dial, tried a new frequency.

Static.

"Hello? I need help!"

Static.

With each new frequency, she paused to listen for long minutes. She listened so intently for a response, straining hard to hear a break, a click, a voice, that she began to think she *could* hear something in the static—whispered, indistinct voices, garbled mutterings reminding her of the voices she'd heard in the forest before they'd found the Volker Institute.

A chill shook through her. What if the Pseudo could weave itself into the electronics? What if it could communicate through the frequencies, the sound waves?

She shut off the radio.

Though every fiber of her being fought against what she was about to do, she knew it was the only way. If she got back to the cabin, she could follow the road from there. She wouldn't be able to find it just by wandering the woods. If she could find the creek, she could feasibly follow that back, but she was so turned around that she didn't even know where the creek was in relation to the Volker Institute.

But she *did* remember the file Lou had been looking over when they were trapped in that enclosure on level 4.

With shaking hands, Harlow dug around in the desk drawers until she found a key card—it had a little yellow square on it, which must have meant something she did not remember, but she could only hope it had the right clearance for where she was going. On her way to the hallway, she scooped up her dead phone and slid it into her back pocket, its weight offering a strange sense of security even if it didn't work.

Armed with the card and the flashlight, she pressed the button to summon the elevator.

The doors slid open on cue. It had been waiting for her. Of course it had; there was no one left below.

Inside, she entered the key card into its slot and selected the button labeled *2*.

The Hub.

The elevator lurched down, pulling Harlow's stomach into an unpleasant pirouette, ground its way past level 1, then came to level 2 and squealed to a halt. The doors lumbered open. With the flashlight, she was able to find a switch on the wall to light up the space before her and found a large round room with freestanding empty doorways— metal detectors?—arranged in the center. Along the curved walls lay half a dozen arched openings into darkness.

God, she hoped she was right about this.

Metal placards glinted above each opening. *Marion Way. Ponderosa.* When she passed one labeled *Sugar Pine Residence Hall*, she began to wonder if she should try one of these passages. Then again, what if these places had been destroyed? What if their tunnels led nowhere— merely to razed earth and dead ends? She had no way of knowing what she would find.

She kept looking, using her flashlight to see the placards where the overhead lighting failed. The next one stopped her.

Trail Creek.

This was it. Within lay absolute darkness. She returned to the panel of switches near the elevator and flipped more of them. Two other tunnels buzzed to life, strings of intermittently set bulbs vanishing into the distance. Despite flipping the rest of the switches, all the remaining tunnels—save one with a few lights so badly flickering they might have induced a seizure—had clearly burnt out long ago.

Including the tunnel that led to Trail Creek Cabin.

She was already not looking forward to traversing the tunnel, but she *especially* was not looking forward to doing so in the dark. Maybe she should try one of the lit-up tunnels, after all. At least she would be able to see where she was going.

Her gaze returned to the entryway of the tunnel labeled *Trail Creek*.

Once they'd run from that place, she'd told herself she would never return. Now it pulled her back, the only place in this wilderness that might feel even a little familiar.

The place where Thorn had died.

Her throat closed, and she had to bend over and breathe through her nose as a wave of dizziness spun through her. She realized she *had* to go back. Even though she knew there wouldn't be a body—the Pseudo left very little behind—she had to bear witness to the scene of his death.

What was walking down a creepy tunnel compared to that?

The flashlight beam receded into its depths, manifesting the strand of dormant lights above, the rounded cement walls.

She started forward.

Regret found her as soon as she looked back and could no longer see the entrance to the Hub.

The walls rang back every breath and footfall, close enough to amplify the tiniest of sounds. Despite the underground chill, sweat beaded and dripped from her forehead along her hairline, prickled her scalp. Her skin buzzed. She hadn't thought she was claustrophobic, but she supposed she would be after she got out of this tunnel.

If she ever did.

It was an insane thought—she knew the tunnel had an end, she knew she would arrive, at some point, in the basement of Trail Creek Cabin—but still she felt like she was wandering into the unknown, that there was no end to the tunnel, no end to the forest, no end to this nightmare...

She pressed on.

The problem with this tunnel, aside from having no working lights, was that she knew what was in here. What she would have to encounter at some point. What was growing out of the wall.

Anticipating this frayed her nerves. She thought she heard voices muttering, the way she thought she'd heard voices within the radio static. Hilarity bubbled up inside her. Maybe she was cracking up. Maybe the cracks in her own mind were growing, like the ones in the tunnel wall, letting in the dirt and rot that would poison what remained of her sanity.

Such a lovely thought.

A faint scrabble. She stopped.

It had come from somewhere ahead of her.

The beam of light shook. Her legs eked out one tentative step, then another. She couldn't turn around now. Going back to the Volker Institute felt like a death sentence.

Another step. She peered into the edge of darkness.

Fine cracks spiderwebbed the wall, grown thick with dirt.

She heard a faint sound like a chuckle.

If she went too slowly past it, maybe it would reach out from the wall, ensnare her like a fly in its web, trap her down here while it digested her.

She would have to pass it quickly.

But what if it had fully crawled out of the wall? What if it had grown a body, was standing in the tunnel somewhere just ahead? The thought sent a deep shudder through her.

Taking a few breaths, Harlow took off at a run.

She tried to keep the flashlight steady, but it swung as she pumped her arms, spasming its mercurial illumination in all directions. As she ran, she caught a glimpse of a pale shape on the wall, a face that was not quite a face staring out at her, mouth open, eager, hungry—

"*Don't you leave,*" it sang, partially Brynn, partially Rhys, partially something else entirely. "*Won't you stay?*"

Harlow leapt past the sound that echoed all around her, the song she could not help but mentally continue.

Won't you come with me—out of the fire, into the dark?

Out of the mire, into my heart?

Oh, won't you stay, down here with me in the dirt?

"I—fucking—*won't!*" she shouted as she ran, leaving the voice behind her, and she could see the end of the tunnel now. Her heart throbbed in her chest as she bolted for it, gasping, tumbled through the archway, and threw herself onto the steps.

In the cellar, she found the ladder, grabbed its rungs, and hauled herself up. Pressing on the underside of the trapdoor, she worried the rug might lie too heavy over it, that she wouldn't be able to open it, that she would be trapped down here—

...down here with me in the dirt.

The door swung up and away from her.

As she crawled over the edge, she discovered the rug still pushed to the side from the night before. She cast around the room, searching for the webbing that had covered the cabin the last time she was here, but found only a black smear on the floor where Wendy had died and a charred lump in the wood stove.

The Pseudo had followed them instead of staying here.

The passage was clear.

Before she threw open the front door, she stopped in the kitchen and hesitated between a bottle of water and the bottle of vodka. One would numb the pounding in her skull and melt the horror from her mind. She could sit down and drink the whole thing. Her body craved it. If she drank it, she wouldn't be going anywhere. She would be staying right here.

She took the bottled water and stepped outside, wondering what would happen if she lingered here, if they would hear her particular vibrations and begin to pull themselves up from the dirt to reach for her. For the moment, she was alone.

The thought settled in her gut.

She was alone.

The urge to lie down in the dirt weighed her down again, but she forced herself to step out onto the grass.

She couldn't give up now. Not after making it all this way. Not after all she had survived.

She would live.

Even if it meant she was alone.

Broken glass glinted in the grass. It was a bottle, jagged edges black and crusty, clotted with what might have been blood.

She made a careful course around it to the worn set of stairs curving down to where the cars were parked. As she went slowly down—not wanting to go too fast and slip, crack her skull open like an egg, and wouldn't *that* be the most ridiculous way to go out at this point?—she wished she knew how to hotwire a car. She imagined hauling ass out of here behind the wheel of Rhys's Camaro and would have laughed had she had any remaining energy to do so. Rhys would roll over in his grave.

If he had a grave.

Her bag, she remembered, was in Wendy's car. Maybe it was unlocked and she could grab it. She came around the side of the Escape and tried to shine the flashlight in the windows but instead was met by the glare of its blinding reflection, until she heard a dull thump from inside the car, and saw, pressed up against the glass, a bloody hand.

THIRTY-SEVEN

Light blinded him.

He sat up, a wave of nausea surging through his body, head swelling into a toxic balloon, and he reminded himself: *You got through the burn unit as a kid. You got through the healing process. You can get through this.*

The wandering blare of light, though—what was that? A UFO? An angel? If angels were real, that would *really* mess with his worldview, even more than the murderous fungus already had.

No, it was a flashlight.

He pressed his hand against the window, peering out, trying to make sense of it. Maybe it was another trick. He thought he could see a familiar shape behind the light, and he figured, well, if this was the time they finally got him, so be it.

He pushed open the door.

The light hit him full in the face, then lowered. Stars dazzled his vision, and he heard the darkness sing with his sister's astonished voice.

"Thorn!"

Thorn wasn't fully aware of how much time had passed, as it had passed in a fever of pain. Night had swirled like an endless dream, then daylight had pressed in on him, heating the car until he passed out, and then darkness again, and now the light that was actually a flashlight.

"What the hell happened?" Harlow demanded. "What happened to your *eye?*"

Yes, he knew he would have to explain that.

After Harlow had taken off with Jacqueline and Lou, Thorn turned to the three pale figures before him—the pseudo-versions of Brynn, Rhys, and Wendy—and prepared to go out fighting. At least his last act would be a heroic one.

But he knew the broken bottle would do no good against them, as it had done no good against Pseudo-Wendy back in the cabin, and he knew it was already crawling through his blind eye, chewing through it to get to the rest of him.

That was when he had the idea. He remembered what they'd done to his face in the burn unit: the way they'd had to scrape his dead skin to remove potential infection.

Maybe he could cut out this infection.

He turned the bottle around.

If he hadn't been filled with the numbing horror that he was about to die—in the same awful way Rhys and Wendy had died—and if he had been able to see out of that eye, to see the sharp edges of glass drawing closer and closer to the pupil, then perhaps he wouldn't have been able to do it. But there was nothing left to lose, and every second that elapsed was another opportunity to wonder if it was already too late, if it had already burrowed past his eye and into his brain, if his final act would be one of excruciating stupidity for nothing.

He drove the broken glass into his eye.

It burst like a cherry tomato—there was a pop and a lightning strike in his head—but he had to keep going, had to scrape out the infection, so he used the glass to dig around the edges of the socket, which welled with blood, and cut through the nerves that tethered the eye—which left him screaming—until the pale orb fell free, squirming, as the tendril within tried to reach back toward him like a severed nerve, desperate for the warmth of his skull.

Thorn could barely see through the bauble of tears over his remaining eye, and his face shrieked with pain, but he laughed, because —well, hell, he didn't even need that eye, anyway.

All of this had happened so quickly, a moment's decision and action, but the three figures still wanted him. He stumbled back, somehow managing to elude their reaching tongues, their hair-thin probing fingers.

Harlow, Lou, and Jacqueline were gone, far into the trees, and he would have no hope of finding them.

The cabin was still infested, overgrown.

And then he thought: the car.

They had tried the Escape earlier, and he didn't think Wendy had bothered locking it afterward. He was sure she hadn't. Even so, as he ran for it, falling over himself down the stairs, he couldn't help but wonder what would happen if it *was* locked. If he grabbed the handle, pulled, and they got him anyway, the whole ordeal of cutting his eyeball from its socket for nothing, after all.

Mercifully, the door clicked open.

He slid inside, hit the locks, and collapsed onto the backseat. Outside, the Pale Forms loomed, features indistinct through his blurry vision. They had gotten into the engine, he remembered. Would they be able to get in here?

It was going to be a long night.

Consciousness slipped and spilled. His eyelids closed, and one of them scraped over an empty hollow that screamed through a tunnel straight into his brain. Hot blood dripped down his cheek, and he wiped it away, then couldn't get the sticky substance off his fingers.

On the other side of the glass, Wendy's face stared in at him, and though she did not speak, he knew what she wanted him to do.

Open the door.

Let her in.

Grief braided into his physical agony and made him want to open the door for her, but luckily he was in too much pain to move.

In moments of lucidity, he reminded himself it wasn't really Wendy out there, but lucidity was a fleeting thing. Sometimes he thought she was coming to prod him awake to get ready for a concert, or even to yell at him for falling asleep in her car—until he remembered Wendy was dead.

He lay back against the seat and fell into the twilight between sleep and waking, a place he had inhabited during much of his time in the burn unit, swimming in morphine, surfacing to that awful burning-itching of being in his damaged body. Craving the former but knowing the latter was necessary, too. The worst part was the eternity of it: time slowed and stuttered, a languid second stretching like taffy, then an hour gone, but everything still the same, still the pain that would not end.

It had no definitive end, either, which was even worse. It hadn't stopped abruptly, leaving him high on endorphins; no, it merely tapered, receding by its half-life, which meant it was never really gone, a half of a half of a ghost echoing even in the scarred flesh.

He stared down that eternity again now as the night lasted eons of cursed twilight, the horror of *forever* flooding him. If he opened the door, at least it would end. She wanted him to do it. He owed it to her, after letting her go over the railing. Death would end the pain. Death would end the restless stretch of twilight.

Wendy pinned him with that empty stare. Her lips curled into a coy smile, full of promises, and he could read her unspoken intention.

Open the door.

He woke to the sight of his curled fingers, grooves of skin lined red with old blood. Morning sun refracted through the window. A seatbelt buckle dug into the small of his back.

Despite the light, his body felt cold. Muted.

Then the pain returned, roiled through him. The urge to vomit crested like a wave, but he hesitated to open the door, knowing what was out there. He blinked, tried to focus on the world beyond the window where trees stood yawning.

He did not see Wendy—or anyone else, for that matter.

Taking the risk, he opened the door, leaned out, and puked onto the gravel. He remembered Rhys vomiting back at the cabin, that tarry liquid of putrefaction, and he stared down at the puddle he had created, wondering if he would find tiny white things wriggling in it like maggots.

When he pulled the door shut, he was left unsure. That creeping worry came over him again: what if he hadn't gotten it out in time? What if even a single piece of the mycelium had been left behind and was, even now, infecting him from the inside out?

He looked up at the rearview mirror and cringed.

The edges of his socket were ragged, pink, and inflamed, crusted with dried blood.

If he hadn't looked like enough of a freak before, he certainly did now. A laugh made its way out of him until it hurt too much to do even that.

Now seemed to be a good time to get out and try to find help, but his body vetoed this plan. Even sitting up made him woozy. He needed to rest more. He needed to be sure he'd gotten it all out of him.

Almost as soon as he lay down again, he passed out.

Again he woke, and this time he was flushed with heat, skin sticky. Daylight had been baking into the car for hours.

He looked out, waiting for the pale figures to show up again. He wondered where Harlow, Lou, and Jacqueline were. Why hadn't they come back yet?

What if they didn't come back?

He checked his face in the mirror again and immediately regretted it. The wound looked even more gruesome, a chunky hole. Even if he was no longer infected with the fungus, he wondered about the kind of infection that might occur from stabbing yourself with glass. He wondered if the blazing heat filling his empty eye socket was a growing infection or just your typical carved-my-eye-out-with-a-broken-bottle sensation.

The stupor of twilight reclaimed him, only this time it was an unbearably hot version that left him feeling parched, filled with dreams of eating sand.

And then it was dark again.

Despite the uneasiness of no longer being able to see into the woods outside the car, at least he was no longer burning up. He didn't know how much longer he could stay here, though. The entire world had become the pain and the twilight of semi-consciousness, and the car like a metal tomb.

Then he saw the light coming down the stairs, beaming through the glass, and the figure behind it.

Harlow.

THIRTY-EIGHT

Thorn was alive.

The discovery spurred Harlow to action. She tipped the bottle of water against his dry, chapped lips. The drink seemed to energize him. She slid her arms under his and helped him out of the Escape.

He was alive, and she clung to this even when he said, "Lou? Jacqueline?" And she had to shake her head in reply, not ready to detail the whole excruciating yarn of it just yet. But Thorn was alive, and she wasn't alone.

"Should we..." She leaned into the car and unzipped her duffel. Inside she found a clean shirt, ripped off one of the long sleeves, and tied it around Thorn's head. He hissed when the cloth made contact with his wound, but at least it would protect it from dirt and anything that might get in and infect it. She slung the bag over her shoulder.

They stepped onto the road and started walking.

With every step, they moved further from the cabin, and this helped keep Harlow going even as her legs ached from all the running she had done through rugged terrain. The cabin, the Volker Institute, all of it receded behind them, but she could still feel eyes on the back of her neck, watching, hoping to catch up to her. She fought the urge to look back over her shoulder at the winding stretch of road behind them, worried she would see Brynn there, just waiting for her to turn around, waiting for her to come back.

Long hours stretched as they limped along, their strides slowing to half the speed at which they'd started, but still they kept going, and they didn't stop because they both knew, somehow, that if they did, they might not be able to start again. It's a wonder what the body can push through in times of absolute necessity.

Their feet finally left the dirt and gravel, met a paved road as the sky began to lighten. A sound rumbled in the distance.

Harlow stopped.

A silver Honda was coming up the road, and she planted herself in the center of the lane, arms up and waving, until it slowed on approach.

The middle-aged couple inside the car was shocked by their appearance, but they ushered them both into the car without hesitation, looked up the nearest hospital on their GPS, and turned the car around.

The leather seat was utter luxury to Harlow. She sank into it and closed her eyes, feeling the hum of the car beneath her, lulled by it, listening to the woman tell them it would be okay, they were going to get them help, and Harlow allowed herself to believe her as dawn broke over the sky.

She took Thorn's hand in hers and did not let go the rest of the way.

She wanted to tell him she was sorry for leaving him at the cabin, but she was too tired to speak, and her mind would not allow her too much of a respite, anyway, for even as the warmth and comfort of the car ride filled her with hope, she could not help but wonder.

Though she hadn't wanted to mention it—her near-contact with the spores in the air—didn't want to add that extra worry to Thorn's plate. Still she wondered: did she put on the mask in time?

Was she sure that not even a single spore had made it inside of her?

How could she know?

muse music sickness nestle nest zest rest jest fest guest guess glissando
glisten glitter gilt guilt tilt windmills windfall wind-tunnel funnel funny
sunny son born barn farm harm alarm fire dire liar lie cry die fly flee
flaw flower power sour dour doubt drought draft drift riff cliff jump
dump stumped stuck stucco stymie die-me diamond monday
monotony monotone tune soon moon monsoon monophonic hooked-
on-phonics phony fickle pickle picture tincture tinnitus tinny tender
fender bender blender bled bleed blood flood food good mood muse
music mucus custard cutter cuttlefish swordfish shellfish selfish self-
centered centerfold gold platinum numb gnome home who am I die I
hear fear see her she is near ear here how haunt hag flag flagellate
flaunt savant savior salvage garbage stage rage mage magic tragic
trapped tapped rapped rapt sapped stark dark park prow row woe low
places faces bases chase embrace erase replace

the dead collect
in low places
their faces are no longer faces
staring up from empty corpses
anyone, no one
everyone
I think my corpse is haunting me

the inevitability of it
and the morbid curiosity: what is she like,
my corpse? what strange places can she show me?
she is my muse, my own death
inviting me
driving me
toward her
the tune is the key
that unlocks her world
another layer too far for ours to reach
except for in places so low
they cannot help dipping into it
touching, tasting each other
why does she haunt me? this non-self
not me, just the corpse I will become
why can't I stop thinking about her?

THIRTY-NINE/AFTER

At least the dead have stopped coming to visit.

Clarity returns by slow degrees as Harlow gets accustomed to the medication, as the alcohol withdrawals leave her more starkly sober than she can remember being in years. Her dad visits, awkwardly asks how she's doing, gives her a bone-crushing hug on his way out. Her mom never shows, but that's no surprise.

Thorn, however, keeps coming back.

"I've been seeing them," she confesses to him. "Lou. Wendy."

He sits there, quiet, for a moment. "I've heard trauma can do that." He leans back, and she can see him struggling not to scratch around the eye patch. "We can get you out of here, you know. I can tell them we want to check you out soon. But you have to prove that you're getting better. That you're not a danger to yourself."

"I'm not."

"You sure?"

Harlow scoffs. "What's that supposed to mean?"

"Truth?"

"Please."

Thorn exhales, pops his knuckles. He looks haggard, face lined with worry. "You want to pretend cutting yourself in the bar was about thinking the infection was inside you. But by then you knew you were clear. Think about how long it lasted inside Rhys—less than twenty-four hours. Even if it was a microscopic fraction of a spore, a single cell of mycelium slowly blossoming inside you, don't you think it would have overtaken you by now?"

Maybe he is right, but still she feels the urge to dig into her flesh, to make *sure*, and she wonders if he has felt that same urge—to dig into his hollow eye socket, desperate to scrape out any remnant that might have lingered. She wants to tell him that *is* the reason she took the knife to her flesh, of course it is, but he isn't done talking.

"Even if that's what you tell yourself—that there was something other than yourself inside your flesh, something toxic you wanted to get out—we both know the truth. The only thing inside you is *you*, Harlow, and you can't stand it because you think *you're* toxic. The only person you've ever really been a danger to is yourself."

"Bullshit." She bristles, shoulders curling inward as she folds her arms across her body, hunching low in her seat.

His gaze is too piercing for her to look directly at him.

"Okay, I'm not sure why I need to say this, because it seems so fucking obvious to me, but look: setting the fire was an accident. You were a kid. That fire could just as easily have burned *your* face off. I know you wish that's what really happened. You're still trying to make it happen. And who's been looking out for you, all these years, to make sure it *doesn't*? How many times have I dragged you home and poured water down your throat when you were on the verge of alcohol poisoning? Just... stop punishing yourself, okay?"

Something breaks in Harlow's chest. She closes her eyes and sees the charred house, the rotting memories lurking within, and reminds herself the remains of that house were demolished years ago; a new house is standing there now, a new family living there, not a trace of what happened any longer.

Maybe it's time to let the house collapse to ash.

She doesn't want to open her eyes yet. Her hands press against her eyelids, trying to keep her there in the dark, refusing the window Thorn has opened for her.

His voice finds her. "So that's why you're here. You were drunk, and you cut longways, not across. This place seemed like a good temporary solution because I didn't have it in me to keep an eye on you 24/7."

Harlow sniffs and blinks at him. "Especially since it's just the one eye, now."

A guffaw explodes out of Thorn. A man sitting on the couch in front of the TV turns to stare at them. Harlow can't help herself; she starts laughing too, and they only get themselves under control when a nurse comes by to ask if they're okay. Harlow waves her off. She feels pleasantly drained, the laughter having wrung poison from her gut. "Hey, what about all that stuff with the Escher Society?"

Thorn shrugs. "I thought it would be good if you had something to focus on."

"So it's not real?"

"Oh no, it's real." He feels around his pockets until he produces an envelope. "And what's more—they got back to me."

"What? *Seriously?*"

The envelope has already been ripped open, and he pulls the paper from it, unfolding it on the table.

As Harlow leans forward to read, she feels her stomach drop.

Dear Mr. Sorenson,

Thank you for informing us of your concerns regarding one of our properties. We have investigated this matter and will be rectifying any potential negligence that may have occurred during this period of inactivity. Thanks to your diligent communication, we have rediscovered the potential of this property and look forward to renewed work after necessary safety upgrades have been made to the facility, which will ensure its security moving forward. For this, you have our gratitude.

Further, we would like to remind you that trespassing on private property is strictly prohibited and will be prosecuted to the fullest extent of the law. We hope you will keep this in mind in your future endeavors.

Regards,
Escher Industries, Inc.

FORTY/AFTER

"Does that mean…" Harlow's eyes have gone round. "Oh, hell no. They can't reopen that place. They can't restart whatever messed up experiments they were doing."

"Sounds like that's exactly what that means."

Thorn folds the letter into tiny squares, more folds than necessary, and shoves it back into the envelope. Not even a name on it. Return address is a P.O. Box. The Escher Society seems to be a dead end. "I guess that's it."

"Are you joking? That's not it. I *told* you—she knows where I am. She's going to keep trying to get to me. She'll find a way. She can travel through the cracks."

Thorn leans his elbows on the table. "I know. She's after me, too."

"What?" Harlow's voice is a quick blade. "Since when?"

"Since I got out of the hospital."

***

When Thorn left the hospital, it was with a pressure bandage over his missing eye. He had to wear it for five days after the enucleation surgery to remove any remaining tissue from the eyeball he'd haphazardly carved out. They cleaned the socket and sent him on his way—all in all, a much less terrible and painful experience than enduring the burn unit as a kid.

He knew he wouldn't be able to explain what he had done when the police came to question him. Everything seemed so strange, so unreal. He wasn't sure why he said it was a bear attack, only that it made sense at the time. It attacked their friends, swiped him in the eye with its claw. Surely that would explain the injury well enough.

He hadn't known, at the time, what Harlow had told them. Maybe she thought they would believe her, or maybe she was just sick of that look from their mom—that look asking for an answer—so she decided to give that answer to the police.

She told them the truth.

Of course, they didn't believe her.

When Thorn called it a bear attack, it made Harlow seem like a lunatic. He felt bad about that, but how could he have known? She'd hightailed it out of the hospital as soon as he was out of surgery.

"You'll be staying with us while you recover," his mom said, allowing for no argument. She and her husband, Nelson, put him up in his old room where he had once spent so many weekdays blasting music through headphones and neglecting his homework. It was no longer wallpapered in band posters, and the black sheets he'd used as curtains had been replaced by faux wood blinds, but the twin bed remained, not rumpled with heaps of dirty socks but crisp and presentable with a navy blue duvet. The pillows were still flat as paper, though.

The first time he saw Wendy, he thought it was a dream.

He was still high on painkillers, trying to sleep, trying to lie very still so as not to jostle the bandage against the raw cavern in his skull, and he wasn't even sure if his other eye was open or closed. It was dark, but he could see, which is why he thought it was a dream. He could see her so clearly: Wendy, coming to him now because maybe he *was* infected, after all, and he was dying, and she was coming to escort him to the afterlife. Or maybe she was just coming to yell at him for letting her fall over the railing.

A low hum filled the air, a vibration he could feel deep in his bones, and it made his skin want to crawl off his muscles and scurry away.

Then she was gone.

Maybe he fell asleep, or maybe he woke up. Either way, it was just a dream. That's what he had to believe.

A few days later, he had his bandage removed and was fitted with a temporary prosthesis. "You can go back to work in two weeks," the doctor said, smiling as if this were good news. Likely, she didn't know Thorn worked as a fry cook, a job he'd taken after Brynn disappeared, when the gigging dried up with the band incomplete, forcing him to make ends meet somehow. At least he got to eat a lot of burgers.

Better, perhaps, than Nelson's meatloaf and his asking, "How you doing, champ?"

Better than his mom's compulsive worrying. "Do you need anything? Are you in pain? Do you want me to call and ask for a refill? I'll do it, you know. They never give you enough. The drug addicts have ruined medication for everyone else. Are you hungry? I have some frozen waffles—"

When he suggested he cook, since clearly he was the only one in the house with a sense of taste, his mom balked. "Don't you dare lift a finger. That's my job. You relax."

They both commented on the prosthetic, too, but he could tell they were insincere attempts to be reassuring. "It looks so natural! Even better than before!"

"I hate it," he said.

"It's temporary," his mom assured him. "Once they fit you for the permanent one, no one will even be able to tell. Really, it's so amazing what they're able to do with glass eyes these days."

She wanted so badly for him to feel good. For him to be healthy and happy and, most importantly, look *normal*. Maybe that was why she'd married the most boring human ever to walk the earth two years ago: Nelson the dentist, wearer of plaid collared tee shirts and khaki shorts, with a face so nondescript his own mother wouldn't be able to pick him out of a police lineup.

When Thorn excused himself to stare at his fake eye in the bathroom mirror, trying to reconcile yet another significant change in what his face looked like, he felt his hair stand up, flesh breaking out in goosebumps as a low vibration unsettled the air.

Then, in the mirror—behind his face, or overlapping it—he saw Wendy.

She put her arms out to him, humming, without words asking him to come to her. As the tone buzzed over his skin, bringing with it a sensation of dread, he almost wanted to. He wanted to reach back for her and let her embrace him, and he had to remind himself that she wasn't really there. She was dead. It was just his broken mind wishing he could see her again.

He believed this fully until Harlow came to visit.

She had kept away for the most part—no surprises there. She often said she would rather have her fingernails pulled out with pliers than visit Mom.

They hadn't had a chance to talk, and Thorn was desperate to know what exactly had happened while he was lying delirious in Wendy's car. He and Harlow closed themselves in his room, and she told him everything, straining to get out the details of Lou's death and Jacqueline's confession.

What he couldn't shake, though—what Harlow had tried to gloss over—was something one of her captors had told her: that the fungus wasn't just a mimic, that it was sentient, that it somehow contained the people it had consumed. He asked her everything she could remember about the Volker Institute, and when he could tell he had worn out her storytelling stamina, he changed the subject, made a few jokes, tried to get her to crack a smile.

When she asked him how he was doing post-surgery, he frowned and looked away, remembering the glass orb in his socket. "You know what's fucked up? It actually feels... *wrong*... having two eyes." He raised an eyebrow. "Is that weird?"

"I don't think it's that weird," Harlow said, and he felt a rush of gratitude for how nonchalant she sounded.

"Whatever, I like the patch better anyway." He pulled it out and held it up in front of the glass eye. "I was thinking of getting into pirate metal."

A knock, and the door opened. "Need anything?" Their mom asked. She leaned against the door frame, hair pulled back in a clean ponytail, face carefully set, mouth pursed, eyebrows up. A rehearsed expression. Thorn remembered this look from when he was a kid. A face at war with itself: pitying while at the same time wanting to act as if nothing were out of the ordinary. It said she found it hard to look at him.

It didn't exactly help that bloody tears had begun to weep from beneath the glass eye, something the doctor told him might happen. Mom backpedaled, announcing her intention to get a washcloth, while

Harlow stuck out her tongue, threw him the devil horns, and said it was the most metal thing she'd ever seen.

"You shouldn't be having company," their mom said when she returned with the washcloth. "You should be resting."

Harlow rolled her eyes behind her back. "I'm not *company*, Mom. I used to live here too."

"It's too much stimulation." She pressed the washcloth to Thorn's face, and he took it from her, tried to wave her off.

It was enough to send Harlow slinking away. Thorn missed her as soon as she was gone.

He could also tell that she had been a little drunk.

***

A vibration in his bones.

He could feel her approaching like a storm: the way his skin prickled with chills, nausea tracing its way through him as that inexplicable feeling of dread rose up from his bowels.

Wendy was coming.

The house was dark and quiet just past midnight, and he had turned off the bedroom light to crawl into bed, when he felt her. At first, he was alone. The tilted blinds admitted the sodium-yellow glow of a streetlight that did not quite reach the corner of the room. There was nothing in that corner.

Not at first.

Then a shape. A figure. As if someone *was* there, and suddenly he felt like he was not alone.

By degrees the form solidified, his eye adjusting to it. The darkness thinned to accommodate her presence, so pale she faintly shone. Her arms were out, waiting for an embrace. When he was able to see her face emerge from out of nothing, he saw the smile carved beneath her blank white eyes.

And all the while—that low hum droning deep in his eardrums, almost too low to hear.

When he'd thought she was a dream, her presence hadn't frightened him so much as made him miss her. But now?

She was here, she was real, and it was both Wendy and *not*. Both her and something *other*, holding out her arms and smiling, humming lower than any human could hum, swimming up from the darkness in the corner of his bedroom.

"What do you want?" he asked.

Even though he could see her right in front of him, at the same time she seemed somehow distant, as if he were looking at her from far away. And that was it, wasn't it? She wasn't *really* here: she was pressing up from the other side of something, peering through a window in the fourth dimension. Maybe her humming created a little hole through which she could peer. He didn't know, he didn't understand, but his chest ached and sorrow weighed him down and fear made him want to run from her—at least, it made him press his back against the wall behind him.

She closed her fist, though she hadn't been holding anything, and now it seemed there was something inside of it, behind the curled fingers. The smile never left her face as she turned her hand palm-up and opened it like a flower.

Sitting on her palm was a small orb, tendrils forming a thin tail on one side. He didn't know what he was looking at until he found himself leaning closer, compelled by curiosity, and the glint of his temporary prosthesis—which he'd left sitting on top of the dresser, having finally taken it out—caught the sodium lamp.

He swallowed.

It was his eye. The only part of him she'd managed to get before he took it out.

She held it there as if to say, *I want the rest.* As if to say, *I see you.*

He sprang across the room and hit the light switch, breath coming hard, but by the time he turned again, she was already gone. His hands wouldn't stop shaking. He cracked the window open and lit a cigarette, not even caring if he stunk up his mom's house. By the time he got control of himself, he couldn't help thinking it was funny: he hadn't wanted Wendy to go when she announced she was moving to Los Angeles, and now he wanted nothing more than for her to leave him alone.

He never put the prosthetic eye back in after that. He felt better wearing the patch, even though it irritated the back of his ear. It was just the falseness of the fake eye, like the falseness of a mannequin, that he could not stand.

Like something inhuman imitating him.

He was almost glad, a few weeks later, to go back to work, if only to have something to take his mind off these nighttime visits. Having been mothered quite enough for one lifetime, he moved back into his own place, subsisting on burgers, burgers, and more burgers. He spent his free time researching the Volker Institute, which led him to the Escher Society. A vague curiosity at first, which quickly morphed into a desperation to rid himself of Wendy.

He needed Harlow's help, though. He hadn't been to the Volker Institute like she had.

She wasn't answering her phone, and he knew she was drinking too much, but he couldn't babysit her. He knew, too, that she was upset about those news articles that had insinuated she'd had something to do with their deaths—as the only person to make it out of the woods both alive and unharmed—but that only frustrated him because they both knew it was untrue, and they both knew no one was actually accusing her of anything.

It was just Harlow, unreliable as ever.

He hadn't realized how bad things had gotten until he found out what she did with a knife in a dive bar.

"She wants us both," Harlow says. "She wants to complete the band. Get the whole set."

"Collect 'em all."

"More like kill 'em all."

"That's a good album." Thorn looks around at the slate blue walls and the analog clock on the wall ticking away the afternoon hours, the tile flooring and plastic chairs. "So what are we going to do?"

"First things first," Harlow says, and there's a spark in her eye he hasn't seen in weeks, not since before she entered this place, which has made her dull, vacant. She looks like herself again. "Let's get me the fuck out of here."

FORTY-ONE/AFTER

Bills pile on the dining table, rent is late, and Harlow—who had been bartending before her hospitalization—is pretty sure she doesn't have a job anymore, but she can't bring herself to care about any of that right now.

Brynn's notebooks, her research, scatter the apartment in a flurry of paper. Before they went to the woods, Thorn had told Harlow to stop looking through that stuff. "It's not good for you. It's not helping." She feels vindicated now that he is poring through the notebooks alongside her, asking, "How much did she know about it when she went out there? You think she knew what it was?"

They flag anything that seems remotely relevant, stick Post-it notes to pages, pass them back and forth. "She went out there specifically to summon her muse," Harlow says as she puzzles over a page of word salad.

"And we think her muse was…?"

She nods. "I think so. It communicated with us through music. It did the same with Brynn." It's a dreadful realization: Brynn spent her life haunted by the Pseudo, the monster she would become. "She found a way to summon it. Maybe she also knew how to do the opposite. To banish it."

The hours pass, and when they come no closer to finding a solution, a way to get rid of Queen Carrion, a little worm grows in the back of

Harlow's brain. A sudden desire. Just one drink, to take the edge off. A little whiskey to warm her, soften her.

"Hey, Thorn?"

He puts a finger on a page to hold his place and glances up.

"Could you pour…" She takes a breath and exhales. "Could you pour out the alcohol in the kitchen?"

He grins. "I thought you'd never ask."

Liquid glugs down the drain. She wants to call out to him to stop, to pour her a drink instead; she's changed her mind; she can't do this sober, but she keeps her mouth shut until it is too late. Empty bottles clatter in the recycling bin.

She feels oddly relaxed. Now that the booze is gone, the craving has passed, too, and Harlow realizes what she *really* needs:

She needs to drum.

Three weeks of dust has settled over her kit. Her palms gently swipe it from the drum skins. It clouds the air when she blows it from the cymbals. The sticks find their way into her hands like extra limbs, becoming a part of her that she forgot how much she missed.

A quiet drum kit is a storm cloud: laden with energy, ready to release it at the first crash of thunder. As soon as she sits, her body is already humming for it, craving the release of sound. Thorn keeps paging through notebooks as she tightens the batter, adjusts the tension of drum heads until they speak, tunes the bass drum until the attack and tone feel just right. It's like stretching her muscles after a long nap.

Sticks meet skin, and she sinks into the patterns, the rhythms, the things that have always made sense to her and taken her outside of herself. Different rhythms line up and intersect, washing over her as muscle memory takes over. It clears her mind to work through other things.

She read once that drummers' brains are different from those of non-musicians, the activity resulting in thicker fibers between hemi-spheres and allowing for a more efficient exchange of information. Maybe that's why the Pseudo is drawn to musicians. It's learning the right construction of connections to transfer information and consciousness across vast distances where it stretches beneath the forest floor.

Maybe there is a way to shut down that exchange.

The surefire way Harlow has always shut down her own brain is through alcohol. Poison. What is poison for a fungus?

Too quickly, she tires. She needs to get back in shape. Her back screams and her wrists are tight.

Still—it feels good.

She has spent so much time over the years trying to hone her body, to control it, by mastering drumming—muscles working in sync, like a dance. When she dropped the match as a kid, no longer in control, her mom ever after told Harlow to tuck in her elbows, watch where she was going, be careful, don't drop that. In hearing it so much, Harlow came to believe she was prone to disaster. She had to keep careful control over her body—long and lanky as it was—or something terrible would happen. She could never simply let her body exist. Each movement had to be monitored, born of conscious intent. When she wasn't drumming, she felt clumsy and stiff in her own skin. What if her body decided to defy her? What if it got up and walked around at night while she was sleeping? What if her muscles spasmed? What if she turned into the monster her mother had always believed her to be?

Now that she is sober, Harlow is acutely aware of herself in her own body, something the alcohol had numbed. After drumming, she finds herself comfortable in her skin for the first time in weeks, maybe months.

"You should check this out," Thorn says in the ringing silence. "I'm reading about infrasound. Did you know that a lot of supposed hauntings are actually a result of infrasonic vibrations? Super low tones can lead to feelings of dizziness and fear." He sets down the paper. "Every time Wendy has shown up, there's always this really deep hum. This low vibration."

Wiping sweat from her face with the side of her forearm, Harlow flops onto the couch beside him. "Okay… so she communicates with tones, but maybe there's something else to it, beyond communication. Something to do with frequencies." A frown tugs her lips. "You know how we were playing 'Midnight Ritual' when the lights went out at the Wonder Room?"

"You mean our cursed song?" Thorn deadpans. "No, I'd completely forgotten."

"There was something about the tune… and I know Brynn had been working on that song for a long time, because she shared snippets with me for probably years before it was done. Years. Who takes that long to write a song? Maybe she knew… she knew it would unlock something. Like a key."

"Play the right series of notes, open a door," Thorn says, nodding slowly as he continues to read the page in his hands. He sucks in a breath. "Holy shit. I have an idea."

When he tells her the idea, Harlow's first reaction is *absolutely not*.

"I don't think it'll work if we're not physically in the same place," he explains. "We have to be near her."

"I'm not going back to the woods."

"What if we could summon her somewhere a little closer to home? Another Low Place?"

Harlow balks. "And bring her *here*? To a city with thousands of people she can murder? It would be like a feast from hell." She shakes her head. "And what if it doesn't work?"

"Then I guess we're all fucked."

They order pizza as dusk chokes out the day, and Harlow knows he is wondering, just as she is, whether they will look up to find a figure staring at them from the corner of the room, a blank eye peering around the edge of a doorway. She can feel tension crackling in the air as they chew.

"Okay," she says at last. "How do we do it?"

nature can hear us. it's always listening
like violin strings, sensitive to vibrations
fungal electronics: can mycelium convey electrical signals?
fragile connections
superstrings
information
the pulse of life
the dead will be eaten by fungus
it is what feasts on us in the end
all life shall be consumed
I read somewhere homo sapiens evolved after eating psilocybin
mushrooms
which sparked higher consciousness
language, art, religious experience
that psychedelic mushrooms are an alien intelligence
with its own language
feeding us the stuff of life, then feeding on us after life
when we are no longer ourselves, when we become the no one of a
corpse
fungus will return our meat to the earth
where it might become something else
a hemlock or a fly

we will be gone
but something of our selves will remain
tiny fragments cycling through life and death
returning
as the fungus returns them to the cycle
is this how we transcend death?
by becoming death?

STUDY: "THE EFFECTS OF LOW-FREQUENCY SOUND WAVES ON MYCELIAL GROWTH"

…observed the high frequency of lightning strikes upon mushrooms in comparison to other organisms, which may reveal a clear evolutionary advantage. Preceding lightning strikes, the rolling thunder of low-frequency tones signals impending rain. Through millions of years of evolution, mushrooms have learned to respond to these tones to prepare to absorb water and electricity, which spur their propagation. In this way, low-frequency sound waves behave as an alarm clock that awakens the mushrooms and stimulates growth. The study observed that the higher the wave frequency, the higher the inhibition of growth…

CHAPTER FORTY-TWO / AFTER

How to break into a nightclub after hours:

Step one, get a job there.

It's no secret that the Wonder Room profited from the tragedy that occurred at the Queen Carrion show, drawing in rubberneckers, people interested in the occult, ghost hunters, and anyone with a morbid sense of curiosity about the place. So when Harlow tells the owner she has experience bartending and is looking for a job, he practically falls over himself to offer her a position, probably wondering how he can tactfully get the word out to fans and dark tourists. Especially with her recent notoriety as the key suspect in her bandmates' mysterious deaths.

Yes, she knows he sees her merely as a sideshow attraction. He probably doesn't even care about her cocktail-slinging skills. But Harlow doesn't plan to be working there for very long.

Just until she gets her first closing shift.

It's only her and the manager, Cory, a stout, amiable man only too happy to offer in-depth answers to each of her questions, delighted by her curiosity. She feels bad taking advantage of his kindness and tries to make up for it by doing a thorough job mopping the sticky floors, wiping down the bar, and organizing glasses. She even polishes the handle of the door to the old bank vault where the bar sits, not that anybody uses the handle, as the door is soldered open, just decoration now.

It feels strange, looking at the raised stage where she remembers sitting frozen at her kit while the room plunged into darkness, broken then by screams. She looks at the front door and cannot help but imagine dozens of people crushed in their desperation to exit. Murphy Dunning, his lungs compressed as the life slowly leaked out of him.

After he finishes balancing the till, Cory shows her how to set the security alarm, as well as how to disarm it. He explains the process for locking up the back door, which leads to the alley with the dumpster, and exiting through the front.

"I always like closing up. Nice and quiet," he says as he shuts off the lights. "Only thing you got to worry about is getting the stragglers out, especially if they're sloppy drunk. But you already know—this ain't your first rodeo." She follows him out, and he locks the front door from the outside. "That covers it for tonight. Good work."

"Thanks," she says, again feeling sorry for what she is about to do, hoping Cory won't be blamed for it. He couldn't have known, after all, that she disabled the alarm when he wasn't looking, before they stepped out. He couldn't have known that, rather than lock up, she propped open the back door.

She checks the glowing face of her phone—just about 3:30 am. Wet pavement swims under the streetlights. Dark buildings hulk on the other side of the street. She is surrounded by the eerie quiet of a city asleep.

Once she has seen Cory get into his car and drive away, she turns the corner and heads around the block to the alley, greeted by the fetid funk of the dumpsters. A car has already pulled up to the back of the Wonder Room and sits with its headlights off.

Thorn steps out. Harlow pulls open the back door to the Wonder Room and props it wide with a loose brick. Then she turns to the car, where several large bags form lumps across the backseat. "All right," she says. "Let's do this."

It takes about half an hour to set everything up, even though Harlow's is a compact kit, and she left some pieces, like the cymbals, at home, taking only the basics she was sure she'd need. The stage looks somewhat forlorn with just her kit, an amp, Thorn's guitar, and a microphone, but it will have to do.

While she was on the clock, Harlow had spent the hours of her shift buzzing with anticipation, counting down the minutes to closing time, mixing drinks, trying to get a look at the sound system controls. She was so busy she didn't have time to even want a drink, despite being quite literally surrounded by alcohol.

Now that it's just her and Thorn in the empty bar, and the sick dread in her gut, palms going clammy, she thinks how easy it would be to grab a bottle from behind the bar. Pour a shot. Down it before Thorn even notices. Just one swig.

But she knows as well as any other heavy drinker: it's never just one drink.

So, at least for now, at least tonight, and maybe tomorrow, and the next day—it will have to be zero.

She needs to be sharp, clear, prepared.

"You ready?" Thorn asks. They sit on the edge of the stage, lit only partially, as they didn't turn on the full stage lights, which seemed far too bright for this intimate affair. Harlow has a bottle of vodka beside her, but it's one she isn't going to drink.

She nods.

It's showtime.

She settles in at her kit, trying to get a good grip on the sticks with her sweaty palms, as Thorn pulls his guitar strap over his head and tunes his instrument, plucking out tender, quiet notes until he is satisfied.

Then they play.

Maybe it isn't the full song with all the parts—Thorn moves back and forth between rhythm and Rhys's part—but it is enough for the song's key tunes, rhythms, patterns to manifest themselves, and something about playing it live feels more potent, anyway, than if they went with a recording.

The Wonder Room fills with the sounds of "Midnight Ritual."

Halfway through the song, Harlow feels the temperature plummet. She shivers, plays harder, heating her body through movement. The cold feels unnatural. It wasn't this cold when she was closing the bar.

Darkness seems to flood in from the corners of the room, like a creeping wave, and it brings with it the smell of rot. Not the nasty garbage and urine smell of the alley, but an earthy, vegetal smell, like produce left in the fridge long enough to mold.

She recognizes it now. They are playing their way *lower*, pulling this place closer to the Underneath.

If Queen Carrion has been traveling through the cracks between worlds to watch them from the other side of things, then she should be able to hear their call. She should be able to come to them, into this Low Place. Space doesn't seem to operate the same way between worlds as it does on the surface.

"Repeat!" Harlow shouts, her voice sounding distant in her own ears as darkness thick as smoke fills the room, and when they reach the end of the song, they start over.

This time, it isn't just their instrumental version of the song that blasts through the Wonder Room.

Someone is singing.

She hears her, as if from far away, and then the voice grows stronger, drawing closer. Brynn's voice.

Queen Carrion is coming.

Harlow keeps playing even as fear twists her gut and sends her heart hammering up her throat, pulsing in her head in time with the beat of her drumming.

On the floor—coming up from between the tiles where the grout has cracked—a rising thread. Another. Twining together, reaching.

Bit by bit, Queen Carrion pulls herself up through the cracks, threads creeping up from across the floor to gather at the center, to stitch together, to weave her form, drawn in by the music. A skeletal figure. A department store mannequin. A person.

Then: Brynn.

She stands in the center of the Wonder Room, and there is a feathery smile on her face. Though her eyes are blank, without iris or pupil, Harlow knows she can see them, and she is delighted by what she sees. She is exactly where she wants to be. Her feet begin to glide across the floor, pulling her closer to the stage.

Harlow's rhythm goes erratic. A drumstick slips from her hand and clatters across the stage. Even without the drum, Brynn's voice continues to sing, to scream, the song.

"I will drink your blood.

I will swallow you whole.
You will never escape me,
I live in your soul."

And Harlow thinks, yes, Brynn has always lived in her soul, hasn't she? Just as Brynn's muse always lived in *her* soul. If Harlow has a muse, then surely it is Brynn. She will drink your blood like a vampire—that's Brynn, too. Sucking in love and never returning, never reciprocating. And there's something alluring about her, a hypnotic quality that has always compelled Harlow. Maybe she's always had it, or maybe it came to her when she was five years old, playing with a Simon toy. Maybe it was her muse, the thing that haunted and inspired her, that hungry thing.

Fine tendrils fan out like wings from behind Brynn's back. They envelop her for a moment, like a cocoon, and her form begins to change. Her face reshapes itself and her body slims until Harlow is staring down at Jacqueline. Jacqueline, singing Brynn's song. Jacqueline, trailing white threads behind her like the long train of a wedding dress, or the cape of royalty. Jacqueline, who, like the Pseudo, just takes what she wants, leaving death in her wake.

She smiles, showing off those little white Chiclet teeth, and it's a smile that says: *I won.*

"Thorn!" Harlow shouts. "Now!"

Thorn stops playing and pulls out his phone. The frequency generator app is already open and set to the highest frequency available: 20,000 Hz. He hits "play" and holds the phone up to the microphone, which gives an initial whine of feedback.

And then—nothing.

Dread rises in Harlow. She doesn't hear anything, and she wonders if it's even working, she wonders if this was a terrible mistake, she wonders what it will be like when Queen Carrion climbs over the edge of the stage, she wonders what it will feel like to die—

But Jacqueline has stopped.

The edges of her form have gone fuzzy, static, individual threads jumping and vibrating and going haywire, unraveling like yarn. Her face loses definition; her hands become loose tangles of thread; her skin leaps and spasms and seems to melt.

The frequency is playing. It's just too high-pitched for Harlow to hear.

Queen Carrion can hear it, though.

Jacqueline's body falls apart, loses shape, becomes a diffuse ball of squirming hyphae, and Harlow is so mesmerized and repulsed by the sight she almost forgets the bottle, corked with a dishcloth, sitting on the stage beside her kit. She grabs it and pulls out Lou's lighter, snapping it to life, igniting the end of the cloth.

She's always been good at starting fires.

The Molotov cocktail smashes into the writhing remains of Queen Carrion, and the tangled ball of thread goes up with a *whump*. White fuzz quickly blackens, flames leaping, sizzling, popping. Her scream is like the shriek of woodland insects, burning cicadas, and long thin limbs flail out, try to escape the engulfing flames—snap out at the drums, the stage, the lights overhead. One pops, rains a tinkle of glass.

Harlow has never enjoyed the sight of fire so much in all her life.

"Burn, bitch."

The screaming rises, becoming Jacqueline's high shriek, becoming Brynn's Queen Carrion scream that she's used in so many of their songs. The long filaments whiplash out again, grasping for anything, still spasming from the fire and the high-frequency tone blasting through the microphone.

Harlow sees faces try to form in the fire, ephemeral, rising and sinking again into the bubbling froth of creation—Brynn, Jacqueline, Audrey, Lou, Wendy, Rhys, Victor, and other faces she does not recognize. The last one she sees is blank, eyeless, the face of a corpse desperate for life, hungry for it.

And then all that is left is a clump of charred material.

Thorn leaps off the stage and returns in a blast of white foam. When the fire is covered, he drops the extinguisher with a metal clang.

For a moment, they both stay where they are, poised, listening, waiting for another figure to draw itself out of the floor. Eventually, Thorn sits down with his back against the edge of the stage, eye patch slightly askew, and Harlow slides down beside him, both of them staring at the scorch mark on the floor, the mess of burnt matter and white foam.

Thorn tilts to the side to reach into his back pocket, which disgorges a smashed pack of Winstons. He pulls one out, brings it to his lips with shaking fingers. Harlow holds her hand out until he slides a second cigarette out of the pack and gives it to her. She flicks Lou's lighter against hers and then does the same for Thorn.

They smoke, for a moment, in silence.

Then Thorn says what she's already thinking. "There's more of it out there, in the woods. That wasn't all of it."

"I know." Harlow takes a long drag. She realizes Brynn will never really be gone. Harlow will carry her muse with her, perhaps for the rest of her life, just as Brynn carried Queen Carrion. Maybe she will catch glimpses of her in her peripheral vision, see a white eye peering out from the cracks in the world. Maybe that familiar voice will whisper strange tunes in her ear. Maybe she will never, truly, be rid of it. "But… now she knows we can kill any part of her that comes for us. She might not want to try again. Maybe it will be enough."

Thorn nods. "Yeah. Maybe."

The darkness has receded, and now it is just the Wonder Room again. Empty. Quiet. Smoke drifts up from their cigarettes, and Harlow thinks Thorn should really quit. These things taste terrible. She frowns at the cigarette between her fingers as it drips ash onto the foam-covered floor. "You know, I think this is a no smoking bar."

Thorn's laugh is a cloud of smoke. It's music.

FROM "WHAT EVER HAPPENED TO QUEEN CARRION?"
THE CURIOUS CASE OF ONE BAND'S   SELF-DESTRUCTION

… Afterward, the Sorenson siblings moved on to form a duo act a la the White Stripes. Calling themselves the Vile Hornets, they enjoyed moderate success on the local circuit. In an interview, their band manager, Caspian Benedetti said, "What happened to them was tragic. Thorn and Harlow have been through a lot, and they're dealing with it in the best way they can: by making music."

When asked if they were looking to revive Queen Carrion, the response was an emphatic *no*.

Over the years, Queen Carrion has fallen into obscurity, largely forgotten, though there remains a small but dedicated online following still invested in uncovering the truth about this seemingly cursed band and its mysterious fate. Some have even gone as far as to try to find the place where they stayed in the Umpqua Forest, seeking to track down the exact cabin and dig up any clues about what really happened out there.

Perhaps we'll never know the true fate of Queen Carrion. Perhaps some mysteries are better left unsolved.

ACKNOWLEDGMENTS

No one creates alone (not even Brynn Werner). Many thanks go to Jake, my partner in all things; my agent Jill Marr; the CLASH team, including Christoph and Leza who gave this book a home; Angela for her excellent copyedits; my own band, Guerra/paz, especially Mona, for helping me realize my weird little dream of being a cellist in a band; all my fellow musicians in the Symphony of the Verdugos; the fine folks who put on StokerCon in San Diego, which allowed me to connect with Christoph to pitch this book, and all the other horror writers I met or reunited with there; the members of the HWA LA, particularly my chapter co-chair Kevin Wetmore; my colleagues at GCC for always asking about and supporting my writing (even if some of them are too scared to read it); and all musicians, writers, and people who create.

ABOUT THE AUTHOR

Jo Kaplan is the Shirley Jackson Award nominated author of *It Will Just Be Us* and *When the Night Bells Ring*. Her short stories have appeared in Fireside Quarterly, Black Static, Nightmare Magazine, Vastarien, Horror Library, Nightscript, and numerous other anthologies and magazines. In addition to writing, she teaches English at Glendale Community College and is the co-chair of the Horror Writers Association's Los Angeles chapter. She also plays cello in both the Symphony of the Verdugos and the band Guerra/paz.

ALSO BY CLASH BOOKS

BEYOND THE PLANET OF THE VAMPIRES

Ulrich Baer

BLACK BRANE

Michael Cisco

8114

Joshua Hull

EVERYTHING THE DARKNESS EATS

Eric LaRocca

STRANGE STONES

Edward Lee & Mary SanGiovanni

A PLAY ABOUT A CURSE

Caroline Macon Fleischer

EMINENCE FRONT

Rebecca Rowland

ON SUBMISSION

Michael J. Seidlinger

BELOW THE GRAND HOTEL

Cat Scully

I CAN FIX HER

Rae Wilde

OF BEASTS

M. Jane Worma